BEYOND RISK

CONNIE MANN

Published by Sourcebooks Casablanca, an imprint of Sourcebooks, Inc.
P.O. Box 4410, Naperville, Illinois 60567-4410
(630) 961-3900
Fax: (630) 961-2168
sourcebooks.com

Printed and bound in the United States of America.
OPM 10 9 8 7 6 5 4 3 2 1

For my son, Ben Klopfenstein, whose endless creativity, incredible work ethic, and fabulous sense of humor inspire me every day. May this next chapter be your best one yet.

Chapter 1

TODAY IS JUST ANOTHER DAY.

Florida river guide Charlotte "Charlee" Tanner grimaced at the mess her all-night baking marathon had wreaked on her little kitchen. When she couldn't sleep, she baked. Later, she'd take the cupcakes to her best friend, Liz, to sell at the Corner Café.

But first, Charlee had to survive her kayak tour on the river. She had taken dozens of groups out over the years. All she had to do was pretend today was like any other day.

Just in case, she grabbed her Taurus 738 .380 handgun and tucked it into her dry bag, then slung her backpack over one shoulder. Cupcake carrier in each hand, she marched down the porch steps of her little tin-roofed cottage with her chin up, shoulders back, no sign of the guilt and anxiety sloshing in her gut. She was a former Florida Fish & Wildlife Conservation Commission officer, for crying out loud. As former state law enforcement, she knew all about projecting confidence. Besides, what choice did she have? Any sign of weakness, and her family and former squad members would hover and cluck like sandhill cranes protecting their only chick.

She tried to enjoy the fifteen-minute stroll through the pines between her cottage and Tanner's Outpost, the earthy smell, sunlight glinting off the Ocklawaha River, the chirp and rustle of birds waking and night creatures bedding down.

But when she reached the gravel parking lot, she narrowed her eyes. At 7:07 a.m., there were already over a dozen cars in the parking lot—and she recognized too many of them.

"Morning, Travis," Charlee called, and watched a blush race over his pale cheeks when she smiled at him. Travis attended the community college and worked at the Outpost part-time. Right now, he was loading kayaks and canoes on the rack for transport to the put-in at Ray Wayside Park.

"Don't forget to check the straps on all the life jackets," Charlee added as she headed inside.

His smile faded. "Like I don't check them every single time," he mumbled.

She wanted to shout every safety admonition she'd ever learned at him. "You can't be too careful out on the water." "Things can go from calm and serene to life-threatening terror in an instant." "An ounce of prevention is worth a pound of cure." *Steady, girl. Just another day on the water.*

She took a deep breath before she stepped through the screen door into the tin-roofed office.

Her oldest brother, Pete, in his green Marion County Sheriff's Office uniform, strode over and swept the cupcake carriers out of her hands. "Hey, squirt, are these cupcakes?"

She should have known he'd show up. Big, bossy, and bull-headed, he was the family's self-appointed protector—whether they wanted protection or not. No one in the family had been surprised when he followed their father into the sheriff's department. And since he'd always been annoyingly vigilant where Charlee was concerned, she'd bet every last cupcake he'd organized this morning's family ambush.

He grinned as he opened the first plastic lid. "Man, these look great."

Charlee planted her hands on her hips, but before she could light into him, her father stepped up behind her and wrapped her in a big hug. "How's my girl today?" He loosened his grip and stepped in front of her so he could study her face.

He was as tall as Pete, but thinner and grayer these days. His eyes were anxious, which made her widen her smile. After her mother's stroke last year, Frank Tanner had enough on his plate without adding worry about her to the list. She reached up and kissed his leathery cheek. "I'm doing fine, Dad. Doing fine. Thanks for coming in today." Charlee had been running the family business since she resigned as a Florida Fish & Wildlife Commission officer last year, but her father ran the office when she took groups out on the river.

The bell above the door jangled, and Charlee shook her head as her other brother, Josh, sauntered in, a handful of pink roses in one hand. Even in his khaki FWC uniform, he looked like he'd just stepped out of the pages of a magazine, hence the nickname Hollywood. He was ruggedly handsome, never a blond hair out of place, and women fell all over themselves for one of his dimpled grins.

He stepped over and gave her a one-armed hug, handed her the flowers. "Thought you'd enjoy these."

She raised a brow, sent him a teasing grin. "Been raiding Mom's rose garden again?"

He shrugged, his eyes steady on hers, his worry obvious. She buried her face in the flowers and refused to meet his gaze. He'd always been able to read her too easily, and somehow, in the six months since pancreatic cancer had taken his fiancée, Elaine, he'd gotten even better at it. But she wouldn't let him. Not today.

When he finally gave up and headed for the cupcakes, Charlee let out a relieved breath.

At that moment, Charlee's youngest sibling, Natalie, stumbled into the office, yawning. "I smell coffee." Then her eyes popped all the way open. "And cupcakes." She spun around and wrapped Charlee in a giddy hug. "I knew you'd have cupcakes today."

Charlee's temper spiked. Pete had shanghaied Natalie, too? "Why aren't you at school?" Natalie's dorm at the University of Florida was more than an hour away.

Natalie ducked her head as she poured coffee. "I had some time, so I stayed over last night." She pulled out a newspaper. "Besides, I wanted to show you the article in the *Gainesville Sun*. The Corner Café made the 'New Eateries to Check Out' list, and your cupcakes were one of the main reasons why. It's not every day one of my totally lame siblings gets media attention."

The minute the words slipped out, Natalie froze, a horrified expression on her face. "I'm sorry. I mean—"

Last year's nightmarish headlines flashed through Charlee's mind, but she pushed them firmly away. She sent Natalie a smile and then eyed the rest of her family. "Look, guys, I appreciate what you're trying to do, I really do, but—"

The old-fashioned bell over the door chimed. A prickle of awareness slid over Charlee's skin, and she knew without turning that Hunter Boudreau had just sauntered in. Pete's longtime Marine Corps buddy, Josh's newly appointed FWC lieutenant, and the one man who had breached Charlee's self-imposed isolation over the past six months. He had coaxed her back into going four-wheeling in the forest, showed up with pizza, beer, and an action movie on Saturday nights, and engaged her in witty banter and made her laugh. Best of all, he never asked about what had happened last year, so she could let her guard down and be herself.

Charlee watched Pete, Josh, and Hunter exchange measured looks, so different from their usual camaraderie. Josh's chin came up, and he slipped on his mirrored sunglasses without saying a word.

Pete's voice was cool. "Morning, Lieutenant." He spat out the title like he'd swallowed a bug. "Surprised to see you here. Thought you'd be busy moving into your new office and digging up dirt on your fellow officers."

That was a low blow. Hunter stiffened, and the tension that crackled in the air made Charlee want to snarl at her brother. The whole thing was such a mess. Two days before, Lieutenant Rick Abrams, their former boss and a longtime Tanner family friend, had been fired for taking a bribe to overlook a poaching incident. Apparently, Hunter had seen Rick take the money and had reported it. Which he'd had to do, no question. But the process was supposed to be anonymous, which could only mean that Rick was talking about it, trying to make Hunter look bad.

When Hunter got promoted to take Rick's place, Pete and Josh started stomping around like angry elephants.

Both Hunter and Josh had stellar records, but everyone had expected Josh to get the job, since he'd been with FWC longer, and Rick had been grooming him to move into the lieutenant's slot.

She shook her head. She was still furious with herself for not seeing Rick's true colors sooner. She'd always liked the handsome, forty-year-old divorced father, and had thought she might be falling in love with him. But somewhere along the way, everything changed. He'd made her doubt herself and her instincts, and even after she'd ended it six months ago, he was still trying to get her back. Now this. How could she not have known him at all? What did that say about her ability to read people?

Hunter's tempting smile brought her sharply back to the present. She'd recently developed an unexpected and unsettling attraction to him, but he treated her like one of the guys. Or like a kid sister.

"I saw the article in the paper and went by the café to congratulate you and Liz, but she said you were working here today." He gave an endearing shrug. "I was hoping you'd brought cupcakes."

Between the sexy rumble of his voice and the smile, Charlee smiled back like an idiot, but wiped it from her face when she met Hunter's piercing green eyes. She didn't buy his reason for showing up, either, but if she let her guard down a fraction of an inch, her family would wrap her in one of Mom's old quilts and lock her away from the world. Bad enough they all knew she'd been up all night baking. She crossed her arms and raised an eyebrow. "You guessed right. Help yourself." She waved at her family, all with cupcakes in their hands. "Everyone else has."

His steady gaze captured hers, and she read his unspoken question. *Are you okay?*

She ignored him. Like Josh, he saw through her too easily, and today, she needed all her armor firmly in place.

As the bell above the office door jangled again, Charlee squared her shoulders, wondering if the rest of her FWC Ocala squad would show up, too. She hid her relief and upped the wattage on her smile as her guests walked through the door.

"Good morning, everyone. Y'all enjoying your stay at the Outpost?" After three days with his teenage son and daughter, Paul Harris's smile looked strained around the edges. "Are you ready to go? It's going to be a great day out on the river." She turned to the teen girl, who was inappropriately dressed in a short sundress and flip-flops, and said, "You might want to pack that phone in a waterproof bag, though. We have some over there." She pointed to a display case.

Brittany scowled at her father and mumbled under her breath, "I hate this place. It's hot and it stinks and there are bugs everywhere."

The door banged open, and two lanky, college-age guys barreled in, laughing, teasing, each carrying an open energy drink. They stopped short when they spotted Brittany.

As Charlee turned to welcome them, another voice asked, "Are we ready to go?"

Charlee jumped. Oliver Dunn had been at the Outpost for several days and had a bad habit of sneaking up behind her. He was dressed in his usual khaki shorts, fisherman's shirt, and wrap-around sunglasses, and his bleached blond hair and tanned skin pegged him as a middle-aged outdoorsman.

"Let's get the paperwork started so we can head out." She glanced out the window and saw Travis checking the kayaks strapped to the racks on the trailer.

As Paul, Oliver, and the two guys filled out liability release forms, Pete kissed her cheek. "Be safe out there, squirt. Thanks for the goodies."

Josh came up behind Pete, gave her a steady once-over. "You going to be okay today, Charlee? You look tired."

The two middle children, they had always been close. Josh understood her sleepless nights better than anyone, especially lately. She made a shooing motion. "Go, already. Geez. I'm fine."

Charlee grabbed her pack from under the counter as the group trooped out the door. She could do this. She looked up at the sky, clear despite the thick humidity. Her weather app said no storms predicted until later. Nothing like that stormy day on the Suwannee River a year ago. No rapids to navigate here on the Ocklawaha, either.

Stay focused on today.

"Charlee, wait up!"

She looked up, not really surprised when Rick Abrams hurried over from his truck. Dollars to doughnuts he hadn't come to offer support, but to plead his case. She kept walking. "I have to get to work, Rick."

He grabbed her arm to stop her. Hard. "Just hear me out, okay? I can explain."

Charlee stopped, fixed him with an icy glare. "Take your hand off me."

"What?" He glanced down in surprise and dropped his hand, but didn't budge from where he stood, too far into her personal space. "Look, Charlee, you need to understand, I—"

Charlee kept her voice calm, implacable. "You need to leave now."

"Just five minutes, that's all I need." He smiled. "Come on, Charlee. Just—"

"I believe the lady asked you to leave, Abrams."

Charlee looked over Rick's shoulder to where Hunter stood in the universal law-enforcement pose, face impassive, hands on his utility belt and in reach of either his gun or Taser.

Rick stiffened and turned to face him. "This doesn't concern you, Boudreau," he spat.

"Anytime a guy puts his hands on a lady against her wishes, I make it my business."

"Really? You're going to blow this out of proportion, too?"

In one smooth move, Hunter positioned himself between her and Rick. "Go home, Abrams. If she wants to talk to you, I'm sure she knows how to find you."

Charlee expected Rick to take a swing at Hunter, but instead, he muttered a string of curses as he stormed off toward his blue pickup, then sped out of the parking lot, flinging gravel in his wake.

Hunter hitched his chin toward her arm. "Did he hurt you?"

She glanced down, surprised at the imprint of Rick's fingers on her skin. "No. He just annoyed me."

Hunter's face was set. "Let me know if he bothers you again."

She tipped her head back so she could see his face, make sure he understood. "I can handle him."

"No doubt. But he's lost everything he cares about. He's angry, and he's fighting back."

Charlee shook her head. "I get why you and my whole family showed up this morning, but I'm fine, okay?"

He folded his arms over his chest and studied her intently, like an insect he'd never seen before. Charlee matched his stance and stared back, drawn, as always, to his quiet strength and the air of danger that surrounded him. Solidly built and sleekly muscled, he moved like a Florida panther. He'd slipped into her life and had become her best friend, almost without her realizing it. For the past six months, he'd also stood between her and the world, giving her a safe space to heal. But she couldn't hide there forever.

He raised an eyebrow and stepped closer, right into her personal space. She didn't back up an inch. He didn't make her feel threatened. Instead, his sexy combination of sandalwood and man beckoned her closer. She held her ground.

"They hover because they care, Charlee."

"I know. And I appreciate it. But I'm former FWC, remember? I can take care of myself."

"No question." His vote of confidence and slow smile warmed her all the way to her toes.

A little shiver slid over her skin as he leaned over and whispered in her ear, "Have a good time out there today, okay?" Then he turned and walked away.

Her cheeks flamed with heat when she saw Paul and Oliver watching the exchange with a little too much interest. Paul's son, Wyatt, fiddled with his backpack, and Brittany had her face buried in her cell phone, oblivious. The two college guys were too busy eyeing Brittany to notice.

"We ready to go?" she asked as she reached them, professional smile in place.

As they pulled out of the gravel parking area, Charlee glanced in her side mirror. Hunter touched the brim of his FWC ball cap in a two-fingered salute that gave her an added boost of courage. She nodded and squared her shoulders. She could do this.

What was it about that stubborn woman that got under his skin? She had family who loved her, but she didn't seem to get how important it was to listen to people who not only cared about her but knew what they were talking about. Hunter knew why the family had shown up in force this morning. The same reason he had.

Hunter had read the official incident report from last year. Charlee had taken a side job with an outfitter at Big Shoals on the Suwannee River to lead kayak/canoe trips on her days off from FWC. It was one of the few Class III rapids in Florida. A year ago today, a storm cell had blown in, and the group of four Charlee was leading got separated in the rapids. The teenagers capsized. Charlee was able to reach them in time to save the girl, but the boy was swept downstream and drowned.

Hunter understood regret and the guilt that gnawed at your soul better than most. His brother's devil-may-care smile haunted him every single day—and most nights. If he could go back in time, he'd find a way to keep Johnny alive. Or die trying.

Instead, he was trying to figure out how to live with his failure—and keep those he cared about from making the same mistakes.

He did another quick scan of today's weather reports. Except for the usual afternoon thunderstorms, everything should be fine. Charlee and her group should be back from their four-hour paddle by lunchtime, well before the predicted 3:00 p.m. storms.

Yet he couldn't shake his unease. Maybe it had nothing to do with the weather. Or what had happened last year. Maybe it had to do with the way her smile drew him to her like he was a puppet on a string. Or the way she looked in her cargo shorts and snug T-shirt. Or the way she always smelled like cupcakes. Maybe it was her fierce love for her family that drew him ever closer.

His eyes narrowed at the cloud of dust Abrams had left behind. He didn't like the way Rick had grabbed her. One more thing to add to the man's list of sins. Hunter would keep an eye on him, make sure he didn't do anything stupid where Charlee was concerned.

But right now, he had a job to do. He walked over to his FWC vehicle and climbed into the gray-and-green Ford F-150 pickup. He'd been working toward a promotion to lieutenant, had already passed the exam and had his board review, but Abrams getting fired wasn't the way he'd hoped to get the job. It would take time for him to earn the respect of the officers now under his command—especially Josh's. Everyone had expected the longtime local boy to get the job. Which meant Hunter had to get his head in the game. Pronto.

Since this was his first day as a lieutenant, he touched base with the members of his unit by phone, rather than simply checking their GPS locations via the computer-aided dispatch, or CAD, system on the laptop in his truck. Officers set their own daily agendas, so he kept things casual, friendly, not wanting anyone to think he was looking over their shoulders. He ignored the grunts and cool responses he got in return.

Then he headed into the Ocala National Forest and touched base with a few of his contacts at a local bait shop. Since he was there, he wandered down to the marina, checked a few fishing licenses and the contents of several coolers, listened to the local gossip, and shot the breeze with a few old-timers who'd claimed the bench in front of the store. But Charlee's tired brown eyes and the guilt she couldn't hide haunted him.

Two hours later, he launched his FWC patrol boat at Ray Wayside Park. He'd take a quick run down the Ocklawaha River, say hello, make sure everything was fine.

Just in case.

Chapter 2

Charlee set her paddle across her kayak and ignored the fine trembling in her hands. Even though no wind churned the placid Ocklawaha River and the cypress trees shading the banks stood still in the warm sunlight, she couldn't settle. She pulled out her smartphone and checked the radar yet again. A scan of the cloudless sky above the tree canopy confirmed there were no storms in the area. She sighed and glanced at the time. Only one eternal hour before she could get off the river.

She heard a bark of laughter and looked around. As usual by this point in the trip, the teens had started getting restless. Troy and Wyatt stood in their kayaks, while Luke filmed them falling in slow motion.

"Enough, y'all," Charlee called, and all eyes turned in her direction.

"Quit trying to be somebody, Wyatt. Geez, you're nothing but a total dweeb," Brittany sneered.

Charlee looked in Paul's direction, surprised again that he didn't put a stop to Brittany's name-calling. Charlee and her brothers had always ragged on each other, but it was never this mean-spirited.

When Paul turned his back on the group and glided away, Wyatt hung his head. Charlee paddled in the boy's direction, pushing aside how much he reminded her of JJ. She couldn't, wouldn't, think about last year.

Right now was what mattered. "Just ignore her, Wyatt," she said quietly. "You're not the dweeb, she is."

That got a sideways smile from the teen, and Charlee smiled back.

"For a guy who's never been in a kayak before, it looks like you're enjoying yourself."

Smiling shyly, Wyatt nodded. "It's pretty awesome out here. I can't believe this is, like, your job."

His words reminded her of Hunter's earlier encouragement to enjoy herself and made her grimace. She wanted to be glad she was out here, but she couldn't, not anymore.

"Brittany! Brittany! Where are you?" Luke called.

Charlee's head snapped around at the panic in the boy's voice. Three quick strokes had her alongside Luke, who held on to an empty kayak. Wyatt pulled up right behind her.

"What happened?" Charlee asked as she slipped off her life jacket, voice calm. She pushed everything aside and focused on the boy, trying to ease his panic.

"Brittany said she dropped her phone and dove down to get it. But she didn't come up, so Troy went in after her."

Paul rammed his kayak into the others as he paddled over, eyes wild as he stripped off his life jacket. "Where's Brittany?"

"We don't know." Luke's eyes were miserable. "Troy dove in after her."

Charlee eyed the life jackets both teens had left behind, and she turned to Paul. "Is Brittany a good swimmer?"

"I don't know! Maybe. She used to be."

Charlee turned to Wyatt, who shrugged, eyes wide and panicked. She turned to Luke. "What about Troy?"

He nodded, and she heard a splash as Paul dove in after Brittany.

Seconds later, Troy popped to the surface. "I can't find her!"

She glanced at all three boys, expression stern. "Stay here. I'll get her." She waited until they all nodded, and then dove into the river, straining to see through the tea-colored water. It was clear but brown from tannic acid. She spun in a circle, waving her arms and legs as she turned, trying to connect with Brittany. She counted the seconds in her head as she expanded the search area, reaching wider, deeper. *Come on, come on. Where are you?*

A suffocating sense of déjà vu wanted to paralyze her, take her back to that day at the shoals, but she shoved it aside. If she let herself go there—for even one second—she wouldn't be able to function. *Just find Brittany.*

She dove deeper. *Yes. There.* She reached a flailing arm and tried to pull Brittany up with her, but the girl wouldn't budge. Was she stuck? Charlee felt her way down the girl's torso and legs, finally realizing her foot was wedged under a log. She tugged and tugged, her lungs screaming for air, but she couldn't pull Brittany free.

A flash of movement caught her peripheral vision, and suddenly, something grabbed her ankle in a viselike grip, clamped tight, and tried to drag her downriver. Her brain shouted *alligator*, but she didn't feel teeth, just an unbreakable hold she couldn't escape even though she kicked with all her strength. *No. No. No. Let go.*

Frantic, Charlee kept kicking with both legs, desperate to free herself. If she didn't get more air, quickly, she and Brittany would both drown.

She finally broke free, sent up a quick prayer of thanks, and latched on to Brittany's arm. She fought the current as she felt her way down Brittany's body to find the submerged tree that trapped her. Charlee braced her feet against the trunk and pushed with everything she had. She managed to move it just far enough to slip Brittany's foot free.

Lungs screaming for air, Charlee grabbed the girl to guide her to the surface, but Brittany just floated in the water. Another wave of panic clawed at Charlee's throat.

Not again. Not again. Not again.

She grabbed Brittany around the waist and used her legs to propel them to the surface. Once they popped up, Charlee spun Brittany faceup so she could get air while she towed the girl to shore.

Her feet touched the bottom near the banks, and she staggered through the mud until she found solid footing near a fallen cypress tree, then stood, pulling Brittany up with her. She had to get the girl up on shore, start CPR.

As she straightened, the water around her suddenly exploded, and she heard several loud bangs in rapid succession. Water splashed her face, momentarily disorienting her. But then the noise registered. Someone was shooting at them!

She heard the boys yell as the shots kept coming.

Charlee raised her voice to be heard above the gunfire. "Get down! Everybody down. Under your kayak, behind a tree. Whatever is closest. Just get down! *Now!*"

She heard splashing as they scrambled to obey.

Even though she crouched with Brittany beside the half-submerged tree, they were still too exposed. The shots stopped for a few seconds, and Charlee scanned the trees, trying to spot the shooter. This might be her only chance. Brittany would die if she didn't start CPR. Charlee tightened her grip on the still-unmoving girl.

She braced her feet on the muddy river bottom as best she could and leaned a hip against the tree trunk as she got a tight grip on Brittany. Once she'd locked her wrists around the girl's back and knees, Charlee lunged up out of the water and made a mad dash for the banks.

She was almost to shore when two more loud cracks sounded in rapid succession. Pain exploded above her ear, and seconds later, her head hit the half-submerged tree trunk.

Noooo.

She struggled to keep her grip on Brittany but could feel the girl slipping from her grasp. A loud rushing sound filled her ears while a gray cloud settled over her vision. She fought it with everything she had, but the gray kept getting thicker, darker, deeper. *No, no, no.*

Charlee dimly heard more shouting as Brittany slid from her slack fingers. "Save Brittany," she pleaded, but she knew no one could hear.

Her world went black.

The second he heard the first shot, Hunter hit the throttle on his official Florida Fish & Wildlife Conservation Commission boat, and his eighteen-foot SeaArk shot forward. After his time in the Marines, he knew automatic gunfire. This wasn't a machine gun, but it wasn't the single shotgun blast or two from a hunter, either. Not in rapid succession like this. It sounded like a semiautomatic rifle.

He dodged and weaved around partially submerged tree trunks that littered this stretch of the Ocklawaha. The 115 HP Mercury outboard motor kept the boat up on plane, and he hoped that was enough to avoid the endless logs and other obstructions. The shots came from where Charlee's kayak tour should be now. When several shouts followed the shots, dread settled in his gut.

He sped around a bend in the river, saw the commotion in the water, and ran the bow of his boat up onto the bank, using a big cypress tree as cover and taking in the scene at a glance. Three young men huddled several yards from shore, using their kayaks as makeshift shields from the gunman. Smart thinking.

A pool of blood stained the water near them. *Charlee, where are you?*

He hopped over the bow of his boat, crouched down, and scanned the banks along both sides of the river, gun in hand. The shooting had stopped, so he couldn't tell if there was more than one gunman. Silence didn't mean the danger was anywhere near over, though.

"I'm Lieutenant Boudreau with Fish and Wildlife. I'm here to help. Everybody stay down and stay put," he called.

"They're both bleeding bad," one of the three young men shouted.

Charlee. Oh God, no. Hunter scanned the banks with his Glock as he slogged over to the group.

Paul, the father he'd seen that morning, held his teenage daughter in a desperate grip. The other man held

Charlee's head above water. Her eyes were closed, and that same ominous crimson swirled around her.

He reached over and checked the girl's pulse. Nothing. He checked again and met her father's panicked expression. "Let's get them on shore, behind some trees, so we can start CPR and see how badly she's hurt."

He checked Charlee's pulse next, and his breath whooshed out when he found it, though it was weak and thready. The gouge in her scalp bled like crazy, but he couldn't tell how deep it was from here, whether her skull had been fractured.

He heard a splash and glanced over his shoulder just as a ten-foot alligator slipped into the water on the opposite bank, aimed straight for their location, no doubt attracted by the splashing and blood. "Everybody out of the water. Now. Get down behind the trees."

Paul carried the girl, and Hunter scooped Charlee into his arms and lunged for shore. More shots hit the water as Hunter raced up the banks, the rest of the group behind him. Thankfully, no one else was hit. He found a high spot farther up behind a cluster of cypress trees and gently set Charlee down. Her eyes fluttered open, and she gripped his arm, hard. "Save her, Hunter." Her voice was raspy, desperate. "You have to save her."

"I'll do everything I can, *cher*. You rest." He pulled his soggy handkerchief from his back pocket and wiped the blood from her face, then positioned it over her wound. He took her hand and pressed it over the handkerchief. "Hold this, *cher*. Firm pressure." He hoped she had the strength to hold it in place.

He quickly moved to where Paul had set the girl down a few feet away, behind another tree. He checked. No pulse, and she wasn't breathing. He tapped her shoulders. "Can you hear me?" He turned to Paul. "What's her name?" he asked.

"Brittany," several voices said.

"Brittany, can you hear me?" She didn't respond, and he lifted her slightly and checked her back. The bullet had not gone all the way through. He swallowed a curse as he laid her back down. Charlee's plea rang in his ears as he started compressions, afraid they were out of time. "Paul, right? Do you know CPR?"

"No. I should. But I don't. Oh God. Brittany. Don't let her die." He collapsed, sobbing as a teenage boy came up next to him and wrapped an arm around the man.

"She'll be okay, Dad. She's tough."

The other man spoke up. "I'm Oliver. I just took a refresher class."

"Take it easy, Paul. Stay calm. What's your name?" he asked the boy. "Okay, Wyatt, you stay with your dad." He nodded to Oliver. "I'll keep doing compressions, and you start breathing. Paul, you and Wyatt check Brittany for other injuries."

Hunter kept up a steady rhythm, relieved that Oliver knew what he was doing. Paul ran his hands over Brittany, crying out when he found the bullet hole. Wyatt stripped off his T-shirt, wadded it up, and handed it to Paul. The distraught father didn't notice she wasn't bleeding, just pressed the cloth over the wound.

"What happened?" Hunter demanded.

"Troy went after Brittany, and—"

"There was a loud bang, but we didn't—"

"We're not sure—"

"Where did the shots come from?" Hunter barked, interrupting them. He met Paul's eyes.

The man paled. "I-I don't know. I couldn't tell."

The word *shots* silenced everyone. Hunter scanned the trees. The shooter hadn't taken off. He was waiting. Hunter could feel it.

Who the hell shot at kayakers? Sweat poured off his forehead as he kept up the compressions, and Brittany's anguished father stroked her hand and murmured prayers.

Come on, Brittany. Breathe.

Finally, she jerked, and Hunter rolled her to her side as she coughed up water. *Thank God.* She gasped and sputtered and finally whispered, "Daddy." Paul swept her into his arms and cried.

His breath heaving, Hunter met Oliver's eyes. "Good job. Thanks." Then he gently eased Brittany from Paul's grasp and positioned the shirt back over the wound. He met Paul's eyes. "She's not out of the woods yet. Keep pressure on the wound, okay?" Now that her heart was beating again, the wound was bleeding. Paul swayed and swallowed hard. Wyatt paled, but he moved in beside his father and positioned his hands over the shirt while Hunter checked on Charlee again. Her eyes were closed, and her hand had slipped down from her head and rested on the ground, but her pulse was steadier.

He eyed the two young men. "Either of you know first aid?" He didn't want to leave her, but he had to get that shooter.

One of the young men moved next to Charlee and put his hands next to Hunter's. "I'm Troy. I lifeguard in the summer. I'll take over."

"Thanks. Keep the pressure on while I grab the first aid kit from my boat. Everybody stay low."

Hunter raced back to his boat in a crouch and called dispatch. "719-Ocala, need EMS at my 20. Shots fired, two injured, group of kayakers. EMS should be able to get pretty close on the old logging road," he added. Though the CAD system kept track of every officer's location, he'd learned as many of the back roads and trails in this part of the Ocala National Forest as he could since he'd joined Fish and Wildlife's Ocala law-enforcement division over a year ago.

"10-4, 719, EMS en route to your 20. Is the shooter still in the area?"

"Affirmative."

"10-4. Backup en route." He knew any officer patrolling the area would be headed his way.

As he reached the group, another shot rang out, splintering bark from above their heads and earning shocked gasps from the teens. Hunter dropped low over Charlee, offering what protection he could as he looked up. Either their shooter had terrible aim, or this was some kind of warning. It had been too high to do any real damage. Still, they were out here, unprotected.

He opened his first aid kit, took out gloves and several gauze pads, and handed them to Wyatt and Troy. "Keep pressure on those wounds, okay?"

"Charlee. Ohmygod, Charlee."

Hunter looked up as Travis, the dark-haired college kid who worked at Tanner's Outpost, stumbled over from the river, his kayak still wobbling from his quick exit. "Travis? What are you doing here? Get down." The kid had been at the Outpost, loading kayaks that morning.

"Is she okay?" Travis gasped, eyes wide as he stared at Charlee's still face.

"Travis. What. Are. You. Doing. Here?" Hunter repeated, grabbing his arm and yanking him to the ground.

Travis finally looked at him, and a dull flush spread over his pale skin. "I, ah, got off work early and thought I'd, ah, take my kayak out."

Hunter narrowed his gaze. He'd question Travis's suspicious timing later.

His eyes went to Charlee and the bleeding that didn't want to stop. Brittany had lost consciousness from the pain, was still losing too much blood, but at least she was breathing.

He met Oliver's eyes. The other man nodded. "Go. We've got this."

Then he turned to Troy. "You're doing good. EMS will be here shortly. I'm going after the idiot with the gun." He checked his Glock and stayed low as he headed into the swamp.

It didn't take long to pick up the trail. With daily thunderstorms this time of year, this part of the swamp turned into a muddy mess, providing a nice easy trail to follow. He moved silently from tree to tree, every sense on alert, just like his military days. Though back then, Pete Tanner had been by his side, and they'd been in the desert, not the swamp.

Hunter peered around a tree and heard a small noise off to his right. He eased that way, and the ground at his feet exploded. He jumped back behind the tree, noted the gunman's location, fired, then moved quickly to another spot.

Back and forth, back and forth, they fired and waited,

fired and waited, though some of the shots aimed his way went wild.

Enough. Hunter stepped out from behind the tree and started running a zigzag pattern, careful of the mud, determined to catch the man before he got away.

Several shots rang out in quick succession, giving away the shooter's location. Hunter fired back and ran toward the sound.

He reached a small clearing just as he heard an engine start. He broke free of the tree line in time to see an aging blue pickup truck roar out onto the logging road. He shot out the back window and took out one of the tires, but the driver didn't slow.

He ran after the vehicle, still shooting until it disappeared from sight.

He muttered a string of curses and stopped, hands on his knees while he caught his breath. Not only had the shooter escaped, the truck didn't have a license plate.

He called dispatch as sirens sounded in the distance, hoping someone could intercept the truck based on his description.

Then he headed back to Charlee and the others, mind cataloging, processing. Given what had happened to Charlee a year ago, today's attack made alarms clang in his head. But he wouldn't make assumptions, let himself get tunnel vision. Right now, he had to focus on this scene, piece together what had happened today.

Then he'd figure out how it intersected with last year. It was too soon to be sure, but every instinct told him someone had Charlee in their sights.

He wouldn't stop until he found them—and stopped them for good.

Chapter 3

An EMT named Drew looked up as Hunter approached Charlee's gurney, eyeing her pale face above the cervical collar. "She's still bleeding more than I'd like, but her vitals are stable, and she knows who's president. They'll do a CAT scan before they stitch her up."

Hunter clenched his jaw, then inclined his head toward the other gurney, where Drew's partner and two other EMTs were working on Brittany. "Will she pull through?"

Drew shrugged and looked away. Hunter understood. Kids were the hardest. "She lost a lot of blood, and we can't tell how much damage that bullet did. They're taking her to the trauma center at Ocala Regional."

"Thanks, Drew." Hunter moved away and started a mental checklist for the investigation.

"Hey! What are you doing?"

He spun around to see Brittany's father take a swing at Oliver, who didn't fight back, just tried to dodge the blows. He hurried over and stepped between the two men, hands on Paul's chest to keep him at a distance.

"My baby could die, and it's all his fault!"

"Easy, Paul. I'm Lieutenant Boudreau with Fish and Wildlife. I know we were all a little busy when I introduced myself before. How about we go over here, and you tell me what happened today?"

"I'll tell you what happened. He tried to kill my daughter." On the last word, all the fight went out of him, and he would have collapsed if Hunter hadn't grabbed him. They sat on a nearby log, and Hunter gave the man a moment to collect himself.

"Paul, I know this is hard, but I need you to walk me through what happened."

"I told you, he—"

Hunter held up his hands in a stop gesture. "How old is Brittany?"

"She is...oh God...sixteen."

"Besides Charlee, your guide, there were you and Brittany, your son Wyatt, right? Plus Oliver and two young men, Troy and Luke." At Paul's nod, he asked, "What time did you all leave the Outpost this morning?"

Paul's eyes flashed in annoyance. "Right after you did. Weren't you there?"

"Yes, sir, I was. Just want to make sure I have everything clear in my mind. So you launched from Ray Wayside and headed downriver."

He waited until Paul picked up the story.

"Everything was fine. Charlee was amazing. She got Brittany to stop texting and even take a few pictures. It was the happiest I've seen her since..." He stopped, blinked back tears.

"Everything was going fine. I, uh, pulled my kayak on shore to uh, make a pit stop, and when I came back, they were shouting for Brittany. They said she dropped her phone and went in after it. One of the boys, Troy, I think, tried to find her. And then Charlee and I dove in, too. But no matter how hard I searched, I couldn't find her."

Paul raked his fingers through his hair as he continued. "I came up for air and saw Oliver dive down. For a minute"—he swallowed hard—"I thought they'd never come back up. But they finally did. Charlee tried to get Brittany to shore, and all of a sudden, someone started shooting." His shoulders sagged. "You know the rest."

"Paul, why do you believe Oliver tried to hurt your daughter? It sounds like he and Charlee tried to save her. He helped do CPR."

"He wasn't there when Brittany first went under."

"You said you had gone ashore. How do you know he wasn't there?" Hunter asked.

"I just know. He was watching her all day, always popping up in the wrong place." He buried his head in his hands. "What am I going to tell her mother?"

"Mr. Harris, would you like to ride to the hospital with your daughter?" one of the EMTs asked as he walked over.

Paul nodded and stood, then turned to Hunter. "I want whoever hurt my daughter punished." He scowled in Oliver's direction, then climbed into the back of the ambulance without once looking over at his son, who sat on a nearby log.

Hunter watched the teen aim a look of pure malice toward his father as the ambulance doors closed. Then all the anger seemed to drain out of him as he pulled his feet up and buried his face in his bent knees.

Hunter walked over to the boy, sat down beside him. "They're going to take good care of her, I promise."

Wyatt nodded. "It doesn't matter. This is all my fault."

"Why do you say that?"

He shrugged, still not looking up. "He hates me. They both do," he mumbled against his knees. "I should never have been born."

Hunter studied him, made a mental note to dig into the family's background, figure out the dynamics.

"Today was a hard day, but you did good, comforting your father, trying to help your sister."

Wyatt shot him a sideways glance. "I tried."

"Of course you did." He paused. "You heard what your father said about Oliver. Do you agree?"

Wyatt shook his head, hard. "No. Yes. I don't know. I mean, that Oliver guy was watching Brittany all day. But he was watching Charlee, too, and was always around both of them. But he was in the water with us, so there's no way he could have shot at us."

Smart kid. "What about when Brittany went under? Where was Oliver?"

Wyatt went very still, then shrugged. "I don't know. Everything happened really fast. I was just worried about Brittany."

Hunter patted his back, and the boy winced. "Did you get hurt today?"

Wyatt looked away, mumbled, "Probably."

"Can I have a quick look?"

Wyatt gave one jerky nod, and Hunter raised his shirt, noted the bruises on his back. They didn't look fresh. He'd definitely need to check for a history of abuse. "You're a good brother, Wyatt. She's lucky to have you."

Wyatt snorted, but then he looked up with such hope in his eyes, it was painful to see. "Believe it, Wyatt. You were tough today." He stood and motioned to a nearby sheriff's deputy. "Let's get you a ride to the hospital, okay?"

As the deputy escorted Wyatt to his cruiser, Hunter went back to work, replaying the conversation. And the one with Paul earlier.

Charlee woke with a gasp of pain. The insistent throbbing in her head felt as though someone was banging on it with a rock. She tried to open her eyes, but the lids felt too heavy, so she left them closed. Gradually, the voices around her started to make sense.

Someone gently brushed the hair back from her face. "You all right, *cher*?" Hunter's Cajun drawl rumbled in her ear.

This time, she pried her lids open and waited for her vision to clear. She must have been hurt worse than she'd thought, because Hunter looked worried, and he didn't strike her as a worrier. She tried to turn her head and realized she was wearing a cervical collar and was strapped to a gurney, not far from the riverbank.

He loomed over her, that tempting hint of stubble right in her face, those piercing green eyes studying her and seeing too much. "Hurts like getting beat with a baseball bat, but you'll be all right."

Like pieces of a kaleidoscope, the last bits of memory fell into place. "Brittany is okay, right? You saved her?"

His gaze never wavered. "They're doing everything they can."

Charlee struggled to focus. "What does that mean? Is she alive?"

"She was when they transported her to the hospital."

"What aren't you saying, Hunter? My brain's too fuzzy to read between the lines."

"You know she was shot. She lost a lot of blood. But she's young."

Tears threatened, but she swallowed them back.

"She's stubborn, too. That should help, right?" Her heart felt like someone had pierced it with a stick, and guilt sloshed queasily in her stomach. How could she have let this happen? Again?

As though he could read her mind, Hunter tucked the blanket around her and said, "Not your fault, *cher*. Blame the shooter who put a bullet in her."

"Did you catch him?"

He shook his head, his gaze direct. "Not yet. But we will, I promise you that."

The panic she'd felt underwater rushed back, along with the suspicion she hadn't been alone. Which was crazy, right? "Someone was down there." The words popped out before she thought them through.

Hunter's gaze sharpened. "What are you talking about, *cher*?"

She eyed him, desperate, suddenly, that he believe her. "Brittany had her foot caught under a log, which could happen. It took everything I had to pull her free. But…as I was trying to find her, it felt like somebody grabbed my ankle, tried to pull me down, too."

Hunter immediately walked to the end of the gurney, pulled back the sheet. "Which one?" He ran his big hands lightly over her skin, his touch raising goose bumps in his wake. "Here?"

When he ran a finger over her left ankle, she winced. He leaned closer, gently turned it this way and that. "It's bruised, no question." He pulled his cell phone out and snapped pictures from every angle. "Did you see anyone down there?"

"No. I couldn't make out anything in that tannic water. But I'm not crazy. And I didn't make this up."

One corner of his mouth turned up in a half smile. "You are one of the sanest people I know."

Not exactly reassuring. "You need to believe me."

He tucked the sheet more securely around her. "I believe we have a lot of puzzle pieces to track down before we see the whole picture."

Everything inside her rebelled at the verbal pat on the head, and she fought against a frightening sense of déjà vu. Rick had said the same things a year ago, had dismissed her concerns about JJ's death, had made her doubt what she knew. But before she could argue, the pounding in her skull increased so fast, it pulled her into the darkness beyond.

He raced away from the river, down the two-lane highway, heart pounding and hands gripped tightly on the steering wheel, trying to keep the vehicle on the road. It kept pulling to one side because of the flat tire, and he fought it with everything he had. He just wanted to get home, away from the noise and the shouting. He couldn't think when it was loud, when there were angry voices inside and outside his head.

Everything had happened so fast, and none of it had gone the way he'd thought it would. He was only trying to help, to do what he'd been told to do. He'd created a distraction, hadn't he?

He eyed the rifle on the seat beside him, and his stomach got a little queasy when he remembered the blood in the water. He hadn't wanted to hurt anyone.

Especially not Charlee.

His head pounded and his vision blurred, so he shook

his head to clear it. A car horn blared, and he snapped his eyes open and veered back into his lane before he hit an oncoming car head-on. The driver shot him the finger as he went by, and he wanted to cry. No matter what he did, it was the wrong thing. All he'd tried to do was help. Make things better.

Why couldn't he get it right?

I'm sorry, I'm sorry, I'm sorry.

The words echoed in his head the whole way back to town. He stopped at a traffic light, tried to think. What now? He needed a new tire. And a back window. He had to bring the truck back as good as new. That was the rule.

A car honked behind him, and he started driving, but he got turned around, unsure which way to go. After another mile, his breath heaved out of his chest, and he pulled into a parking lot and put his head on the steering wheel. If he waited awhile, the chaos in his head would stop, the shouting would settle down, and he could think.

Sure enough, after a few minutes, he raised his head and looked around. There, the ice cream place. He looked the other direction and saw the highway. Now he knew where he was—and how to get where he needed to go.

He pulled into the junkyard the two of them had gone to before. When the man named Joe who worked there asked what he needed, he pointed to the tire and carefully counted out crumpled dollar bills to pay for a mostly new one. He checked the treads before he paid for it, to see how deep they were, just like he'd been taught. This one seemed to be okay. Tool Man would be happy with him and wouldn't shout.

"What happened to the back window?" Joe asked, a curious expression on his face.

He chewed his lip, unsure what to say. Finally, he just looked down and shrugged. "Got old, maybe?"

Joe chuckled. "If you say so, buddy."

"My name isn't buddy." As soon as he said the words, he ducked his head. Tool Man got mad if he told anyone his name. He said that was their secret. "Do you have another one?"

Joe eyed the truck. "I think maybe I do. Come with me."

He looked up and smiled as he followed Joe. Yes, that would be good. If he came home with everything all fixed, Tool Man would be happy. He'd be glad he'd taken care of it. And he wouldn't shout. "Thank you. Will it cost lots of money?"

"We'll get you squared away," Joe said.

He waited patiently while Joe found an old truck that looked just like the one he was driving, popped out the back window, and brought it back and installed it. Then, after he carefully handed over more crumpled bills, he drove away, smiling, unaware that the other three men in the place had been watching his every move.

Someone was down there. Hunter studied Charlee's still face, jaw clenched. What the hell?

He turned as Pete hopped out of his sheriff's SUV. Josh raced from his FWC truck, both headed for their sister before their vehicles came to a complete stop.

Pete's face was tight with worry. "Is she okay?"

"Bullet grazed her. Possible concussion. They'll do a CAT scan before they stitch her up."

"Bullet? What the hell happened out here, Boudreau?"

Pete demanded. The look he shot Hunter confirmed why his nickname was Bulldog. "It was just a freaking paddle trip."

"Right. We don't have all the—"

"Why aren't the EMTs taking care of her?" Josh interrupted. He shoved his sunglasses up on his head and glared at Hunter from Charlee's other side.

Hunter kept his eyes steady on Josh. "They are. But they were busy trying to save the teenage girl. Brittany. She's headed for the trauma center at Ocala Regional."

As soon as the words sank in, Josh's breath whooshed out, and he swore. "She going to make it?"

"Hopefully. She got shot, too, and lost a lot of blood."

"Run us through the timeline, Boudreau." Pete crossed his arms and waited.

Since this was their sister, Hunter ignored the commanding tone—for now—and filled them in on what he knew. "Looks like Brittany dove down for her dropped cell phone and got her foot caught under a log, but Charlee managed to pull her free. She wasn't breathing when Charlee pulled her out." He decided not to mention what Charlee had said about someone trying to pull her down. Yet. He'd wait and see if she still thought that after her head cleared. "But as Charlee was trying to get them out of the water, someone started shooting."

Pete muttered under his breath and started pacing. Josh pulled off his FWC cap and slammed a hand through his blond hair. "Charlee doesn't need this, not with everything else she's had going on."

Hunter pierced him with a look. "Agreed. But she's tough. She'll handle it."

Pete looked from one to the other. "This can't be a coincidence. Not today."

Hunter thought the same thing but kept that to himself for now. "Before we jump to conclusions, we need to gather the facts, see where they lead."

"You gather facts, Lieutenant. I'm going to find out what idiot went after my sister." Pete spun away, but Hunter stepped in front of him and blocked his path.

He stared his friend down. "I'll appreciate all the help I can get from you and the sheriff's department, Pete, but this is an FWC case." Since the incident had happened on the water, Fish and Wildlife would take the lead.

Pete narrowed his eyes and glanced over at Josh before scowling at Hunter. "It may be your case, but this is our sister we're talking about."

"I know that quite well." But the last thing he needed was Pete or Josh screwing up the investigation by going off half-cocked. "We'll find who did this, and I'll make sure nothing happens to your sister."

"Like you protected your brother? Or your lieutenant?" Pete fired back.

Hunter didn't flinch as the words hit home. His guilt over his brother's death could not be part of this. He turned to Josh. "Why don't you interview Oliver? Get his statement. Pete, why don't you get statements from Brittany's brother, Wyatt, and the two college guys, separately."

He turned away without another word, banking on their training to get them to cooperate. He didn't want to fight them on this. The EMTs were just loading Charlee into the ambulance as he walked over. He gave her hand a quick squeeze, relieved when her eyes fluttered open and she squeezed his in return.

When he saw Pete talking to one of the young men while the other two waited nearby, he walked over to where Josh sat on a log beside Oliver. Josh tucked his notebook back into his shirt pocket. "This is Oliver Dunn, in case you didn't get his name earlier. Oliver, this is Lieutenant Boudreau, FWC."

Hunter met Josh's eyes, nodded at the use of his new title. It was a start.

Oliver looked up, eyes sad. "This sure wasn't the day I expected."

"I'm sure it wasn't. Mr. Dunn, you may have already answered this for Officer Tanner, but why does Mr. Harris think you had something to do with his daughter's near drowning?"

The man shook his head again and looked at the ground. "I have no idea. I did everything I could to help, same as he and Charlee did. I heard Brittany might not make it. I guess he needs somebody to blame."

"Are you from around here, Mr. Dunn?" Hunter asked.

"No, sir. From Alabama, Mobile area. Took a little vacation."

Hunter kept his tone casual, friendly. "What kind of work do you do?"

"Mechanic, mostly. Handyman jobs on the side."

Hunter kept his eyes on the man's face as he asked, "Was there anyone else on the river while all this happened with Brittany? Anyone on shore nearby?"

Oliver stopped, head cocked. "I think Paul went up on shore, and a couple canoes passed us earlier. And then that kid from the Outpost showed up." Oliver pointed to Travis, who was giving a statement to another FWC officer. "It was weird how he just appeared all of a sudden. I got the feeling he has the hots for Charlee, so that might explain it."

From what Hunter had heard from Josh, Travis's interest in Charlee wasn't news. His sudden appearance, though, was something else. "Thank you for trying to help today. How can we reach you if we have more questions?"

Oliver scratched his head. "Well, I was planning to head out today, but I could stay a day or two longer, if you need me to and my cabin isn't booked."

"You're staying at Tanner's Outpost?" At Oliver's nod, he said, "Yes, sir. We'd appreciate it if you stick around a few more days."

Hunter stood and walked over to several FWC officers who had arrived on scene within minutes of his call to dispatch. He pulled Officer Lisa Bass aside. Her athletic good looks made men notice her, but Hunter was more interested in her sharp mind. "Hey, Fish. Do me a favor and see what you can track down about the shooter and the gun he used."

She stiffened, hesitated, but then nodded and headed toward the trees. "Anything for Charlee," she said over her shoulder.

Pete and Josh stepped up beside him. "I don't like this," Pete said. "Not today."

"I'll talk to Charlee, see if she can fill in the gaps," Hunter said.

"We'll *all* talk to Charlee," Josh corrected. His features hardened, as did Pete's, as they dared Hunter to argue.

Hunter understood. In their shoes, he'd want to talk directly to his sibling, too. "I'll finish up here and meet you both at the hospital. But don't get any ideas. We do this by the book. For Charlee's sake." He eyed them both. "We clear?"

He waited until both men nodded. Then he strode over to Marco Sanchez, another FWC officer, and put him to work tracking down the truck. He asked Brad "Byte" Griffin to collect physical evidence and then run background checks on everyone involved. As an investigator and computer whiz, Byte did most of his work online, but when word got out about Charlee, her former squad had all shown up.

Hunter wanted to head straight to the hospital, but he wouldn't rush and risk missing something critical. His laptop was in his truck at the boat launch, so he called his captain to give him a verbal update, used his phone to fill out a status report, and then checked in with dispatch. He made another careful circuit of the scene, going over everything again.

Once the scene had been processed and everyone else had left, he cranked up his boat and headed back to the boat ramp and his vehicle.

He knew that itchy feeling between his shoulder blades wouldn't let up until he'd gone by the hospital and made sure Charlee was okay.

Charlee floated in that half state between sleep and wakefulness, trying to get her bearings. She knew she was in the hospital because she remembered being poked and prodded and questioned and having lights shined in her eyes. Finally, they'd given her something to ease the pounding in her head and left her alone.

"Charlee, wake up."

The voice was gruff, demanding. Not like Hunter's soothing Cajun drawl or her brothers' familiar rumble. Did she know who this voice belonged to?

"Quit pretending. I know you can hear me."

Charlee struggled to focus. Who was angry with her? Why? What had she done?

A hand grabbed her arm, hard, and she automatically jerked away. The grip tightened, and she froze.

"You want to play games, act like you can't hear me, fine. We'll play. But I'll win... I always win."

A chill slid down her back. She strained to clear the cobwebs from her brain so she could identify the voice, but it didn't sound familiar.

"You ruined my plan before. And you got in my way again today. You'll pay for that. And so will your family." He clamped down hard on her arm and then let go.

Goose bumps raced over her skin, and she blinked rapidly, trying to get her eyes to adjust. Who was this? The room was dark. Night. Nothing but shadows. She caught the faint outline of a body, but nothing else.

Before she could move, she heard the door to the room click shut, felt the change in the air, and knew he was gone.

No. She had to think. Tell someone. Hunter. She fumbled for the call button on the bed, swung her legs to the floor, but couldn't get the room to stop spinning enough to stand.

By the time a soft voice asked what she needed, Charlee knew it was too late.

Chapter 4

AFTER A RESTLESS NIGHT, CHARLEE WOKE SLOWLY. SHE knew Hunter was nearby before she opened her eyes. Which made her foolish heart skip a beat, even as it irritated her. How could she sense the man? She forced her mind to think and shivered as yesterday came flooding back. Memories of last night weren't much better. She'd dreamt terrifying dreams of being held down under the water, of gators attacking with gaping wide jaws and huge teeth. She thought someone had come into her room and threatened her, too. But that couldn't be right, could it? The images had tangled up with memories of Brittany and JJ and Nora and made her cry out in terror.

But Hunter's voice was there, every time she jerked awake, murmuring in her ear and soothing her fears, helping her tense muscles relax enough for her to doze off again. But as soon as she did, the nightmares continued.

She slowly opened her eyes and then slammed them shut against the sunlight bursting into the room. He must have noticed, for she heard the blinds close, and the bright light behind her eyelids faded. She slowly opened them again to find Hunter peering down at her, a worried frown between his brows. She glanced away, unnerved. He looked like he hadn't slept a wink. Dark stubble covered his chin, and his hair stood on end as though he'd spent the night running his hands through it. So maybe she hadn't imagined his voice. A vague memory of him holding her hand sent a little thump straight to her heart.

"How's the head, *cher*?" he drawled.

Dang, but that lazy Louisiana cadence got to her every time. "Sore." She winced, corralled her unruly thoughts. Asked the question she didn't want to ask but had to know. "How's Brittany?"

"Holding her own. She's a fighter, *cher*, just like you." He sat down beside her and patted her arm like she was his maiden aunt. Or kid sister.

Her heart clenched as she remembered Brittany's sudden smile at seeing a huge gator snoozing on the banks, a great blue heron taking flight. "This shouldn't have happened," she whispered.

"No, it shouldn't have. We're going to figure out who did this, *cher*."

Before she could grill him for details, the door burst open, and her best friend Liz bustled in, a wicker basket in her arms, a flowered sundress swirling around her legs. Where Charlee's wardrobe ran to jeans and T-shirts, Liz was as girly as they came. Flowing dresses, painted nails, heels—and a heart as big as all outdoors.

"Morning, Char, how you doing?" Liz stepped over and kissed her cheek, and Charlee saw the worry in her eyes. "I came by last night, but you were sleeping, and your bodyguard over here"—she aimed a long, pink nail in Hunter's direction—"kicked me out. But it worked out, since Sammy came by looking for you at the café this morning, so I just brought him along."

Charlee looked past Liz to the tall young man shifting from foot to foot, a blush staining his cheeks. He thrust a bouquet of grocery-store flowers in her direction. "Miz Liz said you like flowers, so I brought you some. I hope you're feeling better, Charlee."

Liz gently took the bouquet and brought it closer so Charlee could smell the flowers. "They are beautiful. Thank you, Sammy. It's so nice of you to look out for me."

He shrugged and studied his worn tennis shoes. "I heard you got hurt. I'm sorry."

"I'll be fine." Charlee figured he was in his mid-twenties, but he had the demeanor of a young boy. She and Liz guessed some sort of brain injury somewhere in his early life. "How are things at the carnival? Have the crowds been good?"

At the word *carnival*, a wide grin split Sammy's face. "It's been really fun. Lots of kids are playing my game. I like it when they win and I can give them prizes." He looked toward the door to be sure no one was listening, then leaned closer. "Sometimes I give the little ones prizes even when they don't win. I don't want them to cry."

Charlee laughed, which moved her head against the pillow and made her wince. "You're a good man, Sammy."

"I grabbed all those cupcakes you left in your kitchen, and Sammy here ate four all by himself," Liz said. "The rest were sold within an hour."

Sammy grinned. "You make good cupcakes, Charlee. You have to get better so you can make more."

"I second that," Hunter said, pushing off from the wall where he'd been leaning.

Sammy took one look at Hunter's uniform and visibly paled. "Are you a cop? Your uniform is different."

Hunter smiled, but Sammy still looked like he wanted

to bolt. "I'm a different kind of cop. I work for Fish and Wildlife." He stepped closer, and Sammy backed up a step. "Did you hear anyone talking about what happened to Charlee, Sammy?"

His eyes jumped around the room, finally landing on Charlee. "I-I heard people say she got hurt. Someone shot her and another girl."

"You don't know who that someone is, do you?"

Before Hunter finished talking, Sammy's head swung from side to side. "People shouldn't hurt other people, even if it's not on purpose." He wrung his hands, mumbled, "I have to go," and rushed from the room.

"Did you have to scare the poor kid away?" Liz demanded.

Hunter glanced from one to the other. "He might know more than he's saying."

Liz scoffed at that, but Charlee said, "Maybe. But scaring him will never help."

"He's with the carnival?"

"Yes, he was here last year, too," Charlee said. "Rides his bike all over the place. Started coming to the café."

"He loves Charlee's cupcakes," Liz added.

Hunter glanced at his watch. "I need to grab a shower. I'll be back. Don't go anywhere." He leaned over and patted Charlee's hand again, and a little thrill shot through her at his touch.

The moment the door closed behind him, Liz turned to her. "Okay, spill. Why was he hovering like an expectant father?"

Charlee's eyes widened, and she felt an embarrassing flush steal over her cheeks. "I don't know what you mean."

"Stop. This is me, remember? The girl who knows you have a thing for that sexy man. I still don't know why you let yourself get involved with that loser, Rick."

"I got shot, Liz, and Hunter's a cop. Rick is..." Her voice trailed off. How could she ever explain the way he'd confused her, made her insecure and tentative, when she still didn't understand it herself.

"Rick's a control freak, and apparently, takes bribes, too. A real prince." Liz glanced at Charlee and sobered. "Right. Sorry. And you're not stupid, just confused about your feelings." She took a deep breath. "Tell me what happened, everything, from the beginning."

Charlee looked at her friend and realized she couldn't relive it again. Not right now. "I'll tell you later, okay? Sammy is waiting for you."

Liz studied her a moment, then turned to her wicker basket. "Let me just unpack these and get out of your way." She pulled out a flowered travel mug and held it up. "Coffee, of course. And a few of your own cupcakes." She pulled more things out of the basket. "A book and magazine."

Charlee saw the cover and laughed. "You brought me a cooking magazine?"

Liz shrugged. "Hey, you're really good at cupcakes. I figured maybe you could branch out."

Charlee sent her a smile. "Thanks for coming, Liz. You're the best."

Liz gave her a quick pat on the cheek. "I'll check back in later."

After Liz left, Charlee reached up and winced when she felt the bandage on the left side of her head. Her skull still pounded like a jackhammer, but she wasn't seeing double anymore, so that was good. She forced herself to go through everything that had happened yesterday, step-by-step, but when she got to last night, she wasn't sure. Had she been threatened? Or was it all part of the nightmare? Why couldn't she remember?

She must have dozed, because it seemed like only moments later that the door swung open again. With the exception of her mother, her entire family trooped in to take her home from the hospital. Even Hunter. She raised the head of her bed, letting the concerned kisses and multiple conversations swirl around her as she steeled herself to handle her family.

She cleared her throat, and the noise level dropped. "Thanks for bringing the clothes, Natalie." When she turned to smile at her sister, the motion made her head throb, but she hid her wince, hoping no one would notice. If they did, they'd never leave her in peace.

She eyed Pete and Josh, both in uniform. "I'm pretty sure Natalie and Dad can get me home without an armed escort. Go back to work, guys. I'm going to be fine."

"We just want to make sure you're okay, squirt," Pete said, leaning down to kiss her cheek.

"And now you know I am. Go. Catch bad guys. I'm going home to sleep. Sure didn't get much here last night."

"That's because they—" Josh started, and she held up a hand.

"I know the drill. Sheesh. Would you guys go, already?"

Josh also gave her a kiss on the cheek, then both men exchanged some mysterious man-look before they nodded to her dad, kissed Natalie, and left. Hunter,

Charlee noticed, hadn't budged from where he leaned against the wall. Her brothers had pretended he wasn't even in the room, the big lugs. She looked him over, from his freshly shaven jaw to the way his crisp uniform stretched over that hard chest. No man should ever look that good. When he caught her eye and sent her that slow, easy smile, she suddenly felt ugly and self-conscious in her hospital gown and tangled hair.

Charlee eased out of bed and changed clothes in the bathroom, wincing at her reflection. She carefully ran a brush through her hair, but there was no hiding the white bandage or the dried blood streaked near the wound. She pulled her shoulders back and forced a smile as she stepped into the room. *Never let them see you sweat.*

When the nurse came in with a wheelchair to escort them out, Hunter stepped forward and turned to her father. "Why don't you let me take her home, Mr. Tanner, let you and Natalie get back to the Outpost. I know Charlee appreciates you covering for her while she recuperates."

Natalie looked from Charlee to Hunter and back again, shaking her hand in a "hot" motion where Hunter couldn't see. Charlee felt a blush creep up her cheeks and sent her sister a glare. At twenty, Natalie was all about hot guys.

Charlee looked up in time to see another man-look pass between Hunter and her father. "What aren't you telling me?"

Her father turned to her. "Nothing, sweet girl. I know he'll get you settled." He checked his watch. "I really don't like to leave your mother for too long, but if you need me to stay—"

She interrupted before he could finish. "Dad, go. Please. It's just a few stitches and a concussion. Certainly not a first for this family."

He laughed, as she'd meant him to, and some of the anxiety faded from his eyes. Charlee turned to Natalie. "You need to get back to school. I won't have you missing classes on my account."

Charlee wasn't the only stubborn Tanner. Natalie's chin came up. "I'll help at the Outpost another couple days while you rest up. I'm doing some online classes this semester."

A load of guilt slammed into Charlee, on top of the guilt she already felt. Shortly after JJ drowned last year, her mother had had a stroke, a bad one, and recovery was slow. They said Mama's stroke wasn't from stress over Charlee's situation, but what if it was? She'd resigned from FWC, moved into a little cottage on the property, and had taken over Tanner's Outpost, so Dad could focus on Mom. It was the least she could do.

Since then, Dad had talked about her taking over permanently, mentioned having legal papers drawn up to make it official, since none of her siblings wanted the place. But Charlee didn't want it either, didn't want to be anywhere near the water, but somehow couldn't work up the courage to tell them. Because if she didn't want it, then what? They sold the place to strangers?

And if she didn't run the Outpost, what would she do? Did she want to go back to FWC? She had no idea, and with Mama's recovery going so slowly, she'd shoved it aside.

Right now, Natalie needed to go back to Gainesville, but without Charlee to run the office, that only left

Travis, who worked part-time around his class schedule at the local college in Ocala.

She should head straight there, but her head still felt like the entire high school marching band, complete with cymbals, stomped around in there. What she wanted and what her body could do today were two different things.

Frustrated, she bit back the guilt and smiled at her sister. "Thank you for filling in for me. I'll make it up to you, I promise."

"You don't owe me a thing. We're family."

After more kisses and hugs and promises to check in, a nurse wheeled her out of the hospital, Hunter walking alongside. They waited while he went to get his FWC truck.

"You are one lucky woman to have a man like that hovering over you, child," the nurse commented. "You ever get tired of him, you just send him my way, you hear? I'll take *real* good care of that boy. Um, um."

Charlee sputtered and finally laughed because, if he was her man, oh yeah, she'd take *real* good care of Hunter Boudreau. As long as he quit hovering like the rest of her family.

Her unruly brain conjured up several more wholly inappropriate ideas, so she was grinning when he helped her into his truck and went around to climb in. "What are you smiling at?"

Charlee felt her cheeks redden and hitched a thumb over her shoulder. "The nurse just told me that if I ever get tired of you, I should send you her way. She'll take *reaaall* good care of you."

He flicked a glance in the side mirror at the dark-skinned nurse waving in front of the door, and a flush crept up his cheeks. Hunter, blushing? Would wonders never cease?

He didn't respond, just drove away from the hospital with the same economy of motion he did everything. Smooth, unhurried, as though he had all the time in the world. He reached behind the seat and handed Charlee her backpack.

She reached inside, relieved to find her gun and knife right where she'd left them. "Thanks for taking charge of this for me." She'd worried, when she woke this morning, where it had ended up. She should have known Hunter would take care of it.

"Why did you kick everyone out?" she asked.

"I didn't kick anyone out. They all had things to do."

"And you, Lieutenant, have nothing better to do than chauffeur me around?"

He sent her a quick glance and didn't say another word for the next ten minutes. Charlee bit her tongue to keep from babbling to fill the silence. She wasn't really a silence kind of girl. She liked noise and voices and laughter.

"Do you believe someone tried to pull me under?" She hadn't meant to ask it right then; it just popped out. But after her experience with Rick, she had to know.

He kept his eyes on the road. "I don't doubt what you said or what you believe. I saw the bruises myself. The implications open up a whole host of ugly questions."

Something inside her settled at his matter-of-fact tone. She bit her lip, then told him the rest. "I think someone came into my room last night. Told me I'd messed up his plans, but I wouldn't be able to do it again."

His head snapped in her direction, and she shrugged. "But I had really weird dreams, so maybe I imagined it."

They stopped at a light. Hunter shoved his sunglasses up on his forehead, speared her with those green eyes. "When? I was in your room most of the night."

Charlee ignored the happy little twang in her heart at that statement and focused on the question. "Before you came, I think." She thought harder. "Yes, I'm pretty sure. It was after they stitched me up and I fell asleep. Someone woke me. I thought it was a nurse, but it wasn't. The voice was male, gravelly. After he left, I pressed the call button, hoping they could find him, but by the time someone came, I knew it was too late." She looked away. "I felt dumb for calling, so I asked for some pain meds. Or maybe I imagined the whole thing."

"Doubtful, but we'll find out, *cher*. And if you're right, we'll track him down."

She glanced over as he slid his sunglasses back in place and drove through the intersection. His face had gone hard, and he looked every inch a warrior.

Sure, this was his job, but the way he took her words at face value shored up another piece of her battered confidence. She sat up straighter. "What happens now?"

"I take you home to rest."

"And then you're going back to work."

He glanced into the side mirror. "After a while."

So much for his belief in her. "Oh, no. You're not going to hang over my shoulder like everyone else in my family." He pulled up in front of her tidy little cottage and cut the engine. She laid a hand on his arm, then pulled it back, feeling a snap of awareness at the contact she'd think about later. Right now, she had to make sure he understood. "Look, Hunter. I appreciate it. I do. But

I'm a big girl. I've had stitches before. And a concussion, too. I'll be fine."

He ignored her. Just came around and opened her door, extending a hand to help her down. She ignored the hand, but her knees started to buckle, and he grabbed her arm before she fell flat on her face, completely ruining her "I'm fine" speech. "Okay, so maybe I'm not one hundred percent yet, but I will be."

Once her feet were firmly on the ground, he put both hands on her arms, effectively caging her between his hard body and the car door. She was always surprised, somehow, by his size and strength. "Your family hovers because they care. You want them free to do what they need to do, then you're stuck with me for a while." He reached into his truck and slung her backpack over one shoulder.

"You don't have work to do, Lieutenant?" she asked again. Somehow, using his title kept him at enough of a distance that she could at least draw breath. It also reminded her that throwing herself into his arms was probably a very bad idea.

"I have some phone calls and paperwork, which I can take care of from your kitchen as well as anywhere."

He was right about her family, dang it, and that just made her more irritated. They all needed to get back to work. "I don't like anyone hovering."

He turned her toward the house, keeping one hand on her upper arm. "Duly noted." She let him guide her up onto the porch and into the living room. Had it always been this far in from the car? She stiffened her spine. She would not collapse at his feet like some helpless ninny.

She made it into the bedroom, suddenly aware she hadn't made the bed yesterday morning. Flowered sheets, pillows, her duvet were still in the tangled mess they'd been after a sleepless night. Thank goodness there were no lacy unmentionables lying about. Of course, given she didn't own anything with lace, that wasn't an issue. She plopped down on the bed. Her brain was a complete mess.

Before she could stop him, Hunter gave her shoulder a gentle shove and pushed her down on her side. He tucked a pillow under her head, slid her flip-flops off her feet, and tucked her in.

Then he set the backpack by the bed, pulled out her gun, and set it on the nightstand. "Get some rest, *cher*. Doctor's orders. I'll be in the kitchen if you need me."

She met his gaze, touched that he understood her need to have her firearm nearby. But still, he was hovering. She should protest. Say something. But the sense of safety Hunter's nearness provided was all her body needed to slide into sleep.

Hunter surveyed her kitchen and shook his head. The results of her cupcake baking marathon littered every available space. He didn't bake, though his grandmere used to, so he knew the dozens of cupcakes she'd brought to the Outpost took a while to make. She obviously hadn't slept much the night before last. Not surprising, given what had happened a year ago.

Had the lack of sleep affected her judgment? As soon as the thought registered, he discarded it. Charlee was not only a trained cop, she was a protector at heart, with a big dose of nurturer. He'd been drawn to that from the moment he'd met her. She wanted to protect people, care for them. Especially her family. She'd smack him if he told her she did exactly what she accused her family of doing: she hovered. And like her family, she did it because she cared.

She could pretend all she wanted, but she hadn't been fine yesterday morning. He'd seen it in the tension around her chocolate-brown eyes, the slight tremor in her hands. But she'd put on a good show for her family, her guests. Tried to distract them with cupcakes. He knew it hadn't worked, but he gave her points for trying.

He pulled out his cell phone and dialed the hospital while he ran hot water in the sink, squirted dish soap onto a sponge. The hospital operator transferred him to the nurses' station covering Charlee's room, and he asked if she'd pressed her call button during the night. He spoke with a nurse, who confirmed Charlee had requested more pain meds about nine p.m. last night. Hunter thanked her and hung up. So someone had been in her room. He'd have Sanchez check the hospital security cameras, see if they got lucky and caught the person's face. He didn't think they'd catch the shooter that easily, but he could always hope.

Once the baking utensils were washed, he turned to scrub the counters and stopped. At the far edge of the old wooden table in the middle of the kitchen, a piece of paper peeked out from under a dusting of flour. He picked it up by the edge, shook the flour off it, and used the side of his hand to wipe off the rest.

No wonder she looked rattled yesterday. "I'll make sure you never forget" was scrawled in red marker over last year's newspaper article. He swore. She shouldn't have kept this reminder in front of her, tossing guilt in her face all night long.

He marched to her bedroom to demand answers, but she was curled up on her side, sound asleep. Something stirred in his heart at how vulnerable she looked, so he eased the door shut and went back to the kitchen. He'd grill her later.

He grabbed his laptop from his truck. Like her brothers, his radar twitched at the timing of these two incidents. Even though last year's drowning had been ruled an accident and Charlee proclaimed a hero for saving the girl, the boy had died. That didn't help you sleep nights. It could also make family members seek revenge.

He logged in and reread the report of the incident on the Suwannee River in White Springs, about two hours north. Charlee had worked for an outfitter there on her days off from FWC. Rick Abrams had been working with the lead investigator. He set that aside and focused on the report. The weather had been iffy, at best, when they set out. Charlee's boss was quoted as saying that he'd trusted his guides and told them all to make their best decisions when it came to weather. At the time Charlee's group set out, so had three others, and all of those had returned from their trip down the rapids wet but without incident at the appointed time.

So what went wrong on Charlee's trip? How had they gotten separated? That it had taken her a while to get back to them, he understood. He'd paddled plenty of rapids, knew about fighting the current. He was more impressed that she'd been able to get back to them at all.

He was halfway through Rick's pompous-sounding

essay when he caught a whiff of her vanilla scent. "What are you doing?" she asked, voice rough with sleep.

He closed his laptop. But he hadn't had a chance to move the newspaper clipping.

She looked around, blinking. "You cleaned up. You didn't have to do that."

He shrugged. "I needed a place to work."

She casually grabbed the article, but he stopped her with a hand on her wrist. "When did you get this? Does your family know about it?"

She shook off his hold, but wouldn't meet his eyes. "Of course they know, since I came home afterward."

He stood, moved in until she had to meet his eyes. "Don't play dumb, *cher*. It doesn't become you."

She sidestepped him, folded her arms around her middle, and paced the small space. "It came in the mail three—no four—days ago."

"Did you keep the envelope?"

Her eyes snapped to his. "No, but it was postmarked Lake City. I figured it was from either Tommy or Sally Jennings, JJ and Nora's parents. They were obviously devastated by the whole thing. Or maybe James, Tommy's brother." A haunted look slid over her face, telling him she was reliving that awful day.

"Did you tell your family about this?" His tone snapped her back to the present.

She frowned. "Why would I? They all have enough on their plates. It was sent to me. I understood Tommy—or his ex-wife—needed to make sure I didn't forget." She snorted. "Like that will ever happen."

"It wasn't your fault, *cher*. You know that."

"Really, how do I know that, exactly? They were my

group, damn it, and their safety was my responsibility." She slammed a fist on the table, then winced and held her head in her hands. "I failed, and JJ died. How can that not be on me?"

He pulled her into his arms and held tight, offering comfort without words. He refused to think about how good it felt to have her plastered against him, how much he'd like to nuzzle that sweet spot right behind her ear. She needed him to be a friend, never mind that he wanted to blow past those boundaries. *Focus, Boudreau.* He couldn't let his growing need for her distract him, or worse, cloud his judgment. She needed his A game in this investigation.

She looked up at him, anguish in every line of her body. "It's happening again. Brittany might not make it. Someone shot her, for crying out loud. Who does that?"

"She's tough. The doctors are optimistic she'll pull through, *cher*. Don't give up on her."

She pulled back and glared at him. "I'm not giving up. I'm furious that someone would do this."

"Can you walk me through it? The whole trip?"

She nodded, and he watched her spine stiffen as she started talking. She was as tough as she was beautiful, and his admiration grew. "Everything was going fine. I got Brittany to stop texting and look around. The other two boys took Wyatt under their wing, and they all goofed off together, which was nice, because Brittany spent most of her time saying mean things to her brother. She dropped her phone and dove down after it. When she didn't come back up, Troy dove in after her."

She swallowed hard. "I was talking to Wyatt and didn't see it happen. I should have."

"You can't have your eyes everywhere at once, *cher*," he said.

She ignored him. "Troy popped up and yelled that he couldn't find her, so I dove in after her. Paul dove down, too. The water's so murky, I couldn't see anything, so I was trying to find her by feel. I'd finally located her when something clamped down on my leg and tried to pull me downriver. I kicked until I got free, but by then, I was almost out of air. Brittany's leg was caught under a log, and it felt like forever before I managed to pull her free. I got her to the surface, but she wasn't breathing. As I tried to get her to shore, someone started shooting." She swallowed hard. "You know the rest."

Hunter's expression was intent. "You didn't see anyone else down there?"

She frowned. "You know how dark that water is." She chewed the inside of her cheek. "Maybe I got trapped under a branch and it just felt like someone grabbed me." She stopped, studied his face. "You don't believe that."

"Neither do you, not after someone threatened you last night. I'm checking backgrounds of everyone who was on the river with you." He paused. "Tell me about Travis."

"He's a good kid, big-time into video games, socially awkward."

"He has a crush on you."

She grimaced. "I know. I spent some time gaming with him when I first came home, and he took it as more than it was."

"Would he try to hurt you?"

"Travis?" She laughed. "No. I can't picture that. He's harmless."

Without warning, the laughter turned to tears. Hunter stopped, surprised. Charlee was not a crier. She turned her head, swiped at her cheeks, and fought to regain control.

He refused to offer easy platitudes, but he could help her think, process. "What was Travis doing there? He wasn't with your group."

Charlee cocked her head, blinked several times. "No, I thought he was working all day, since I would be gone with the group. But with Natalie there, maybe Dad let him go early."

"Did it strike you as odd, him showing up like that?"

"Not any more than usual."

Hunter's senses sharpened. "What does that mean?"

Charlee shrugged. "He's always watching me."

Hunter raised a brow. "That doesn't make him odd; it makes him male, *cher*. You're lovely to look at."

A blush raced over her cheeks, and she ducked her head.

When he picked up his cell phone and started dialing, she asked, "Who are you calling?"

"I'll get someone to stay with you while I check on something."

She narrowed her eyes. "I told you, I don't need a babysitter. I'm fine."

"The doc said we should keep an eye on you for the next day or so. Make sure those stitches stay put and that sharp brain of yours didn't get too banged around."

She folded her arms over her chest and drew his eyes to the way her snug T-shirt hugged her curves. Even with her bandaged head, her tough stance and hot body made it hard to look away. But he forced himself to meet her eyes.

"If you're going to keep acting like my family, we're going to have a serious problem, Lieutenant."

He studied her implacable expression, weighed the risk, nodded. He wasn't going far. "Okay. Get some rest. I'll be back in a while."

Chapter 5

He'd backed down, just like that. Instead of the fight she'd expected, Hunter had simply nodded and left. Confused, Charlee sank down on the couch and snuggled under a crocheted throw her mother had made years ago. The more she got to know him, the more she was drawn to him, and she wasn't sure what to do with that.

Right now, she had other, far more important things to think about. What happened on the river? If Tommy Jennings had sent the newspaper article, it wasn't a huge stretch to imagine JJ and Nora's grief-stricken father might have taken shots at them.

But that didn't explain who'd grabbed her underwater. Had the same person deliberately trapped Brittany under the log? And what about the threat last night? Was that Tommy?

A chill started deep inside, and Charlee wrapped the afghan tighter around her middle, never mind the mid-nineties temps outside today. But the more she thought, the more her anger grew, until her fury burned white-hot. Grief-stricken father or not, nobody shot at children and got away with it.

She slid the blanket off and slipped her feet into her flip-flops. Let Hunter conduct his official investigation. She'd start her own. She stood up too fast and grabbed the back of the sofa as pain banged in her skull like a steel drum. The doctor had told her to expect that for a day or two, but it was still annoying.

She decided against more pain pills, since they made her drowsy. Instead, she slowly climbed into her Jeep. Out of habit, she'd grabbed her gun and slid it under the seat. Even though she wasn't going far, since her cottage sat just on the far reaches of the Outpost property, she'd been carrying a gun long before she became an FWC officer. Dad had taught all his kids to shoot, making sure they could protect themselves from both four-legged and two-legged threats at any time.

But before she did anything else, she had to stop and reassure her mother. Mama would have heard about what happened. Charlee didn't want Mama seeing her like this but knew she'd worry more if Charlee didn't show up.

She parked behind her mother's little sedan and then walked around the house to the big screened porch that overlooked the Ocklawaha River. She found her mother in her favorite wicker rocking chair, dozing.

The screen door squeaked, and Mama woke with a start, then a lopsided smile broke over her face. Charlee's heart clenched, as it always did, at seeing this once-active woman trapped in a body that struggled back to life inch by agonizing inch.

Charlee placed a gentle kiss on her forehead, then sat in the rocker beside her. "Hey, Mama."

Her mother's eyes widened, and she made a sound of alarm as she studied the bandage on the side of Charlee's head. "Charlotte."

Charlee grinned. "Don't worry. It's not nearly as bad as some of Pete and Josh's injuries."

Her mother's right side was still weak, and words came slowly, often still garbled. She forced out one word. "Hurt?"

"Nah. Not too bad. I'm a hardheaded Tanner, remember?"

Alice sent her the "Mom look" that called her bluff.

Charlee laughed and squeezed Mama's good hand. "Okay, yes. It hurts a little bit, but I'll be fine in a couple days. I just wanted to stop by and say hello, tell you not to worry."

"I. Always. Worry. I'm. A. Mother."

"I know, but you don't need to."

Alice looked toward the river. "Miss kayaking with you, Charlotte." Charlee had to blink rapidly. Before the stroke, Mama spent time on the river almost daily, hiked in the forest. Seeing her like this was agony.

Charlee leaned over and hugged her gently. "Me, too. But we'll get out there again. Before you know it." Though after a year of therapy and hard work, Alice was still using a wheelchair. It discouraged her. Discouraged all of them.

"Cupcakes soon?"

Everything in Charlee's heart wanted to say yes, let's do that right now. But she had to get to Oliver's cabin. "Cupcakes soon. Promise."

Alice lifted her good hand and cupped Charlee's cheek. "Rest, sweet girl."

"I will. Love you, Mama."

"Love you more."

Charlee took a steadying breath as she hurried down the steps and climbed back into her Jeep. She drove past the office and the canoe/kayak pullout and kept going until she came to the row of small cabins that lined the perimeter of the camping area. She pulled up in front of Oliver's cabin and found the door open, Hunter standing on the tiny porch. She parked next to his official F-150.

He looked her up and down like she was a misbehaving five-year-old, arms folded over his chest. "I thought I told you to stay put."

She propped her hands on her hips. "And I told you to stop telling me what to do."

He shook his head, sighed. "What are you doing here, Charlee?"

She swept a hand to indicate the now-empty space where Oliver's car had been. "The same thing you are. Looking for Oliver. I need to ask him some questions."

"Which would be my job." Hunter had his phone to his ear, but his eyes stayed on hers as he spoke into it. "Natalie, you have the phone number Oliver Dunn gave when he registered?" He propped the phone between his shoulder and ear and scribbled in a little notebook. Then he hung up, dialed the number, listened. "Hello, Oliver. This is Lieutenant Boudreau with FWC. Please call me at this number as soon as you get this message."

"Let me guess. It goes straight to voicemail."

"Right."

"Which could mean he has his phone turned off."

"Maybe. I told him not to leave town." He indicated the cabin. "He's cleared out." He dialed again, asked whoever answered to track the GPS signal on Oliver's phone.

"Now what?" She tried to sound casual, but her head pounded hard enough that she leaned against the side of her Jeep to keep from swaying. Dang, this was annoying.

Hunter glanced her way, then rolled his eyes. "I'll follow you home."

So much for looking like she had it together.

Charlee stayed upright until they were inside her cottage, then slowly lowered herself to the sofa, determined not to collapse and have Hunter call in her family.

He went to the kitchen, came back and shook two pills into her hand, handed her a glass of water. He watched her, keys in hand, eyeing her with concern. "You'll be okay for a while?"

"Where are you going?"

"To work. I need to find the shooter. Your job is to rest."

Before she could protest, he leaned over and dropped a brotherly kiss on her forehead. Once he disappeared, Charlee fought to stay awake. She had to tell him something, but her thoughts were muddled. She was still struggling to figure it out when her eyes slid closed.

Hunter drove back to the scene, shaking his head at Charlee's stubbornness. The woman didn't quit, which impressed him more than it should. But he couldn't think about her. Not now. He pulled up and found Pete and two members of the sheriff's department crime scene unit combing the area inch by inch. He strode over to Pete, who straightened and crossed his arms in a belligerent stance.

"Find anything new, Bulldog?" Hunter kept his tone level.

"Not yet."

Hunter glanced around, saw the female tech look

away, and motioned Pete out of earshot. "I'm going to assume you were planning to call me immediately with any new information. We both want answers, Pete. But you know FWC is lead on this case."

Pete exhaled and looked away, then locked eyes with Hunter. He saw worry there, and anger, both of which he understood.

"Someone took shots at my sister, exactly one year after a kid died on her kayak trip."

"I don't believe in coincidence, either. We're going to find him. Together."

Pete looked away again, scrubbed the back of his neck, then pierced Hunter with a look. "Rick has been a good friend to our family, a good cop."

"No argument. But he made some bad choices."

Pete got right in his face. "For good reason. He needed that money. His kid is sick, Boudreau."

Hunter kept his gaze level. "I know. And I'm sorry to hear it. But that doesn't make it okay to take a bribe."

Pete shifted uncomfortably, mumbled, "Extenuating circumstances."

"The brass didn't see it that way."

"They wouldn't have had to see anything if you'd kept your mouth shut."

Hunter studied his friend. "Come on, Pete. You know me better than that. I couldn't ignore it, not when I saw it happen. Neither could you."

Pete glared, worked his jaw, then nodded once. "Right. Doesn't mean I'd have wanted to turn him in, though." He paused, jabbed a finger in Hunter's face. "Josh should have gotten that promotion, not you."

Hunter met his gaze head-on. "Also not my decision."

"You going to tell me you didn't want the job? Then you should have turned it down."

"I wanted it, and I worked hard to get it, though that wasn't how I planned for things to go." He paused, chose his words with care. "Don't fight me on this, Pete. We both want to know what the hell happened, so we need to work together. And not just because we have to."

Pete rubbed a hand over the back of his neck, studied Hunter for a long moment, then nodded. "Let's get to it, then." He walked toward a cypress tree and pointed. "We recovered the first shell here."

Hunter followed him. It was a start.

Charlee woke with a crick in her neck and a growling stomach. When had she last eaten? Her tongue felt like it was wearing wool socks, so she downed a glass of water, then stood in front of her open fridge, hoping something edible would materialize. A jug of milk of dubious vintage, baby carrots, a jar of homemade pickles, plus a jar of grape jelly with about an inch left in the bottom. She slammed the door, winced, and opened the freezer, hoping for better luck. She found two leftover pizza slices, two scoops of vanilla ice cream, and a bag of frozen strawberries. She put the pizza in the oven and decided to grab a shower while it heated.

She stayed under the spray so long, her fingers were pruned and her knees felt a little wobbly, but being clean was worth it. She tightened the belt on her short robe as she walked into her bedroom and stopped short as several things registered at once. Her bed was neatly made. Had she done that? She couldn't remember, her eyes riveted to the ball cap in the middle of the bed.

She swallowed hard. That was the memory she'd been trying to recall. She could have sworn she saw a ball cap exactly like that on the ground when she came to by the river yesterday. It looked just like the one JJ had been wearing a year ago.

Was she having some sort of hallucination? She gripped the doorjamb and closed her eyes. Opened them again. *Breathe, Charlee. Think.*

She squinted, focused all her energy on what she was seeing. No, the cap was definitely there. It was navy-blue, with some sort of logo embroidered on it.

Charlee took a step into the small room, and her law-enforcement training kicked in. Someone had been here.

The closet door stood open, so there was obviously no one hiding in there. Both windows were closed and locked. She'd grab her gun, check under the bed. Then get her phone, take a picture of the cap. Call Hunter. Probably.

But before she could quietly ease away, she heard a noise. Some sort of clacking, like a baby's rattle.

Oh God. She knew that sound. And it terrified her.

Chapter 6

Charlee's breath backed up in her lungs as a rattlesnake poked its head out from under the ball cap and stared straight at her, tongue flicking in and out, shaking its rattles. It was as thick around as her wrist and easily six feet long. She froze. Couldn't move. Couldn't breathe. Nothing in this world scared her more than snakes. When she was six, Pete had dared her to run from one to keep her from following her brothers through the woods. Big mistake. She still had the scar on her ankle, and Pete still felt guilty. No matter how much she tried to talk herself out of it—and despite her FWC training—she'd never been able to get past her fear.

She gripped the metal footboard in front of her. How was she going to get away?

For now, she'd wait. She forced herself to take slow, even breaths so she wouldn't hyperventilate. In, out. In, out. The snake eyed her. She kept breathing, slowly, so very slowly. No sudden moves.

She eventually brought her heart rate under control and deliberately eased her death grip on the bed frame. The snake looked around, seemed to calm down.

She dropped her hand to her side and bumped the frame. The sound drew its attention and garnered another ominous rattle.

Charlee froze again, swallowed hard. As long as the snake stayed where it was, things should be fine, right?

Eventually, it'd give up and go to sleep or something, wouldn't it? She tried to remember everything she'd learned, but her brain couldn't seem to think beyond her terror. For now, she'd stand here "until Jesus came back," as Mama always said.

She didn't know how long she waited, but it was long enough for her feet to ache from standing and her bladder to start clamoring for relief.

The snake kept watching her, looking around.

She heard a car out front, and her instant relief turned to panic. If someone knocked on the door, it would startle the snake. She cocked her head, listening, poised to run if she had to. There was a slight chance she could clear the doorway before the snake could strike.

Nobody knocked. But the car didn't leave, either. Maybe it was one of her brothers. They had keys to her place, though they hadn't used them since she'd read them the riot act for barging in one night last year to check on her. She didn't know who'd been more surprised, her brothers or Rick Abrams, who'd jumped off the couch, gun drawn, when they burst through the door. That had been the first and last time they'd let themselves in.

She didn't hear a key in the lock, no whispered call from a family member in case she'd been sleeping.

Instead, she heard a footfall on the back porch and then Hunter's face appeared in her bedroom window. He cupped his hands against the glass, looked around, then held up both palms in a "don't move" gesture before he disappeared. Like she had any intention of moving an inch. She didn't know what he planned to do, but just knowing he was outside took her panic down a notch.

She eyed the snake again, which had now crawled completely out from under the cap and started investigating her bed. As long as it didn't get any closer, she'd be fine. *Come on, Hunter. Where did you go?*

What felt like two years later, she heard a slight creak on the wooden floor in the hallway. For a big man, he moved like a cat.

He eased up behind her with a trash can in one hand and a snake hook in the other. His warm breath sent an unexpected zing down her back as he leaned close and whispered, "Start easing back. When I count to three, run."

She barely nodded as she inched backward, eyeing the snake, which had suddenly come back to attention, coiled up again, and issued a warning rattle.

His voice was a mere breath of sound. "One. Two. Three—"

Before he finished the word, Charlee turned and tore down the short hall to the living room. She collapsed on the couch, panting, the shakes setting in now that she was out of striking range.

She heard his low voice, several thumps, and after a few minutes, Hunter walked by carrying the closed trash can, the snake presumably inside. He went out to his truck, then came back in and sat down beside her. "I'll take it out to the forest and release it. Any idea how it got in?"

Charlee tried to respond, to find words to thank him, but nothing came out. When he pulled her against his side, she didn't hesitate, just curled up against his hard chest, trying to control the shakes. He simply held her, the steady beat of his heart under her ear. His hand stroked her back in a slow and steady rhythm that eventually allowed her to draw a deep breath. And another. "Don't like snakes," she finally murmured.

"Most people don't." She could hear the smile in his voice.

She sat up suddenly and immediately missed the warmth of his arms. "Somebody put the snake there on purpose."

Hunter nodded. "Looks like. I didn't see any obvious entry points. With the AC on, it wouldn't have come inside, anyway. Somebody probably caught it in the forest and brought it here. I'll have Fish check with the local dealers, just in case."

"How did you get in?" she asked.

"When I saw what was happening, I called Pete. Asked if you had a key hidden anywhere. Seriously? You put it under a fake frog? That's like putting a neon sign out front."

Which was probably how whoever was behind this had gotten in. With her heart still hammering, she wasn't up for a lecture, too, so she put her hand over his mouth. When she realized what she'd done, she jerked her hand back, mortified.

Quick as a snake himself, he caught her wrist. "You did good, *cher*."

He turned her hand over and brushed a quick kiss over her palm. Charlee froze as a snap of electricity raced up her arm and warmed her from the inside out. Their eyes met for one long moment, and she saw that same flash of attraction reflected back at her. He glanced away and dropped her hand like he'd been burned. Charlee wrapped her arms around her middle, that darn flush heating her face again. She should act like it was no big deal, right?

Footsteps pounded up the steps, and Pete swung the door open, eyes narrowing as he saw them on the couch. "Everybody okay?"

Charlee jumped to her feet and immediately regretted it. Her head throbbed, but she ignored it and propped her fists on her hips. "I thought we already talked about you barging in without permission."

He mirrored her stance. "After Hunter said he had to get in your house, fast, and then didn't answer his phone, yeah, I barged in."

Hunter slowly stood. "I'll show you." He turned toward the bedroom, and Pete followed.

Charlee stayed where she was. She didn't want to see the ball cap or remember the coiled snake slithering over her new comforter. Call her crazy, but now she'd have to buy a new one. Which made her mad. She'd really loved that pretty thing. Had spent months finding just the right shade of blue.

Pete reappeared almost instantly, Hunter behind him. "Walk us through what happened, squirt."

Hunter holstered his phone and sat down beside her again. "Crime scene techs are on their way."

Charlee took a minute to corral the thoughts racing around in her head. She looked up at Pete, who paced in front of her small fireplace. "Sit. You're making me dizzy."

He plopped into an armchair next to the sofa, eyes brimming with concern. "You sure you're okay?"

She nodded, then said, "After Hunter dropped me off, I fell asleep on the couch. When I woke up, I was hungry, so I put some pizza in the oven to defrost while I took a shower. Afterward, when I went into the bedroom, I didn't see it immediately. I saw the ball cap."

Hunter went still, alert. "What about the ball cap caught your attention?"

She swallowed, tightened her grip on the robe when she felt his eyes on her. "I wanted to tell you earlier, but with everything going on...anyway, I'd seen a cap just like it before. Twice, actually. The first time was a year ago. JJ was wearing one just like it the day we kayaked the Shoals." Her voice wanted to shake, so she took another deep breath to steady it. "The second time was when I came to the other day. There was one in the mud, near Brittany. But I hadn't seen anyone in the group wearing it beforehand. I would have noticed." She wrapped her arms around her middle and looked at Pete. "I know you probably think I'm crazy, or that I'm imagining things, but I know what I saw."

The two men exchanged glances. Charlee tensed, waiting for them to tell her she was overreacting or "misremembering," as Rick used to say, but neither one did. Hunter's voice took on the same soothing rumble as before. "You're not crazy, *cher*. Not a bit." He looked at Pete. "Did your guys find a ball cap like that at the scene? I don't remember anyone on my team mentioning it."

Pete already had his phone in his hand. "We're about to find out."

Charlee turned to Hunter. "What now?"

They heard several vehicles pull up outside. "That's the crime scene unit."

She eased to her feet, steadied herself. "I need to get

out of here for a while." It was one thing to be the one tracking down bad guys, but quite another to feel like someone was stalking *her*. Knowing they'd been in her house while she showered rattled her more than she wanted to admit.

Hunter let the techs in, had a word with Pete, and then reappeared. "We'll go get some food in Ocala while they do their thing here."

Charlee nodded, went to turn off the oven, get dressed. "I need a new comforter."

~

The techs were gone by the time they got back. They'd taken her old comforter set with them, as she'd requested, but they'd left fingerprint dust and sandy footprints everywhere. "You relax, *cher*. I'll clean up."

Charlee snorted and carried three sacks of groceries in from the car.

He shook his head and followed, wondering when mule-headed stubbornness had become such a turn-on.

Once the food was put away, she held up a dust rag and a broom. "Name your poison."

"You dust. I'll sweep."

She simply nodded, and that, more than anything, told him how badly the snake had shaken her. Charlee talked, laughed. This subdued version wasn't the real woman. Pete had filled him in on the snake scenario from her childhood, and now Hunter had forced her to run from another coiled snake. But she hadn't hesitated. Her unexpected trust in him and mental strength delivered a one-two punch that left him reeling.

Especially when he brought in the new flowered sheets and comforter.

As they made the bed together, he refused to think about how much he'd liked the feel of her in his arms earlier. Or how much he'd like to hold her again, to curl up with her under all those roses, run his hands over every inch of her smooth skin. He shoved the thought away. *Not going to happen.*

Charlee wouldn't meet his gaze, but the blush staining her cheeks made him wonder if she wasn't thinking similar thoughts. He shook his head. Or maybe she was just embarrassed to have him in her bedroom.

The minute they were done, she hurried back to the kitchen. She glanced up when he walked in, hands clenched on the back of a kitchen chair. "Thanks for being there today, Lieutenant. I appreciate it."

He knew she used his title when she needed distance. He studied her eyes, saw exhaustion and a flash of anger. Guilt slapped him. "I screwed up. I should have made sure the house was secure before I left you alone."

"You couldn't have known."

He remembered his brother's fear that someone had discovered he was snitching for the cops and how Hunter had dismissed his worry. "Yeah, I should have. It's my job to know."

When she opened her mouth to protest, he said, "Where do you keep extra bedding? I'll take the couch tonight."

She narrowed her eyes, shook her head. "You're not staying here."

He'd expected that. "Either I stay, or you can move in with Pete or Josh for a while. But I figured you'd be more comfortable at home." He grinned. "Besides, I don't snore as loud as your brothers."

Her chin came up. "I'll be fine. I'm trained law enforcement, remember?"

"I know." He stepped around the table and put his hands on her shoulders. When she stiffened, he let his hands drop. "You're tough *and* smart, so you know you have to be careful. Some nut job is sending you messages, and until we catch him, I'll be around as backup."

She narrowed her eyes. "I won't let you run my life, Lieutenant."

"Not my intention. But I'm not leaving until this is over. Me or your brothers. Your choice, *cher*."

He hoped she wouldn't fight him, but he wouldn't back down. Their gazes locked, held, and when she finally nodded, some of the tension eased out of him.

She slipped down the hall, returned moments later with a stack of bedding. "Help yourself to anything you need in the bathroom."

"I'll check the perimeter before I bed down." He couldn't listen to the water run, wanted to avoid the mental image of her peeling off her clothes before climbing into bed, so he went outside and called the hospital, relieved that Brittany had come through the surgery just fine. The bullet hadn't nicked any major organs, and the doctor expected her to make a full recovery.

He hung up and walked around the cottage, testing the locks on all the windows, then made a wider sweep of the woods surrounding it. He didn't come back inside until long after her bedroom light went off and he'd convinced himself that climbing under those flowered sheets with her would be a very bad idea.

Charlee tossed and turned, but she couldn't sleep. Every time she closed her eyes, she saw shiny black snake eyes staring back at her, that scary tongue flicking in and out. She wanted to cover her ears to keep the sound of rattles from echoing in her head. Hunter had taken care of the snake. It couldn't hurt her. It wasn't in the bed.

Her head understood completely. The rest of her still tended to shake, huddled under the covers.

Finally, she slid the blankets back and stumbled to the kitchen. It wasn't until she had the lights on that she remembered Hunter trying to sleep on her too-short sofa. She slowly eased the door to the kitchen closed behind her, turned on the oven, and started assembling her baking supplies.

The simple motions of beating the butter and eggs, stirring the batter, centered her like nothing else. No electric mixer tonight. She needed the steady rhythm of the wooden spoon. As she stirred, she finally let her mind slide back to the day JJ died. For months, she'd tried to block it all out, but more and more, the nagging sense that something was not quite right about the whole horrible day slithered into her mind at odd hours. She took a deep breath for courage and decided to wade back into her memories, see if something popped.

Once she slipped the first pan of cupcakes into the oven, she set out another bowl and started on a batch of chocolate chip cookies. As she added ingredients, she imagined she was viewing last year's scene through a camera lens. She couldn't quite get her mind to focus on JJ's lifeless body, so she let her memory slip over to Nora and how she'd found her. Charlee saw her, lying half in the water, eyes closed, a branch over her neck, bruises coloring her skin.

Charlee went over it all several times, until her head hurt from trying to think so hard. Frustrated, again, that no answers leaped into her mind, she tucked the memories back into the box she kept them in and turned her focus to her baking.

The first cupcakes were ready to frost, and several dozen cookies cooled on racks when Hunter eased into the room, looking far too wide awake for…she glanced at the clock—two thirty in the morning. He wore only a pair of low-slung jeans, the top button undone, no shirt.

She swallowed hard, forced herself to look away. *Oh my*. She'd known he had a rock-hard chest, had felt it, but knowing and seeing were two very different things. She gripped the spoon to keep from reaching out to see if that crisp chest hair felt as good as it looked.

She turned and crashed into him with a small yelp. "I, ah, didn't hear you come up behind me." She held the bowl of frosting in front of her like a shield. When would she stop stammering like an idiot in his presence?

Hunter grinned that slow grin and scrubbed a hand over the stubble on his chin. "Smells so good in here, I feel like a cartoon character being drawn along. Woke me up, and I couldn't resist." He looked at her like a starving man at an all-you-can-eat buffet.

A delicious heat started in her midsection. Then his eyes went to the cupcakes, and she gave herself a kick. Of course. Her baking put that longing in his eyes. Not the tomboy little sister with her unimpressive curves and fear of snakes. But one silly corner of her heart wondered what it would be like if he did look at her that way.

She pasted a bright smile on her face. "Eat. That's what they're for."

He grabbed two, put the first in his mouth and made a humming sound in the back of his throat that she felt all the way to her toes. "*Cher*, these are amazing."

Charlee nodded and kept her eyes on the frosting to hide the blush staining her cheeks. She jumped, surprised, when Hunter stepped beside her and tucked a finger under her chin, tilting her to face him. With his mesmerizing green eyes locked on hers, he took his index finger and swiped at her cheek, slowly wiping off a smear of frosting. Time stopped as he licked the frosting off his finger, his eyes dark and hungry on hers.

Charlee felt his heated gaze in every pore of her body, and it sent a delicious warmth through her. She gripped the bowl tighter so she wouldn't toss it aside and snatch him close. She wanted to run her hands all over his hard chest, the sleek muscle, feel his calloused hands on her. He always had that effect on her, making her want things she'd never known she wanted. Never known she might be capable of. With Rick, things had been… comfortable. Pleasant. But the storm Hunter stirred up inside her with just a look threw her completely. She had no idea how to react.

He reached into the bowl and scooped up another blob of frosting, then slowly licked it off his finger.

Charlee watched, mesmerized, as those green, green eyes pierced through all her defenses, glinting wickedly. Everything stilled as she read the invitation in his eyes, daring her to get closer, to drop her guard and come play with him. The metal mixing bowl slid from her grip and crashed to the floor, bounced once. She started at the sound, and that lazy grin reappeared.

"You have the same effect on me, *cher*." He scooped up the bowl and set it on the counter. Then turned back to her and pulled her closer, his big hands cupping her shoulders as he stopped suddenly, stilled.

Had he really said that? About her? Her breath hung suspended as she waited for him to take that last step, to bring her flush against his body, to kiss her. Instead, his gaze roamed her face, and she watched a storm rage in those piercing green eyes, despite the want clear in every hard line of his body.

Her heart pounded at the way he was looking at her, and she almost, almost pulled him in for a long kiss just to break the delicious tension. *Kiss me, already.*

The oven timer buzzed.

Charlee leaped back, face flaming. *You're an idiot.* This was Hunter, another overprotective macho male who'd try to take over her life if she let him. Hadn't he already maneuvered his way into her house? She wouldn't risk letting him into her heart, too. Been there, done that.

Hunter stepped away from her and rammed a hand through his close-cropped hair. His obvious frustration made her feel much better.

The timer buzzed again, and he hitched his chin at her. "Are you going to get that?"

It took her brain a moment to catch up, then she grabbed the oven door. Her hand was halfway inside when he shoved a pot holder in her direction. "Don't burn yourself."

Charlee shook her head as she pulled the tray of cookies out and set them on a cooling rack. The man made her stupid.

By the time she had herself under control enough to look at him again, he lounged against the counter, arms crossed over his chest, expression blank.

He straightened, his tone crisp and professional. "You should get some rest. It's been a long couple of days."

She blinked at the sudden change, but then a yawn escaped as exhaustion seeped through her defenses. She turned off the oven, headed for the sink.

Hunter nudged her aside with his hip. "You put things away. I'll wash up."

When she started to protest, he tapped a brisk finger over her lips. "It's not an offer I make often. Take advantage."

Within a few minutes, the cupcakes and cookies were in air-tight containers, and her counters and table gleamed. Hunter guided her back to her room with a hand on her back, and her heart started pounding. Would he expect to climb under the covers with her, get pushy, the way Rick had?

Before she found any words, he eased her down on the bed, pulled the covers to her chin, placed a brotherly kiss on her forehead, and disappeared.

His easy dismissal stung, but then she reminded herself she didn't want him to want her. It would be so much easier being good friends if she didn't feel this unrequited attraction. It sometimes made her feel awkward around him. When she wasn't feeling awkward or itching to touch him, he made her feel comfortable, accepted. She sighed. He made her feel safe.

She slept.

~

Hunter knew he'd never get back to sleep. Not with Charlee in the next room, temptation wrapped in the smell of vanilla, those big brown eyes like a punch to the gut.

Instead, he opened his laptop and went over his notes, trying to figure out who had shot at them. He didn't want to limit his focus too soon and overlook other possibilities, but between the newspaper clipping, the threat in her hospital room, her feeling that someone had tried to pull her farther under the water, plus the snake and the ball cap, everything seemed to connect what happened yesterday to last year's drowning.

Why? Revenge? Then Tommy Jennings topped the list. It was the anniversary of his child's death, and that could make sane people do crazy things. He'd have to check if Byte had gotten a lead on Jennings's whereabouts yesterday. He'd check on the ex-wife and daughter, too.

What about the missing Oliver Dunn? He'd left several more messages, with no response.

Then there was Travis and his crush on Charlee. Had he crossed the line into obsession? Maybe he shot at them and then showed up to play the hero? He'd arrived by kayak, but that could have been staged.

What about the two teenagers? Troy and Luke? Had they been friends of JJ Jennings and wanted revenge? But they all seemed genuinely shaken and eager to help Brittany. He'd seen some scary, crazy teens in his work as a detective in New Orleans, but he didn't get that lifeless vibe when he looked into either of their eyes. They seemed like good kids.

Paul Harris, Brittany's father? No question he'd been

frantic, but that could have been faked. He'd been on shore, but he'd been with Brittany during the shooting. He couldn't be in two places at the same time. Though the fact that he blamed Oliver seemed a little too neat and tidy to suit Hunter. And what about young Wyatt's feeling that this was somehow his fault?

He yawned and rubbed a hand over the stubble on his face. He had lots of questions but no clear answers. Yet.

He glanced at the clock, closed his laptop, and started a pot of coffee.

Before it finished brewing, his cell phone rang.

Chapter 7

Hunter checked the caller ID before he put the phone to his ear. "Lieutenant Boudreau."

"Lieutenant, this is Dr. Morgan at Ocala Regional. I think you need to get over here right away."

Hunter's grip on the phone tightened, and dread pooled in his gut. "What's wrong?"

"Brittany Harris is dead."

He clenched his jaw and asked the question he was pretty sure he knew the answer to. "Were there complications from the surgery?"

"None. She'd shown signs of regaining consciousness earlier, and all her vitals looked good."

"What happened?"

"Looks like she was murdered. I wanted to call you right away, before the media gets wind of it. You'll call the sheriff's department?"

"Yes." Hunter rubbed the back of his neck. "Start at the beginning, Doc."

"We had a situation. The fire alarm went off about an hour ago. It turns out someone threw a lit cigarette into a trash can in one of the restrooms on the third floor. It was chaos, patients trying to get out, others yelling in panic, trapped in their beds. After the fire department put it out and we got everyone back to their rooms, I had the nurses on my floor go room by room to check on all the patients."

The doctor sighed. "One of the new nurses went into Brittany's room, saw the duct tape over her mouth, ripped it off, and attempted CPR. But it was too late. She couldn't save her. She's pretty shaken up. Brittany's father was still here at the hospital, so I let him know there were complications—but I didn't get into details. He's understandably upset. I secured the room and haven't let him or anyone else in."

"Thanks, Doc. You did the right thing. Sequester that nurse somewhere until I get there. And keep Paul Harris out of the way. You didn't tell him she was dead?"

"Given the situation, I thought it should come from you."

"I agree. I'll be there in twenty minutes." Hunter hung up, bit back a curse, and turned to find Charlee leaning against the doorframe.

"What happened?" Her voice was scratchy from sleep but pitched high with worry. She looked uncharacteristically fragile in her tank top and sleep shorts, arms wrapped around herself, dark circles under her wide eyes.

He wanted to protect her from the truth, at least for a little while. "I'll fill you in later. I need to get to the hospital. You should go back to bed."

She stiffened at that and gripped his arm as he tried to move past her, eyes blazing. "Don't you treat me like a five-year-old. You'll tell me now." She searched his face, and some of the stiffness left her spine. "It's Brittany, isn't it?" Her voice was quiet, knowing.

He nodded. "Yes, she didn't make it."

She sagged against the doorframe. He reached for her, but she shrugged off his hold and stiffened her spine. "What happened? I thought she was going to be okay. You said the surgery went well."

Hunter glanced away, then met her eyes, gave her the truth, straight up. "Somebody killed her."

Charlee's jaw clenched, and her eyes blazed. He could almost see her cop brain start to sort and process and formulate a list of questions. She straightened, and those beautiful brown eyes settled on him, determination burning from deep inside. "I'm coming with you."

"You know I can't do that, *cher*." Former FWC or not, he couldn't take a civilian along.

She eyed him and raised an eyebrow. "So now, after the whole I-won't-leave-you-alone speech, you're leaving me alone?"

"You know procedure as well as I do. Besides, you can protect yourself."

She sent him a sardonic look, and he knew he'd trapped himself in his own words. "Grab your gun, lock the door behind me. I'll be back as soon as I can."

He checked his gun and gear belt before he hurried out the door. Then he waited until he heard the dead bolt slide home before he hopped in his FWC-marked F-150 and raced toward Ocala.

Charlee gave him four minutes' head start, which was how long it took her to throw on jeans and a T-shirt. She took a couple of ibuprofen to ease the lingering pain in her head and carefully locked the dead bolt on the cottage's front door before she climbed into her Jeep.

The whole way into Ocala, she tried to figure out how she was going to get near Brittany's body. In light of what she'd been thinking about earlier, a nagging question had popped into her brain and wouldn't let go. But she had to know. Did Brittany have bruises on her neck like Nora's? And if she did, what did it mean?

Charlee had no idea. But if there were, it would be another "coincidence"—which she didn't believe in—another supposedly unrelated fact that nagged at her like a sore tooth.

Of course, whether Brittany had bruises or not, they still didn't have motive. Why would someone kill a teenager? Because if it was obviously murder, and Hunter had said as much, there had to be motive.

She pulled into the hospital parking lot and blew out a breath when she saw the local news trucks starting to arrive. It wouldn't take long before the Orlando and Tampa stations showed up, too.

She was glad she'd grabbed her hoodie on the way out. She pulled it on and tucked her hair into the hood, careful of her bandaged head. She tucked her hands into the front pocket as she slipped inside. Hospitals were always freezing, though that wasn't why her hands were like ice. She blinked back furious tears. Sure, Brittany had been mean to her brother and rude to her father—weren't all teens?—but that hadn't hidden the pain in her eyes. Charlee had so wanted to make a great memory for the girl. And now…this.

She forced the anger and hurt aside so she could think like a cop. First, she had to get past Hunter into Brittany's room. Charlee was ninety-nine percent sure this had something to do with her, because someone had threatened her and accused her of messing up his plans. Priority one was identifying him so she could

huddled further into himself. “I’m so sorry, Wyatt,” Hunter murmured.

It seemed to take Paul a few moments for the words to sink in. “Murdered?” he whispered. “Somebody murdered my baby?” He hissed out a breath. “How is that possible while she’s in the freaking hospital?”

“We don’t have all the answers yet, Mr. Harris. But we’re going to get them. I’ll check in with the staff and let you know when you can see Brittany. But first I have to ask, when was the last time you saw her?”

Paul looked off into the distance as if in a trance. “Must have been about midnight, I guess. I went to see if she’d woken up yet, because the doctor said it could be any time. I didn’t want her to wake up alone.”

Wyatt let out a quiet snort of disbelief.

Hunter turned to the boy. “What about you, Wyatt? Did you go in to see your sister at the same time?”

“No. He went alone. He said that since Brittany didn’t really like me, she wouldn’t want my face to be the first thing she saw when she woke up.”

Hunter kept his expression bland for Wyatt’s sake. Who said that to their child?

“You misunderstood, Wyatt. That wasn’t what I meant. What I was trying to say—”

“You just wanted to be alone with her so I wouldn’t hear whatever you said to her.”

“Wyatt,” Paul warned.

Hunter kept his tone casual. “What did you want to talk to your daughter about, Paul?”

Paul rubbed a hand over his face. “Just father-daughter stuff. I wanted to tell her I loved her. And that I was sorry.”

Wyatt snorted again, and Paul shot him another warning look.

"Sorry for what?" Hunter pressed.

"For the divorce, all the hard times lately. For making her come on this trip."

Wyatt shrank further and further into himself. Paul brushed a hand over his son's leg, and he flinched.

Hunter kept his voice low. "Wow, Wyatt. You got really bruised. Did that all happen on the trip, too?"

Wyatt shrugged. "I guess."

"I want to see my daughter," Paul demanded.

"And you will. After your dad talked to Brittany, Wyatt, did you go in to see your sister?"

"Yeah, just for a minute. She was sleeping, so I didn't stay."

"What did you do next?" Hunter asked Paul.

"We were hungry, but the cafeteria was closed, so we grabbed some snacks from the vending machine. Wyatt fell asleep curled up on the floor, and I dozed in the chair. Until the fire alarm went off. They forced us to leave. I wanted to stay with Brittany, but they said no." Paul spun, tried to grab Hunter by the shirtfront. Hunter neatly sidestepped. "Who killed my baby?"

Hunter put more distance between them. "I don't know. Yet. But I will. Stay here until the nurse comes back for you."

He hurried down the hall and stopped short when he saw Pete, along with Sanchez and Fish, clustered outside Brittany's room, with Charlee in their midst.

~

Charlee knew he'd spotted her when everyone went

silent. Hunter marched down the hallway, and without slowing down, he leaned in and took her by the arm, steered her away from the others. "We need to talk."

She'd expected him to chew her out in front of everyone, so she appreciated the gesture. In his place, she wasn't sure she'd have been as considerate.

Just out of earshot, he let go and folded his arms over his chest. "I told you to stay home, Charlee. You can't be part of an active investigation. You know the rules."

Charlee didn't say anything, just mirrored his stance and waited until he ran out of steam. Her silence seemed to give him pause.

"What did you come here to find out?"

"I needed to see Brittany's body."

"Did you find anything?"

Caution made her shake her head. "I'm not sure yet." She had suspicions, but until she had time to think, to compare these photos to the ones from last year, she didn't want to say or do anything that might unwittingly create tunnel vision for Hunter and his team. They needed to look at all the evidence with an open mind. Rick had told her she was imagining things. Maybe she was.

She watched Hunter's growing impatience and was debating what more she could say, when Pete stepped up behind him. "We need to get in there. The media is starting to circle."

Hunter turned to Charlee. "Stay here. I'll be right out."

"I was just going to go talk to the nurse—"

"You and I are not done. Stay put."

He didn't wait for her agreement, just went into the

room and closed the door in her face. Charlee bristled, but she understood.

She leaned against the wall, hands in her pockets, tried to think. Then she pulled out her cell phone, studied the pictures. Were these bruises a match to the ones from Nora's neck? A chill passed over her skin, and she straightened, looked up and down the empty hallway.

She didn't see anyone. But she knew this feeling, had learned not to ignore it.

Someone was watching her.

Inside Brittany's room, Hunter pushed aside his frustration as his team went to work. Fish took pictures while Marco Sanchez pulled on gloves and bagged the duct tape and other items that might have trace evidence. Hunter and Pete stood off to the side. Neither man spoke while they studied the scene.

"Pretty ballsy, coming in and slapping tape over her mouth while she's connected to all those machines," Pete said.

"Machines that would start beeping the minute she stopped breathing. So he created a diversion with that cigarette. Thrown in a third-floor trash can. While there's chaos, he walks in here, suffocates her, and walks out without anybody noticing."

Hunter took one more look at the crime scene. "Make sure you get everything we need before I let her family in." Sanchez nodded. Hunter glanced from Fish to Sanchez. "What was Charlee looking for in here?"

The two officers glanced at each other, then Fish said, "She just wanted to see the body. She wore booties, didn't touch anything. She knows the drill. She took a few pics with her cell phone and left."

"The whole body or one area?"

"Ah, mostly the upper body."

Hunter leaned closer, saw the bruises around Brittany's neck. He motioned to Fish, who snapped several more close-ups. Charlee had no business in this room, but every single person understood why she'd needed to be there. Or maybe they didn't. He'd question her later. "I'm going to have a look at the hospital security cameras. See what we can find out there."

More sheriff's department officers and crime scene techs waited outside the room. Pete talked to a detective, then turned to Hunter.

"What did the father have to say?"

"Says he saw her last about midnight. Some tension between the siblings. Byte—Officer Griffin—is checking into the family background."

Charlee straightened when they walked into the hallway, but there was no hint of apology in her eyes.

"Stay with us," Hunter said and was relieved when she fell into step with them.

"You hanging in there, squirt?" Pete asked.

She gave him a half smile. "Yes. Thanks. Where's Josh?"

"He caught a call to fly search and rescue near Clearwater," Hunter said as they got into the elevator. She didn't seem to have heard him, though. She scanned the hallway, brow furrowed, body tense, as though she was looking for someone.

Chapter 8

Charlee hid her surprise when Hunter motioned her into the tiny security office along with him and Pete. She'd expected to wait in the hall. The guard, a balding, heavyset older man, had smile lines that creased his face and a uniform shirt that strained over his belly. The rolling chair creaked when he sat down at his keyboard. Most of the wall was taken up with monitors pointed at different hallways, the parking garage, entrances to the building.

"Such a sad thing that happened. We sometimes have family members get a little out of control with grief over a loved one, but murder..." He shook his head. "It don't make a lick of sense to me."

"We appreciate the help," Hunter said. "Can you bring up the tape for the fourth floor from last night, starting just before midnight?"

The man leaned over, punched keys, then sat back as grainy images sped backward on the screen.

Charlee's heart pounded as she leaned closer, squinted to make out faces as the tape rewound. Hal, according to his name tag, stopped the tape at just after 11:30 and then started playback. Charlee's hands gripped the back of his chair, willing a face to jump out at her, to give them a name, someone, who could have done this. At the same time, she prayed it wasn't someone she knew. She knew people did terrible things to each other. She'd certainly dealt with enough of it at FWC to keep her up nights. But kids dying was the worst. A kid being murdered? It defied comprehension. Brittany had come through the surgery like a champ. She was young and would have made a full recovery. Why had someone shot at her to begin with? And why had they come back to finish the job?

Silently, they watched nurses walk up and down the hall, go into and out of various rooms, go back to the nurses' station. Then a doctor appeared in a white lab coat and did the same. Just before midnight, they watched Paul Harris come down the hall, go around the corner. Shortly after that, a man in a ball cap walked down the hall, then disappeared around a corner.

Something about him caught her attention. Before she could figure out what, she felt Hunter and Pete both stiffen beside her. "Do you have a camera where we can see Brittany's room?"

Hal just shook his head, face sad. "Unfortunately, no. The cameras are pointed at the elevators and nurses' stations, the hospital entrances and exits. But that's it."

"Go back," Pete barked, and Hunter shot him a look before his eyes went back to the screen.

Hal rewound again, stopped. Charlee leaned closer still, her shoulder brushing Hunter's, bringing the usual jolt of awareness, but she couldn't think about him now. Who was that…?

Beside her, Hunter muttered a curse as Pete did the same. When it clicked in her mind, she bit back her own. "That's Rick!"

Hunter nodded, eyes glued to the screen.

Rick Abrams? What was he doing here in the middle

of the night, heading down the hall toward Brittany's room?

The tape kept scrolling, and they watched the same doctor they'd seen earlier go down the hall, then Dr. Morgan appeared several minutes later. He disappeared around the corner too, and that must have been when the fire alarm went off. The tape didn't have sound, but suddenly, there was a flurry of activity. Nurses sprang into action, hurrying up and down the halls, call lights flicked on outside doorways, patients rushed from their rooms. You could feel the tension in the air.

Several minutes later, a uniformed firefighter stepped off the elevator and headed for the nurses' station. The chaos slowly eased, patients shuffled back to their rooms, but then a nurse came charging around the corner to where Dr. Morgan had just exited a patient's room. She gripped his arm, and they disappeared down the hall toward Brittany's room.

Hal moved to stop the tape, but Hunter said, "Keep going."

They watched for several more minutes, but there was no sign of Rick or anyone else who shouldn't have been there.

"Go back again," Hunter told Hal. When they reached the segment where Rick appeared, he said, "Print that frame for me, would you?" Hal nodded, clicked a few buttons. "Keep going." Whenever a nurse or doctor appeared, Hunter had Hal print out their faces.

Stack in hand, they thanked Hal and left the security office.

They took the elevator back to the fourth-floor nurses' station. Hunter went straight to the unit supervisor, a no-nonsense woman with a sturdy build and tidy look. He introduced himself, and she asked, "What can I help you with, Lieutenant?"

"Can you identify these people for me?"

She grabbed the glasses on a chain around her neck, balanced them on her nose, and went through the pictures one by one. As she rattled off names, Hunter jotted them down on the back of the photo. When she got to the one of Rick, she paused, shook her head. "Don't know who that is. Never seen him before."

She paused again when she got to one of the doctors, who had his back to the camera. "Not sure who this is, either." She held the picture closer, studied it. "Could be Dr. Franks or maybe Dr. Hillman, based on the build. But neither of them have patients on this floor." She looked up as Hunter came to attention. "Though that might not mean anything," she was quick to add. "Sometimes, the vending machines on three don't work, and people come up here to use ours." She shrugged.

"Thank you, you've been most helpful. We'll be in touch if we need more information."

Her expression turned fierce as she looked at Hunter. "Find out who did this, Lieutenant."

"Yes, ma'am. We plan to do just that."

They moved into a small alcove. Hunter looked at Pete, handed him the picture of the unknown doctor. "Ask around, see if you can find a staff member who can identify him. Then track him down and see what he has to say for himself." Pete nodded and left.

Hunter turned to Charlee, pulled out his cell phone, and called Sanchez. "As soon as you're finished there,

I need you to find Rick Abrams, ask him what he was doing here last night."

There was a pause. "Abrams was here?"

"Yes. Go find out why."

"Okay, Lieutenant, though I'm sure there's a good explanation."

"If there is, we need to know it, sooner rather than later."

"10-4," Sanchez said.

Charlee shook her head in disbelief. "Maybe, like the nurse said, he was here to get something out of a vending machine while visiting someone on another floor."

Hunter nodded once. "Maybe. Sanchez will check."

She rubbed her hands down her arms again, fighting a chill that was deeper than the frigid air-conditioning. She met his eyes. "None of this makes any sense."

"Not yet. But it will." He turned and held out his hand. "Let me see the pictures you took of Brittany."

Charlee hesitated, then opened the photo app and handed him her phone. He studied the photos, handed the phone back. "What are you thinking, *cher*?"

"I'm not sure yet. I need to get back to the cottage and check on something."

His eyes narrowed. "Why won't you just spit it out?"

"Because it could be nothing, and if it is, I don't want to send the investigation down a rabbit trail that will waste time."

"Let me be the judge of that. Tell me the whole story."

He was right, but after the way Rick had dismissed her concerns last year, she was loathe to say anything. Still, if it meant finding Brittany's killer, how could she not? "I'll tell you everything as soon as we're back at the Outpost."

They went back to Brittany's room, found Wyatt crouched on the floor outside the door, hands over his ears as though to block out his father's wailing. Hunter went into the room, but Charlee slid down beside the boy. He lowered his hands, and in his eyes, she saw pain, certainly. The clear knowledge that his oft-annoying sister was gone forever. But there was...more, she decided, something more. It looked a lot like fear.

"How you doing, Wyatt?" she asked quietly.

He looked away. Shrugged. Then speared her with a hard glance. "I heard people talking. They say somebody, like"—he swallowed hard—"suffocated her. Is that true?"

Charlee returned his look. "I wish it wasn't, but yes. It's true." She watched the emotions race over his face. There was that fear again, along with all the rest.

"That lieutenant guy, he thinks my father did it, doesn't he?"

Charlee shook her head. "They don't know anything yet. But they'll ask questions, keep digging until they figure it out." Charlee winced. Not the most encouraging thing to say. "But I'm sure your father had nothing to do with it."

She waited for Wyatt's vehement declaration of his father's innocence, some outburst about accusing him unfairly, but it didn't come, and another chill slid over her skin. "Wyatt, do you have a reason to think your father had something to do with this?"

Abject misery and a split second of what looked like guilt flashed in his eyes before he sprang to his feet. "Don't say things like that about him! You don't know him!"

He raced down the hall before Charlee could stop

him. She debated following but decided to give him a bit of space. And give herself time to think through his reaction and figure out what to say next. Several minutes later, Hunter came out of the room, glanced around. "Where's Wyatt?"

"He took off to get some air, I think."

When Hunter simply looked at her and waited, she sighed. "He seemed worried, scared maybe. I asked if he thought his father had anything to do with Brittany's death, and I guess it spooked him."

Hunter's eyebrows shot almost to his hairline. "You guess?"

Charlee shook her head, tried to make him understand. "It's hard to explain, but he wasn't acting right. Something is off about his relationship with his father." She met Hunter's knowing look. "You've thought it, too. And how he flinches whenever someone touches him."

Hunter rubbed the stubble on his cheek. "I've noticed. And I need to ask him about it."

They walked out the main exit of the hospital, found Wyatt pacing on the sidewalk. He stopped right in front of Hunter, chin up, eyes desperate. "He didn't do it. You can't make it sound like I don't trust him. He's my father. He loved Brittany. He didn't do it."

"No one is accusing anyone of anything right now, Wyatt." Hunter's voice was calm, and Charlee felt her own racing heart slow just listening to that easy Cajun drawl. "It's way too soon. Right now, we're just asking questions, trying to get a sense of what happened. Can you tell me what you remember?"

"We already told you. Why are you asking again?"

When Hunter just waited, Wyatt spoke, every word

clipped. "We were in that stupid waiting room. They said one of us could go see her. Dad wanted to go, so I stayed. He came back, said she still hadn't woken up, so I could go in." He looked away. Bit his lip. "I didn't really want to, but I did. She was just sleeping. It wasn't like she could talk or anything." He shrugged. "I came out, we got snacks from a vending machine. Then Dad said he was going for a walk, and a few minutes later, the fire alarm went off and everyone went crazy."

"Did your dad come back then?"

Wyatt seemed to consider. "Yeah, after a while. He brought me another soda from the vending machine."

Hunter opened his mouth to ask another question when Paul Harris burst through the door. "There you are, Wyatt." He turned on Hunter. "Why are you questioning my son without me present? How dare you."

Hunter raised both hands, palms out. "We just asked him what he remembered, that's all."

Paul put an arm around his son, and Charlee saw Wyatt wince, then cover his reaction. She met Hunter's eyes.

"You want to talk to my son again, you do it with me present. Understand, Lieutenant?"

"Of course. Again, I'm sorry for your loss."

"When can I have my daughter? Take her home?"

"Soon. I'll let you know as soon as I can. In the meantime, I hope you'll both go get some rest."

"You think I can sleep, knowing my baby is dead?" His voice rose with every word.

Wyatt took his arm, tugged gently. "Let's go, Dad. It's okay."

In an odd role reversal, the son led the father away, glanced over his shoulder as they did.

"He's scared," Charlee murmured. "And he knows more than he's saying."

Beside her, Hunter nodded. "I agree. Let's go. You're dead on your feet."

It was almost dawn when they got back to her cottage. Charlee dreaded the conversation, wanted to avoid seeing his skeptical look, but it had to be done. As soon as she got inside, she went into her bedroom and pulled a cardboard file box off the top shelf of the closet. Before she'd resigned last year, she'd made copies of everything she could get her hands on having to do with the case. Call it a cop's sense, but beyond her guilt over JJ's death, there had just been something... off about what had happened, and she couldn't quite let it go. But she'd never found anything more concrete than a feeling, and Rick had convinced her that maybe she wasn't cut out for police work, since she couldn't emotionally separate from the case. Maybe he was right.

But now, a year later and another death, with her the only obvious link. It was past time to figure out what really happened. She pulled out a file folder, flipped through it until she found the picture of Nora, JJ's sister.

She grabbed the photo and went back to the kitchen where Hunter sat at the table, sipping coffee. She slid onto a chair, set down the photo. Then she pulled up the photos of Brittany and held the phone up next to it.

Beside her, she felt him stiffen as he studied the bruising on both necks. The ones around Brittany's throat appeared to be from strangulation. Which didn't make much sense if the killer covered her nose and mouth with tape. Why do both?

Hunter's sharp gaze flicked back and forth between the photos. "Who is this, Charlee?" he asked, pointing to the photo on the table.

"That's Nora Jennings. JJ's sister. I was able to save her, but not JJ."

"Someone tried to strangle her?"

"No. I don't think so. Maybe." Charlee ran her hands through her hair, winced when the movement pulled on her healing stitches. "When I got to Nora, there was a branch over her neck, and her head was underwater. She almost didn't make it."

He shot her a look. "But she did, thanks to you."

Charlee waved that away. "She doesn't remember what happened, says it's all a blur, but those bruises have always bothered me. They don't look like something a branch would cause."

"What did the investigator on the case say?"

Charlee looked away, couldn't meet his eyes. "He told me to let him do his job, and since she was alive, the bruises really weren't important. JJ got swept away and drowned. It was tragic, but it was an accident." She sighed. "Rick said the same thing."

"Rick is an idiot," Hunter said immediately. Then he fell silent, and Charlee could almost see the wheels turning in his head. She waited for him to dismiss her concerns, but instead, he asked, "What about the bruises—or about the scene—seemed off to you?"

Charlee's mouth dropped open, and she wondered if she'd heard right. When she didn't respond, he said,

"Think, *cher*. You have good instincts. What bothered you?"

"Like I said, it was always the shape of the bruises." She stopped. "And the fear in Nora's eyes when she said she couldn't remember what happened."

"Is it possible brother and sister fought, and she accidentally pushed him in?"

"Yes, anything is possible."

He studied her for a long moment. "But it's still like an itch you can't scratch. I'll have the techs see if there's a way to match up the bruising patterns."

Charlee sucked in a breath. Once again, he had taken her opinion seriously. His easy acceptance made several more bricks in the wall around her heart tumble to the ground, letting in glimmers of light. "Thank you."

He looked at her in surprise. "For what?" He paused. "You were a great officer. You ever think about coming back?"

Yes. No. Maybe. She turned, pushed to her feet. "Not having this conversation right now, Lieutenant. I'm beat."

Hunter checked the perimeter around the cottage, then sat in his FWC truck and used his laptop to catch up on paperwork. After he was sure Charlee was asleep, he went inside to try to catch a few hours shut-eye on her too-short sofa.

He'd barely drifted off when her shout woke him. He came off the couch in one smooth motion, gun in hand, already racing down the hallway. When he burst into her room and saw her thrashing around, he stopped, realized she was caught in a nightmare.

He huffed out a relieved breath, sat down on the side of the bed. "Easy, *cher*. It's just a dream."

"JJ! Oh God, JJ. Where are you?" Her head thrashed back and forth, hands clenched.

He put a hand on her arm, felt the tension there.

She jerked away. "No! I have to find him. JJ!"

He leaned closer, ran his hand slowly up and down her arm. "Wake up, *cher*. It's just a bad dream."

Slowly, her eyes blinked open, fear still lurking in their depths. "Hunter?"

He pushed the tangle of hair out of her eyes. "Yeah. You're okay." The first fingers of dawn crept through the window, highlighting her bare shoulders and slender neck. He swallowed hard, nudged the strap of her tank top back into place, determined to ignore the temptation of her creamy skin. "Go back to sleep."

He started to rise, but she reached out and stopped him with a hand on his forearm. She sat up and propped a pillow against her back. "Stay." She closed her eyes, swallowed hard, opened them again. "Please? I can't go back to sleep yet."

He studied her, caught by the effort those words had cost her.

All the reasons this was a very bad idea crowded his tongue, but somehow, he couldn't say no. He nodded and scooted next to her, tucked her hand in his.

She looked at their joined hands, then ran a finger over the heavy silver bracelet he wore. "You never take this off, do you?"

He'd told her funny stories about his younger brother late one night after a few too many beers. He'd mentioned that he'd bought Johnny the bracelet but had glossed over his brother's death, unwilling to admit it had been his own fault. He really didn't want to tell her now either, but this was Charlee.

His eyes met hers, and he found himself telling her the truth. "I wear it to remember him. He died because I wasn't paying attention. I got cocky."

Her eyes widened, but her voice was quiet. "Tell me what happened." He was tempted, but when he opened his mouth to tell her, the words locked in his throat.

The silence lengthened. Charlee didn't push, and finally, he just shrugged, shook his head to push the memories away.

She let it go, just kept running her finger back and forth over the silver links in a soothing motion. "I like it. It's very sexy," she murmured.

His eyes shot to hers, and even in the predawn light, he caught her startled expression, as though she hadn't meant to say the words aloud. He took the out she'd offered him, eased away from the memories, and grinned, turning the tables on her. "Glad you think so, *cher*. I think you're sexy, too, by the way."

He saw the slight shiver that raced over her skin as he pulled her closer, ran his palms over her bare shoulders, and touched his lips to hers in one featherlight kiss. She pulled back, eyes wide, and they stared at each other for long seconds. He saw the longing in her expression, the indecision. He waited, completely still, while that clever brain of hers warred with desire. When she slowly leaned into him and kissed him back, he let out a sigh of relief.

The kiss deepened slowly, gradually, until his tongue slipped between her teeth and she pulled him closer and closer, until there wasn't an inch of space between them. His body urged him to tug her closer still, but his mind told him to hit the brakes. Charlee wasn't at the top of her game just yet, and he would never take advantage.

He inched back, saw the wide-eyed shock on her face.

"What are we doing?" she whispered.

He sent her an easy grin, ran the back of his hand down her cheek. "Being there for each other." He saw the way her longing glance ran over his bare chest, but he eased her back down on the bed, then pulled the covers over them both. "Get some rest, *cher*. You've had a long day."

"Good night, Lieutenant," she said and rolled onto her side, snuggling against him until her back hit his chest. He gritted his teeth, tucked her in close, and wrapped his arm around her waist. Every nerve ending in his body wanted more of the way her body curved into his, but he held himself stock still.

Comfort, this was about comfort. Everything else could wait. To distract himself, he started mentally reciting every fact of the case.

He must have drifted off, because he woke to her calling Brittany's name, tears running down her cheeks, panicked. He ran his hands up and down the smooth skin of her arms, inhaling her sweet vanilla scent as he murmured in her ear, "It's okay, it's just a dream. I've got you, *cher*."

He kept up the soothing motion until she drifted off again, content to hold her so she could rest.

Somehow, having her in his arms soothed him too, and he slept, holding her tight.

Charlee woke disoriented. She remembered the nightmares, and...Hunter. She turned, smelled him on her pillow, and a warm fuzzy sensation expanded in her tummy right before an embarrassed flush washed over her cheeks. He'd held her, calmed her. And she'd kissed him silly. But he hadn't pushed, despite the desire building between them.

Unsure what to do with the emotions he stirred in her, she grabbed a quick shower and found him at her kitchen table, wearing a crisp, clean uniform, laptop open in front of him. She hesitated. *What to say?*

He sent her a slow, lazy smile. "Morning, *cher*. You look better. Rested. Coffee's ready," he added, then turned back to his laptop. "I ran home for clean clothes while you were sleeping."

She poured a cup, watched him work. "Want me to scramble a couple eggs?"

He stood, closed the lid on the laptop. "How about you sit while I make eggs?"

She narrowed her eyes. "I can make eggs."

"I know you can. But from what Josh said, I can make them better." He grinned over his shoulder as he pulled the eggs from the fridge.

"Nobody complains about my cupcakes."

"And they won't. You bake amazing cupcakes. But I have it on good authority that your cooking is another story."

She grimaced, appreciating this lighter side of the intense lieutenant. He was trying to relieve some of the tension from last night, as well as break through the darkness surrounding them, and Charlee was grateful. She waved a hand. "Carry on, then. I can handle being served."

"Glad to hear it." He put a skillet on the stove, cracked eggs into a bowl. "How's the head this morning?"

She touched the stitches, winced. "Headaches are getting better, but the wound is still tender."

"Then quit touching it."

She smiled as he'd meant her to. They bantered back and forth while he scrambled eggs with an expert hand. She made toast, poured more coffee.

But too soon, the meal—and the reprieve—was over. "What's on today's agenda?" she asked.

"I have some more people to talk to. Wouldn't mind you coming along."

She raised a brow. "Not exactly protocol."

He propped both fists on the table and leaned closer, the clean scent of his aftershave making her lean in, too. "If I left you here alone, would you stay? Or go off digging on your own?"

Charlee took a sip of coffee to hide the flush that crept up her cheeks.

Hunter straightened. "Former cop. Case related to you. I get it. Just don't get in the way, okay?"

Once again, his calm acceptance of her skills and opinions threw her off balance. Before she could formulate a response, he started clearing the table. "We're out of here in five minutes."

"Let me get my shoes and my phone."

Out of habit, she also grabbed her backpack and tucked her gun inside, just in case.

Chapter 9

She expected them to go farther than just down the dirt road. "What do you want with Travis?"

Hunter parked his FWC truck in the gravel lot in front of the Outpost and turned to look at her. "Follow my lead, okay?" He came around to her side before she could ask what he meant.

He took her arm in a surprisingly gentle hold, once again throwing Charlee for an emotional loop. Just when she thought he was rock-hard, through and through, he showed these glimpses of softness that had her insides puddling at her feet. She straightened and shoved such nonsense from her mind. Right now, they had to talk to Travis. And she had to convince her family she was fine, so they wouldn't worry.

They found Natalie behind the counter, talking on the phone. Her eyes lit up, then narrowed as she eyed Charlee up and down. She ended the call, then came around the counter to wrap her in a careful hug. "What are you doing out, Charlee?" She glared at Hunter. "I thought the doctor said she should rest."

"He did, and I did, but I'm much better now." She looked around. "Is Travis here?"

Natalie raised her eyebrows. "He's out by the shed, doing some maintenance on the canoes and kayaks. Why are you looking for him? Usually, you're avoiding him."

"We need to ask him a few questions about what happened," Hunter said from behind Charlee.

Natalie planted her hands on her hips and studied her. "You sure you're okay, Charlee?"

Charlee crossed her eyes and stuck out her tongue, hoping to get her little sister to laugh, but ended up swaying slightly, mortified when Hunter steadied her from behind. "Getting better all the time. I should be back to work tomorrow."

Natalie looked at Hunter, then back at Charlee. "Take your time, Sis. It's all good."

"We'll just go check in with Loverboy Travis," Hunter said and casually took Charlee's arm again.

"Loverboy Travis?" Charlee couldn't help laughing. "Don't let him hear you say that. The last thing I want is to encourage him."

Hunter grinned, the hand on her arm distracting her. They found Loverboy in the shed, sitting on a sawhorse, playing a video game on his phone.

"Hey, Travis," Charlee said.

He jumped and spun around so fast, the phone landed in the dirt. He scooped it up, then hurried over. "Charlee. I didn't expect to see you today. Are you okay? You look good."

Hunter interrupted his nervous chatter. "I need to ask you a few questions about what happened the other day."

"Sure, of course. Whatever you need."

Hunter waved him back to the sawhorse and leaned against a rack of canoes. Charlee stood beside him, determined to see Travis's face as he answered the questions. "Walk me through what happened, Travis. You were here at the Outpost in the morning…" He let the statement trail off.

Travis picked up the story. "Right. Once Charlee and the group left, I did a little work for Mr. Tanner, and then he told me I could have the rest of the day off, since Natalie was there."

"Did you ask for the time off?"

Charlee saw Travis freeze at Hunter's question.

"I, uh, yeah. I wanted to get out on the river for a while."

Charlee narrowed her eyes. "You followed me. Why?"

Travis fidgeted with his phone, head down, not meeting their eyes. "I knew it was going to be a tough day for you. I just wanted to make sure you were okay."

"What made it tough for Charlee?"

Hunter's question made Travis look from one to the other. "The anniversary. Everyone knew that."

"Not everyone." Hunter crossed his arms and leaned forward in interrogator pose. "How did you know about it?"

Again, Travis fidgeted. "I heard Mr. Tanner and Pete talking about it a couple days ago." He paused. "It wasn't hard to find on the internet."

Charlee stiffened. "Why did you think I wouldn't be okay?"

Beside her, she sensed Hunter's focus sharpen.

Travis's head snapped up. "You're awesome, Charlee. A great guide. I just thought you might want a friend along. Especially with that Oliver guy around." He snapped his jaw shut as though he'd said too much.

"What's wrong with Oliver?" Hunter asked.

Travis's chin came up. "He just seemed like he spent too much time watching Charlee."

"Afraid he was poaching on your territory?" Hunter demanded.

"What? No. Nothing like that." He turned pleading eyes on Charlee. "I just wanted to make sure you were okay. That's all."

"Maybe you got there and saw Oliver paying a little too much attention to Charlee, so you thought you'd play the hero. Create a little accident and then show up to save the girl and win Charlee's affection."

Charlee didn't think Travis had it in him to devise such a plan.

He jumped to his feet. "No. That's crazy. I would never hurt anyone."

"Do you own a gun, Travis?"

His face paled. "No. I hate guns. I've never even fired one."

Hunter motioned for Travis to sit back down. "Okay. Where were you when you heard the gunshots?"

"Not far. Just a few minutes. But as soon as I heard them, I started paddling like crazy."

"Why? Gunshots aren't that uncommon out here."

Travis shrugged. "They sounded different, sorta like a machine gun."

"How do you know what machine guns sound like? I thought you said you hated guns."

His head shot up. "I play a lot of first-person-shooter video games. Shotguns sound different."

"What did you see when you arrived?"

"You were there. You know. Why are you asking me?"

Hunter just waited.

Travis swallowed. Shook his head. "It was horrible. There was blood in the water, and I didn't see anyone at first. Everyone was hiding in the trees. I thought"—he swallowed hard—"I thought at first that Charlee was dead. That the girl was dead, too."

"But they weren't."

"No." He looked at Charlee. "I'm really glad you're okay."

"When did you call 911?"

A flush crept up his cheeks. "Um, I didn't. I saw your boat and thought you probably did that."

Charlee leaped toward Travis, but Hunter's grip on her arm kept her from getting to him. "Why didn't you call 911? Did you help do CPR on Brittany?"

When he looked down, shook his head, Charlee shouted, "What is the matter with you? You've been trained better than that."

Travis hitched his chin toward Hunter. "He was already there, doing that. I had to make sure you were okay first. Don't you see?"

"No, I don't see at all." Charlee broke free of Hunter's grasp to tower over Travis. "We had a guest in trouble, and you did nothing."

Travis swallowed hard. Hunter made a calming motion with his hands, then looked back at Travis. "Did you pass anyone else on the river on your way there? Anyone who can verify your whereabouts at the time of the shooting?"

Travis paled so much, you could see the veins under his blotchy skin. "I didn't hurt anyone. You have to believe me." He looked from one to the other. "I know there was another group of canoes on the river." He slumped back down. "But I don't really remember when I passed them. I didn't shoot anyone." He looked up, expression stricken. "I'd never hurt you, Charlee."

"Let's go," Charlee said.

Anger spurted through her veins, and she wanted to shake Travis until his teeth rattled. She stomped back toward Hunter's truck. "That measly coward. He's done working here. I'll make sure of that. He should have started CPR right away. He—"

Hunter stepped in front of her. "Take a breath, *cher*. He thinks he's in love with you, so his brain is scrambled. What we don't know is if he fired those shots."

Charlee took several deep breaths to calm her racing heart, get her anger under control.

Hunter helped her inside the truck, cranked up the air conditioner. "I'll let your sister know we're leaving."

When they pulled up in front of her cottage, she turned to Hunter. "He could easily be the shooter. He knows the river, knows the woods around here. And if he plays those shooter games, he'd know how."

"Concussion or not, your mind is sharp, *cher*. I'm thinking along those lines, too."

As she opened her door, her cell phone rang. She glanced at the screen, then put the phone to her ear. "Hey, Liz. What's up?"

"I've been trying to reach you. The news about the girl is all over town. It's horrible. Are you okay?" Before Charlee could answer, Liz fired off more questions.

Charlee understood her worry and waited until Liz finally wound down. "If you stop and take a breath, I'll answer all forty-two of those questions."

"Sorry. I'm worried, that's all. People care about you,

and they're sad and angry—and scared. They're coming here for comfort food and answers. Do you have any information I can give them?"

"No. That would be up to Hunter. The investigation has barely gotten started."

"Can you stop by? I need to see you, hug your neck, make sure you're okay."

Charlee glanced at Hunter. "Can we pick up some cupcakes and drop them off at the Corner Café?" At his affirmative nod, she said to Liz, "It's going to take me a little while to get them frosted."

"That's fine. As long as I know you're okay. I really appreciate you bringing more. Are you still with Mr. Yummy?"

Liz had a voice that carried, and when Hunter quirked a brow at that, Charlee felt the blood rush to her face. "Yes, I'm still with Lieutenant Boudreau."

Liz laughed. "Right. Bet your face is red now, too, isn't it?"

"Thanks for that, girlfriend."

Liz chuckled. "Just get over here. Bring cupcakes. And him." When Charlee started to protest, Liz's laughter died, and she added quietly, "Be safe, okay? Promise me, Charlee."

A lump formed in Charlee's throat. "I will. Thanks."

He watched her climb out of the FWC pickup and scowled. He didn't like the way the lieutenant hovered around her. Didn't he have other things to do? Like try to figure out what had happened to Brittany? He hadn't wanted to handle her death that way, and it annoyed him that he'd had to modify his plans. He could, of course, if he wanted to. But he hadn't wanted to. He liked coming up with a plan, a perfect plan, and then executing it brilliantly. The plan was for Brittany to die on the river. Like Nora.

He ran a hand over his head. No, not like Nora. Because of Charlee, Nora hadn't died. JJ had. Beautiful JJ, who hadn't done anything wrong except have females around who constantly belittled him and criticized him and made him feel small. He knew what that was like. Knew what happened when you didn't have a champion to stand up to the bullies, those ugly female creatures who smiled so sweetly but had all the power and used it to beat you down. JJ should never have died.

And that was Charlee's fault. If she hadn't been so worried about stupid Nora, she would have gotten there in time.

He narrowed his eyes when that Boudreau jerk put his hand at the small of Charlee's back to guide her. Like she was his. Like he'd put his own stamp on her.

Anger tried to burst out, break free. Had the cop dared to do more than look? He'd pay for that. Charlee would pay for that, too. Charlee was his, and it was time she understood that. They had a connection, he and Charlee, a bond, strong and permanent. It had been forged on the Suwannee a year ago and had only gotten stronger in the time since. She might not realize it, but he'd seen how she'd changed this year, how she'd gotten sad, seen how much she needed him. Some Johnny-come-lately wasn't going to get in the way of that. Not while he was around to stop it.

No, Charlee was his. Until he decided her time was

up. Then she wouldn't be anybody's. But he would decide when that time came. He alone.

"I'm hungry. Can we eat soon?"

He started at the voice. Had forgotten he wasn't alone. He took all the anger and all the anticipation and carefully hid them inside so there was no trace of his agitation on his face. He turned, smiled gently. "Of course. What would you like? Should I grill us a couple of burgers?"

A big toothy grin accompanied vigorous head nodding. "Can we get more cupcakes? At the Corner Café? They're really good."

He reached over and ruffled his hair. "How about burgers first, then cupcakes later, before we have to work. Sound good?"

The big goofy grin was answer enough. He took meat out of the freezer and then went outside to fire up the grill. The Corner Café was always a good place to pick up the local news and gossip.

Charlee was surprised at the size of the crowd at the café when she and Hunter arrived.

Liz elbowed her way through the well-wishers and swept the cupcake holders out of Charlee's hands, then pulled her into a desperate hug.

Charlee tried to lighten the mood as Liz swiped tears from her cheeks. "Great, now you look like a raccoon, with mascara everywhere."

"Don't ever scare me like that again, okay?"

Charlee rolled her eyes. "I'll do my best."

She spent the next few minutes getting hugged and

questioned by the locals, giving vague answers, and trying to ignore the ache behind her eyeballs. Time for a few more ibuprofen.

Hunter had positioned himself at a little table in the back corner and alternately watched her and everyone coming and going. Which was both unnerving and comforting. As a former cop, she found herself studying people she'd known her whole life with a new and uncomfortable suspicion.

Sammy bounded through the door and wrapped Charlee in a hug that knocked the breath out of her. "Charlee! You're here. Did you bring more cupcakes?"

She laughed. "For you, Sammy. Always." She nudged him toward the counter, met Liz's eyes. "Sammy wants at least two cupcakes, Liz."

Liz smiled. "Coming right up. Show me which ones you want, Sammy."

Charlee swept her gaze around the café and had a sudden, unbidden urge to leave, right then. She glanced at Hunter, and something must have shown on her face, because he stood and reached her in three quick strides. "You ready to hit the road?"

She nodded, hugged Liz, and they were out the door.

But as they crossed the threshold, Charlee stopped, scanned the parking lot. Then looked over her shoulder, studied the faces in the café. Someone was watching her. She could feel it.

Hunter stepped up behind her. "Something wrong, *cher*?"

She studied the parking lot again. Nothing looked out of place, and no one seemed to be paying her any attention. But the feeling persisted. "No, let's go."

Hunter stood behind her as Charlee opened the door to her cottage. She crossed the threshold and almost landed on her butt when she stepped on an envelope and it slid out from under her flip-flop. She took several stumbling steps into the living room but managed to stay on her feet.

"What in the world?" She reached down for the envelope.

"Don't touch it." Hunter went back to his truck for gloves and an evidence bag. He carefully opened the manila envelope and pulled out a photo.

Charlee leaned over his shoulder and gasped when she realized what it was. The picture was of her, standing on the porch, holding the newspaper clipping of last year's death. Her head snapped up, and she looked around. "Somebody's watching me. Whoever sent this was here the day the clipping came." A shiver passed over her skin, and she rubbed her arms as she paced.

Hunter slid the photo and envelope into the evidence bag. "Maybe. Maybe not. They wouldn't have known exactly when it would arrive. It came in the mail?"

Charlee thought back. "Yes, definitely. I saw the Lake City postmark." She stopped, looked at Hunter. "Someone is trying to creep me out, and they are succeeding."

"It's more than that, *cher*, and you're too smart not to know it."

"I do. But until Brittany's murder, I figured it was Tommy or Sally Jennings, maybe even James, Tommy's brother, trying to make me pay for some of their anguish, like I said. Now I don't know what to think."

"We need to talk to them."

"Tommy and Sally's relationship wasn't great to begin with. I can't imagine trying to deal with the loss of a child."

"It's got to be the hardest thing in the world. But if one of them crossed the line from grieving to revenge, we'll find out."

Charlee nodded, her mind spinning. Despite the temperature outside, she felt chilled all the way to her bones and rubbed her arms, wondering if she'd ever feel warm again.

She stood at the kitchen window, looking out. Sunlight flashed between the branches of the huge live oaks that surrounded her cottage, giving the area a fairy-tale feel. The breeze swept through the strands of Spanish moss that swayed from the branches, rustling the leaves.

Something glinted, then disappeared.

Charlee watched, waited.

There.

"Hunter." The word came out a whisper. He didn't respond, so he must not have heard her. She said his name again, and he appeared at her elbow.

"What's wrong?"

She ignored the way the words whispered across the back of her neck and pointed. "There's something—or someone—in the tree out there. See?"

Together, they waited, watched the moss and leaves.

Whatever is was flashed again, and Hunter muttered, "Stay put," before he pulled his gun and eased out the back door.

Chapter 10

Hunter approached the tree from the back, where the trail camera was mounted, to make sure whoever had put it there wouldn't get a glimpse of him on camera. He'd like nothing more than to stomp the thing to bits, but this might be just the break they'd been looking for. On the older models, you had to physically get the SD card from the camera. But on the newer ones, you could connect to your cell phone, and they'd send images to you via email or text. If that was the case, it just might net him the cell number of Charlee's stalker. But either way, Hunter planned to watch the watcher. He headed back to his truck to get what he needed.

When he came inside a few minutes later, Charlee stood up from the couch. "A trail camera?"

"Yes. I'll see if we can track down the serial number. If we're really lucky, maybe a cell number it's tied to. Either way, we'll be ready if our guy comes back." He grinned.

He could almost see the wheels turning in her head. "You installed another camera?"

"You bet. I'm covering all the bases. If it's a cellular model and Byte can trace it, great. But if it's one of the older models, our guy will have to come back to get the SD card or replace the battery. We'll be watching."

Charlee rubbed her hands up and down her arms. "It all makes perfect sense. I just don't like knowing someone's been watching me. Even worse to think they'll still be doing it."

He shrugged. "Don't worry about it, just act—"

She held up a hand. "Seriously? Do not tell me to act natural."

His eyes were steady on hers. "Just trying to catch this guy."

"Right. I know. I don't want to miss the big picture, so to speak." She shuddered.

Every protective instinct sprang to life. He wanted to pull her close and promise her it would all be okay. But nobody could promise that, and he respected her too much to offer empty words. Still, the need to hold and protect her gnawed at his good sense. The best thing he could do right now was figure out who was after her. Frustration made his voice gruff. "I need to make some calls. Why don't you lie down for a while? You look like you've been staked out in the desert for days."

She batted her eyelashes at him, à la Scarlett O'Hara, and drawled, "I declare, you say the sweetest things."

She surprised a laugh out of him, a real laugh that made him shake his head.

"You should laugh more often, Lieutenant," she quipped, then sashayed down the hall and closed her bedroom door.

He stared after her. He couldn't remember the last time he'd laughed, truly laughed. She had a way of bringing things out in him he'd thought long dead.

Focus, Boudreau. He gave Byte the camera's serial number, hoping it was connected to a cell signal, but he doubted it. It appeared to be one of the older models. Then he updated his captain and responded to the regular two-hour check-in from dispatch, confirming all was well. He also checked in with Fish and Sanchez for an update and checked the CAD log to see what issues his other patrol officers were facing today.

Finally, he called Josh, who had planned to do an aerial patrol of a section of the Ocala National Forest this morning. "Tanner."

"Hey, Hollywood, Boudreau. No issues on that fly-over this morning?"

"No, sir."

"Did you have a chance yet to check if anyone saw any other cars leaving the area of the shooting?"

"Of course. I always do my job, Lieutenant."

Obviously still ticked off about Hunter's promotion. Hunter let the silence stretch. "And?" he finally prompted.

Josh heaved a long-suffering sigh. "I checked with all the first responders, talked to a couple old-timers who don't live far from there, and questioned anyone else I could think of. No one saw another car in the area. But I did find an elderly couple at the Corner Café who said they'd been coming back from a trip to Ocala for doctor's appointments when they saw a dark-blue pickup truck barreling away from the forest like, and I quote, 'The hounds of hell were after him.' They didn't get a license plate or good look at the face, though they did say they thought he was a pretty big guy and wearing a ball cap. Which could describe just about any male who lives out here between the ages of eighteen and sixty-five."

"Any luck at local tire shops?"

"I called both places along SR-40, then called every shop on that end of town, but got nothing. On a hunch,

I stopped by Joe's junkyard out that way, too. Nobody claimed to have worked on a blue pickup lately."

Hunter huffed out a curse. They needed a solid lead. "Thanks, Hollywood. I appreciate it."

"Like I said, Lieutenant, just doing my job."

Hunter ignored the chill. In Josh's place, he'd have been frustrated at being passed over, too. He'd give the man some space. They'd find their way eventually. "Charlee and I spoke to Travis. He's got a crush on your sister, does Travis. Left work early the other day to make sure she was okay. Says he had overheard mention of the anniversary. Charlee read him the riot act for fretting over her instead of starting CPR on Brittany when he arrived."

"Slimy little coward. I bet she did." There was a pause, then Josh added, "It's damn coincidental that Travis just 'happened' to show up there at that time."

"Agreed. But to what end? That he has a thing for Charlee, I get. That he let it distract him from what he needed to do, I also get. But that he would want to harm Brittany for some reason? It's a big leap I'm not sure I'm ready to make."

"Why don't I run his background? I think he grew up around here, but I can't be sure."

"Do that and let me know. Thanks, Hollywood."

"How's Charlee?"

"Sleeping right now. Brittany's death hit her hard, and she didn't get much sleep last night. And I'm sure her head is still pounding. But she's tough. She'll handle it."

"I can come spell you for a while."

"No. We're fine here." In the ensuing silence, Hunter

realized he'd answered too fast. "If you'll get me the background on Travis, that'll help."

Hunter checked on Charlee throughout the night, but she never stirred. At six, he made coffee and did a search for Brittany Harris's name. Not surprisingly, she was all over social media, especially Instagram. There were lots of pictures of her "enduring" the trip to Florida with her lame brother and stupid father, but none of that was out of the ordinary. Wyatt didn't show up there, but he was all over the online gaming forums and chat rooms. It didn't take long to find out which games he played most often, who his gaming partners were, that he couldn't wait to graduate and get away from his family, and that he thought school was a waste of time. He was particularly vocal about a certain math professor at his private school who, to hear Wyatt tell it, picked on him all the time for no reason.

By the time Charlee mumbled, "Morning," as she wandered into the kitchen, Hunter had just typed the professor's name into the search engine and the school's website popped up.

She walked behind his chair and stopped when she saw his open laptop. "Why are you looking up JJ and Nora Jennings's school?"

Hunter turned to face her. "I wasn't. I was looking up Wyatt and Brittany Harris's school."

All the color drained from Charlee's face. "Tell me that's some kind of sick joke." She poured a glass of water, and a bit sloshed over the rim as she sat down across from him.

Hunter typed in JJ Jennings's name and found himself on another page of the school website, with an "in memoriam" listing for James Junior Jennings.

He checked several more pages on the website, and that twitchy feeling at the back of his neck intensified. "No joke. According to the website, all four kids went to the same private school in White Springs."

"And one child from each family died exactly one year apart? No." Charlee shook her head. "Can't be coincidence."

"I agree." Something stank about this whole scenario. His phone rang. "Boudreau. What have you got?" He shifted away so he could focus without being distracted by Charlee's questioning gaze.

"You said you were looking for information on the Brittany Harris autopsy right away, Lieutenant," the medical examiner said.

"Yes, thanks for getting back to me so quickly."

"Your initial assessment was correct. Brittany Harris was suffocated. There was no indication that any system failed that would have caused her death. There were no puncture wounds, no drugs in her system except what was prescribed. Someone put tape over her nose and mouth and suffocated her."

Hunter tapped his fingers on the table, thinking. "You're sure?"

"Absolutely. The who and why will be up to you, Lieutenant."

"It is possible she was strangled? She had bruises on her neck."

There was a pause. "I considered it, but I don't think so. The bruising was too light."

"Thank you, Doctor." He hung up and faced a wide-eyed Charlee. "I'm sure you heard all that. The ME confirmed Brittany died of suffocation, not the gunshot." He picked up his phone.

"Why strangle her *and* use the duct tape?"

"Good question. To buy time? To keep her quiet?"

"Who are you texting?" Charlee asked.

"Your brothers and Sanchez and Fish. I want to get everyone together for a meeting."

Then he called his captain and updated him.

All the while, Charlee didn't say a word, just paced the small room, arms locked around her middle, equal parts sadness and fury in her eyes.

When he couldn't stand it anymore, he stepped around the table and pulled her into his arms. After a moment's hesitation, she wrapped her arms around his neck and tightened her grip like she'd never let him go. He rubbed his hands up and down her back in a soothing motion, struggling not to notice the way her breasts pressed against his chest or how perfectly they fit together. Her sweet vanilla scent made him want to nuzzle her neck, but he didn't let himself. The more time he spent with her, especially lately, the more he admired her. And the more he wanted her. She was sharp and beautiful, and lately, she was starting to shed the insecurities that had surrounded her the past year. The fire rekindling inside her made him want to get close enough to absorb some of her heat. But she was his friend, and he knew if he pushed, he could put their friendship in jeopardy. He wouldn't risk that. She meant too much to him.

Even as he told him himself that for the tenth time,

she shifted back slightly in his arms so she could see his face. His hands settled at her waist, and he pulled her closer, ran his hands over that sleek back and down her very sexy butt. Their eyes met. Held, and the mix of vulnerability and strength in hers was almost his undoing. Especially since she was looking at him as though he were a mirage that had suddenly appeared after a long, dusty trek through an endless desert. And she was ready for a deep drink.

Electricity crackled and sparked between them, and his hands reached up to cup her smooth cheeks, run his thumbs over the soft skin. Time stretched and froze, and before he could force himself to move away from the temptation in her beautiful eyes, she slowly leaned forward and lightly brushed her lips over his.

The contact shocked him like a jolt from a Taser, and his hold on her tightened. Their lips met again, and the fire burst into flame. She made a sound at the back of her throat and opened her lips wider. He plunged his tongue inside, wanting more of her sweet taste. More of her heat. When she wrapped her arms around his waist and plastered her curves to his, reality slapped him. Hard. She wasn't ready for this. They weren't ready for this. The timing sucked.

It took every ounce of his self-control to take that one necessary step back, to put some distance between them. Her eyes blinked open, wide and confused. His hands didn't want to let go, so he backed up another step for good measure, until he could breathe again.

A flush climbed Charlee's cheeks, and she turned and straightened some mail, not meeting his eyes. But somehow, her self-consciousness just made him want her more.

No. Absolutely not. He couldn't let himself get close, couldn't get involved with Charlee, especially not now, while they were in the middle of a case. She mattered too much. His feelings for her could distract him, cause tunnel vision. And if that happened, people died. He wouldn't risk that with her. He touched Johnny's bracelet, put the barriers firmly back around his heart. Johnny's death would always remind him of what happened if he let emotions cloud his judgment. He would never make that mistake again.

He scrubbed a hand over the back of his neck, took a deep breath. "You can sit in on the meeting, but you need to let us do our jobs." Really, could he have made a more idiotic statement?

Her eyes met his, and her expression went hard. "Right. Civilian. Murder investigation."

She whirled around and would have slipped past him, but he stopped her with a light touch on her arm. "You're beautiful, Charlee. And you make me crazy."

"I'm not anyone's toy."

His eyebrows shot to his hairline. Where had that come from? Rick? "No, you're a lady who should be treated as such by a man who will treat you right."

She tossed her head and kept walking.

He let her go. *Distance*, he reminded himself. *Professional distance. Friendship.*

Charlee had no idea how sexy she was. She was smart and strong, but she was also picket fences, babies, and forever. The one woman he sensed could change his life forever. If he let her. Which he could never risk, certainly not in the middle of a case. No matter how strong the pull.

He would protect Charlee. And he had a killer to catch.

If she made him feel things he'd never felt before, he'd ignore it. It was better that way. Safer for their friendship, safer for his relationship with her brothers, altogether safer for his heart.

Charlee paced her bedroom, trying to gather her scattered wits. What had she been thinking, throwing herself at Hunter again? Hadn't she learned her lesson about macho males with Rick? And Hunter had backed away like she was a live grenade. Fine. Whatever. They were friends, good friends. Actually, the best friend she'd ever had. Around him, she felt like she could be herself, without fear of judgment. If lately he looked at her with the same growing hunger she felt for him, it was better, safer, if they both ignored it. She didn't want to lose the ease between them, the closeness, by behaving like an idiot. She took several deep breaths and walked back out to the living room.

He looked up from his laptop, expression carefully blank. "You up to some more questions?"

She could pretend, too. She sank down on the sofa, since the annoying dizziness still hit at odd times. "Ask away."

"Did you sense any hostility toward Brittany or Wyatt from Paul Harris?"

Charlee considered. "No. He came across as a divorced dad trying to do right by his teenagers—neither of whom wanted to be around him, which is typical. Brittany liked playing the martyr, and Wyatt hid behind his video games. There was anger on Brittany's side." She thought about it. "Wyatt's, too, given the way he avoids his father. I worry there's some abuse, but I'm having trouble seeing Paul in that role. I got the sense that the three had once been close, and Paul was desperate to regain that. I can't picture him trying to kill either one of them."

Hunter nodded. "What about Oliver Dunn? Besides his stalker vibe, anything else stand out to you?"

Charlee looked away, then met his gaze. "Honestly, I just tried to avoid him. But he tried to help Paul connect with his kids, to engage them in conversation, make jokes."

"How did Paul feel about that?"

Charlee searched her memory. "At first, he didn't look happy, but after a while, they all seemed to be having a good time."

"Where did Oliver say he was from?"

"If he said, I don't remember. I was only focused on two things: making sure everyone had a good time and getting them all back safely."

"And surviving the one-year anniversary," Hunter added, brow raised, though he hadn't asked a question.

She swallowed hard. "Right, get through the day and convince my family I was fine."

"They care—"

She held up a hand. "I know. Which is why I don't want to add to their burdens. Next question."

"Why do you think someone shot at you and Brittany?"

"Shooting at me, I get. But Brittany? It doesn't make any sense."

"Not to us. But it does to whoever did it. We'll work every angle until we can see the whole picture."

It was how an investigation worked. But this was different. Personal. A young girl was dead, and it had something to do with Charlee. She had to think. She walked into her bedroom without a word and put on her tennis shoes, running shorts, and tank, and strapped a knife to her ankle. She passed through the living room and said to Hunter, "Let's go for a walk. I need to clear my head."

"Give me two minutes." He returned in running clothes, gun at his back, and motioned for her to precede him.

Every fiber of her being wanted to go by herself and escape the tingly awareness whenever he was near. But she wasn't stupid. "I need to process, so keep up."

"Yes, ma'am." Hunter grinned as they set out at a fast walk.

Just being outside, moving, helped settle her mind. Hunter kept pace without a word, and she couldn't decide if that was good or bad. The way his T-shirt stuck to his skin and outlined his chest messed with her equilibrium, and the silence made her want to fill it. But she kept quiet, thinking about the case. She had to keep her priorities straight.

By the time they got back, she felt much more settled, but she was still glad to head for the shower and escape his nearness. When she walked back into the living room, she was surprised to find him alone.

"Where is everyone?"

She leaned over his shoulder as he checked the CAD log, which showed GPS coordinates of each officer's whereabouts. He pointed to a spot on the map where Sanchez's and Fish's call signs were clustered together on a call. For some reason, Josh was there, too. She knew his call sign. Hunter opened the details tab and read the call description out loud. "Resident claims there's a large gator in his yard and asked for help to remove it."

Charlee's eyes widened at the address. "That's Rick's place."

"That's what I thought." He dialed his cell phone. "Let's see if Pete is there, too." The sheriff's department had their own system, so Pete's location wouldn't show up on Hunter's screen. "He's not picking up."

Charlee was already by the front door, sliding her feet back into her tennis shoes. Rick lived out in the woods, and she never wore flip-flops when she went there. His grass always needed cutting, which meant there could be snakes.

Hunter notified dispatch he was heading to that location and then didn't say anything more, though his irritation grew with every mile.

"Cell service is always sketchy out there," she began, but he shot her a look that made her swallow the rest of her words.

"Don't make excuses for them, Charlee. That's not your job, and they don't deserve it."

She looked out the window. Sure, she'd spent most of her life fighting with her older brothers. But she'd also defended them, always, against outsiders. They'd done the same for her. She didn't quite know what to do with this. They'd flat-out ignored Hunter. In the middle of an important investigation. That wasn't like any of them. There had to be another explanation.

Though given the look on Hunter's face, he didn't seem inclined to find out.

Chapter 11

Hunter's jaw locked as they pulled down the long gravel drive to Rick's place, and he pulled up behind several official FWC vehicles and Pete's sheriff's department SUV. Abrams's small, aging mobile home sat right on the banks of the Ocklawaha. It was about two miles past the Outpost's property line, right next to Josh's place, which sat on the opposite end of the property from Charlee's cottage.

Hunter marched over to the group. "Is there some reason you all weren't at the meeting at Charlee's I asked you to attend?"

Five pairs of official eyes widened at the accusation. A few feet away, Rick Abrams stood silent, a smug expression on his face.

Josh was the first to respond. "What meeting?"

"I sent every one of you a text."

Josh, Sanchez, Fish, and Pete all pulled out their cell phones. "I got nothing," Pete declared. "There's no signal out here."

Fish held up her phone. "Sorry, Lieutenant. I didn't get it. Or maybe I did, but like Pete, I have no signal out here."

"Me, either," Josh said. Sanchez nodded agreement.

Hunter scanned the group again but saw no belligerence, which took his temper down several notches.

When he checked his own phone, he didn't have a signal either. "What are you all doing out here?"

"We caught a call," Josh said, though he wouldn't meet Hunter's eyes.

"Right. Large nuisance gator." He looked at Abrams, spread his arms to indicate the surrounding area. "Where is he?"

Abrams stepped forward, hands on hips. "Sorry about that, Boudreau." He didn't look a bit sorry. "My bad. After I called it in and asked for help, crazy beast just wandered back into the river and disappeared."

Josh looked uncomfortable, Sanchez wouldn't meet his eyes, and Fish fiddled with her phone.

At that moment, Charlee appeared, and Abrams's whole demeanor changed. He hurried over and tried to hug her, but Charlee stepped out of his reach. Hunter instinctively moved closer.

"Good to see you, Charlee. Are you okay?" He stepped into her personal space again, and Hunter watched her back up another step. "I was so worried when I heard what happened. I came by the hospital, but you were sleeping, and I didn't want to wake you. Don't worry, we'll figure out who did this to you."

"I believe that's my line," Hunter drawled.

Abrams spun around. "This is none of your business, Boudreau."

"Actually, I think it is." He scanned the faces around him. "Since you're all here, I have a few questions for you, Abrams. First of all, when was it exactly that you went by the hospital?"

"What? Why are you asking me this?"

"Just answer the question."

"Two days ago, not long after they brought Charlee in, after Brittany was shot." He glared at Hunter. "You can't believe I'd hurt her?"

Hunter didn't answer. "What were you doing at the hospital the following night, say between midnight and three a.m.?"

He shook his head, folded his arms. "I wasn't at the hospital then."

"Really? Then who is it we saw on the security footage, stepping off the elevator?"

His eyes widened. "That wasn't—" Abrams began, then he stopped, and all the arrogance leached out of him. "Fine. I was there. I was keeping an eye on things, you know? Just in case."

"In case what? Charlee had already been released."

He scrubbed a hand over the back of his neck, blew out a breath, wouldn't meet Hunter's eyes. "My boy had to go back to the hospital for some tests. My ex won't let me visit, so I came by late at night to check on him, make sure he was okay."

Hunter studied him. Abrams's frustration was so genuine, Hunter believed him. "It still doesn't explain why you manipulated everyone out here on a false call."

"It wasn't false. There really was a gator."

Hunter merely raised a brow.

"Okay, I shouldn't have done that. But I wanted to tell my friends"—he put extra emphasis on the last word—"about what really went down with the so-called bribe."

Hunter let that go for now and eyed his team. "Head over to Hollywood's, and we'll have that meeting."

He turned to Abrams. "I'm sure the guys will call you later, but right now, you'll have to excuse us."

Abrams stiffened. His whole body coiled as though ready to strike, but then he thought better of it and stormed past his blue pickup truck and into the aging mobile home, slamming the door with enough force to rock the entire structure.

The others glanced at each other, clearly uncomfortable. Hunter scanned the group. "I get that he's your friend and was the squad leader. He was mine, too. This whole situation sucks, but for right now, we have a murderer to catch."

Without waiting for a response, he turned back to his truck and slid inside. Charlee, he noticed, climbed into Josh's FWC truck. Sanchez and Fish headed to their own trucks, while Pete headed for his sheriff's SUV alone.

Within minutes, they were at Josh's place, sitting on the screened porch out back. Hunter gave them a rundown on the camera he'd found, the private school both Brittany and JJ Jennings had attended, and finished up with what the medical examiner had said. They fired questions at him, and he gave them everything he knew, then asked, "How are we doing on background on Oliver Dunn and Paul Harris? We need to find out everything we can on Tommy Jennings, too, right away. Josh, anything on Travis Humphries's background pop?"

"Actually, it did."

Hunter shot him a look that clearly asked why he hadn't called him right away. Josh held up a hand and said, "Sketchy cell service, remember. But there's enough coverage here that everything just came through." He scrolled through his phone as he talked, giving them the summary. "Apparently, our friend Travis spent a good bit of his childhood in Miami, shuttled from foster home to foster home before coming here to Marion County to live with an elderly aunt and uncle when he was fifteen. He ran away several times, and they kicked him out when he turned eighteen. The reports said his relatives felt he was 'mentally disturbed' and needed more help than they could give him."

"So they kicked him out?" Charlee asked from where she sat on the porch swing.

Josh nodded. "Right."

"Dig deeper," Hunter said. "See what they meant by 'mentally disturbed.' Sanchez, Fish, you guys see what you can find out about this Oliver Dunn. His answers seemed too vague. Talk to Paul Harris again, too. Charlee and I will go talk to Tommy Jennings and his ex-wife, Sally."

Pete and Josh exchanged glances. Hunter narrowed his eyes. "What?"

Pete's chin came up. "Josh and I took a ride out to Jennings's place the morning after Charlee got shot, couldn't find him. His boss said he hasn't been in for a couple of days."

Hunter thought his jaw would break from clenching it. "You didn't think to mention it?"

"At the time, nope," Josh answered. "We were thinking of Charlee." He paused, met Hunter's eyes. "But in retrospect, it was childish to keep it from you."

Beside him, Pete nodded, expression sheepish. "Since the Harris girl got killed, I've made sure you're kept in the loop." He worked his jaw, then met Hunter's eyes. "Should have done it from the beginning."

Hunter eyed each one, then nodded. "Appreciate it." Before he could say more, dispatch called on his radio. He answered using his call sign. "719-Ocala. Go ahead." He listened, then said, "10-4. Hollywood is with me, and his boat is ready to launch. We'll check it out." He disconnected, then turned to Charlee, whose whole body had gone tense. He couldn't blame her. Seemed every time a call came in, more bad news arrived.

"Dispatch got a call about some dead gators here on the Ocklawaha, near the confluence of the Silver River." He turned to Josh. "I'll drop Charlee off at the Outpost, and you can pick me up at the dock there."

"10-4. Be there in twenty," Josh said, the earlier hostility finally gone. He gave Charlee a quick kiss on the cheek before he headed for his boat.

Pete bussed her cheek, too, before he took off, Sanchez and Fish not far behind.

Hunter climbed into his truck, relieved they were finally working together again.

On the short drive to the Outpost, Charlee watched Hunter slide into warrior mode. Intense, focused, lethal, it was far fiercer than simply cop mode, which was as natural to him as breathing.

She understood priorities, but she was still irritated that he'd taken her compliance for granted. "Never thought to ask if I was okay with this plan?"

His head snapped in her direction. "Weren't you planning to work at the Outpost today?"

"Yes."

He looked at her, eyebrow raised as if to say *So what's the problem, then?*

Charlee carefully pulled on her Outpost ball cap, cautious around the stitches in her scalp. She pulled her ponytail through the hole in the back and sighed. She wouldn't be petty. "Never mind." She wasn't FWC anymore. Her job was here at the Outpost.

Hunter slid out and came around the vehicle, dark sunglasses hiding his expression. "I'll wait for Josh on the dock. You'll be okay here for a couple hours?"

Charlee raised her backpack, in which he knew she kept her gun, and saluted. "Scout's honor."

He huffed out a laugh and shook his head as he walked around the side of the building.

The bell overhead chimed when Charlee walked into the office. "Hey, Dad. How're things?"

Some of the fatigue left his face when he saw her. He wrapped her in a careful hug, then leaned back to study her face. "How's the noggin? How many of me are there today?"

Charlee grinned and kissed his cheek. "Only one, but that's always been more than enough."

Her father threw his head back and laughed, and Charlee realized how much she had missed that sound. She couldn't remember the last time he'd laughed like that.

"Natalie went back to school, right?"

Her father grinned. "You could see the cloud of dust for miles. I'm still wondering if the stork dropped the wrong baby off all those years ago. She couldn't wait to put on those crazy high-heeled sandals and her fancy little outfit and blow on out of here."

"Glad she's able to get back to 'the real world.' I hated keeping her exiled here a minute longer than necessary."

Her father eyed her carefully again. "You sure you're okay, Charlee? We're not real busy today. You could take another day. I'm fine here."

Charlee looked up and saw Travis watching her through the window. "Travis is working today?"

"I asked him to come in, just in case you weren't up to it yet."

She wanted to fire him on the spot. But maybe it was better to keep him around for now. It gave her father extra help in the office and let them keep an eye on him.

The bell above the door chimed, and Charlee smiled when she saw who it was. "Hi, Sammy. What brings you out here?"

He grinned from ear to ear and pulled a handful of rather bedraggled bright-pink wildflowers from behind his back. "I was riding my bike, and I saw these pretty flowers." He held them out to her. "I know you like flowers, so I brought them for you."

Charlee buried her face in the blooms and then leaned up to give Sammy a kiss on the cheek, watching him duck his head and blush. "Thank you, Sammy. These are beautiful. It was so nice of you to bring them for me."

The bell above the door chimed again, and Charlee sighed when Rick Abrams strode through the door and headed right toward her. "We need to talk, Charlee." He brushed past Sammy, who narrowed his eyes and stepped in front of him.

"I was talking to Charlee. She's my friend."

Abrams dismissed him. "Right, but now it's my turn. Scram."

Charlee turned her back on Abrams and gently touched Sammy's arm. "Ignore him. I'm glad we're friends, and thank you again for the flowers."

Sammy flashed an angry look at Rick and then turned and left.

Charlee turned back to Rick, hands on her hips. "Why did you follow us over here, Rick?"

He chewed the inside of his lip in a gesture she'd always disliked. "Just hear me out, Charlee. What happened at work—"

Charlee's temper spiked. At him, but mostly at herself. When they'd first started dating, he'd been great. He'd treated her like a princess, so she'd ignored the warning bells about the things he said, the little ways he undermined her. It had taken months before she'd realized how subtly he'd gotten her to doubt herself and lose her confidence. She was still trying to get over that—and forgive herself for allowing it.

Now he'd taken a bribe? What did that say about her ability to read people, a critical skill in law enforcement? She'd told him they were through months ago, and he was still pretending he hadn't heard. Now he'd been rude to Sammy, the sweetest guy in the world.

Decision made, she brushed past Rick, kissed her father's cheek, and headed for the door, backpack over her shoulder. "As long as Travis is here, I'll just go with Josh and Hunter. They have a report to check on."

"Are you sure you—"

"Love you, Dad. I'll be fine."

"Hey. We're not done, Charlee. We need to talk."

She glanced over her shoulder. "We've been done for months. I have nothing to say, and you have nothing

I want to hear." She almost added *sorry* but stopped herself in time. Not sorry.

She almost ran over Travis, who smiled when he saw her. "Hey, Charlee. I wasn't sure if you'd be in today."

She poked the black T-shirt that covered his skinny chest. "You'd better do your job today, Travis, and do it right, or I'll fire your sorry butt."

She hurried down the dock, afraid she'd literally missed the boat.

Josh's SeaArk idled at the dock while he and Hunter studied a cell phone. Josh stepped to the helm, and Hunter started untying the lines.

"Wait." Charlee broke into a jog. Both men looked at her in surprise when she hopped aboard.

Josh pulled away from the dock.

"Hold up, Josh. What are you doing, Charlee? I thought you were working in the office with your dad."

Charlee studied his face but couldn't see his eyes behind the dark shades. Some silly corner of her mind had hoped he'd be glad to see her. She kept her voice light. "Travis showed up to work, and I figured he and Dad could handle it without me."

He folded his arms and studied her. "And you didn't want to watch him drool all day."

She grinned. "That, too. And Rick showed up."

Hunter stiffened. "What now?"

"Said he wanted to talk. I said I didn't." She shrugged. "Just let dispatch know I'm riding along. I can't think of a safer place for me to be, can you?"

Behind them, Josh snorted. "She's got you there, Lieutenant."

Hunter whipped his head around, and Josh quickly added "sir." But he was grinning as he said it.

Hunter let out a sigh and turned back to Charlee. "You are making me crazy." His expression hardened as he glared in her direction. "Just don't do anything stupid."

Charlee saluted smartly and saw him smother a grin before he shook his head and turned away.

She turned to Josh, kept her tone light. "Hey, Bro, how's your basketball team doing?" Elaine had been a tutor at the forest community center and had convinced Josh to start a boys' basketball team. Since her death, those boys seemed to be the one thing that gave him purpose.

He smiled, a real smile this time, and a seed of hope took root in Charlee's heart. He was starting to heal. "We're going to have a tournament soon. Will you bring cupcakes?"

She nudged him with her shoulder. "Of course. You don't even have to ask."

The woman would drive him completely nuts before this thing ended. Hunter found himself watching the way she moved, checking to see if her head hurt, for when it did, she'd get this little frown line between her brows. He understood, better than ever, her brothers' need to wrap her up and keep her safe. Charlee was unlike any woman he'd ever known. From the time they'd become friends over beers with the whole FWC squad, he'd been drawn to her wit and quick comebacks, never mind her ready smile. Then, after what happened at the Shoals, she'd needed a friend, someone to be there while she worked through her guilt. And when she'd finally ditched that douchebag Abrams, he'd seen the uncertainty in her eyes and been determined to help her regain her confidence. Seeing the self-assured woman he'd first met reemerge was incredible to watch.

Like now, seeing her standing next to Josh as he sped along the river, she looked like she'd been born on a boat. He caught the glimpses of anxiety as she eyed the water, but she didn't back down from her fear. Charlee didn't shy away from dirt or hard things. The fact that she would move heaven and earth for her family got to him. That unwavering devotion was achingly familiar. He understood, and he never wanted her facing the kind of guilt that would haunt him until the day he died.

As though she sensed him thinking about her, she stepped up beside him with a playful smile.

"Those are some very deep thoughts, Lieutenant. Care to share?"

He pushed memories of Johnny aside as one corner of his mouth kicked up. She'd blush to the roots of her hair if she knew how badly he wanted to pull her flush against him, run his hands over every inch of her skin, and kiss her until the flames consumed them both.

"Just trying to figure out which crazy person is after you."

He watched the playfulness fade from her expression and wanted to call the words back. But it was better this way. Distance was good. Safe. For both of them.

They smelled the dead alligators before they saw them. Josh came around a bend in the river, and the stench slapped them like running into a wall of awful. Charlee covered her mouth and nose as Josh slowed down, and they all looked around, trying to identify where the gators were.

It didn't take long.

They were lying along the banks, vultures circling overhead. Charlee had spent her life on this waterway, so she'd seen dead alligators before. As an FWC officer, she'd found several that poachers had gotten hold of, missing their heads and tails. But she had never seen one hacked up like this. Never mind three.

She looked over her shoulder and saw that Hunter and Josh wore the same shocked expressions.

Hunter motioned to Josh, who eased the boat closer. Hunter grabbed a camera and took pictures of the scene from every angle he could get from the water. They didn't want to mess up any potential evidence or footprints when they stepped ashore.

Hunter put the camera down and studied the dense swamp. Charlee shaded her eyes from the afternoon sun, trying to see into the shadows. "The swamp goes way back at this spot," he said. "There's no way someone came in by truck or even ATV. They had to have come by water."

Hunter glanced at Josh. "I agree. You couldn't get a vehicle back in there."

Josh nosed the boat up between two cypress trees, and both men pulled on rubber boots. Charlee glanced down at her shiny white tennis shoes. "I'll just wait here."

Hunter let his sunglasses dangle around his neck and slid over the side and into the mud. He looked back over his shoulder and winked. "Don't go anywhere."

Charlee rolled her eyes and watched as they slogged

around the area, looking for something, anything, that might help them identify who had done such a horrible, senseless thing.

Hunter had seen a lot of things in his life, but this kind of animal cruelty made him sick. This wasn't someone looking to earn a buck by selling a hide or a tail to a restaurant. This was a seriously sick individual.

He and Josh climbed back into the boat, and he met Charlee's questioning look. "Whoever did this was one angry son of a gun and took his fury out on those poor creatures," Hunter said.

"But how would he hack them up? If he's going after one, the other two aren't going to calmly sit around and wait their turn," she said.

Her razor-sharp brain never stopped. "They'd been trapped first. All three jaws had been taped shut."

Charlee's eyes widened. "So somebody caught them and then killed them. Didn't take the tail to eat, at least?"

"No. This was unnecessary violence." Josh fired up the motor, jaw clenched. "And we are going to track down and find the scumbag."

Hunter slipped his sunglasses back on. "Let's head back and see if anyone we know has a wildlife camera near here. Maybe we'll get lucky, and someone will have captured this model citizen coming or going."

Josh turned the boat around, and they started back toward the Outpost slowly, all three of them scanning the riverbank. They passed several canoes and kayaks, but none of the people they questioned could offer anything helpful.

Charlee sat down in the bow of the boat, eyes on the river, watching for obstructions below the surface and pointing them out to Josh.

Suddenly, she stood, cocked her head to listen. “What’s that noise?”

She waved Hunter over. He stepped to her side, taking in her curious look. “Something just started ticking.”

“Ticking?”

“Listen.”

He motioned Josh to idle the motor. Then they all heard it. Like an old-fashioned alarm clock.

Hunter and Charlee both reached for the front cubby at the same time. Hunter opened the latch and lifted the cover.

He froze. The ticking came from a timer.

Which was strapped to explosives.

The red flashing countdown timer was at fifteen seconds, fourteen…thirteen…

He turned to Josh. “We’ve got a bomb!”

He glanced back at the timer, grabbed Charlee’s hand, and yelled, “Jump!”

He and Charlee leaped off the port side, and he saw Josh hurl himself off the starboard side.

Chapter 12

Hunter gripped Charlee's hand and wouldn't let go. Not as they flew through the water, not when they splashed down far too close to the boat for comfort. No way was she dying today.

He looked over his shoulder at the empty boat, estimated the remaining time, and knew it was almost up. He tightened his grip on Charlee's hand and yelled, "Dive! Now!"

He waited until he saw her draw breath before he dove as far and as deep as he could. Thankfully, they were in a deeper section of the river. She kept a tight grip on his hand and matched him stroke for stroke as they swam for the river bottom. Hunter didn't stop until he touched bottom and felt a tree down there. He gripped Charlee with one hand and the tree with the other and braced himself. He didn't have long to wait. The explosion sent shock waves through the water, buffeting them with far more force than he had expected. He almost lost his grip on her, but he held tight. She'd have bruises tomorrow, but he could live with that.

He waited until his lungs burned and screamed for air before he urged Charlee back toward the surface, but at an angle away from the boat. They burst through the water, both gasping for air. He'd never heard a more welcome sound. Everywhere he looked, burning debris floated all around them.

"Josh! Josh!" Charlee shouted her brother's name, and Hunter joined her, spinning in a circle as they tried to find him.

"Josh!"

He tugged Charlee closer, and her frantic eyes met his. She held his arm with both hands. "Where is he? We need to find him."

"Josh!" he shouted again. They waited.

"Here."

They both spun toward the opposite shore. "Over here."

Hunter kept her behind him as they picked their way across the river, fighting the current and avoiding the debris.

It seemed to take forever before they reached Josh, who had collapsed on the muddy bank, holding on to a cypress knee. Blood covered his face, but he didn't seem aware of it.

"Josh. You're bleeding!" Charlee hauled herself out of the water and half climbed, half crawled over to her brother. "Hold still and let me see where the hole is."

Josh angled his head to look at her, his grin macabre with the blood streaming down his face. "Don't make me laugh, Sis. Hurts."

Hunter joined them, and he heard Charlee's sigh of relief. "He's probably got a concussion, but it doesn't look like he'll need stitches." She stuck her tongue out at her brother. "Cheater."

Hunter marveled at her calm, the way she used the hem of her shirt to stanch the bleeding, her sense of humor under fire. She'd have done well in the Marine Corps. He knew she'd been a great FWC officer. Her kind of grace under pressure wasn't the norm for most people.

Hunter checked his phone holster. Empty. "Anyone still have a phone?"

Both Charlee and Josh checked and shook their heads.

"Then I guess we wait. Dispatch will send reinforcements when we don't respond at the next check-in."

Hunter crouched down beside Charlee as she checked Josh's eyes again. Oh yeah. Definitely a concussion, one pupil more dilated than the other. But Josh was able to answer most of the neurological questions Charlee tossed at him, so that was a plus. Just as they had with Charlee, he figured they'd do a CT scan at the hospital to check for brain bleeding, but Hunter's gut said he'd be fine.

As the adrenaline started to wear off, he saw Charlee's hands tremble, but she didn't stop taking care of her brother.

Hunter scanned the river, suddenly aware that they were exposed out here. He hadn't had enough time to take a look at the bomb, so he wasn't sure how it was triggered. Was whoever did this watching them, even now? Did he have a gun, ready to take them out since the bomb hadn't?

"We need to get out of sight," he said quietly.

He saw caution enter Charlee's eyes when his words registered. She scanned the surrounding swamp as he stood. "You grab that side of this big lug, and I'll take the other."

Josh tried to help but didn't accomplish much. Charlee and Hunter half carried him between them. They stopped at a fallen log tucked between two cypress trees and set him down. He immediately tried to lie down.

Hunter exchanged looks with Charlee. "Who's the president, Hollywood?"

Josh mumbled the correct name, touched his head, and winced. "Dang."

He watched Charlee check Josh's eyes again, relieved the pupils were almost the same size. So they let him sleep while they waited.

And wait they did. Their wet clothes had dried and gotten damp again with sweat by the time an FWC boat flew around the bend and came to a rocking stop before it crashed into the debris.

"Lieutenant Boudreau! Hollywood!" Sanchez manned the boat, searching the riverbank.

Hunter looked over at Charlee. "Stay here and stay down."

She nodded, and he made his way to the bank, all the while making sure they didn't have company watching them. He didn't get the sense anyone was out there, but he wasn't taking any chances with Charlee's life or either of his men.

Hunter grabbed the line Sanchez tossed him and tied the boat off to a cypress tree. Sanchez scanned the area, wide-eyed. "What the heck happened?"

"Someone blew up Josh's boat."

The other man cursed. "Are you all okay? Let me get EMS out here."

"Thanks. We also need to get the crime scene techs to collect evidence before it floats downriver. Josh has a concussion, but we need to make sure that's all it is."

Sanchez spoke into the radio strapped to his shoulder, letting dispatch know he'd found them and asking for EMS and the crime scene unit. He finished up and spotted Charlee. "You okay? Didn't expect to see you here, too."

Charlee rolled her eyes. "I somehow thought I'd be safer with them." She nodded toward Hunter and Josh.

One corner of Sanchez's mouth quirked up as he shook his head. "That'll teach you. Glad you're okay, Tanner."

Almost another hour went by before two more boats arrived on scene, one to process the evidence and take what they could salvage back with them, the other to transport Josh, Charlee, and Hunter back to town and the hospital.

Sanchez walked up beside Hunter as Fish and the EMTs helped get Josh aboard her boat. "This is getting really out of control, fast."

Hunter watched Charlee help her brother and nodded. "I know. We need to figure out who this perp is and stop him, quick."

Despite outside temperatures in the midnineties, Charlee couldn't seem to warm up. It seemed like she was always cold lately, right down to the marrow of her bones. The ER staff had checked her stitches and pronounced them healing just fine, but still, she shivered, and not just from the subzero temps in the emergency room.

They'd come within seconds of dying today.

This was no accident. She couldn't explain it away, couldn't convince herself it wasn't exactly what it looked like: attempted murder.

The only thing not clear was the intended target. Was it Josh, since it was his FWC boat? Was it Hunter? Or her? But she wasn't supposed to go along today, so how would someone have known to set off the bomb?

She paced back and forth in the waiting room, trying to make sense of it all while the doctors ran tests on Josh. Hunter huddled with Sanchez and Fish and with Pete, too, who'd come flying into the room a few minutes ago.

She just wanted to go back in time, to last week, or maybe last year, before the world as she knew it went completely crazy.

She couldn't wrap her mind around someone who would kill a teenager. Or slaughter innocent animals. Never mind deliberately setting a bomb. In a boat.

Hunter materialized beside her, and she jumped. "Josh is okay, right?" Maybe he could get more information out of the nurses than she could. So far, all they were saying was, "You'll know something soon."

"They are keeping him overnight for observation, and Pete got a deputy assigned to stay outside his room and make sure he isn't disturbed."

Charlee heard what he wasn't saying. "You think whoever did this will try again when they realize he's still alive."

"We still don't know who the intended target was. It might have been Josh. But it could have been me, or even you, though that's a stretch, with your last-minute arrival."

He was thinking the same things she was, which bolstered her confidence in her thought process. "What's next? How do we catch this guy?"

His smile was grim. "For now, we let Josh rest." He checked his watch. "And we grab something to eat and get some rest, too. The crime scene wizards will do their magic with the bomb fragments, and you and I will go see Travis in the morning."

"Travis? You think he had something to do with this?"

"He has a history we just found out about." He used his badge to get her past the nurse's station and into the cubicle where Josh dozed.

"Hey, Hollywood. You okay?" Charlee stepped over to the bed and brushed a hand over his arm, trying not to cry at how vulnerable and battered her big, tough brother looked against the stark-white sheets.

His eyes opened slowly, and he sent her a loopy-looking grin. "Hey there, Sis. You doing okay?"

"Yeah, I'm fine. I'm not the one that got banged in the head, remember?"

He squinted, like he was trying to think. "Yeah, you did." He glanced from her to Hunter and back. "Didn't you?"

Her smile was a little shaky. "I did, Big Brother. But not today. Today was apparently your day to get smacked in the head."

The curtain parted, and their father raced in, stopping short at the sight of Josh in the bed.

"Hey, Dad. Today was my turn to get whacked."

"Don't say things like that," Charlee snapped, and Josh looked momentarily confused.

Then he blinked several times and apparently realized what he'd said. "I meant smacked in the head. Don't go getting all dramatic on me, Sis." He squinted, as though trying to think. "Will you call Sanchez, ask if he'll cover basketball practice for me at the community center today? He's usually there tutoring at the same time. I don't want the boys to think I ditched them."

"Of course, I will." Charlee smiled, so relieved he was okay, her throat closed with emotion. Hearing that the boys were his first concern, she knew his heart was going to be okay, too. Eventually. A day at a time. She blinked back happy tears.

Hunter turned to her father. "Charlee and I need to go check on some things. Josh is staying the night here, and Pete requested a deputy stay outside his door to make sure he's able to rest."

Her father looked from one to the other, understood what they weren't saying. He ran a hand over his face, eyes worried, but nodded. "Keep my girl safe, Boudreau."

Hunter nodded gravely. "Yes, sir. You have my word on that."

Charlee felt like she was staggering on the last tattered dregs of her strength. Every muscle ached, and her head had begun throbbing again. They'd picked up fast food on the way back to her cottage and eaten all the fries in the truck while they were still hot. Once at the cottage, she barely managed to choke down the burger. She wasn't hungry but knew she needed to keep her strength up.

She stayed in the shower long enough that she almost used up all the hot water before she remembered Hunter. He didn't deserve a cold shower just because she couldn't stop her teeth from chattering.

Finally, clad in sweatpants and a long-sleeved T-shirt, she crawled under the covers and, thanks to the pain meds, eventually dropped off to sleep.

In her dreams, she fought against hands that tried to

squeeze the air from her throat and ran from alligators with gaping jaws and bouquets of wildflowers on their heads, strapped to explosives.

He settled at his computer and inserted the SD card he'd pulled from the trail camera outside Charlee's cottage earlier today. They'd almost spotted him as he'd climbed out of the tree, when Hunter and Charlee suddenly burst out the door and headed down the dirt road, walking and talking. Actually, they were doing more than that. They were flirting, and it infuriated him. The way they snuck glances at each other when the other wasn't looking made bile rise in his throat. His hands clenched into fists.

Charlee was his. Why didn't anyone understand that? He wouldn't let anyone get between them.

He started scrolling through the photos, grinning as he watched Hunter run around the cottage when he'd left the snake on Charlee's bed. He wondered if she remembered telling him about her fear of snakes.

He squinted, frustrated that the quality on some of the photos wasn't clear enough to see her expressions up close. He'd really wanted one of the new cell trail cameras, so it would send the photos directly to his cell phone, but the signal out at the Outpost wasn't always strong enough, and he didn't want to miss anything important. Like when she realized Josh was dead.

She would grieve. He longed to see her face as she cried, to absorb her every teardrop and gather them like a balm, a soothing ointment for the ache in his heart. Oh, yes, he would enjoy her grief.

Sleep tight, Charlee. You'll need your rest for the days ahead.

He wished he could see the look in her eyes when she first woke up and realized anew that her brother was dead. He lived for her pain, actually. She'd understand, finally, what he'd been going through. She'd fully experience how one person's actions could snatch away someone you loved, changing everything. Forever.

He looked forward to watching her suffer, even if he couldn't watch it in real time. He'd waited a long time for it.

He took his eyes off the monitor to watch the small television mounted to the wall. Time for the news. He grabbed the remote and clicked back and forth between the stations, his agitation growing as the minutes ticked by. Where was the breaking story about an FWC officer's death? Why wasn't anybody reporting it?

He spent the next half hour going back and forth, back and forth, but there was nothing. Were they keeping it quiet? But why? There was no reason to.

In disgust, he turned off the television. He was tempted to throw the remote against the wall, but he didn't want to make too much noise, didn't want to wake him. That would put him all out of sorts.

He cruised the internet instead, and finally, finally found an obscure little tidbit about some dead alligators and a boat explosion.

It took a minute to register what hadn't been said. When it did, his blood ran hot. Josh hadn't died. Her brother was still alive.

He lunged to his feet, gripped the remote until the plastic cover popped off and cut his hand. He tossed it on the floor and strode outside. He paced, desperate to get his roiling emotions under control. He wanted to rage and smash things, but that wouldn't help. Would only draw unwanted attention.

No, he needed calm. Control. He gripped his head and forced his breathing to slow. Gradually, he calmed down, and his brain kicked back in.

This was merely a minor setback. His plan was still in play.

All he needed was patience.

Her suffering would come.

And after...she would die.

Chapter 13

Bleary-eyed and stiffer than she'd have thought possible, Charlee shuffled into the kitchen the next morning and stopped short to find Hunter standing at the stove, scrambling eggs. "Morning, *cher*." He pointed with the spatula. "Coffee's ready. Eggs coming right up." He reached over and put bread in the toaster, then went back to the eggs.

Charlee poured coffee, then slid into a chair and watched him. His dark hair glistened, still wet from his shower, and he was freshly shaved, already wearing his FWC uniform. She could get used to seeing him in her kitchen every morning. The smile disappeared. No. She couldn't. Shouldn't.

They were best friends. Best to leave it at that. Besides, she had a future to figure out.

Once they solved this case and Mama got a little better, Charlee would work up the courage to tell her parents she didn't want to take over the Outpost. Liz wanted her to move into the spacious apartment above the café and become a full-time baker. Then she could create a life separate from her overprotective family and the river she'd come to hate. It was what she wanted, wasn't it?

Hunter turned off the burner and slid a plate of eggs and toast in front of her. She pushed her conflicted feelings aside. Now was not the time.

"Eat up, *cher*. Today will probably be another long day."

She watched his face as she asked, "Have you heard how Josh is?"

"I spoke to the nurse a little while ago. He's tired and grouchy, but the scans showed no fractures or any bleeding, so they'll release him later today." He smiled. "He's got a hard head, like someone else I know."

Charlee smiled back. "No argument there." She scooped up some eggs. "Thank you for checking. And for breakfast. Again."

"Eggs and steak are my go-to foods. But after all this is over, I'll make you my famous jambalaya." He grinned. "I'm told it's world-class."

Charlee's heart stuttered at his casual comment, and temptation crooked a finger. What if they took it a step further, gave in to the attraction that kept getting stronger? She choked on her eggs and tried to regain her equilibrium. Right now, they both had more important things to think about.

A sudden urge to check on Mama hit her, so she started clearing the table. "Liz needs more cupcakes, so I'll head over to the folks' place this morning and have Mama help me bake." She was also the one person who could help Charlee sort out her jumbled feelings for Hunter.

"I've got a briefing with the captain, then I'm going to the Outpost to talk to Travis, so we'll catch up in a while." Hunter looked up from his cell phone, met her eyes. "How's the head?"

Charlee thought a minute. "Everything else is sore this morning, but the head is getting better every day."

His sexy grin warmed her all the way to her toes. "Good. I'll drop you off on the way."

Charlee found her mother in her usual wicker rocker on the screen porch, gazing out at the water. She smiled her lopsided smile, and Charlee's heart clenched, as always. "Morning, Mama." She gave her a kiss on the cheek, then sat in the other rocker. "It's sure peaceful out here this morning."

"My Charlotte." Mama smiled, and Charlee saw the worry in her eyes. "How's…Josh?"

Charlee smiled and patted her hand, always startled by how thin she'd become, how fragile. "He's going to be fine. The nurses said he was grouchy and complaining this morning, so that's a good sign."

Sudden tears ran down Mama's cheeks, and Charlee gently brushed them away. "He's okay, Mama. Truly. They'll release him later."

"Could. Have. Died…You. Too."

Her body might be struggling, but her sharp mind cut right to the heart of things. "God was looking out for all of us. We're okay. Please don't worry."

At this, Alice tried to roll her eyes, and the result surprised a laugh out of Charlee. "Right. Mother's worry. Check." They rocked in silence for a few minutes, then she said, "Liz needs more cupcakes, so I figured we'd bake some this morning. That okay with you?"

Alice beamed and gripped the arms of her rocker as if to leap to her feet. Charlee grabbed the wheelchair and helped her into it. Within minutes, they were settled in the kitchen with the oven preheating and Alice balancing a bowl in her lap and mixing batter with her good hand, a smile on her face she never had anywhere but in the kitchen.

Mama looked up, watched Charlee's face. "How's… handsome…lieutenant?"

She felt the telltale blush steal over her cheeks. "Handsome." She paused, and then the words spilled out, as always around Mama. "I like him, a lot, but I'm afraid. Things with Rick were okay for a while, but then everything got all turned around." She paused. "I didn't like the way Rick made me feel, like I was stupid and inadequate. Maybe I am. What if I start to feel that way with Hunter?"

Alice thumped the bowl on the table with a clatter that made Charlee jump. She wheeled the chair around and tugged Charlee down until they were face-to-face. She cupped her cheek, eyes fierce, as she forced the words out. "You are not stupid. Smart. Good instincts. Hunter good. Man." She paused. "Rick weak. Manipulator." Her mouth worked. "Used you, Charlotte."

Charlee reared back in surprise. "I never knew you felt that way about him. I thought you liked him."

"Never asked."

Chagrined, Charlee smiled. "True, I didn't, did I?"

Mama smiled. "Stubborn Tanner." Then she turned her wheelchair and rolled from the kitchen. Charlee followed, surprised when Mama dug around in the magazine basket in the living room and thrust a dog-eared education journal at her. Mom might be retired, but the teacher in her was still going strong. She tapped an article on the cover.

Charlee looked down, then back at Alice. "Gaslighting?"

She nodded. "Rick. Read."

Before she could ask more, the oven timer dinged, and they went back to the kitchen. By the time Hunter came by to pick her up, they had several dozen cupcakes ready to go. Charlee cupped her mother's cheeks and looked into her eyes. "I love you, Mama. Thank you for this morning. I needed that time."

Her mother's eyes filled, something new since the stroke, since no Tanner had ever been a crier. "Love. You. More." She pointed to the forgotten journal on the table. "Read."

Charlee gave her a kiss and scooped the magazine into the old backpack she'd unearthed from the back of her closet after losing hers in the boat explosion. Along with her spare weapon. "I will."

Hunter had found Travis behind the counter at the Outpost, playing a video game on his phone.

When he saw Hunter, all the color drained out of Travis's face. "Is Josh okay? Mr. Tanner said he got hurt. He's in the hospital." He glanced around, then lowered his voice, though there was nobody else in the store. "He said Josh's boat blew up. That can't be right, can it?"

Hunter rested a hand on his weapon as he focused on Travis. "That's why I'm here. What do you know about it?"

Travis jumped up, and the stool he'd been sitting on crashed into the wall behind the counter. "What do I know about it? Are you crazy? I don't know anything about it. Why would I?"

Hunter folded his arms over his chest and narrowed his eyes. "Let's try this instead. What do you know about some dead alligators?"

"You mean the three that were down on the bank a couple miles downriver?" He shrugged. "Yeah, they stank pretty bad."

"When exactly did you see them?"

Travis's eyes bounced back and forth across the room. "Uh, yesterday morning, before work. I, ah, took a ride in my kayak." He looked away. "I'm trying to get in shape."

Since he looked like the only thing he bench-pressed was a video game controller, Hunter figured he had a long way to go. But he never criticized anyone trying to improve.

"Why didn't you report the dead alligators?"

"I didn't know I was supposed to." He cocked his head. "I'm supposed to tell you guys stuff like that, huh?"

Hunter suppressed a sigh. "Yes, Travis, you're supposed to report stuff like that."

He shrugged. "Sorry. I didn't know. But what's the big deal? They weren't hurting anyone. They were already dead."

"When did you kill them?"

Travis's head whipped around so fast, Hunter thought he heard a snap. "I didn't kill them. Why would I?"

Hunter stepped around the counter. Travis inched backward until his back hit the wall. "You've done it before. Why did you do it again?"

Travis's eyes narrowed, and his fists clenched at his

sides. "You had no right to go digging in my past. That happened a long time ago. When I was a kid. I don't do that anymore."

Hunter kept his eyes on Travis, voice low. "Because you're hunting people now?"

Travis's eyes blazed, and he lunged toward Hunter, who stepped back, hand in easy reach of his weapon.

"You don't want to do that, Travis," Hunter warned quietly.

Travis took a step back, threw his hands in the air, and shook his head. "I didn't hurt anybody. I didn't kill those gators either."

"Where were you three days ago?"

"What day was that?" He huffed out a breath, whipped out his phone, checked the calendar app. "I had class, I think. Yeah, I had class." He tapped the phone. "Then I went out in my kayak for a while. After that, I went back to my cabin, played video games."

"Can anyone vouch for any of that?"

He shrugged. "I didn't know I'd need an alibi for my life. Geez." At Hunter's look, he shrugged. "My professor should be able to vouch for me. And people saw me on the river."

"What people?"

"I don't know. People people. Geez. I didn't hurt anybody."

Hunter took down the professor's name. "Mind if I look around your cabin, Travis?"

His eyes narrowed. "Don't you need a search warrant for that?"

"Why would I need that if you're innocent? I just want to look around."

A family with two small children came into the office, wanting to rent a canoe. Travis hurried in their direction. Over his shoulder, he said, "Go ahead and look. But I haven't done anything wrong."

But Hunter noticed that his hands were trembling as he handed out release forms.

~

Charlee leaned against the open doorway of Travis's one-room staff cabin and covered her nose. It smelled like a locker room and looked like a storm had torn it apart. "Find anything?"

Hunter looked up, frowned. "You shouldn't be here."

"Travis said he didn't care if I came, too." When Hunter opened his mouth to say something, she added, "Don't worry. I'm staying right here. Civilian. Evidence. I know."

Hunter had opened the blinds and turned on the ceiling fan to let light in and the stench of sweat and old pizza out. He wore gloves and poked here and there, but nothing caught his attention until he moved the mouse on the computer and the big monitor clicked to life. The screen filled with images of Charlee.

He uttered a string of curses and turned the monitor so she could see. She gasped as row after row of pictures of her filled the screen, starting right after she'd gotten home last year and continuing until recently.

"He's been following me." She tried to process what she was seeing. And what it meant. "Could he be the one who put the camera outside my cottage? Did he send the clipping?"

Hunter already had his phone out. He held up one

finger. "Byte, this is Boudreau. You've processed everything from the gator scene, right? Great. I need you to get over to Travis's cottage at the Outpost and see what you can find, especially on his computer. See if he's the one who set up the camera outside Charlee's cottage, or if he's spying on her in any other way. I'll send Sanchez to grab the SD card out of the camera I installed, too. Yeah, thanks."

Charlee's stomach churned. She'd known he had a crush on her, but this took it to a whole new level. "He's been taking pictures of me, following me, for a whole year." She should stop repeating herself, but the words kept coming.

"That seems clear. How he fits into the rest of it, we don't know yet." Hunter stepped closer, put a hand under her chin, and forced her to look at him. "I want to kick his sick butt into next week, but we need to keep him close, keep an eye on him until we figure out his part in all this, okay?"

His words snapped her back into investigative thinking. "He'll know we found the photos."

Hunter nodded. "And I'm sure that's making him very, very nervous. But we don't want him to run. We may need him."

Fury and bile filled her throat. "I need to get outside."

She hopped off the small porch and walked to the edge of the woods surrounding the cottage, where she paced while she cleared her head. Could Travis have killed Brittany? Possibly, but unless he had been play-acting all along, she didn't think he had the smarts to plan such a thing or the guts to carry it out. But she couldn't be sure.

One thing was crystal clear. Until they had someone in custody, she had to protect her family. Someone had tried to kill her brother yesterday, no matter what Hunter said. The bomb was on Josh's boat. Whoever put it there had no way of knowing she or Hunter would be aboard.

She didn't know who or why—yet—but because of her, someone had targeted her family.

She marched back to Hunter's truck and grabbed her backpack. She pulled out her spare Glock, checked the magazine. She'd been keeping the gun nearby out of habit. From now on, she'd do more than that. She'd keep it on her person. She tucked it behind her back, in the waistband of her shorts, and pulled her T-shirt over it. No one was going to hurt the people she loved. Not without going through her first.

Chapter 14

Hunter scanned the patrons coming in and out of the Corner Café, surprised at how busy they were on a Friday, long after the early-morning coffee rush. Liz had chosen the location well, making it an easy stop for people heading west on SR-40 to go to work in Ocala or for anyone heading east toward Daytona Beach. The coffee and cupcakes were awesome, but he figured most people came for the company as much as the coffee, as in most small towns. He glanced around the renovated Victorian. The wood floors gleamed, and the bold paint colors and quirky artwork gave the place a comfy vibe, without making a guy feel like he was drowning in lace.

He'd run home for clean clothes and now sipped his coffee and watched Charlee work the counter with Liz. They made a great team. Charlee looked relaxed here in a way she never did while at the Outpost. While he couldn't fathom not being near the water, he understood how a place you once loved could make you want to run. He hadn't been able to go back to his Grandmere's place outside New Orleans since she'd passed. Her death, so soon after his brother's, made his insides knot and the walls feel like they were crushing him with guilt. So he didn't go back.

Charlee laughed at something Liz said, and he looked up, struck again by her unconscious beauty. From what he could see, she never wore more than the tiniest hint of makeup, but she took his breath away. Every time. Part of it was her reemerging confidence in herself. Even though she wasn't FWC anymore, that cop presence was coming to the forefront more and more, too. She'd never wait to be rescued but would organize it herself—and save everyone else, too.

He forced his attention back to his laptop and finished the status update for his captain. They still didn't have all the pieces to the puzzle, and it was making him crazy. He looked up as Pete pulled out a chair, turned it around, and straddled it. "Anything new on your end?"

"No. How about you? Did you find Tommy Jennings?"

"Not yet. He hasn't been to work, and I asked a local deputy to stop by. He said the place looked deserted. No signs that anyone had been there recently." He took a breath. "Look, about yesterday—"

Before he said any more, Hunter interrupted. "Appreciate you following up. Is it possible—"

"Hear me out," Pete said, eyes steady on his. "I didn't blow off the meeting, none of us did. But Rick did call us out there, and we went. That's on us. Won't happen again."

Hunter nodded, the relief quick and sharp. This was the Bulldog he knew. Honest to a fault, responsible, a team player. Sometimes hotheaded? Sure. But a guy you wanted watching your back if bullets were flying. He kept his eyes on his friend. "Any possibility Abrams is somehow connected to all this?"

Pete reared back at the unexpected question. "Now hold on just a minute—"

Hunter held up a hand. "I have to ask, Pete. You know I do. And in my shoes, you'd do the same."

Pete let out a frustrated breath. "Yeah. I know. Doesn't mean I have to like it."

"There's a lot about this case none of us like."

Pete scrubbed a hand over the back of his neck. "Our sister has caught the eye of a killer, Boudreau. You, more than most, should understand how that feels."

Touché. "I do. We'll need to work together to stop him."

"Agreed. This is your investigation. But I think you're way out in left field thinking Abrams had anything to do with it."

"It makes sense, though. He and Charlee had a thing, even though it was a while back. Now he's been fired. If he shows up and solves the case, he's a hero. Maybe has a chance to win her back, maybe even get his job back."

Pete's brow furrowed. "They'd never hire him back, but as for the rest, I can't see it. Sure, he had a thing for Charlee, but I know this guy. He's not like that."

"We don't always know what churns underneath. You know that, Pete."

Their eyes met and held for a long moment. When Pete nodded, Hunter knew they'd found their footing again.

"Yeah. Sometimes reality bites." Pete stood. "I need to get going. I'll be in touch. Keep an eye on Charlee. This guy isn't done."

"Watch your back, too. My gut says Hollywood was the target yesterday. Which could make you next."

Pete's look said he'd been thinking the same thing. He gave a two-fingered salute. "Roger that."

Hunter watched him give Charlee a kiss on the cheek before he left. He hadn't written another sentence before Charlee slid into the seat Pete had vacated. She still had dark circles under her eyes, but a bit of her usual bounce was back in her step.

"Josh looked better than he did last night, didn't he?"

"Much better." They'd stopped by the hospital on the way at Charlee's insistence. Personally, he thought Josh looked like he'd been keelhauled, but he didn't say that. "He's going to be fine, *cher*. It'll just take time."

She propped her elbows on the table. "I know you're just humoring me, since he looks terrible, but thanks for letting me pretend. I'm ready when you are."

He got a refill for his coffee, and as he paid for it, his cell phone rang. "Boudreau."

"Hi, Lieutenant. Byte here." Young and eager, Officer Brad Griffin could make computers stand up and dance, a skill Hunter definitely appreciated. "I finally got all the background info you wanted on Oliver Dunn, and unfortunately, there isn't much. Nothing, in fact. He owns no property, doesn't have a social security number, no bank accounts or credit cards, no school records, no military. Nothing. On paper, the man doesn't exist. Oh, and his phone was a burner. Sorry."

Hunter cursed softly. He had suspected as much. "Thanks, Byte. Appreciate it."

"Sorry, Lieutenant. I'm working on everything from Travis's cottage and computer next. I'll be in touch once I finish."

He tucked the phone back in the holder and met Charlee's concerned gaze. "Oliver Dunn doesn't exist in any database. There is no record of him anywhere."

Charlee cocked her head, thinking. "He told me he sold his house a while back. Said he loved the adventure of the open road, of being able to come and go with nothing more than a duffel bag." She swallowed hard. "He also said he didn't like the whole big-brother way technology was going, so he paid cash for everything." She took a sip of water. "But...he had a cell phone, right?"

Hunter nodded. "Burner. Pretty much untraceable. We might be able to find where it was purchased, but not much more than that."

"We need something we can use," she muttered, and he had to agree.

When they got back to the cottage, Charlee curled up on the sofa with the magazine her mother had given her. Hunter sat at the kitchen table with his laptop, urgency nipping at his heels.

He opened a new file and started two lists: everything he knew as of right now and everything he didn't. He looked up a while later when he saw a flash of lightning, followed by a crack of thunder that shook the cottage.

The storm blew in quickly, Florida style, with howling wind, swaying trees, and bolts of lightning followed by thunder bursts rumbling overhead. Hunter figured they were through the worst of it when the power suddenly went out.

Probably just the storm, but he wasn't taking chances. He grabbed his flashlight and went into the living room, where Charlee had just lit several candles and two kerosene lamps. He saw her scanning the area outside the window.

"I'm going to take a walk around outside, take a quick look."

She turned to him. "You think someone cut the power?"

Her sharp cop mind made him feel like they were a team, and he found it sexy as hell. "It was probably the storm, but I want to be sure."

Outside, the rain pounded down in what locals called a frog strangler. He couldn't see past the end of his arm and was soaked to the skin in seconds. Still, he made a careful circuit around the house. The power lines were all intact, and there was no evidence anyone had tampered with any of the windows. With this rain, there were obviously no footprints to be found, but he was confident no one was lurking around.

Charlee met him on the porch with a stack of towels. He scrubbed his hair dry and then stripped off his shirt, tossing it to the floor. He looked up and realized Charlee hadn't moved, just watched him dry his upper body, her features shadowed in the eerie glow of the storm. The rain pounded just beyond the porch, creating a curtain and enclosing them in their own little world. He stepped closer and met her eyes, surprised by what he saw. He stilled at the storm raging in her chocolate-brown eyes. It rivaled the one beyond the metal roof and made desire slide over his skin. He saw want and doubt reflected back at him, uncertainty and desire. The same confusing, tempting, sexy mix he'd been battling for days. Months. Knowing she felt it too loosened something inside him that had been nailed shut.

He took another step closer.

Charlee's mouth went dry at the sight of Hunter's bare chest. She'd seen him shirtless before, but this time, she couldn't seem to stop staring. She studied his wide shoulders, washboard abs, and that intriguing patch of chest hair that disappeared inside his waistband. Without thought, she reached out a hand to touch his chest and then snatched it back before she made contact, embarrassed.

Slowly, he tipped her chin up so he could see her eyes and then gently took her other hand and placed it on his chest. Her eyes widened, and she curled her fingers in his chest hair, loving the way it felt under her palm. When he sucked in a breath, she felt emboldened and ran her hand over his pecs, over the flat male nipples and down his stomach. He shivered, and an answering quiver spread through her belly.

He reached out and ran a finger down her cheek, then cupped her face. "You are so beautiful, *cher*."

His words shattered the fantasy. "Don't lie to me," she whispered and tried to move away. She couldn't take it, not from Hunter.

He gently tightened his grip, eyes steady on hers. "I'm your best friend. You know I'd never lie."

He picked up her hand and traced a finger over her palm, over the calluses from the gun range and holding a kayak paddle. She tried to close her fist. She didn't have soft, pretty hands. But he wouldn't let her.

"Your hands are strong, capable. And when you touch me, I go up in flames." He placed a kiss on those calluses and then reached up and cupped both her cheeks.

His tenderness undid her. Where did such a hard guy find such soft words?

He leaned in and kissed each eyelid. "You are tough and tender and the most amazing woman I've ever met. And if you don't want me to kiss you, you'd better run. Right. Now."

Charlee's hand on his chest froze, and her eyes met his. Could she trust his words? Did he mean what he'd said? His eyes gleamed like green fire as he slowly pulled her closer and leaned in, giving her time to change her mind. She ignored the doubts, the insecurity clanging in her head as his lips met hers in a kiss that felt like...home. He kept the pressure light as he explored and tasted and let her get used to him.

Charlee sighed and leaned into the kiss, but suddenly, it wasn't enough.

She gripped his shoulders and pulled him closer until her breasts pressed against his chest. She sighed with relief as his hands settled at her hips, then he reached around and pulled her even closer, cupped her backside until there wasn't an inch of her not plastered to every inch of him. She cupped the back of his head as he nuzzled her neck, breathing in that unique combination of sandalwood and pure male. His skin felt amazing, but it still wasn't enough.

Some dim corner of her mind knew he was letting her set the pace, take what she wanted. So she opened her mouth and slid her tongue inside. The kiss went from smoldering to wildfire in the blink of an eye, and she felt the heat spread out from her core over every inch of her body, pooling low in her belly.

Hunter kept one hand around her waist, anchoring her to him, and buried the other in her hair as the kiss went deeper. Charlee ran her tongue over his teeth and growled low in her throat when she felt him shudder. She'd never been kissed like this, as though she didn't know where he ended and she began. Her heart pounded as she pressed closer, wanting more, deeper. Nothing had prepared her for the overwhelming sensations he stirred in her.

His hand slipped under her shirt, and the feel of his calloused palm made her shiver. He eased her back far enough to tug the fabric out of the way.

The lights flicked back on.

He growled low in his throat as Charlee stepped back, blinking against the light. He pulled her back toward him, but it was too late. In that split second, desire turned to doubt. She couldn't do this. Didn't trust these new and confusing feelings he stirred in her. Wasn't sure yet that she could completely trust his motives, but even more important, trust herself and her instincts. The way Hunter acted toward her, the things he said, they were nothing like Abrams. But still, uncertainty churned in her gut. She knew it had to do with her screwed-up instincts, her insecurities, far more than it did with Hunter. Still. Until she was sure of herself, she couldn't risk letting someone get too close, couldn't let down her barriers.

"Charlee," he started, but nothing else came out.

She just shook her head, then turned and escaped back into the house.

Hunter let out a slow breath, then grabbed his soggy shirt and wrung it out. He scanned the sky before he went inside.

The storm was almost past, but the power could still be iffy. With well water, without power, you didn't have water, either, so he figured he'd grab a quick shower while he could. Otherwise, he just might try to change her mind.

He took several deep breaths as he rooted around in his go bag and then showered quickly, window open, making sure he hadn't missed anything outside, but he heard nothing but the fading rumble of thunder as the storm moved away. He lathered his hair, smiling at the sight of his shampoo bottle next to Charlee's on the shower shelf. That felt right. Comfortable. Homey. But he wanted so much more...

Charlee curled up on the sofa, listening to the receding storm and trying to ignore the fact that Hunter was in her shower. Her hands still tingled from where she'd touched him. Even though it had only been a kiss, the words he'd said and the way he'd looked at her had been more intimate than anything she'd ever experienced in her life.

She picked up the journal her mother had given her and glanced at the article she'd been reading before the power went out. She'd heard the term "gaslighting" before, but never thought of it in relation to her. Narcissists and manipulators twisted the truth around so carefully and gradually that they got their victims to doubt themselves, to take the blame for things that weren't their fault, and even, in extreme cases, made them doubt their own sanity. As she'd read the descriptions, she'd felt her chest tighten as her mind catalogued all the times she'd felt that way with Rick.

She jumped up and started pacing. How could she have been so foolish? So gullible? She was trained law enforcement. She should have been able to see through him. But she hadn't, not until it was too late. Was Hunter doing the same thing? She thought about his words and the way he looked at her and thought, *no*. *Maybe?* How was she supposed to tell?

All she knew was that he made her feel safe and protected in ways she never had before. He treated her like an equal, and when he looked at her, she felt like he really saw her—and liked what he saw.

Before she realized what she was doing, she walked down the hall and found herself standing with her hand on the bathroom doorknob, knees trembling. What if she just walked in, eased open the shower curtain and climbed in there with him? The idea was insane, and it made her shiver with want and uncertainty. She wasn't the kind of woman who took sexual risks. Ever. At least she never had been before. She closed her eyes, and her skin tingled at the mental image of Hunter naked, soap running over all that hard muscle.

She swallowed hard. *You are so beautiful*. His words echoed in her mind, and she started to turn the knob. *I never lie*.

She eased the door open a crack and took a deep breath while she argued with herself.

A knock sounded on the front door, and she jumped. She snatched her hand away and spun toward the front door. Before she could get there, someone knocked again, harder this time. Her heart started pounding. Was something wrong with Mama? She rushed over to the old-fashioned glass door but stopped just before she flung it open. She stepped off to the side, away from the glass. "Who is it?"

"Paul Harris. Open up."

What did he want? Behind her, the lights flickered

several times but stayed on. She unlocked the dead bolt and pulled the door open a crack. "Hello, Paul. What brings you out here in this kind of weather?" She looked past him. "Where's Wyatt?"

The man looked awful. The porch light reflected his wrinkled clothes, which smelled pretty rank, too, hair that stood on end from running his fingers through it, grief that twisted his face. Before she realized what he intended, he shoved the door all the way open and moved past her into the room.

"Hey! What are you doing?"

He reached behind him and closed the door, and now Charlee saw the wild look in his eyes. This was not the same pulled-together businessman she'd met before his daughter died and his world got turned inside out.

Charlee widened her stance and kept her voice low, but firm. "I'll ask you again, Paul. What are you doing here? And where's Wyatt?"

He must have noticed her tone, for he finally stopped pacing and looked her square in the eye. Something dark floated there and kicked her caution up several notches. When they'd gotten home earlier, Charlee had tucked her gun into her bedside drawer, while Hunter had stashed his service weapon in the end table next to the sofa where he'd been sleeping. She started edging in that direction.

Her question about Wyatt seemed to surprise him. "He's back at the hotel. Playing one of those stupid video games." His eyes darted around the living room, then bounced back to her. "You have to find out who did this, Charlee. You have to find out who killed my baby." His voice broke on the last word, and he swallowed hard.

"I know FWC is working with the sheriff's department, and they're doing everything they can to figure out what happened."

"She shouldn't have died. That should never have happened. My baby should still be alive."

Charlee kept her eyes steady on his. "Yes, she should. Everything in me wishes she were."

He stepped closer, and Charlee eased around the sofa, keeping it between them. Two more steps to get the gun.

"Why haven't they arrested anyone?"

No way would she tell him Oliver was the prime suspect and he was in the wind. "I don't know all the details of the investigation, Paul. I'm a civilian, just like you. But I do know they're working very hard to find answers."

"You're lying. You know exactly what's going on, since you're having sex with Boudreau. Is that why you're doing it? So he'll tell you what's happening?"

Charlee took the insult without flinching. She casually leaned on the end table, kept him talking as she slid her hand into the drawer. "How did you find out where I live, anyway?"

He snorted. "You're not that hard to find, Charlotte."

Just as her hand closed around Hunter's weapon, Paul pulled a gun from behind his back, pointed it at her.

She had Hunter's gun pointed at Paul almost before he could blink. "Put the gun down, Paul. For my safety and yours."

He acted like he hadn't heard. "Tell them to stop harassing me. Tell them to stop following me, stop asking questions, stop blaming me, and find the real person who killed my daughter!"

Charlee kept her eyes locked on Paul's as Hunter

quietly stepped up behind Paul and snatched the gun from his hand. He had Paul's arm twisted behind his back before the other man realized he was there.

"Ow, you're hurting me."

"You should have thought of that before you pulled a gun on Charlee."

"I didn't hurt her. I wasn't going to. It's not loaded. I just..." He broke down and started sobbing.

Hunter pulled a wooden side chair out with his foot and shoved the other man into it. He checked to make sure the gun really wasn't loaded, then tucked it behind his back. "Sit. I need to make a call."

While Hunter called dispatch and requested someone from the sheriff's department come transport Harris, Charlee handed Hunter his gun, then pulled out another chair and sat down, facing Paul—but safely out of his reach—as he sobbed into his hands. "Paul, talk to me. What's going on?"

He swiped at his tear-stained face, looked from Charlee to Hunter and back again. "I'm sorry. I'm acting like a crazy person. I'm usually not like this. Losing Brittany..." He wiped his nose on the shoulder of his shirt. "I can't seem to get it together. And instead of trying to find whoever did this, they keep questioning me, keep asking what I had to gain."

"Who keeps questioning you?" Charlee asked quietly.

He pointed an accusing finger at Hunter, who stood just out of reach of Paul's chair, arms folded, cop face firmly in place.

"Sheriff's office, FWC, I don't even know anymore. They all want to know about stuff that happened a long time ago. I don't care about any of that. I just want to know what happened to Brittany. I want whoever did this to pay for it."

"Brittany went to White Springs Academy, right?" she asked.

"You already know that."

"Did she know a boy named JJ? He had an older sister, Nora."

Paul leaped from his chair, and Hunter said, "Sit down," in a tone that froze him in his tracks. "That's what they keep asking me!" He sank back down on the chair.

"Did Brittany know JJ?" she asked.

"That's the boy who died last year. The sister didn't go to the school. I think she already graduated." He pulled on his hair. "I don't even know anymore."

"What was Brittany's reaction to JJ's death?"

"All the kids were really shaken up by it. It was horrible."

Hunter and Charlee exchanged glances, then Hunter asked, "What do you remember about the day JJ died?"

Charlee knew Hunter was looking for a connection, tugging threads to see what unraveled. She kept her eyes steady on Paul, who looked genuinely bewildered. "Why would I remember anything about it? I didn't know the boy."

"Because it was all over the news, and your daughter would have talked to you about it."

"Okay, so?"

"So where were you that day?"

He started to get up again, but Hunter put his hand on his weapon, so Paul settled for glaring at him. "I sell pharmaceuticals. I travel a lot. I would have to check my records, because I don't remember."

"We already checked. You didn't have any appointments that day, and you didn't check in with the office. Where were you?"

Paul shrugged. "If I wasn't working, I would have been home. Things weren't good between my wife and me. I spent a lot of time driving around, thinking." He speared a finger in Hunter's direction. "But that doesn't mean I killed anyone."

"But it does mean you don't have an alibi for the time in question."

Paul jumped up. "Why would I need an alibi? I thought the papers said it was an accident."

"I told you to sit." He waited until Paul complied, then said, "We're going to find out." Hunter walked over to the front door as footsteps came onto the porch. He greeted the sheriff's deputy, gave him the info he needed, then waited while the other man entered the room, cuffed Paul's hands behind his back, read him his rights, and escorted him to the door.

"You can't arrest me! It wasn't even loaded!"

Hunter's expression was as hard as steel. "Child protective services will take care of Wyatt until you're released. After that, you should take your daughter home for burial. The ME has released her body."

Paul aimed a malevolent look at Hunter as he was escorted to the waiting patrol car. Another deputy climbed into Paul's car and followed them.

Hunter shut the door and redid the locks, then leaned against it, arms crossed over his chest. "Why did you let him in?"

Charlee went on the defensive. "I didn't. I saw who it was and opened the door a crack. He forced his way in."

She'd assumed Paul posed no danger, which had been stupid. A rookie mistake. She was already kicking herself for it, but she didn't need him to rub it in.

As she walked past him, Hunter spun her around. She slammed into his hard chest, and he wrapped his arms around her. "If that gun had been loaded, he could have shot you."

Charlee fought the urge to wince and narrowed her eyes, tried to bluff her way through. "Give me a little more credit. The man is a wreck. Completely destroyed by his grief."

"Which we both know significantly upped the chances of him shooting first and thinking later."

It galled her to admit he was right. "Okay, yes. I shouldn't have let him get past me. Satisfied?"

His green eyes speared into hers. "I won't be satisfied until we find whoever is behind all this and I know you're safe."

She wanted to protest that she could keep herself safe, but given the last few minutes, she couldn't say the words. Here she'd been starting to think maybe she did have what it took to go back to FWC and to protect her family, and then she'd proved once again that her instincts were completely screwed up. If she couldn't make smart decisions on the simple stuff, how could she be trusted to handle bigger things, life-or-death things?

Self-doubt swamped her, and she looked down, tried to hide. Hunter tucked a finger under her chin until she had to look up. Everything in her stilled at the emotion swirling in his eyes. Worry. Concern. Want.

"I care about you, *cher*." Time seemed to stretch as they looked at each other, all the words they couldn't say pulling them closer. Charlee wasn't sure who moved, but next thing she knew, Hunter was kissing her like a soldier just returned from war. This kiss wasn't gentle, it was harsh and primitive, and Charlee felt his hands on her like a brand, making her feel safe and protected. As always.

But therein lay the problem. She couldn't just stand in his shadow, hide behind him. She had to be an equal partner. She had to know she could protect herself and her loved ones on her own. And right now, she had nothing but doubts. She broke the kiss and eased away.

Until she knew herself, had learned to trust herself and her instincts again, she couldn't get involved. Not even with Hunter.

"I'm sorry," she whispered and let her head fall against his chest. His hands gentled, rubbing up and down her back, a stark contrast to their harsh breathing and the way his heart thundered against her ear.

"Look at me." Hunter cupped her cheeks, brought her face up so their eyes met. "It's your call, always. Trust your gut." He paused, and his expression hardened. "You can trust me, too. I'm not Abrams."

Charlee stammered and tried to find the words to explain. "I wasn't… I didn't…"

Hunter had the nerve to laugh. "Never play poker, *cher*. You'd lose. Whether this"—he made a back-and-forth motion between them—"ever goes any further or not, we're best friends, and we'll stay that way. I'll have your back, always." Then he leaned in closer and whispered, "But that doesn't mean I don't think about touching every gorgeous inch of you."

He let her go, and Charlee stepped back, swallowed

hard. She hurried to the kitchen for a bag of chips and jar of salsa, trying to wipe the tempting images from her mind and calm her racing heart. How could she explain what she didn't completely understand herself?

When she got back, Hunter lounged on the couch, bare feet stretched out on the coffee table, pretending the last several minutes never happened.

They watched some inane comedy, and she tried not to notice his muscular legs or the way his T-shirt hugged his hard chest. Every nerve ending felt alive in ways she'd never felt before, so she never expected to fall asleep. But then she knew, somehow, that she was in the dream. She clawed and fought against the hands gripping her throat, sucking in huge gulps of air as she broke free and raced toward safety. But safety kept getting farther and farther away, and behind her, the gator was gaining speed, a bomb tied to the top of its head. She had to get to Brittany, but the mud kept slowing her down. No matter how hard she tried and how fast she ran, she couldn't reach her. She kept sinking under the water.

"Brittany! No! Please! Hold on!"

Warm arms surrounded her, and a deep male voice rumbled in her ear, "It's okay, *cher*. You're safe now. I've got you."

Charlee twisted and thrashed, trying to reach Brittany, but he just kept murmuring in her ear and stroking her back. She felt him carry her down the hall and gently tuck her into bed. She sighed as he pulled the light blanket over her shoulders and kissed her forehead. She couldn't bear the idea of being alone, so she grabbed his arm and tugged until she felt him climb in beside her.

The soothing motion of his hand on her arm slowed her frantic heartbeat, and she snuggled in next to his hard body, her back to his chest. He was warm and solid and smelled like soap and man and safety. For long minutes, he rubbed her arm in a steady rhythm, whispering nonsense in her ear, his steady heartbeat soothing her in ways she'd never been soothed before.

Charlee tried to lift her head to thank him, but she couldn't seem to summon the energy.

"You're a good man, Hunter Boudreau," she murmured. She pulled his arm around her waist, covered it with her own to keep him there, and slept.

Even though it was very late at night, he'd made sure every inch of his disguise was in place before he approached Charlee's cottage. You couldn't be too careful. Boudreau's F-150 was a dead giveaway that he was still around, which made him angry, but he'd deal with him later, after Charlee. Still, the fish cop was smart, so he was extra cautious as he climbed the tree and swapped out the camera's SD card. He knew he probably should have waited a few more days before he risked coming back, but he had to know what was happening. Anticipation built just thinking about what he had planned.

The moment his feet touched the ground, he caught a flash of movement in his peripheral vision. He didn't stop to think, just raced off into the forest in a zigzag pattern, heart pounding. He finally slowed and hid behind a tree to listen. There was nothing but the normal sounds of the forest at night.

When he eventually wound his way back to his truck, confident no one had followed him, he climbed inside and sat for a few moments, waiting for his heartbeat to settle. Maybe he'd startled a deer or even a possum, out for a stroll.

He wouldn't let himself consider any other possibility.

To keep his spirits up, he took out his cell phone and flipped through the pictures he'd taken of Brittany that night in her hospital room. Oh, they were good. He smiled at the memories they induced. The one of her wide-eyed terror was a particular favorite. He couldn't wait to see the same look on Charlee's face.

He grinned in anticipation but then sobered. He'd picked up enough gossip to know the cops weren't giving up on their search. Let them look.

He and Charlee weren't having their little rendezvous until he decided it was time.

Chapter 15

Hunter had spent a considerable chunk of the night thinking about Charlee calling him a good man and what utter crap that was. His arrogance had gotten his brother killed. He'd also thought about his fury with Paul Harris for threatening her and how damn hard it had been to hold Charlee all night long in that too-short iron bed.

By the time she wandered into the kitchen at eight thirty the next morning, yawning and stretching like a contented cat, his voice came out harsher than he intended. "Thought maybe you planned to sleep all day."

She stopped in the act of pouring coffee and squinted at him. "Sorry. I didn't realize it was so late." She smiled a little sheepishly. "I guess I still need more sleep than I thought."

He should be happy she'd gotten some good rest. "We need to get on the road." He thumped his coffee mug into the sink and stormed out of the room. It was either that or he'd pull her close, and never mind what he'd told her last night.

In far less time that he'd ever known a woman to get ready, Charlee climbed into the truck beside him and clipped on her seat belt. "So where are we going, oh cheerful one?"

He narrowed his eyes, and she had the gall to laugh. "Stop growling, Lieutenant. You don't scare me. Though I do wonder at the source of all this disgruntlement."

"Disgruntlement? We have a murder to solve, in case you forgot, maybe more than one. And some crazy on the loose who blew up Josh's boat. And a suspect who pulled a gun on you. Yes, I know it wasn't loaded. Consider me a shade past disgruntled."

She huffed out a breath. "I get it. I do. Fine, be grumpy. Miss this gorgeous day. I don't care."

He couldn't stay mad at her. He just couldn't. He shook his head, and a small smile turned up the corners of his mouth. "You're killing me, *cher*."

His improved mood lasted another hour and a half, until they got to Lake City and Tommy Jennings's last known address. Apparently, after JJ's death, Nora had stayed with her mother, and Tommy had moved out to a remote cabin north of town. The GPS took them off the paved road and onto a gravel road, which turned into nothing more than a dirt path several miles later.

The GPS said, "You have reached your destination."

Hunter stopped the truck, and they both looked around the small clearing.

"I don't see anything." Charlee squinted into the dense trees, vines covering shrubs and bushes. She shook her head in frustration. Wait. She leaned forward. "Is that the cabin back there?"

"I think so. Stay here while I check it out." He eased out of the truck, hand on his gun. "Mr. Jennings. I'm Lieutenant Boudreau with Fish and Wildlife. I'd like to talk to you."

Only the chirp of birds greeted them. Hunter eased over to the cabin, picked his way up the rickety front porch, and called out again, "Mr. Jennings? Are you home?"

The silence lengthened. Charlee heard rustling from inside the cabin, a door opening.

"Go away and leave me alone. I haven't done anything."

Charlee eased her door open to better hear what was being said.

"I'd just like to speak with you, sir. Please come out where I can see you."

Tommy Jennings emerged from the shadows on the porch, and Charlee gasped. She would never have recognized the man. Just like Paul Harris, loss had eaten him up from the inside out. His short hair and shaved chin had given way to greasy hair that hung past his collar and a matted beard. His clothes hung on his thin frame, and his eyes held the same haunted look as Paul's.

But it was the shotgun he had pointed at Hunter's chest that got her attention. Charlee took out her gun, held it against her leg, out of view, and headed for the cabin. "Mr. Jennings, it's me. Charlee Tanner."

Hunter let out a low growl before he stepped in front of her. "Put down the gun, Mr. Jennings."

"This is private property."

"We're just here to talk. For your safety and ours, I need you to put the gun down."

Tommy squinted at Charlee, and his words came out slightly slurred. "What do you want, girl? It's not enough my boy is gone? You come to gloat?"

Charlee's heart clenched, and she blinked back tears. The smell of alcohol hovered like a cloud around him. "I would never do that, Mr. Jennings. Not a day goes by that I don't think about JJ and wish things had ended differently."

At that, Tommy Jennings set the gun on the bench

beside the door and spit over the sagging railing. "Then why are you here?" He swayed a bit. He'd been drinking. Heavily. Already, or since last night.

"Mr. Jennings, your employer says you haven't been at work the last couple of days," Charlee said.

"I took some time off. They're okay with it."

"Where were you on Monday, Mr. Jennings?" Hunter asked.

He swiped at his tears, looked off into the distance, then swung his gaze between Hunter and Charlee. "I took a walk, had a few drinks, tried to get through the day."

"Can anyone vouch for that?"

He snorted. "Not unless you count the deer out there in the woods. Why?"

"Where have you been since Monday, Mr. Jennings?"

He spat again, cleared his throat. "Here. Lying low."

"A sheriff's deputy came by to talk to you, and he said no one was home. Were you?"

He looked away. "I didn't feel like talking to anybody. Didn't figure it was anybody's business where I was but my own." He looked from one to the other, his expression clearing suddenly, making Charlee think he'd been exaggerating his drunkenness. "Now what's this all about?"

Hunter kept his tone conversational, but Charlee saw the way his hand rested on his gun. She kept hers out of sight. "Mr. Jennings, I know this is hard, but I have a few questions about the day your son died. Has there ever been a question in your mind that maybe his death wasn't an accident?"

The man's head snapped up, and his eyes narrowed. "What are you talking about?"

Hunter took a deep breath, and Charlee knew he was choosing his words carefully. "Exactly one year after JJ's death, a girl was shot on a kayak trip. She later died. The coroner says it was murder. We're trying to figure out if the two are somehow connected."

"Murdered?" His head swiveled from one to the other, then his eyes narrowed. "What's that got to do with me?" He seemed to consider, then he stiffened. "You trying to accuse me of something, Lieutenant? Because I sure don't know anything about any of this."

"We're just gathering information, Mr. Jennings. That's all."

Jennings turned to Charlee. "Were you there?"

At Charlee's nod, he looked at Hunter, then his chin came up and he jerked it at Charlee. "You sure she isn't the one who did it?"

Charlee opened her mouth to protest, but one look at Hunter's face, and she snapped her mouth closed.

"We're looking at all the possibilities. Is there anything you can tell us, anything you remember from that day that might help us now?"

Charlee watched the sadness settle over Tommy. He wrapped both arms around his middle, and his chin started quivering. His feet seemed to collapse under him, and he plopped down hard on the rickety bench beside the cabin's front door. "Jimmy, oh God, Jimmy. Please God, Jimmy."

Goose bumps popped out all over Charlee's skin, and she felt like she'd been snatched back in time to a year ago. Hadn't Tommy sat the same way, mumbling the same thing?

"Mr. Jennings?"

Several minutes passed before Tommy seemed to come out of his trance. "I can't help you. I'm just trying to survive." He stood suddenly, as though he'd just remembered something. "Wait here."

Charlee and Hunter exchanged a glance as he disappeared inside the cabin and then stepped back out moments later.

"I wondered why somebody sent this to me. I guess maybe now I know." He handed Charlee a manila envelope.

Charlee waited until Hunter returned from the truck with a pair of gloves and let him open it. He pulled out a photo of Josh, standing by his boat at the Outpost.

Charlee bit back a sharp cry.

Hunter slid the photo back into the envelope. "When did you get this?"

Tommy rubbed a hand over his stringy hair, shook his head. "Yesterday. It was in my mailbox, but it didn't have a postmark, so I figure somebody just shoved it in there. Seemed strange that it had Charlee's name on it."

"Did you let anyone know you got it?"

He shrugged. "I didn't know what it was. I threw it in the trash, but since you're here, you can have it."

Hunter thanked him, and they climbed back into the truck and wound their way back to the main road.

"Why would someone give him a picture of Josh?"

"To let us know he's watching and that he knows what we're thinking. He knew we'd come out here and question Jennings."

Charlee tapped her fingers on the dashboard, shaking her head. "Someone is trying to pull that poor man back into the nightmare. He's so broken. And he's living out here all alone. It breaks my heart."

Hunter reached over and squeezed her hand. "I feel for him. But I'm also trying to figure out why he acted more drunk than he was, though it may just have been a way to get us to leave him alone." He paused. "None of this is your fault, *cher*. Remember that. And much as I feel for Jennings, we can't get sidetracked. That photo is either proof the two cases are connected or a clever attempt to throw us off the trail. We need to figure out which it is."

She snapped her eyes to him. "The picture of Josh was taken at the Outpost. He was there." Her heart pounded just saying the words. She remembered her terror at seeing the countdown timer, the panic of trying to find Josh after the explosion. Another thought pushed its way in and added to her chill. What if Hunter was next? "You need to be really, really careful, Hunter."

"I plan on it. So do you. That was your name on the envelope."

With her concern for Josh, her brain hadn't made that connection until he said it. She was the thread that connected everything, but they still didn't know how. Who was next? Hunter? Or maybe Pete?

Charlee grew quiet, trying to sort it all out in her brain. Her head still ached off and on, so she turned sideways, facing out the window, trying to get comfortable. She let her mind wander, trying to connect the dots.

The next thing she heard was Hunter growling, "Hang on."

Something slammed into them from behind.

Chapter 16

CHARLEE GRIPPED THE DOOR HANDLE AS THE TRUCK fishtailed on the road. Hunter held the steering wheel in a white-knuckled grip, fighting to keep them on the pavement.

She glanced behind her, desperate for a look at the driver of the pickup truck following them. It was older, blue, with rust and dents, but she couldn't see the driver's face with the sun glinting off the windshield. The truck sped up. "He's going to ram us again."

"I see him. Come on, you coward," Hunter muttered. He alternated between glancing into the side and rearview mirrors, trying to anticipate their pursuer's next move.

Slam. Slam.

The pickup rammed them yet again, and Hunter's truck fishtailed, but he managed to get them back in their lane just as an oncoming car approached. The other driver honked and gestured as he went by.

Charlee couldn't blame him. If not for Hunter's skill, they would have crashed head-on.

"What is he doing?" Charlee's voice climbed as the other vehicle closed the gap between them again. Hunter kept steady pressure on the accelerator, but there were other cars ahead of them, so he couldn't go much faster or he'd get boxed in.

They neared the bridge over the Ocklawaha River,

and Hunter cursed as the pickup gained speed again. "Roll down your window! If we land in the water, we'll be able to get out."

"Oh, dear God." Charlee whispered a prayer as she fumbled for the right button. Hot summer air whipped inside, stinging her eyes. She looked in the side mirror again, but all she saw were dark glasses and a ball cap.

Hunter hit the gas, trying to break away from the pickup, but the other driver kept pace. Just as they reached the highest point of the bridge, the pickup slammed into them with enough force that Hunter couldn't correct, even though he tried with everything he had.

There was a horrible crunching sound as they slammed into the guardrail. The rail held, stopping their forward motion, but Charlee's relief was short-lived. The truck kept going, flipping up and over until suddenly, they were airborne, the river rushing up to meet them.

She braced her feet. *God, please.*

"As soon as we hit the water, get out."

He'd barely finished the words when the truck hit the water, nose first. The impact deployed both air bags, and Charlee fought her way past the bag and unclipped her seat belt. Water poured through the open window, rising fast.

Oh God. Visions of drowning, of Brittany under the water, tried to swamp her, but Charlee pushed them away. *Go, go, go.*

Beside her, Hunter slammed a fist against his airbag, batting it away. "Climb through your window. I'm right behind you."

Charlee nodded and gripped the window frame, fighting the force of the water. The hood of the truck was almost completely under the surface, and the murky Ocklawaha poured in faster and faster.

She pushed through the window frame and held on, waiting for Hunter to follow.

Why wasn't he behind her? Where was he?

The truck shifted and sank farther, and Charlee barely managed to avoid getting pulled down with it. She had to get Hunter. Something was wrong. She wouldn't leave him, couldn't fail him like she had Brittany.

She turned and let the force of the water suck her back into the cab of the truck. There was only a small air pocket left near the roof of the cab. Hunter had his head tilted back to keep his mouth out of the rising water as he struggled and tugged.

"Get out of here! Go!" He pushed her away with one hand while he kept tugging with the other. No way was she leaving him to drown.

She braced one hand on the back of the seat and followed the line of his shoulder with the other until she reached his seat belt. That's what had him trapped.

She sucked in a gulp of air and dove down, patting her way down his body until she reached his utility belt and the knife he kept there. *Come on, come on.*

Her fingers connected with leather, and she wanted to shout in triumph. She reached for the knife, but it wasn't there. *No!*

He must have dropped it while he was trying to cut himself free. She felt him tugging on the seat belt, trying to get the buckle to give.

Don't panic. Think. Frantic, Charlee patted her own

pockets. When her hand connected with something small and metal, she used both hands to pry open the small blade on her pink pocket knife and started sawing the belt. The pressure to open her mouth and draw a breath was overwhelming, but she ignored it, despite the spots dancing before her eyes.

Hunter realized what she was doing, and his hand closed over hers. She released her grip, knowing he could get it done faster than she could. She wasn't sure the little blade was sharp enough to cut through, but it was all they had. She popped up, her head hitting the roof of the truck as she gulped in air. Beside her, Hunter wheezed as he stretched to reach up high enough to get his own air. She heard him inhale, then his head went down, and she felt him sawing like crazy.

Suddenly, the belt popped free, and he gave her a shove, pushing her through the window. This time when she turned, she felt him grab onto her waistband and knew he'd follow.

With the last bit of strength she could muster, she used her feet to push off from the window frame and shoot to the surface.

She gulped in big lungfuls of air, gasping. He popped to the surface beside her and quietly sucked in air. She wanted to shout his name with relief, but before she did, she realized he wasn't looking at her; he was looking up at the bridge above them.

Someone stood looking down at them.

"Dive," Hunter shouted just as something hit the water near their heads.

Charlee dove, gripping Hunter's hand as they swam away from the shore with long, sure strokes.

When they finally surfaced again, Charlee came up quietly, filling her lungs fast, in case they had to dive again. She looked around, saw the bridge behind them.

"We can head for shore now. He can't get here from up there."

Charlee nodded and swam behind him, but the adrenaline suddenly started draining away, taking the last of her strength with it. She swam against the current with everything she had, but she couldn't seem to make headway against the fast-moving water.

Hunter was slowing too, but not quite as much. She saw him look back as the current dragged her farther away. He disappeared and then surfaced right in front of her. "Put your arms around my neck. I've got you."

Charlee wrapped her arms around him and kicked with every bit of her remaining strength, determined to do her part. It was slow going, but they eventually fought their way against the current until they were close enough for their feet to touch bottom. She thanked God they were both still alive.

They stumbled over toward the bank and took cover behind a tree so they couldn't be seen from the bridge. Gasping for breath, they slogged up onto solid ground, slipping in the mud, holding cypress knees for balance. They trudged farther up into the swamp and then collapsed side by side onto a fallen tree.

Charlee looked up at Hunter's face, still panting. "You're bleeding. Cut above your eye."

Hunter swiped a hand over it, winced. "Not too bad. You okay?"

"I think so." She looked back toward the bridge. "That is one determined son of a gun."

Hunter scanned the area, expression grim. Then his expression became thoughtful as he turned back to her. "It always has something to do with water."

Charlee thought it through, her tired brain sluggish. "Josh's boat. This."

"You and Brittany getting shot. Always water."

Charlee shivered. "He almost succeeded today."

Hunter stepped closer, but before he said more, they heard sirens in the distance. Charlee sighed. "This is getting to be way too familiar."

"We'll catch this SOB, *cher*. I promise."

As the sirens got closer, Charlee and Hunter walked toward the nearby road to meet the FWC and the sheriff's officers as they arrived. Hunter took charge of the scene, and Charlee answered questions until her tongue felt numb.

About halfway through the process, her brother Josh drove up, hopped out of his truck, and raced over to her, pulling her to her feet and into a bear hug that knocked the breath out of her. "Don't ever scare me like that again," he muttered, then pulled back to look her over.

Charlee gasped when she saw his face. "What happened to you?" He had the beginnings of a black eye, a split lip, and what looked to be an ugly gash along his temple, held together with butterfly bandages. She looked down. His knuckles were scraped, too.

"Are you okay, Sis?" He ran his gaze over her, much as she'd just done to him.

"Never mind me. I'm fine. Just wet. But what happened to you?"

He worked his jaw, then met her gaze. "I had a long overdue chat with Rick. Told him to back off already. That you were done. He disagreed."

Charlee narrowed her eyes, shook her head. "I don't need you to fight my battles for me, Josh. Haven't for a long time."

"I know you don't. You never have, but we're family. We protect each other. I should have done something long ago, but when Elaine got sick..." His voice trailed off. Then his eyes snapped back to hers, expression fierce. "I didn't like the way he treated you. Then. Or now."

Charlee couldn't believe it. "Why didn't you say anything then?" First her mother, and now Josh.

He shrugged. "Knew you'd figure it out eventually." Then he shot her his trademark grin. "Besides, didn't think you'd want to hear it anyway."

She grimaced. There was that. But why had it taken her so long to see what her family apparently had known from the beginning?

Hunter called Josh's name. He pecked her on the cheek and then got to work.

As she sat on a log, absolute determination worked its way over, around, and through all the noise and activity and bone-deep exhaustion. Despite all her doubts and insecurities, she would protect her family. Or die trying.

After what seemed like days, Charlee and Hunter finally left the scene. They stopped at the Outpost to reassure her folks she was in fact fine, just wet, and then Hunter drove her home in a replacement truck. She nibbled at the takeout he'd picked up on the way but couldn't muster more energy than that.

When her cell phone rang and Liz's number showed up, Charlee sighed and answered. She didn't want to go through it all again, but if she didn't answer, Liz would either keep calling every five minutes or show up in person, and Charlee wasn't ready for that either.

"Hey, Liz. How're things?"

"Charlee, are you okay? I was terrified when one of the café regulars said you and Hunter got run off the road."

Charlee shook her head, amazed anew at how fast news traveled in a small town. "I'm fine, Liz, really. Soggy, but unhurt."

There was a pause. "I don't believe you're fine. But I think you don't want to talk about it."

"No, I really don't. I'm sorry. Maybe another time."

"I'm coming over."

"No!" That came out louder than she'd planned, so she lowered her voice. "Please, don't. I'm tired and just need some rest."

"Is Lieutenant Yummy with you?"

Charlee smiled. "Hunter is here right now, yes."

"Good, then I'll let him look out for you." Before Charlee could point out that she could take care of herself, Liz sniffed, and Charlee knew she was fighting tears. "Just be safe, okay? I need my best friend."

"I'll be fine, and we'll figure out what's going on. Promise."

She meant every word. She wasn't going to sit on the sidelines while Hunter and the rest of her FWC squad figured this out. Or her brothers. She took a quick shower, grabbed a yellow legal pad to jot down notes, and curled up on the sofa with an afghan. That was the last thing she remembered.

While Charlee got some much-needed rest, Hunter gulped down coffee to combat the adrenaline withdrawal and talked on the phone with Sanchez and Fish, Pete, Josh, and his captain, assigning tasks and getting updates. He stared down at the piece of paper he'd been scribbling on and tried to make sense of it all. There was a cluster with JJ and Nora and Tommy Jennings in it. He added Tommy's ex-wife, Sally. Another cluster contained Brittany, Wyatt, and Paul Harris. He added Paul's ex-wife, too. He needed her take on all this. He had circles with Oliver Dunn, Travis Humphries, and Rick Abrams's names in it. He listed Josh and his own name, but in the middle of the page was a big circle with Charlee's name in large block letters. She was the one connection that tied everything together. He just had to figure out how. And why.

He tapped his pen on the page and tried it from another angle. If he started with Brittany this time, who had the means to shoot her? Travis, with his suspicious arrival on the scene? Tommy Jennings as payback for JJ maybe? Oliver Dunn, who had seemed to watch both Charlee and Brittany too closely? What about Paul Harris? It was unlikely Paul or Oliver could have been the shooter, but there were some gaps in their stories he needed to fill. Or maybe they hired someone.

The question was why? What did anyone stand to gain? Nothing in anyone's financials had raised a red flag, so it didn't appear to be about money. Other motives? Travis could play the hero, impress Charlee. Maybe Paul was taking out family frustration? But Hunter wasn't quite buying that. Tommy Jennings had the strongest motive and no alibi for the time of the shooting.

Could the shots have been aimed at Charlee and Brittany simply got in the way? Maybe. He'd keep looking into that.

What about today? Someone obviously had followed them and had known they would head to Jennings's place. That moved Abrams up on Hunter's list, especially after he and Josh had gotten into it over Charlee. Abrams would think like a cop. But why would he want Charlee dead? Because she didn't want him? And why leave the picture of Josh? He clicked his pen, thinking. Still too many pieces missing to get the whole picture.

Charlee walked into the kitchen, and his heart filled with admiration as he thought about the way she'd handled herself today. Then he remembered that she'd come back for him and put herself at risk. His relief turned to fury. "If I tell you to do something, I expect you to do it," he snapped.

She turned from the counter, where she was assembling baking ingredients, one eyebrow raised. "Okaaay…what brought this on?"

"I was clear on that from the beginning. You do what I say."

Understanding dawned, and her chin came up. "Unless following your orders means you die."

He made a slashing motion with his hand. "No. You should have left me, Charlee. I would have gotten out."

She threw up her hands and reached into the cupboard.

"Fine. Whatever. Next time, I'll let you drown. Good enough?"

He let out a slow breath. He was acting like a jerk, but he couldn't seem to stop. Not when it came to her. "My job is to protect you. Stop getting in my way."

She turned her back as though she hadn't heard him, but she creamed the butter with a lot more vigor than usual.

Hunter stalked to the door, then stopped with his hand on the knob. He turned and went back to the kitchen.

She ignored him for a few minutes, then cast him a quick glance. "If you're waiting for an apology, you're going to be there awhile. Best friends protect each other." He thought she muttered "Idiot" under her breath, but he couldn't be sure.

He tried to find the right words and finally just started talking. "My Grandmere raised my brother, Johnny, and me after our parents died in a car crash when I was seven and Johnny was two. We lived in a small town outside of New Orleans. I went into the Marines to get out of being a father figure, and by the time I came home, Johnny had gotten involved with a drug dealer named Ace. I couldn't get him to see the guy's true colors until Johnny witnessed Ace kill one of his own men, and what I had been trying to tell him finally sank in. I was with the New Orleans PD, and Johnny wanted to help me take Ace down. I told him no, absolutely not. If Ace even had a feeling Johnny was working with the cops, he'd be dead.

"But I couldn't talk Johnny out of it, so I told him to keep his head down and let me handle it." He sighed.

"I just wanted to get through the raid. Keep Johnny safe. Get Ace off the streets.

"We'd just pulled into the alley when my phone buzzed again. I was annoyed. There were three messages from Johnny. One from Grandmere.

"Johnny had been calling and calling all day, needing reassurance. The SWAT team was ready. There was no time to respond again." Hunter rubbed a hand over the back of his neck and glanced at Charlee, who just stood, bowl in hand, and listened.

"When I found them, Ace had a gun to Johnny's head. He'd figured it out and decided to use Johnny as a hostage to get away. To buy time, I called off the SWAT team, put down my gun, and pretended to go along. But while we were in the stairwell, Johnny tried to save me. Instead of letting me get him out of there, he tried to grab Ace's gun.

"Before I could get my second piece out of the ankle holster, Ace had shot him. My brother died before I could get to him." He swallowed hard, pinched the bridge of his nose.

"If he'd just stuck with the plan, I would have been able to save him."

The silence stretched on and on, until he finally looked up. He'd expected pity, but this was Charlee. He should have known to expect the unexpected. She had set the mixing bowl aside and propped her hands on her hips, sparks shooting from her eyes.

"I am not your brother, Hunter. I can protect myself."

"No, *cher*. You're definitely not." She looked every inch a warrior goddess. But she wasn't indestructible. The terror he'd felt as the truck hit the water today, plunging them both under water, then his absolute fury that she wouldn't leave, but risked her life to save him all rushed back, hardened his tone. He had to force the words past the fury clogging his throat. "You could have died today, too."

He stalked out the door and around the perimeter—twice—unable to quell his growing frustration. The woman—and this case—were tying him in knots, and he didn't like it. Why couldn't he see the whole picture? And what if he couldn't figure it out in time to protect her?

He would. He had no other choice. He eased into the trees, not making a sound.

He grabbed a fallen palm frond and held it in front of his face as he worked his way over to the trail camera he'd installed to watch the watcher. He hoped the camouflage would keep the suspect from knowing he'd been made. He checked the battery and pulled out the SD card, then went to his truck and plugged it into his laptop. It didn't take long to scroll through the pictures. There were plenty of four-legged visitors who passed by the camera, but no two-legged ones. He was almost to the last picture…wait. He scrolled back. There.

Sure enough, the infrared camera had picked up someone climbing down from the tree. He enlarged the photo, cursed. Their guy was taking no chances. From the shape, he figured it was a man, but he was wearing camo gear, a hat, sunglasses in the middle of the night, and something over his face to disguise his features.

He emailed the image to Byte before he returned the SD card to the camera.

He didn't hold out much hope, but maybe, just maybe, Byte could come up with an ID. In the meantime, he'd have to figure out another way to find this guy.

You won't get to Charlee. Not on my watch.

While Hunter checked outside, Charlee popped the second batch of cupcakes in the oven, his words echoing in her mind. Her heart ached for him over the loss of his brother. She would have wrapped him in her arms and told him how sorry she was if she thought he'd allow it. She, better than most, understood the kind of guilt that gnawed at your heart, the sense of failure when things went wrong that never really went away. She also knew responsibility and the need to protect those you cared about. In that way, she and Hunter were exactly the same. She shook out her fingers to get the blood flowing after clenching the wooden spoon so tightly. She knew every bit of the frustration churning inside him.

But even though she knew things were different with Hunter, he still sounded just like her brothers. Or Rick. She wouldn't tolerate a man telling her what to do "for her own protection." She snorted. Please. Capable woman here. Former cop. No pats on the head or macho swagger, thank you very much.

Hadn't she followed her instincts and done what needed doing today? It had been exactly the right thing—no matter what he thought—and had shored up her battered confidence.

She allowed herself a little smile at that, then let out a breath. Enough. She had far more important things to think about than her muddled feelings for her maddening, altogether tempting best friend.

A bowl of chocolate fudge frosting sat on the table, and she was using her pastry tube to decorate the first batch of cupcakes when Hunter strode back in, his face void of all expression. She glanced up and went back to what she was doing. She didn't have time to decipher what he was thinking. She didn't care, either. At least that's what she told herself.

He walked up behind her, and she could smell his woodsy scent and the heat that emanated from him. "Look, *cher*, I know you don't like it, but I'm trying to protect you—"

He didn't get any further than that. Without conscious thought, Charlee whirled around and shot half the tube of chocolate frosting right in his face, then calmly went back to her cupcakes. "Spare me the macho crap, Lieutenant. I don't want to hear it."

The silence went on for several beats, and Charlee had a moment to wonder if she'd gone too far. But then she heard him start to laugh. She looked up through her lashes and saw him tip his head back and laugh like she'd never heard him laugh, with his whole body.

She tried to keep from smiling, but finally gave up and joined in.

She was so distracted by the pull his laughter stirred in her belly that she yelped in surprise when a big glob of frosting landed on her nose. Followed immediately by another blob on her right check. And then her left. She tried to fight back with her pastry tube, but his assault was relentless, swiping frosting off his own face and transferring it to hers.

"Two can play this game, *cher*, and I'm betting I'll win," he warned, adding another layer to her chin.

"Oh yeah?" She went on the offensive, and they went back and forth, smearing frosting on each other.

Laughing and breathless, Charlee took a step back, stunned at the playfulness from such a serious man. She opened her mouth, trying to decide what to say, when his eyes met hers. Their laughter stilled as they studied each other. Behind the frosting and the laughter still dancing in his eyes, Charlee saw something more. Attraction, certainly. But something that went much deeper, that reached beyond friendship and caring and connected them in ways she was almost afraid to examine too closely.

Almost.

Charlee read the clear invitation in his eyes, and suddenly, her arms were around his neck, his wrapped around her back, and his hard mouth came down on hers. But where she expected aggression, he gave her featherlight kisses and licked the frosting from her lips, a smile on his own.

A shiver shot straight to her core, and she clutched his shoulders as he pulled her flush against him. The bands of muscle under her hands tightened, and she could feel the effect she had on him, but his arms didn't feel like a cage, the way Rick's had. No, Hunter was different. Danger clung to him like a second skin, but it was never directed at her. He growled low in his throat as he nuzzled her neck, and Charlee shivered, burrowing closer.

She shifted, giving him access to her neck, and ran her hands over his shoulders, down his arms, loving the way his hard grip made her feel safe even as his roaming hands and woodsy scent tempted her, invited her to move closer, to explore the fire that erupted whenever their skin touched.

When he nudged her lips open, she opened her

mouth, welcomed his tongue in to dance with hers, hearts pounding, the kiss sparking and bursting to life until all Charlee felt was heat—his, hers, theirs. Being in his arms was like nothing she'd ever experienced before. It felt...right.

The thought startled her with the force of a slap, and her eyes popped open. No, this couldn't feel right, could it? Her thoughts spun and twisted, mind and heart battling for control.

Hunter must have sensed the change in her, because he eased back just far enough to look in her eyes. She saw her own desire reflected there, hot enough to sear them both, but he didn't say anything, didn't move. Simply waited for her to decide. Some cowardly part of her wished he'd pull her close, take the decision out of her hands by overwhelming her senses with the heat between them. But then the truth dawned. He wouldn't push, wouldn't let them get swept along by passion, not without giving her time to make a decision.

He confirmed it when he rumbled, "Your choice, *cher*." Then he smiled, that slow, sexy smile she felt all the way to her toes. "Want to shoot the rapids with me?"

Charlee realized that was exactly how she felt right now. Like she was in her kayak, ready to push off into the raging current where the river would sweep her along on a rush of adrenaline and all she could do was hang on for the ride. Did she have the guts to plunge into the water?

She studied him, stroked a shaky hand down his cheek, poised on the edge. "I don't want it to change things between us," she whispered.

His smile got wider, and mischief danced in his eyes.

"Oh, it'll change things, *cher*. No question. Our friendship, no. Never. But in other ways…?" He waggled his brows suggestively, and she burst out laughing.

And just like that, her indecision slipped away, and she smiled back. She could trust him. And she could trust their friendship.

All the other questions swirling around them could wait.

She cupped his cheeks, enjoying the feel of the stubble under her palms, and pulled him close. "Then show me what you've got, Lieutenant."

He threw his head back and laughed before he wrapped his arms around her and kissed her with an intensity that left her body quaking and seeking to get closer, deeper, more.

They somehow maneuvered out of the kitchen and down the hall, shedding clothes along the way, all without ever letting go of each other, as the fire stoked higher.

Once they finally reached the bedroom, Hunter eased her back on the bed, slid her shorts from her legs. She was tempted to hide under the intensity of his gaze, but he said, "Let me see you, *cher*. Let me touch."

Charlee met his eyes and felt the same heart-pounding swoop of adrenaline as when she shot into the first rapid on a tough course. Poised halfway between the exhilaration of the ride and the terror of possible disaster, she let him look his fill. But the admiration in his eyes, the words he murmured in her ear, allowed her to let go of the fear and get swept away by the thrill of the ride. She opened her arms, and the last of their clothes seemed to melt away as their mouths met and their hands stroked and touched, giving and taking, learning each other.

As the pace increased, their hearts pounded and their breaths came in gasps. The tension built and built until Charlee couldn't take it another second. "Please," she murmured as her head spun and her eyes slid closed.

"Look at me, *cher*," he commanded as he moved over her, melded them together.

Charlee locked eyes with him as he gripped both her hands and began to move.

Together, they raced through the raging currents and clung to each other as the tension built, tighter and tighter until they rocketed over the edge together. Afterward, breaths heaving, both smiling, they slowly, gradually, reached the calm waters on the other side.

Chapter 17

Charlee woke before dawn, her head nestled against Hunter's shoulder and their legs tangled together. She felt a blush race over her skin as memories of the night washed over her, of the way she'd let go of control, but somehow, she couldn't regret it. She'd been raised to believe casual sex was a cheap substitute for love and marriage. The few other encounters she'd had in her life, especially the one with Rick, had left her feeling sad and hollow afterward.

Last night with Hunter had changed everything. He made love with the same single-minded attention to detail that he did everything else, but more surprising was the way it all felt…right. Like this was how it was supposed to be. Only a woman in love could feel this way, she decided. She froze, letting the knowledge flow over and around her. Her smile widened as the reality set in. She loved him. It was as simple and unbelievably complex as that.

But then she sobered. She couldn't tell him. Certainly not now. Number one, they had to find Brittany's killer, and she had to know what had really happened last year. Nothing else could get in the way of that. And two, she figured her big, tough warrior wouldn't want to talk about something like feelings. She almost snorted but didn't want to wake him.

Instead, she eased out of the bed, grabbed clothes,

and headed for the shower. Afterward, she pulled on her favorite swishy skirt and matching top, pulled her hair up in a high ponytail, and smoothed on tinted moisturizer and a bit of blush. She had the coffee going and was packing up the cupcakes, humming under her breath, when Hunter emerged from the bathroom, a surly expression on his face.

Charlee took in his freshly shaved chin, low-slung jeans and bare chest, and her mouth went dry. *Oh my.* "Good morning, Lieutenant," she said primly.

His gaze traveled over her, the smolder in his green eyes making her glad she'd primped a little. "We going somewhere?"

"I need to drop these cupcakes off at the Corner Café." She glanced at the clock on the wall. "If we hurry, we'll have time to grab breakfast there before church."

Hunter raised a brow. "We're going to church?"

Charlee nodded, desperate to get her mind back on the case and away from Hunter's broad chest. She cleared her throat. "Tanner family tradition. Besides, it's the best place I know to find out what's happening around town. Between that and the café, hopefully, we'll learn something useful."

Hunter poured coffee into a cup. "I like the way you think. Thanks for the coffee. Let me get dressed, and I'll load the car."

Rattled by her wayward thoughts, she snapped, "No need. I've got it."

Hunter raised both hands. "Just offering to help, *cher*. Not impugning your independence."

She felt ridiculous, took a deep breath to settle her nerves. "I'll meet you outside."

The café was doing a brisk business, but even so, Liz came around the counter and hugged Charlee like she'd just been dragged from a shipwreck. "Are you okay? How's the head?"

Charlee hugged her, then eased away. "I'm fine. Feeling better today than I have since…well, for a while." She held out the cupcake carriers. "I brought more. Hunter's getting the rest from the car."

"Fabulous. How's it going, having him stay at your place? He still sleeping on the couch?" She raised both eyebrows.

Charlee felt a flush creep over her cheeks. "We're friends, remember? He's there as…protection, nothing more."

"So you keep saying, girlfriend. I'm waiting for you to convince yourself." She looked over Charlee's shoulder. "Good morning, handsome. You just set those treats right here."

Charlee jumped when a voice said, "Morning, Miss Charlee. You look beautiful today."

Startled, as always, at how close Sammy stood to people, she eased back a step and beamed up at him. "Good morning, Sammy. How are you? How's the carnival going?"

His grin stretched from ear to ear. "It's been really fun. Lots of kids are winning, so I get to give out lots of prizes." He eyed the cupcake carriers Liz was unpacking. "Did you bring more cupcakes?"

"I did. Chocolate with chocolate frosting."

"I like those. Can I have some?"

Liz turned around, two cupcakes on a napkin. "Of course you can, Sammy. Here you go."

He leaned forward and kissed Liz on the cheek, then started to kiss Charlee's cheek, too, but a blush crept over his face, and he pulled back, unsure. "Um, thanks for making the cupcakes, Miss Charlee. Yours are the best."

Charlee laughed and reached up to kiss his cheek. "I'm glad you think so, Sammy. You have a good day."

Sammy smiled and waved as he walked out the door to the café just as her brother Pete came in. He was wearing dark jeans, collared shirt, and a tie, so he was obviously headed for church, too. He kissed Charlee's cheek. "Hey, squirt. Ooh, more cupcakes." He smiled at Liz. "I'll take two and a cup of coffee."

Josh walked in then, also dressed for church, which shocked Charlee. He hadn't been since Elaine had died. He ordered the same, and they took a small, round table in the back corner. Charlee bit back a smile when she realized all four of them sat with their backs to the wall and studied the patrons. Cops to the core.

"Any new leads?" Pete asked after he'd devoured his first cupcake in two bites.

"Nothing on my end," Hunter said. "You find out anything new?"

"No, and it's bugging the hell out of me."

"I'm with you on that," Josh said.

They went over everything they knew so far again, but nothing jumped out at her or to them, either. The bell over the door chimed, and Josh looked up and choked on his coffee, sloshing half of it over the table. While he mopped up, Charlee studied the newcomer. "Isn't that Delilah? The monkey researcher?" She'd rented a kayak from the Outpost a time or two and seemed very nice, though shy and quiet.

Josh didn't appear to have heard the question, as his eyes were glued to the lovely young woman with the short pixie haircut as though he'd just been sucker punched in the gut.

"I'll see you guys at church," Josh muttered and headed in Delilah's direction.

They all exchanged raised eyebrows as he made some comment that made her laugh out loud. Now wasn't that interesting? But a few minutes later, Charlee glanced at her watch and stood, that creepy feeling she was being watched stealing over her. "We need to go or we'll be late."

Just as they were walking out, Pete's cell rang. "I'll meet you guys there. Great cupcakes, squirt."

Normally, sitting with her family in the historic clapboard church calmed Charlee. There was something about the connection to the past and the tradition of the old hymns that always soothed her heart. Especially seeing her mom back in their pew next to Dad, holding hands. She smiled when Josh squeezed in beside her just before the service started.

But despite all her reasons to smile, nothing felt right. She glanced over her shoulder, trying to figure out who was watching her.

"What's wrong?" Hunter whispered.

"I'm being watched."

"We're sitting in the fourth row. You probably are."

Charlee rolled her eyes. "You know what I mean."

Hunter casually glanced around. "I do. Any guesses on who?"

"No. Did you see Pete? He should have been here by now."

"Maybe he got held up with that phone call."

An older lady with a big straw hat turned around and glared. "Sorry," Charlee whispered.

She tried to focus on the sermon, but by the time they left, she felt more unsettled than ever.

As they drove back to the cottage, she called Pete's cell three times, and it always went right to voicemail, which was unlike him. He always took her calls.

For a cop, Pete Tanner was stupid. Which was what he'd been counting on. He'd left his truck unlocked while he was at the café, never giving it a thought. And when he'd told Pete he had information relating to the Brittany Harris murder, the idiot hadn't hesitated to arrange a meeting.

Now here he was, driving down the dirt road, swerving and fighting to keep the wheels straight. Good, the drug he'd poured into his travel mug was doing its job. It had been a risk, but a calculated one. Too much, and he might not get all the way out here to the Ocklawaha River. Not enough, and he might put up a fight.

He chuckled to himself as he watched Pete stagger out of the truck. He waited as the other man made his way to the edge of the river, hands on hips, shaking his head as if to clear it.

Silently, he snuck up behind Pete, the branch firmly clasped in his hands.

Something must have alerted him, for Pete started to turn, hand reaching for the gun he wasn't wearing. Probably left it in the truck, the fool.

Before Pete could see his face, he swung out hard

with the branch and knocked the other man out cold. He had a pretty nice swing, if he did say so himself.

He waited a minute to see if he came to, kicked him in the ribs for good measure, then grabbed Pete by the arms and dragged him to the water's edge. Once there, he rolled him over and pulled him into deep enough water that his head would end up submerged.

Nothing would go wrong this time.

He whistled a happy little tune as he walked back to where he'd hidden his truck. This time, Charlee would experience every minute of the soul-deep agony of losing someone you loved.

After a quick lunch, Charlee tried Pete's cell again, and it went right to voicemail. Again. While she called Josh to see if he'd reached Pete, Hunter called the medical examiner's office, on the off chance his contact was working today. "Hey, Doc, sorry to bother you on a Sunday, but I have to ask, did you find anything else that might help us figure out who killed Brittany Harris?"

Pages rustled in the background. "I was just going over the paperwork again, Lieutenant. I'll send you my report. There was one thing you might find interesting. We found traces of some old bruising on Brittany's skin."

"What kind of bruising? Like she fell, or someone beat her up?"

"They were on her biceps, as though someone took hold of her upper arms and shook her, hard."

"They weren't recent?"

"I'd say ten days to two weeks old."

"Thanks, Doc. Anything else?"

"Afraid not. Everything I found is pretty straightforward. Look for the email."

"Appreciate it." Hunter disconnected and made another phone call. As he dialed, Charlee showed up in the doorway and leaned against it, a worried expression on her face, which meant they still hadn't heard from Pete. He was about to hang up when the phone was answered.

"Mrs. Harris. Good afternoon. This is Lieutenant Boudreau again with Florida Fish and Wildlife. I'm sorry to bother you, but I was wondering if I could come by your home this afternoon. I have a few more questions." He saw Charlee raise her eyebrows and turned his back so he could concentrate. "Ah, no, ma'am, I don't guess San Francisco is anywhere near Orlando. Is Wyatt with you? Good."

He paused. "Mrs. Harris…sorry, Ms. Harris, I need to ask. What kind of relationship did you have with your daughter?"

There was a stunned pause, then her adamant response. "We had a terrific relationship, Lieutenant."

"I'm very glad to hear it. I'm sure it definitely makes it easier for a parent if your teenager talks to you about everything."

Hunter grimaced as the woman burst into great big, gasping sobs. "Take your time, ma'am. I know this is difficult…" He waited until the sobbing slowed to a sniffle before he asked what he really wanted to know. "What about her relationship with your, ah, ex-husband? Would you also classify it as good?"

"I should never have let him take Brittany on this crazy trip. But he begged me, said he needed that time with her, with both of them. If I had taken her with me, none of this would have happened."

"Why did he say he needed that time? Was he trying to make up for something?"

"You mean besides being a terrible husband and lousy father?"

"Can you tell me specifically what you mean by lousy father?"

Hunter heard a dramatic sigh and waited. "Look, I don't doubt he loved her and Wyatt, too, even though he was a total jerk. He tried. But he had some…issues. And sometimes Brittany got caught in the middle of them."

"What kind of issues, Ms. Harris? I'm not asking you to create problems for your ex-husband. But I am investigating a murder."

She gasped and sniffled some more at the word *murder*. "He had a temper, okay? A bad one. As long as he kept it under control, everything went okay. But if sales weren't good that month, he got tense. And after our marriage started to fall apart, well, there was lots of stress. He didn't always deal with it very well."

"Did he hit you?"

"He slapped me in the face once, hard. That's when I kicked him out."

"What about Brittany? Did he hit her?"

"I wouldn't have thought he'd ever raise a hand to either of us, but yeah, he slapped her, too. And that night, he grabbed her arms and shook her like a rag doll." She stopped, blew her nose. "After that, we both had very limited contact with him."

"Did he hit Wyatt?"

"I think so, but Wyatt always denied it, wouldn't let me see."

"In your mind, is it possible he suffocated Brittany?"

Hunter held the phone tighter as the silence stretched. He pulled the phone away to see if the call had been dropped. It hadn't.

"I would never have thought I could say this, but I have seen Paul in one of his rages, and if something set him off, yes, I think he could have hurt our daughter and not realized what he had done until later."

"Thank you, Ms. Harris."

"You catch my daughter's killer, Lieutenant Boudreau." She blew her nose. "No matter who it is."

"Yes, ma'am, I plan to."

He hung up and turned to Charlee, who had poured a glass of sweet tea and watched him over the rim, worry in her eyes. "Did you hear from Pete?"

She shook her head. "No. And Josh can't get him on the phone either. It's not like him to blow us off. Or to miss church."

"Why don't we swing by his place and see if he's there before we go talk to Paul Harris again. I want to know if his story matches his wife's version."

"It's weird that he's still here. I would have thought he'd go home after he made bail. Liz said somebody told her they've seen him on the riverbank, pacing, and in the hospital outside the room she was in, crying."

"Grief affects people in different ways, *cher*."

"Or it could be that he killed her and he can't deal with it."

Hunter didn't say anything. He simply nodded as they went out to his truck.

Charlee's agitation grew when they went by Pete's place and there was no sign of him. His house was locked, no truck in the driveway. Charlee called him again, left another message.

Hunter didn't want to jump to conclusions and send out the cavalry if Pete just needed a little alone time, but given all that was happening, he didn't want to under-react, either. He turned to Charlee as they pulled up at the hotel, squeezed her hand. "Let's talk to Harris and then see if we can track Pete down, okay?"

At her relieved nod, he straightened and knocked on the door. "Lieutenant Boudreau, FWC, Mr. Harris. I have a few more questions."

Harris swung the door open, growled, "What now? Vials of my blood? Why do you people keep harassing me instead of finding who did this to my daughter?" If anything, Paul Harris looked worse today than when he'd shown up soaking wet during the storm. Haggard, gaunt, hungover. He'd aged decades in the past week.

"We won't take up much of your time, sir. Just a few more questions."

Paul opened the hotel room door wider and gestured them inside. They stepped over the threshold into what looked like a more expensive version of Travis's cabin, with smelly clothes strewn about and empty pizza boxes littering the dresser.

Once they were inside, Hunter stood, hands in reach of his gun, as always. He gestured Paul toward one of the beds. Paul plopped down, and Charlee sat in one of the two chairs at the little table in the corner.

"So, Paul, I have to ask why you didn't mention your court-ordered anger management classes last time we talked."

Harris leaped to his feet and paced the small space. "What does that have to do with my daughter's death?"

Hunter shifted his weight, demeanor relaxed, but kept his eyes steady on Paul's. "That's what we're here to find out. The medical examiner said there were old bruises on Brittany's upper arms. What do you know about that?"

Paul's face paled, and he wouldn't meet Hunter's eyes. *Gotcha, dirtbag*. But whether the guilt was over hurting his daughter or killing her, Hunter didn't know yet. Paul shoved a hand through his hair. "Yeah, okay, I have some issues, but I'm dealing with them. It was mostly a misunderstanding, anyway. But I got a little angry when my wife announced she was leaving me and taking my daughter and son away from me forever."

"So you hit her."

Paul nodded miserably.

"And you grabbed Brittany to try to make her see your side of it."

Paul nodded again. "I didn't want to lose either one of my girls."

"But your wife called the cops, and you had to go to classes."

"I had it under control. I didn't need a stupid class."

"What about Wyatt? Did you hit him, too?"

His silence was answer enough.

"Did you suffocate your daughter, Paul?"

"What? Oh God, no. Never. You've got it all wrong. If that's what you think, that I'd ever hurt a hair on my baby girl's head..." He collapsed back onto the bed in a fit of sobbing.

Hunter felt for the man's loss. But hitting women and children? Not okay, ever. "Thanks for your time, Mr. Harris."

Charlee followed him out the door and back to his official truck. She hadn't said a word the whole time.

"I think he has a temper, but I don't think he killed Brittany," Charlee said as they headed out of the parking lot.

As much as he wanted to make an arrest, he agreed with Charlee. And they didn't have a single shred of evidence linking him to Brittany's murder. Or linking anyone else to it, either. No fingerprints, no DNA, nothing but speculation and circumstantial evidence.

Which meant the perp was not only smart, but he had a carefully crafted plan.

Hunter dialed Pete's cell again, and when it went straight to voicemail, he left another message.

His gut said they had to find him. Fast.

Chapter 18

Josh hadn't heard from Pete, either, nor had their parents. Beside Hunter, Charlee paced the length of the kitchen. She'd already called everyone who might have seen him and gotten nothing. Josh had done the same.

"Hey, Byte, sorry to call on your day off, but this can't wait," Hunter said into his cell.

"No problem, Lieutenant. What do you need?"

"Can you run a cell number for me, see if you can get a GPS lock on it?"

"Sure." He heard keys clacking in the background. "Give me the number."

He rattled it off and waited. It wasn't long before Byte said, "Got it," and read him the GPS coordinates. "The signal isn't moving. But this is Bulldog's—"

"You're the best, man. Thanks. Do me a favor and don't mention this search, would you?" If Pete was merely taking a break, or maybe had a lady his siblings didn't know about, he didn't want to embarrass him.

Without missing a beat, Byte asked, "What search?"

Hunter thanked him and hung up. He looked at Charlee. "We have a location." They hurried out to the truck, and Hunter kept his foot hard on the accelerator as they headed for another remote spot along the river.

Charlee gripped her hands together, panic in every line of her lovely face. "Can't you go any faster?"

"Easy, *cher*. We're getting there." He smiled to ease the tension. "And just so you know, if for some reason we find your brother along the banks with a fishing pole in the water or having a picnic with a pretty lady, I'm blaming you."

Charlee sent him a weak smile. "I hope that's all it is, but I don't think so." She speared him with a glance. "And neither do you."

Hunter nodded and sped up. When they burst through the trees and saw Pete's truck near the riverbank, they were both out of Hunter's vehicle almost before it stopped.

"Pete!" Charlee screamed as they spotted his body lying in the mud.

They dropped to their knees in the water beside him. He was lying on his back, covered in mud, eyes closed, much too still. There was no visible sign of injury. No blood that Hunter could see. His heart pounded as he shook his friend's shoulders. "Pete! Can you hear me?"

"Pete!" Charlee shouted. "Wake up!"

Hunter leaned over to check for a pulse, and Pete shoved him backward into the mud.

"What are you doing?" Pete's eyes popped open, confusion and pain in their depths. "What's going on?"

"Oh God, Pete. You're okay." Charlee leaned over and kissed his muddy cheek.

Pete struggled to a sitting position, and Hunter put an arm around his back to help him up.

"What happened out here, man? Are you hurt?" Hunter saw the back of his head. "You're bleeding." He grabbed Pete's chin, looked into his eyes, checked for concussion. "What is it with you Tanners and head wounds? Good thing you all have skulls like rocks."

Pete looked around, blinked. He reached back, touched the back of his head, winced. "It's hard to remember."

"What brought you way out here?" Hunter asked.

Pete thought a moment. "A phone call. Yeah. Somebody said they had information on the case and told me to meet them here."

Hunter made a mental note to have Byte check Pete's call log. "And then what?"

"There was nobody here. I was about to leave when I got hit in the back of the head."

"You could have drowned, you dang fool. Why'd you come alone?" Charlee asked.

"We don't have many leads, so I was hoping this would be one. We need a break in the case."

"What else do you remember? Did you hear a voice? A vehicle? Anything?" Hunter wanted the crime scene techs out here, pronto, to see if they could get any footprints or tire treads. Anything that would help.

"No, I can't rememb—wait. Yes. There was someone else here. Not right away, I don't think." He cocked his head. "I remember being turned over onto my back, coughing up water, and a voice saying, 'I'm sorry. I'm really sorry. Don't die.'"

Hunter and Charlee exchanged glances.

"Let's get you to the ER and get you checked out. I'll call it in."

"I don't need—" Pete started.

"Don't start with me. You're going." Charlee's voice brooked no argument.

As they got Pete settled on a log to wait for EMS,

Hunter studied the area and thought this just might be the break they'd been looking for.

I'm going to get you, you slimy son of a gun.

Charlee sat on the log beside Pete while the EMTs wrapped gauze around his head and prepared to transport him. When he protested again, Charlee shoved her face in his and hissed, "Don't argue, Bulldog. This guy has already tried to kill one of my brothers. He won't get to hurt another."

Pete opened his mouth to argue, but something in her expression registered, for he gentled his tone. "I'll be fine, Charlee. So is Josh. Like Hunter said, we have hard heads." He met her eyes, his worried. "And so do you, squirt. He's tried to hurt you, too."

At that reminder, Charlee's worry increased. She kissed his cheek as the EMTs loaded the gurney into the ambulance, then whipped out her phone and called her sister, Natalie.

"Hey, little sister? How are you?"

"What's wrong, Charlee? You sound weird."

"I'm fine. Pete, though, got himself a concussion and is being transported to the hospital as we speak. But he is laughing and talking, and his head is as hard as the rest of ours, so he'll be fine. Just wanted to let you know."

"This is me you're talking to, Charlee. Not Mom. Cut the gentle crap and tell me what really happened."

Charlee sighed. "We don't know yet. Somebody called him saying they had information on the case, but when he got there, they whacked him on the head and knocked him out." She decided not to mention how close he'd come to drowning. "Look, Nat, I think you should come home."

"I can't, Charlee. I have classes, exams. But I'm always around people."

Charlee rubbed her forehead. "If you won't come home, we need to get you some protection."

"What? No. I'll be fine." Then she chuckled. "You're not going to make the stranger-danger speech, are you?"

Charlee hid a smile. "No, since you say you know it." Then she sobered. "We don't know who or why yet, Nat, but it seems somebody has targeted our family. Please, please be careful, okay? And check in regularly so we know you're okay."

There was a long pause, and her voice was more serious than Charlee could remember it being. "I will. I promise. Love you, Sis. Kiss that big lug for me, too, okay?"

"Will do. Love you, too." Charlee hung up and sat on the log, watching Hunter and the other officers work, taking molds of footprints and tire treads, dusting Pete's truck for prints, taking pictures. Part of her wished she was in the middle of the action, gathering evidence. But then she decided there were advantages to being a free agent.

She sat very still, studying the surrounding area, shuffling through the facts of the case, one by one.

It wasn't long before that familiar feeling returned. She'd bet money she was being watched.

Chapter 19

Charlee was relieved when morning finally came. It seemed like she'd spent the night tossing and turning as her mind went over the facts of the case or trying to save Brittany from drowning and waking herself with a muffled scream. It was exhausting, and the guilt weighed her down like a shroud. She'd been tempted to ask Hunter to join her in the bed, just so she wouldn't be alone with her nightmares, but that was selfish, and her pride wouldn't let her. He'd been in warrior mode since they'd found Pete, so she figured he needed sleep even more than she did.

When she dragged herself out of bed and to the kitchen, she found him hunched over his computer, looking like he hadn't slept at all.

"Morning, *cher*. Hospital says Pete's doing fine, no skull fractures. Lab says he was given a mild dose of the party drug GHB, so he'll be released in a bit, but we haven't figured out yet how it got in his system. The sheriff's deputy who kept watch outside his room said all was quiet there last night." He met her eyes. "I also talked to Josh. He's got a sheriff's deputy friend from Gainesville watching Natalie. He says everything was quiet there, too."

Relieved, Charlee poured coffee and sank down at the table across from him. "You've been busy. Did you sleep at all?"

"I'll sleep when we catch this guy."

His simple statement made her love him even more, though she'd never say that out loud. He was putting her family ahead of himself, quietly and without fanfare. "Thank you for checking in on Pete and Natalie. And thanks for the coffee." She took a sip, held the mug with both hands. "I still can't believe someone is targeting our family. It's driving me crazy."

"We don't know why yet, but we will, *cher*."

The house phone rang, and she offered up a silent prayer before she answered. *Please, no more bad news.* "Charlee, girl, how are you this morning?"

"Hey, Dad. What's up?"

"I hate to bother you, but with everything going on, I forgot I have my six-month appointment with my cardiologist this morning. Any chance you can stay with your mom while I go?"

"Of course. When do you need me there? Sure, you go on. I'll be there in twenty minutes, okay? Perfect." She hung up and filled Hunter in.

"That works, since the captain scheduled a meeting this morning about the case. He's assigning more manpower. Some of the sheriff's department will be there, too. I'll drop you off on the way."

Charlee rinsed her cup and grabbed her backpack off the counter, checked her gun. "I'll take my Jeep. I don't want to be stuck without a vehicle if Mom needs something."

"You won't go anywhere else?"

"Scout's honor. I'm not giving this lunatic any more opportunities to hurt one of us."

"Text me when you get there."

Charlee rolled her eyes. "I'm going five minutes away."

His voice hardened. "Text me anyway."

"Yes, Mother," she drawled as he walked out the door. But she didn't argue. Things were coming to a head. She felt it, too.

After Hunter left, her little place suddenly felt too big, too quiet. She'd gotten used to having him with her all the time.

She climbed into her ancient Jeep and patted the dash. "I've missed you, girl."

She hadn't gone far when the heard the ominous *thump-thump-thump. Oh, come on.* She stopped the Jeep and climbed out to walk around the vehicle. Flat tire. Of course.

She got out the jack and tire iron and set to work. The first lug nut came off with relative ease, so she was grinning to herself as she started on the second. These were always the hardest part. If they'd been tightened by machine, she didn't have a prayer of getting them off. The second one wouldn't budge. Neither would the third, even though she jumped up and down on the tire iron, hoping to get it started. Nothing.

Sweating, frustrated, and very aware time was slipping by, Charlee gave up and decided to go on foot. She wasn't that far away.

She jogged through the trees, figuring if she took the shortcut, she should be at her parents' house within ten minutes. She reached in her back pocket to give her dad a heads-up, but her phone wasn't there. Where had she left it?

She mentally retraced her steps as she ran, sweat trickling down her back and the nape of her neck. Nobody ran during the summer in Florida. That's why shady porches, mint juleps, and afternoon naps were invented.

She'd set the phone on the hood of the car as she'd worked the tire iron, in case her dad or Hunter called. Brilliant.

She picked up the pace. She was almost there, so it wouldn't matter. She could get it later.

Her top stuck to her skin by the time she ran up the steps to her parents' big, old farmhouse.

Instead of going around to the screened porch in back as usual, she went to the front door, since it was closer, surprised that it swung open at her touch. Her dad must have left it open, knowing she was on her way. She stepped into the big living room. "Mama, I'm here. Where are you?" Her mother startled easily these days, and Charlee didn't want to scare her.

She checked the kitchen and found it empty. Same with Mama's favorite wicker rocker on the screened porch. Charlee headed down the hall, peeking in bedrooms as she went. Her father's den and her mother's craft room both stood empty. Her mother wasn't in the cushy club chair in the corner of their bedroom, either. So where had she gone?

"Mama? Are you here?" Had her father decided to take her with him and not let her know? Or maybe he'd called, but she—idiot—hadn't brought her phone. "Mama?"

She moved farther into her parents' bedroom, and that's when she heard it: water running. She hurried toward the big master bath that had been carved out of a tiny bedroom and stopped, stunned. Her mother's bare feet stuck up over the rim of the big sunken tub, the one her father jokingly referred to as his wife's indoor pool. "Hey, Mama? You having a soak?"

The hair on the back of Charlee's neck stood up when Mama didn't respond. Charlee raced over to the tub and shrieked, "NO!" when she saw her mother's head under the water.

Chapter 20

"No, no, no, no, no. Mama!" Charlee fell to her knees beside the tub and pulled Mama up by grabbing her under the arms. Careful not to smack her head, she eased her mother's still form up and over the edge of the tub and laid her gently on the floor. Her mother didn't move. Didn't open her eyes, and Charlee's heart threatened to explode.

She put her ear by her mother's chest, listening for a heartbeat through the wet clothes, but she didn't hear or see one. Mama wasn't breathing, either.

Charlee leaped back into the bedroom and grabbed the portable phone, dialing 911 with fingers that shook. "This is Charlee Tanner at the Outpost. I need EMS please, right away, at my parents' house on the property. It's a white farmhouse, west of the office along the riverbank. I found my mother in the bathtub. She's not breathing. I'm starting CPR. The front door is not locked." Then Charlee rattled off the official address and hung up.

She raced back into the bathroom, hoping her mother had started breathing again, but she hadn't. Charlee pushed her terror away and started CPR. She emptied her brain of everything but the count: thirty compressions, two breaths. Then thirty more compressions, two more breaths. She wouldn't let herself think about the fact that this was her mother, that she could lose her if this didn't work. She knew if she let thoughts like that in, she wouldn't be able to do what she needed to do.

Hands shaking, sweat pouring down her face, Charlee kept the rhythm going. *Come on, Mama. Breathe. Please breathe.*

Still nothing, but Charlee wouldn't give up. Finally, finally, when tears of frustration and fear were pouring down her face along with the sweat, Charlee heard sirens in the distance. She heard a knock on the door, then a voice calling, "Ms. Tanner? Are you here?"

"Down the hall. In the back. Hurry." Each word came out between pants, and Charlee worried they hadn't heard her.

But they had, and within moments, two EMTs hurried into the room, one pulling a stretcher, the other kneeling by her side. "I'll take over." He nudged her aside and took her place while his partner unpacked the defibrillator. They attached the leads, then he called out, "Clear." Charlee yelped when her mother's body arched up off the floor and slammed back down again. All eyes went to the monitor they'd connected. Nothing.

Oh God, please, no. Please give her back to us.

"Clear!"

Her mother's body jerked a second time, but still nothing. Charlee hung her head, defeat threatening to crush her. This couldn't be happening. It just couldn't.

"Clear!"

Charlee couldn't watch it again. She tried to stem the tide of tears that wouldn't stop, fighting to draw a breath.

"Atta girl, that's the way," the older EMT murmured, and Charlee's head snapped up and to the monitor. She swiped the tears away so she could see. They had a heartbeat.

Relief almost sent her crashing to the floor, every muscle in her body exhausted. "Thank you, God."

Her mother drew in a breath, then turned her head and threw up all over Charlee's legs. Charlee stared in shock and then laughed out loud. "Gee, thanks, Mama."

But Mama didn't open her eyes. They put her on oxygen and kept the monitor attached to her heart as they readied her for transport, but she didn't wake up.

Charlee moved to the sink and grabbed a washcloth to wipe off her legs and wash her hands, her eyes on the mirror to watch the EMTs. She felt completely numb, like she'd been wrapped in cotton, and everything had been muted and softened.

As they prepared to roll the stretcher down the hall, the older EMT looked over at Charlee. "We'll take good care of her. You saved her life, you know. You should be proud."

They disappeared, and Charlee's knees gave out. She grabbed the doorframe and slid to the floor, his words a cavern that had dropped open under her feet.

Proud? No, she wasn't proud. Her emotions tumbled and spun and made her stomach churn. She was terrified. And angry. And heartsick, because this was her fault.

Someone had tried to kill her mother. Because of her.

At that moment, Josh shouted her name. Two seconds later, he raced into the room and sank down beside her, yanking her into his arms. "Are you okay? What happened?"

Hunter ran in right behind him.

Charlee saw the concern mirrored in both faces and

swallowed back the regret threatening to choke her. They needed facts. Information.

She nodded to Hunter. "I got a flat tire and jogged over, but Dad wasn't here. Wait. Dad. We need to call him."

Josh laid a hand on her arm. "As soon as I heard the address, I called him. He's going to meet the ambulance at the hospital. It'll be faster."

Hunter eased farther into the room, crouched down, and placed a gentle hand on her shoulder. "You all right, *cher*? You didn't answer my text."

So that's what made them come running. Charlee felt the heat of his concern all the way to her toes, and it burned off some of the fear inside her. She looked over and saw Josh frowning at Hunter.

She ignored him, her eyes on Hunter. "I will be. And, please God, Mama will, too."

"Finish the story, *cher*." Hunter helped her up and sat down on the edge of the bed beside her.

"I hadn't gotten far when I realized I had a flat. So I stopped and tried to change the tire."

Josh settled down on her other side. "I can't believe you got the lug nuts off."

"Only the first one. The others wouldn't budge, no matter how much I jumped on the tire iron. I finally gave up and decided to jog over and deal with it later. I didn't want Mama alone for too long." She shrugged. "I left my phone sitting on the hood of the car in case Dad called. When I got here, the door was open, but I figured Dad must have left it that way for me."

"He'd never do that," Josh said, "but I'll check."

"I called her, but she wouldn't answer. I finally found

her back here." She closed her eyes against the terrible image. "She was in the tub with her feet sticking up. Her head underwater."

"Was she hurt anywhere that you could see?"

She followed Hunter's gaze and saw blood on the floor. How had she not noticed that before? "I-I don't know. I didn't check. I pulled her out of the tub and onto the floor and called 911. Then I started CPR and didn't stop until the EMTs got here."

"Which is exactly what you should have done, Sis. You followed first aid protocol to the letter." Josh wrapped his arm around her shoulder and pulled her close, his voice husky. "You saved her life."

Charlee leaped to her feet, furious. "I shouldn't have had to! Somebody did this to her. Because of me."

Hunter spoke quietly. "Is it possible she decided to have a soak and climbed in there on her own?"

Both of them said, "No."

"Since her stroke," Josh said, "she's been in a wheelchair. Her right side is still almost useless." Josh pointed to the step leading up to the big tub. "She'd never have been able to navigate that on her own."

Charlee agreed. "She wouldn't have tried it, either. She's much more afraid these days. And she was fully dressed."

Hunter held up a hand. "I had to ask." He glanced from one to the other. "The perp had the opportunity to kill her outright, but he didn't. He left her for you—or your father—to find. Just like Pete."

Charlee raced back into the bathroom and threw up. Hunter appeared behind her and thrust a wet washcloth in her direction, then rubbed her back while she tried to catch her breath. "I'm sorry to be so blunt, *cher*."

She wiped her face, rinsed her mouth, and turned to face him. "What have I done that someone would do this?"

"Whatever the reason, it makes perfect sense to him. When we figure out how he thinks, we'll be able to get a step ahead of him."

His phrase from the day by the bridge came back to her. "It's always about water."

Hunter nodded. "Yes, somehow it's always about water."

The rest of that eternal day, Charlee turned that phrase over and over in her mind, replaying everything that had happened lately and weighing it against what had happened a year ago. Her frustration mounted when nothing new came to mind. Where was the connection? And why couldn't she see it?

Fury still pounded through Hunter's veins when he got to the hospital later that day to check on Charlee and her mother. Paul Harris, the slimebag, had lied to their faces, more than once. But worse, he'd hurt his daughter and deceived his wife and tried to convince them all he was nothing but a grieving father.

He noticed people stepping out of his path as he passed and deliberately slowed his pace. He didn't want to unload all of this on Charlee. She had enough to worry about.

What nobody was saying was that with all the trauma her mother had already been through with her stroke, the damage from the water this morning may have been too much for her to beat back. He hoped she made a full recovery, but he had his doubts. For Charlee, he would set them aside.

When he entered the darkened room, he saw Charlee on one side of the bed, her father on the other, each holding one of her mother's hands.

Charlee looked up as he entered, and her smile hit him square in the gut. Had anyone ever been that happy to see him in his life? It warmed him from the inside out. And it scared him spitless.

He went to her side, leaned over and kissed her forehead, nodded to her father. "How's she doing?" He kept his voice quiet.

"She's resting. The doctors say that's what she needs most right now."

Her father said, "Why don't you kids go grab a sandwich or something. You've been here for hours, Charlee. You must be starving."

She started to protest, but Hunter didn't let her finish. "Good idea. There are several fast food joints nearby. What can we bring back for you, sir?"

He waved that away. "Anything is fine. Maybe some lemonade, if you can find it."

"Grease and lemonade. We can do that."

Hunter guided her out of the room. Halfway to the elevator, Charlee stopped him with a hand on his chest. "Why are you rushing me out of here? I need to stay with them."

Hunter indicated the elevator, and they started walking again. "You and your dad need to eat. I could use a bite, too. And I didn't want to discuss new developments in front of your folks. Your mom needs her rest, and your dad needs to keep his mind on her."

Charlee nodded agreement, but as the elevator doors slid closed, she turned to him, eyes bleak. "What if she never wakes up?" The words were barely a whisper.

Hunter tugged her into his arms and held tight, offering what comfort he could. She sounded small and afraid, and that made him furious all over again, more determined than ever to find whoever was behind this. "Your mama is tough, like her daughter. Stay strong, *cher*. She needs you." She nodded and burrowed closer, her head tucked against his throat. He breathed in her scent and rubbed her back, murmuring reassurances in her ear, lending her his strength, making sure she knew she was not alone.

When the doors opened, Charlee jumped back. One young guy grinned, and Hunter fixed him with a stern look while heat climbed Charlee's cheeks.

Her chin came up, and he watched her tuck her sadness and worry behind determination as they walked across the street and ordered sandwiches. As soon as they were seated, Charlee took a bite of her chicken sandwich, sighed, and then motioned for him to talk.

He raised a brow. "Don't I get to eat, too?"

She swallowed. "Fine…but hurry up. I need to know what's going on."

"Yes, ma'am." He devoured his sandwich in a few bites, and they both polished off the fries in record time. He watched her wipe the ketchup from her lips and grinned.

She caught his smile and lowered the napkin. "What? Do I still have ketchup somewhere?"

He reached out a finger and swiped a bit from her cheekbone. "Just a little bit."

"You're making fun of me."

"Actually, I was thinking that it's nice to be around a woman who enjoys food and doesn't spend all her time moaning about how she wants to eat but can't."

She waved a hand, grinned back. "Yeah, I gave that up years ago. I love bread and baking too much. I don't want to get as wide as I am tall, but that's pretty much my only criterion."

"No danger of that. You're beautiful, Charlee. Sexy, too," he added with a wink.

She eyed him for a long moment. "I know you're trying to distract me and lighten the mood a little, but I need answers. Start talking, Lieutenant."

He crumpled his napkin. "Right. We brought Paul Harris in a while ago. He's been lying all along. You said there was the usual father-daughter teenage stuff going on, but it went much, much deeper than that. He was putting on an act that day, too. We got the transcript from his phone and found a bunch of ugly texts between the two of them. Texts he'd tried to delete the day she died, by the way. Brittany had threatened to tell her mother about the new girlfriend Paul had—the one he'd hooked up with long before the divorce proceedings started. She said her mother would make mincemeat out of him in the divorce, and she'd be sure to help her."

Charlee sat back in her seat, stunned. "I can't believe it. He seemed so sincere. Genuine."

"He may really have loved his daughter and his wife, but not at the expense of his money and his reputation." He finished his soda. "We also questioned him further about JJ's death, and he can't account for his whereabouts the day JJ died. No one at the office can vouch for him that day. No client records, no receipts from any restaurant or gas station. There's just his word he didn't do it. Which doesn't hold much water, pardon the pun."

Charlee rolled her eyes and started stacking trash on the tray. "We should get Dad's food and go."

They stayed at the hospital until Josh came in after his shift and said he'd spend the night with Mom, just in case.

"I can have one of my buddies stay at your place, Sis."

Before Charlee could answer, Hunter said, "I'm staying with her until we catch this guy. I'll take care of her tire while I'm there, too."

Josh looked like he wanted to argue, but Charlee's ultraconservative dad piped up. "Good idea. I don't want her alone until this is over."

"Then she can stay with me," Josh insisted.

Mr. Tanner looked from one to the other, then fixed Hunter with a stern look. "Hunter's a good man. He'll take good care of our Charlee."

"Yes, sir, you have my word on it."

Charlee didn't start chuckling until they were in Hunter's truck. "You should have seen Josh's face when Dad backed you up about staying with me. He expected Dad to take his side."

Hunter shook his head. He didn't always understand the dynamics in this big family. "I don't want to cause trouble between you and your brothers."

She shook her head, still grinning. "They'll get over it. Trust me. But it is nice to see Dad put Josh in his place. Haven't seen that in a while, since everyone's been tiptoeing around Josh."

Hunter didn't know what to say. They drove to

where she'd left her car, and he changed the tire in no time. Then they drove all the way back to town to get a replacement installed, glad the place was still open. Hunter asked about an old blue pickup, maybe missing a back window, and got a blank look from the kid behind the counter.

The young man pointed to the computer. "If you have a license plate, maybe a make and model, I can help you, but we don't record descriptions like that."

After several more fruitless questions, they thanked him and climbed back in Hunter's truck.

By the time they were finally back at the cottage, Charlee was swaying on her feet. "Get some rest, *cher*. It's been a very long day."

She simply nodded and went into her bedroom and closed the door. Sometime later, when he heard her cry out from yet another nightmare, he found her facedown on the covers, still fully clothed. She must have walked in and collapsed.

He slipped off her flip-flops and pulled back the covers before tucking her underneath. Without hesitation, he climbed in beside her and pulled the covers up. Then he eased her closer until her head rested on his shoulder and he had his arm wrapped around her waist.

"Sleep. I'll keep you safe."

She mumbled something but didn't wake, just burrowed deeper against him. He listened as her breathing evened out again, but he couldn't fall asleep. The jumbled facts of the case ran through his mind, frustrating all his efforts to put them in an order that made sense. Anxiety tightened his chest as the worry built, and Charlee murmured a sleepy protest. "Shh. It's okay, *cher*."

But it wasn't. He felt like he'd gone back in time, before the raid in New Orleans. They were doing all they could, chasing down every possible lead, but Hunter worried that he'd somehow miss the most important thing. That some seemingly innocuous detail would be the key to it all, and he wouldn't see the whole picture in time.

And this time, Charlee's life would be on the line.

He tightened his hold on her and vowed to keep her safe.

Chapter 21

Hunter had already been up for several hours reviewing his notes on the case when the scent of coffee brought Charlee stumbling into the kitchen. He turned away so she wouldn't notice how her sleep-rumpled look affected him. They had other things to worry about today.

He pulled out the last two cupcakes from her recent baking frenzy and offered one. "Breakfast?"

She watched him as she licked off the frosting, a teasing gleam in her eye. He ignored it and grabbed a frying pan like a lifeline. "How about I scramble some eggs while you get ready?"

"Great. Thanks." She planted a quick kiss on his cheek and hurried out of the kitchen.

When she rushed back into the room a few minutes later, he swallowed hard at the sight of her in another tempting pair of shorts and tank top, damp hair up in a ponytail, a faint trace of makeup on her face.

The caffeine had obviously kicked in, and she started shoveling food like she was late for a plane. "Nobody called last night?" When he shook his head, she nodded. "Okay, I need to get back to the hospital so Josh can get to work. I'll convince Dad to go home and get some sleep. Travis is covering the Outpost this morning." She gulped coffee.

He walked over and planted a quick kiss on her

mouth, ignoring her startled "Oh" of surprise. He grinned, enjoying throwing her just a little off balance. "I already talked to Josh, and he said your mother had a restful night. He convinced your dad to go home last night. Said he'd need his strength for when your mother came home. And Phil, the off-duty deputy watching Natalie, said all is well there, too."

Charlee finally sat back, let out a relieved sigh. "Okay. Good. I should go sit with Mama."

"Actually, I want to take you with me. We need to talk to Tommy Jennings again. Let him know we arrested Paul Harris. I want to see his reaction."

She studied his face. "Your instincts say something's still off about Paul as our prime suspect."

He raised a brow and waited to hear what she was thinking.

She sighed. "I've been going over and over what happened this week and comparing it with last year, and I can't make any connection—except the school—but I know there is one. There are no coincidences in a murder investigation."

"Agreed. That's why I want you with me. I respect your judgment."

She smiled, then her eyes narrowed. "And you don't want me alone."

He grinned, then cleared their plates. "That, too. Let's go."

They made the drive back to Lake City in relative silence. Hunter turned on a jazz station and tapped a finger on the steering wheel in time to the music, while

Charlee sat with her arms tightly crossed, jaw clenched, staring out the window. He knew she was worried about her mother. But it was more than that. With every mile, her anger grew, until it exploded into a barely concealed fury he understood well.

He glanced at her, chose his words with care. "Don't let it get you, *cher*."

She snapped her gaze to his. "Don't let what get me? That someone is going after my family?"

"No. The fury. If you give it free rein, it will consume you."

"I don't need you to tell me how to feel, Lieutenant."

"I wouldn't dream of it. That rage is yours to control. Or not." He let out a breath and gave her the rest of his story, telling her things he'd merely glossed over with the police department shrink after his brother had died. "Telling Grandmere that Johnny was dead was the hardest thing I've ever done. After that, I vowed to find every single member of that drug ring and keep shooting until they were all dead. Grandmere must have known, because she got right in my face and told me that if I loved her, I wouldn't do this thing." Hunter shot Charlee a half smile. "Understand, Grandmere was less than five feet tall and under one hundred pounds soaking wet, but she got through. She laid a hand on my chest and told me that it wasn't my fault. Johnny had made his own choices, and vengeance belonged to God. If I tried to mete it out, it would destroy me, and she didn't want to lose me, too.

"So I settled for getting justice for Johnny. By the time I was done, every single member of that drug ring was behind bars." It wasn't enough, it wasn't nearly enough, but it had been the best he could do without destroying his grandmere, too. "She died just before the last one was arraigned."

Charlee reached over and gripped his hand, hard. "It wasn't your fault, Hunter."

He raised a brow. "Isn't that my line?"

Her back stiffened. "This is different."

"No, it isn't. That anger kept me going for months, until it was the only thing I could see, but it didn't bring Johnny back, and it didn't take away a single ounce of the guilt I felt. I don't want that for you."

"He tried to kill my mother." Her voice sliced like a thin blade.

"But he didn't succeed. We're going to find him, and we're going to stop him."

Charlee made a noncommittal sound in her throat and didn't say another word the rest of the way. But she didn't loosen her grip on his hand, either.

Hunter took the turnoff to Tommy's place, and Charlee snapped to attention, focused on the area around them. Pavement gave way to gravel, and finally, they turned down the dirt path that led to the cabin.

They parked in the same place as last time. Hunter climbed out and scanned the area. It had that deserted air, just like before, but something felt off. He leaned into the open window and said, "Stay put and let me look around first."

Charlee ignored him and slid out of the truck, gun in her hand.

He strode around the vehicle and blocked her path, memories of Johnny's stubbornness fresh in his mind. "We do this my way, or I come back without you. Your choice."

There went that stubborn chin. "This is my family he's after."

"We don't know that it's him."

She raised a brow, fairly shaking with fury. "Don't we?"

"Stand down, Charlee. You know we don't have enough yet."

He kept his eyes on hers until she finally looked away. "Stay here. And keep your gun out of sight."

"Okay. But if you're not back in five minutes, I'm coming after you."

"Fair enough." Hunter pulled his gun but held it alongside his leg as he approached the front door. "Mr. Jennings. It's Lieutenant Boudreau. We'd like to ask you a few more questions."

He moved across the open area to the half-hidden cabin, eyes scanning all the while. He sent a quick glance over his shoulder to be sure Charlee hadn't followed. She peeked around the corner of his truck, then ducked back out of sight.

"Mr. Jennings?" He stepped up onto the rickety front porch, careful of his footing.

The door stood open behind the torn screen door. "Mr. Jennings? Hello?"

He carefully stepped inside, surprised at how tidy the small space had been kept. After the way Tommy had looked, he'd expected a mess. Recliner and television set, two-person dinette, kitchen nook in the back. Hunter moved farther in, peeked into the minuscule bathroom and single bedroom, home to a carefully made double bed and a sturdy wooden dresser. He glanced into the small closet and saw several shirts and pairs of jeans, all neatly hung. Two pairs of boots sat on the floor. Tommy Jennings might not have much, but he took good care of what he had. Interesting, in light of his drinking.

Hunter walked into the kitchen, and that's where things changed. Two empty whiskey bottles sat beside the sink. Several more had been tossed into the trash can. A pile of unopened mail sat on the counter. Beside them, he saw a ticket stub and one of those plastic bracelets you get at events and hospitals. It had obviously been cut off, but not thrown away yet.

The back door stood open, just like the front. That didn't seem like something Jennings would do. Hunter would bet money the man locked up if he left.

He walked down the back steps, gun sweeping the area in front of him, eyes scanning the dense trees. He walked to a small lean-to that had been empty on their last visit. The blue pickup inside matched the description the old couple had given Josh of a vehicle seen leaving the site where Charlee and Brittany had been shot. He pulled out his phone and took a picture of the truck and the license plate.

His phone chirped with an incoming text from Charlee. I'm coming around the side of the cabin.

He waited until she appeared, then lowered his weapon.

"Your five minutes are up. Did you find him?"

"Not yet."

Charlee peered into the lean-to, gun at her side. "Isn't that the same truck that old couple said they saw?"

"Very possibly. But Jennings wouldn't have gone far on foot. Not way out here."

Charlee spun in a circle, and her gun came up,

scanning the area. "Does that mean he's out here watching us?"

"Maybe." He raised his voice. "Mr. Jennings, it's Lieutenant Boudreau. If you're out here, please show yourself." He motioned to Charlee. "I'm going to circle the perimeter. Stay here."

He made a complete circuit, stopping regularly to listen, but found nothing out of the ordinary.

When he got back to the lean-to, Charlee had disappeared.

"Charlee, where are you?" He hissed the words. "Charlee!"

He backtracked into the cabin, but she wasn't there. "Charlee!"

Was it possible Jennings had grabbed her in that split second? If so, the man had to be a pro, because Hunter hadn't sensed a thing. "Charlee! Jennings!" Hunter ran out the front door and circled around the other side of the cabin. The truck still sat in the lean-to. "Charlee!"

"No! Don't you dare!" The words seemed to come from far away. But the voice was definitely Charlee's.

Hunter froze, heart pounding as he tried to pinpoint the direction of her voice. "Charlee? Where are you?"

He hurried into the woods, scanning as he went. What if Jennings had grabbed her and was using her as bait?

Every nerve went on high alert as his eyes adjusted to the gloom in the trees. He heard a loud, "NO! NO! NO!" from off to his right. Head down, he moved in a crouch, gun ready.

"This can't be happening again. It just can't."

The forest suddenly opened into a little clearing at the edge of a stream. Charlee crouched at the edge, shaking the shoulder of a man lying facedown at the water's edge. A large tree limb lay on top of him.

He hurried over and crouched beside her. "Are you all right, *cher*?"

Where he expected despair, he saw fury. "He's dead. Just like JJ. And Brittany. It wasn't him. Who is doing this?"

"First things first. Did you check for a pulse?"

Charlee looked at him like he was stupid. "Of course. No pulse. We're too late."

Hunter opened his mouth to say more, but then he looked closer. Tommy's head was submerged in the creek, cocked at a weird angle, the weight of the limb lying across his head and shoulders, making it impossible for him to move. His head was turned sideways, and his wide-open eyes stared out into the clear water. Hunter reached over and checked his neck for a pulse, just to make absolutely sure.

He put his gun away and pulled out his cell phone to call dispatch, asked them to send local law enforcement. Then he took several pictures. "His body is already cooling."

Charlee ignored him and suddenly leaped to her feet. She grabbed one end of the big limb. "We need to get this off him, do CPR. Just in case."

Hunter grabbed her from behind, stopped her from dragging the branch away. Attempting CPR might make her feel better, but it could destroy evidence the killer had left behind. Tommy Jennings was beyond help. She knew it, too. "Stop, *cher*. He's gone."

She struggled against his hold for a moment before she sagged in his arms. He turned her around and held her while she pounded her fists against his chest and silent tears ran down her cheeks. After several minutes, she pulled back, wiped her face, and they went to work.

While he took photos, Charlee stood off to the side and ran an expert eye over the scene as well. By the time the first responders arrived, she gave them her statement and responded to their questions like the efficient FWC officer she'd been trained to be.

Hunter watched her, impressed all over again. She was the kind of woman you wanted by your side in a crisis. She didn't wilt or cower or run. She stood tall and went on the offensive when necessary. If he wasn't careful, he could fall in love with a woman like her.

He ignored the little voice in his head that warned he already had.

Several hours later, Charlee sat in the open door of Hunter's truck, head back, exhaustion a lead blanket weighing her down. She'd answered all the official questions, but the most important one was still unanswered: who was doing this?

That helpless feeling, like she was trying to peer through dense fog, was so like last year that she shuddered in the stifling humidity. Nothing in her world seemed familiar, except the constant numbing parade of death and near-death scenes. Always centered around water. JJ's drowning. Brittany and Pete's near drowning. Josh's boat explosion. She and Hunter getting run off the road into the river. Her mother's near drowning.

And now, Tommy Jennings dead in the creek.

Dear God, they had to figure out who was doing this. Paul Harris was in custody, so who was left?

"You holding up okay, *cher*?" Hunter stepped in front of her, blocking the bright sun.

She squinted to see his face and nodded. He looked as tired and drawn as she felt.

"This is not your fault. The fault lies with the person who killed him." Hunter put a finger under her chin to make her look at him. "Don't take on what isn't yours."

Charlee searched his eyes, saw the truth and the caring there. "I know I didn't kill him. But I'll always wish I'd been able to save him. And Brittany. And JJ."

Suddenly too frustrated to sit, she climbed out of the vehicle and paced while he leaned against the door. "How is this connected to JJ's death? If it wasn't Tommy doing this, then who? And how is it connected to me and my family?"

"We still have more questions than answers, but we are going to find this SOB."

He stepped closer and held out two clear evidence bags. "Any idea what these are? Or where they're from?"

Charlee took the one containing a ticket stub. "This could be from any local event. Maybe a raffle ticket? I'm not sure." She took the other bag. "These look like the kind of wristbands they give you at the carnival for unlimited rides. Josh and I used to go every year when they came to town."

"Do they still come?" Hunter had his phone out, keying in a search.

"Oh, yes. Sammy said he'd been giving lots of prizes away."

"Sammy? The kid who brought flowers to your hospital room, has a crush on you?"

She rolled her eyes. "He's a sweetheart."

"We should talk to him. See if he saw Tommy Jennings at the carnival recently."

Before she could respond, her cell phone rang. She fished it out of the console where she'd set it. "Hey, Dad. How's Mom today?"

"She's the same. The doctors say there's no swelling in her brain, so hopefully she'll wake up soon."

"Did you get some sleep? What time did Natalie get there?"

"I told her not to come. She has a couple of big tests the next few days, and she needs to concentrate. There's nothing she can do here anyway except worry. I told her I'd give her regular updates."

"Have you talked to her today?"

"A little while ago. Why? Is something wrong?"

Charlee bit her lip, decided not to mention Tommy's death. Not yet. Her father had enough to worry about right now. "Just wondering how her tests went. I'll call her later to check in. Give Mom a kiss for me and call me the minute she wakes up, okay? Love you."

"Love you, too, sugarplum."

He drove away from Tommy's place, heartbroken and furious. This should never have happened. Never! Tommy was dead, and it was all Charlee Tanner's fault. She'd caused this. If she hadn't come snooping around with that know-it-all Boudreau, none of this would have happened. It wouldn't have been necessary.

But they'd come to Tommy's place, the two of them, making eyes at each other, asking questions, too many questions. Tommy had crumpled like cheap toilet paper. He'd admitted as much. Had told him he'd been thinking about what happened a year ago and how some of the things he was starting to remember were confusing him. He'd broken down and cried like a baby about his son's death, mumbling all kinds of nonsense. The incoherent ramblings of a drunk.

But some of it wasn't nonsense.

He couldn't let Tommy have some sort of attack of conscience and start telling tales to the wrong people.

He banged a fist against the steering wheel. This was all her fault. He'd never wanted this to happen. Never. Tommy wasn't supposed to die. But Charlee and her meddling had given him no choice. Now his death became one more sin in her long list of sins. She would be punished for it. She'd wish she'd never been born before he was done with her.

He parked the truck and sat for a moment, hands tight on the steering wheel, squeezing, squeezing, wishing it was her neck. He'd enjoy watching the life drain out of her. But no. She wouldn't die like that. He had to stay focused. No matter how tempting it seemed, that would be too easy. He had lots more suffering in mind for her before he let her slip away.

Sweat beaded his forehead, and he slowly let go of the wheel, deliberately slowing his breathing. He had to collect his thoughts, get his emotions under control. He was home. He couldn't let his feelings show, or he'd have to answer more questions.

He stepped out of the vehicle and pasted a smile on his face before he opened the door and went inside.

"Hey, how was your day?"

Chapter 22

As Hunter drove away from Tommy Jennings's place, something nagged at Charlee like an itch in the middle of her back she couldn't reach. She crossed her arms and chewed the inside of her cheek while she tried to figure it out.

"You focus any harder, *cher*, you'll catch fire."

Charlee smiled at his attempt to lighten the mood. "Just thinking."

"Something's bugging you. What?"

The picture of Tommy's lifeless body under the water flashed through her mind, and she forced herself to examine the scene from every angle. "Tommy didn't have any bruising around his neck, like Brittany. Between that and the drag marks in the mud, we know the tree limb didn't fall on him. The killer dragged it over there."

"That's what it looks like, yes."

Charlee took a deep breath. "So Tommy was probably alive when he went into the creek." She shivered and locked her emotions up so she could think logically. She looked at Hunter. "Knocked out?" For Tommy's sake, she desperately hoped so.

"That's the working theory. He had a pretty significant head wound. No blood on the limb, though, so we're thinking the killer hit him with something else first."

Although she really didn't want to think about it,

Charlee's mind flashed back to finding Pete facedown along the riverbank, and her eyes widened. "He didn't try to hold Pete down."

Hunter's eyes snapped to hers. "Which means either we found Pete quicker than he expected, or, he wanted to be sure Tommy drowned. That's good police work, *cher*. Sure you don't want to come back?"

"No, thanks. Two cops in the family is quite enough. I'll just, ah, stick to running the Outpost."

"I get the impression that's not something you really want to do, either."

Charlee wanted to squirm but held herself still. "That's been the plan for a while now. Once Mom recovers from the stroke, she and Dad are going to do some traveling. With this, though, her recovery may be pushed back by several more months."

"But you don't really want to run the Outpost."

Charlee bristled. "How do you know what I do or don't want to do?"

"Don't get riled. It's just an observation. I've seen you when you're baking and when you're at the Corner Café. Your whole body lights up, and you're, I don't know, you. Same when we talk about the investigation. I've seen you drive up to the Outpost, too, and it's like all the life drains out of you. You get out of the car dragging your paws like my old hound dog on his way to the vet. You weren't like that before. You loved every minute on the water."

When Charlee just narrowed her eyes at him, he said, "Plans and dreams can change, and that's okay. Just make sure you aren't giving up what you love because of what happened last year. That would be letting him win."

Charlee thought she might explode. "It's not okay to change plans," she burst out. "Not if that would change your parents' plans, too. I made a commitment. I can't back out now."

He reached over and patted her hand. "I'm sorry I said anything. Now is not the time to make big decisions. First, let's find this guy."

Charlee slapped his hand away. "Will you stop patronizing me?"

He shook his head, blew out a breath. "Either I'm not communicating, or you're not hearing me. It's okay if you change your mind about the Outpost, Charlee. You and your parents will work something out. You love each other. I'd just hate to see you give up what you really love out of misplaced guilt."

Why couldn't the man understand? "I hate being on the river now." The words popped out, and she looked out the window to hide her shame.

The silence stretched for several minutes before Hunter said, "After I made sure everyone involved with Ace's crew was behind bars, I turned in my badge and gun. Said I was done. Then I went home and lost myself in a bottle for a while."

Charlee glanced his way. "What pulled you out? Made you become a cop again?"

He shot her a quick grin. "When I wouldn't answer my phone, my partner finally showed up at my door, poured out my booze, shoved me into a cold shower, and had coffee and a new case file waiting for me after. When I got done cussing him out for sticking his nose in my business, I called my captain, who said he'd stashed my gun and badge in his desk drawer until I got my head on straight. I still had to get cleared by the department shrink, but after that, I went back to work."

"And the first time you had to pull your gun?" She didn't try to hide the accusation in her tone.

His smile turned rueful. "You don't miss a thing, do you, *cher*? I made myself go to the range every single day—until the flashbacks didn't control me anymore and my hands quit shaking."

"Just like that. You make it sound so easy."

He laughed. "No. Not easy. I almost changed my mind because I wasn't sure I could do it. But it was necessary to get back to what I was made to do."

"Well, bully for you. I've been back on the water for a year. It's not any easier. Since Brittany...it's even worse." But she wanted it to get better so badly, sometimes she couldn't breathe. "At least no one will die if my cupcakes are dry."

He snorted at her attempt at humor. "Finding this guy will help. None of it has been your fault, *cher*. I'll keep saying it until you believe it."

Charlee didn't want to hear it. None of it changed how she felt. She forced her mind back to the day JJ died and then thought about Tommy's death. She turned toward Hunter. "Has Byte found any info on James Jennings? Where is he now? And does he have an alibi for the time of Tommy's death?"

Hunter was dialing Byte almost before she finished asking the questions. He listened, then said, "Okay, keep digging. See what you can find." He glanced her way. "Byte's been looking but hasn't found any record of James anywhere. No paper trail. Nothing. Do you know anything that might help find him?"

Charlee replayed the day in her mind and came up blank. "Nothing except that he seemed to make Tommy cower, and Sally seemed to hate him. But nothing that would help us find him."

"If there's anything to be found, Byte will find it."

Her emotions in a knot, Charlee pushed them aside and focused on the carnival coming up ahead. Just seeing the giant Ferris wheel, the mini roller coasters, and the rides she'd always loved helped settle her heart rate. She rolled down the window and absorbed the smell of popcorn and grease. The carnival wouldn't open for another couple of hours, so they should have time to talk to the workers. If they were on-site.

Hunter drove around to the open field where the workers set up their trailers and campers. They headed toward a cluster of people, who immediately stopped talking to glare in their direction.

"What do you want?" a heavyset woman on the wrong side of sixty growled.

Charlee stepped forward. "Hi, I'm a friend of Sammy's and wanted to ask him a couple of questions."

The woman folded her arms over an ample chest and shifted so she blocked Charlee's path. "What kind of questions? Sammy don't need no trouble."

Charlee held both palms up. "He's not in any trouble. Not at all. But I'm hoping he recognizes this picture." She reached behind her, and Hunter put his phone in her hand, Tommy's picture facing out. She held it out. "Have you seen this man here this week?"

She shook her head. "He don't work here."

"Was he a guest? Do you remember seeing him here at the carnival?"

The woman eyed her for a moment, then threw her head back and laughed. When she sobered, she said, "We see hundreds of people every night, more on weekends. Why would I recognize this dude?"

Charlee decided not to mention Tommy's death. "I was hoping you might. And I wanted to ask Sammy the same thing. Could you point me toward his trailer?"

The woman spat into the dirt near Hunter's feet. "If Sammy ain't in no trouble, what's this one doing here?"

Hunter stepped up, slid an arm around Charlee's waist. "Just giving a pretty lady a ride, that's all."

The woman guffawed at that. "You're a slick talker, I give you that. But I ain't no fool." She waved a hand toward an older but immaculate trailer not far away. "Sammy been staying there with Tool Man. But if I hear you gave our boy any trouble, you'll answer to me." She glared at Hunter.

"Yes, ma'am. We just want to show him the picture." He scanned the rest of the group, who eyed them suspiciously. "Any of the rest of you folks seen this man recently?" He held out the phone. None gave it more than a passing glance, and all shook their heads no. "Thanks for your time." He tucked the phone away as they walked toward the trailer.

"Not exactly warm and welcoming, are they?" Charlee said.

"Protective of Sammy, which I can appreciate."

"None of them looked like they'd seen Tommy."

"Didn't appear so, no."

When they reached the Tool Man's trailer, Charlee walked up the steps and knocked on the door. "Sammy, it's Charlee. Are you there?"

The door swung open, and Sammy appeared, a smile on his face but clearly troubled. "Hi, Charlee. What are you doing here? We don't open for a couple more hours." His smile turned down at the corners when he spotted her empty hands. "You didn't bring me any cupcakes."

"I'm sorry, Sammy. Coming here was a last-minute decision, or I would have."

"Did you come to see where I work?" He hurried out, and Charlee backed down before he trampled her, eager as a puppy. He started walking toward the midway, and Charlee and Hunter quickened their pace to keep up.

He didn't stop until they came to one of those shooting games with little ducks everywhere. Sammy pointed to the huge stuffed animals hanging above their heads. "Those are the best prizes. I love it when I can give those away." He indicated some smaller stuffed animals and little toys. "These are the other prizes, in case people don't win. They're called, con-con… I don't know the word."

"Consolation prizes?" Charlee asked.

He beamed. "That's what they're called. You're smart, Charlee. And pretty, too." He ducked his head, and a blush crept up his cheeks.

"Thank you, Sammy." Hunter pressed his phone into her hand, and Charlee held it up so Sammy could see. "Have you seen this man here before, Sammy?"

Sammy's eyes widened, and then he quickly averted his gaze and started shaking his head from side to side. "Don't know him."

"Okay, that's fine. But have you seen him? Has he been here?"

Sammy just kept shaking his head, getting more and

more agitated. Charlee tried another approach. "A nice lady told me you're staying with the Tool Man."

Sammy gave an uncertain nod. "He's been real nice to me. Teaching me things, like how to cook eggs and shoot a gun."

Charlee and Hunter exchanged a look.

"But he doesn't want me to drive the truck. He says I'm not very good at it." He looked up, and his smile reappeared. "But I can ride my bike to the café to get cupcakes."

"I'm glad! It's always good to see you. Is the Tool Man home, Sammy? Maybe he's seen this man."

Sammy was shaking his head before Charlee finished speaking. "We shouldn't bother him. He's in a bad way today, so I just stay out of his way."

"Do you mean he's not in a good mood today?"

Another shrug. "He don't like it when I bother him. And when he's talking to himself, he gets real mad if I answer." He looked up, eyes wide and confused, and Charlee's heart melted. "How am I supposed to know when he's talking to me or himself?"

"Does he ever hurt you when you answer?"

Sammy seemed to pull further into himself, and Charlee glanced at Hunter. "He been real good to me, like a dad, I guess, so I know I have to get punished when I do things wrong. But he takes good care of me."

"Is he home now?"

Sammy wouldn't meet her eyes. "He was. But I don't think he is now." He glanced off behind the trailers. "The Tool Man doesn't like no strangers coming around."

Charlee looked over her shoulder but couldn't see what he was looking at. "Does the Tool Man go by another name, Sammy?"

Sammy smiled then. "He says it's cool to have a nickname, like a movie star. If I do good, he'll let me have a nickname, too." Then his face fell. "But I haven't been doing so good lately."

Charlee knew to tread lightly. "We all make mistakes, Sammy. Have you made some?"

"I was only trying to help!" The words burst out of Sammy, and then he hurried back toward the trailer. "Bye, Charlee," he called over his shoulder.

The door slammed shut. Charlee looked at Hunter, who had both eyebrows raised, and they walked back to his truck in silence.

Once they were back on the road, Charlee said, "He's worried about something but can't put it into words."

"Or he knows exactly what's wrong, and he's afraid to put it into words."

"Could be either one." She sighed. "So how do we find this Tool Man? Come back tonight?" Charlee asked.

"That's what I'm thinking." Hunter listened to several voicemails, then punched an address into the GPS. "First, we need to talk to Sally and Nora." He glanced at her. "You going to be okay with that?"

Charlee would rather have dental surgery than have to deal with more of Sally Jennings's accusations, but she nodded grimly. What choice did she have? She was all in now. She couldn't stop any more than Hunter could. They had to figure out who wanted Tommy Jennings dead. Because maybe that would make all the rest of the puzzle pieces line up to show them who the killer was.

Just as she braced herself to deal with Sally, her cell phone rang. The number was local, but she didn't recognize it. "Hello?"

"Where are you, Charlee?" Travis demanded. "I told you I have a test today, and I need a really good grade on it. You're going to make me late."

"How did you get this number, Travis?"

"From your dad. He's still at the hospital. Oh, but good news, he said your mom is starting to wake up. So, when are you getting here?"

Hunter must have heard the conversation, for he swung the truck in a sharp U-turn that had Charlee clutching the door handle.

"I'm on my way. I'll be there in..." She glanced at Hunter.

"Twenty minutes," he supplied.

"Twenty minutes," she repeated. "Sorry about that, Travis. I totally forgot." She hung up and dialed her father. "Hey, Dad. I hear Mom is waking up."

"She is, and her smile is as beautiful as ever. A little lopsided, but gorgeous."

Charlee felt her throat close at his obvious love for her mother and ability to rejoice in the smallest of victories. *Thank you, Jesus*. "I'm so glad to hear that."

"Are you at the Outpost? Travis called me in a panic. Something about a test today. I gave him your number."

"He called me. Thanks, Dad. He says he'd told me about taking a trip out for him today, but I don't remember." Which really bugged her. Had he told her?

"Easy enough to do with all that's been happening." He paused. "With his crush on you, I just realized I probably shouldn't have given him your number."

"It's okay. You just take care of Mom."

"I'll tell him he's never to use that number again. I'm sorry."

"Stop apologizing. Give Mom a kiss for me. I have to go. I love you."

Charlee hung up and let the relief slide through her. Her breath eased out, and she felt the muscles in her neck and shoulders slowly relax as she leaned back in the seat.

"That's good news, *cher*. Your mama is tough, just like her daughter." He grinned. "Now if we can keep Travis from phone stalking you, you'll be all set."

Charlee laughed. "There's always a fly in the ointment, isn't there? I may have to change my number." She looked over at him, her smile coming all the way from her heart.

Hunter reached over and gave her hand a quick squeeze.

The familiar tension crept in as they approached the Outpost. Charlee hated that Hunter was right. The place she'd loved most in the world now filled her with dread. She squared her shoulders. She'd take that kayak tour this afternoon, just like any other. She could do this.

Pete's official SUV sat in the parking lot, and she hurried inside, heart pounding. "What's wrong?"

In uniform, Pete lounged behind the desk, booted feet propped up, reading the paper. He sat up when she rushed in. "'Bout time you got here."

Charlee looked from him to Hunter, who had come in behind her. "What are you doing here? You should be home resting."

He made a calm-down motion with his hands, which always raised her hackles. "Easy there, squirt. I'm on light duty. I stopped in to see you and found Travis pacing like a caged tiger, worried about some test. He said you were on your way, so I told him I'd man the store until you got here."

"Glad to see you up and around, Pete," Hunter said. "I need to talk to Sally and Nora Jennings." He looked over at Charlee. "You good here for a while?"

Charlee made sure her body language conveyed none of the dread she felt. If either of these macho men knew she was the least bit hesitant, there was no telling what idiotic scheme they'd hatch. "Of course. This is my job. Go talk to Sally and Nora. Tell them..." She stopped, shook her head. "Never mind. They don't want to hear from me."

But after Hunter walked out the door, she hurried after him. She caught him just as he climbed into his truck. "Will you ask Nora about what happened that day? About the bruises around her neck?"

"What are you thinking?" He kept his eyes steady on hers, and she hoped he meant what he'd said about her investigative skills.

She took a deep breath. "I'm not sure. As I said, when I found Nora last year, she had a limb over her neck, just like Tommy. She had bruises around her neck, like Brittany. But she survived." She paused. "Tommy didn't have any bruises."

"You mentioned the bruises before, but there is nothing in the file."

"I told the investigator. Rick told me I was looking for evidence that wasn't there."

At the mention of Rick's name, Hunter's jaw hardened. "What did Nora say happened?"

"She's always said she doesn't remember."

"You don't believe her."

"I don't know. The bruises didn't seem like they could have been made by the branch." Charlee looked at him, waited for him to brush it off, or worse, to laugh at her, as Rick had done.

He nodded slowly. "Between the bruises on Brittany's neck and the similarity of Tommy's death and Nora's near death… I'll ask Nora about it."

Before she could process her relief that he'd taken her seriously, Hunter yanked her into his arms and gave her a mind-numbing kiss that seared her all the way to her toes. He set her back and said, "I love the way you think, *cher*."

Then he climbed into his truck, rolled down the window, and said, "Look for all the things you love about the river today," and drove away.

His words—and that kiss—echoed in her mind as she tidied the front counter and checked their reservations for the day. Pete sat back in the chair and picked up the paper. "Don't you have a job to do? Bad guys to catch?"

He set the paper down and folded his arms across his chest. "What's going on with you, Charlee?"

She focused on straightening the postcard rack. "What are you talking about?"

"I'm talking about you. Look, I get that what happened last year shook you up, but you've always loved this place, loved the water. Out of all four of us, the Outpost was your favorite. That's why Dad wants you to have it. We're all okay with that. But now…" His voice drifted off, and he sent her a worried frown. "You're not the same."

"Knowing someone died on your watch will do that to you. I figure you should understand that."

"It wasn't your fault, Charlee."

She fisted her hands on her hips, feeling like she might explode with frustration. "I wish people would stop saying that! Maybe it wasn't technically my 'fault,' since I didn't cause the storm, but it was absolutely my responsibility. I was the guide. My group. So yes, it's on me."

"Dad said he's tried to get you to sign papers turning the place over to you, and you keep putting him off."

"I've been a little busy here lately, in case you forgot. And besides, how is any of this your business?"

He looked as though she'd slapped him. "Because it's family business. Dad said you've been squirrelly for a while now. Not just lately. Why are you stalling?"

"I'm not stalling," she shot back. Which wasn't entirely true. But she didn't plan to discuss it with Pete. They called him Bulldog for a reason.

He moved closer, trying to back her into a corner to get her to talk, a trick he'd been using since childhood. She put her palm out and shoved him back. "Quit. You know better than to push this way."

He backed up, sighed. "Sorry. Habit. Talk to me. Why won't you sign the papers?"

"Because I'm not sure I want the place." The words burst out and surprised them both. But now that they'd been said, Charlee felt an unexpected sense of relief.

"Oh no. A deal's a deal, Charlee, and Tanners don't welch on deals."

Since he'd put her guilt into words, she had no snappy comeback.

"You have to cut them free of this place, Charlee. You know they want to take their trailer and go exploring. They can't do that until you sign."

"They can't go until Mama is strong enough," she countered.

"And when she is? They still can't leave until you've taken over."

"Then they should sell the place!"

He drew back, genuinely shocked. "Sell it? They don't want to sell it. They want it to stay in the family."

"Then you run it." Charlee crossed her arms and pierced him with a look.

"But I don't want it. Besides, I have a job." He blew out a breath, visibly calmed himself. "What's really going on here, squirt?"

What the heck. She gave him the truth, straight up, no chaser. "I hate being on the water, Pete. I dread every single trip. I don't want to be here anymore."

His eyes widened as understanding dawned. Just as he opened his mouth to respond, the radio on his shoulder crackled to life. He answered, then headed for the door. "I have to go." He stopped, turned back, then pulled her into a bone-crushing hug. "I'm sorry for riding you so hard. We'll figure this out. Don't worry." He kissed her cheek and disappeared.

Charlee sank down in the seat he'd vacated and tried to calm her racing heart.

She almost had things under control when she heard cars pulling into the parking lot. Her kayak tour had arrived.

She put on her game face and was smiling when the two families walked through the door. "Hi. Welcome to Tanner's Outpost."

Chapter 23

ONCE HE GOT ON THE ROAD, HUNTER CHECKED THE CAD system to see who was on patrol near the Outpost, then called FWC Officer Wagner. "Hey, Greg, I know it's your day off, but I could use your help." Greg was a recent transfer from another FWC region, so Charlee hadn't met him yet.

"What do you need, Lieutenant? I'll see what I can do."

Hunter outlined his plan, gratified by Greg's quick agreement. "Thanks, Wag. I appreciate it. Keep me posted, would you?"

"Sure thing, Lieutenant."

Hunter disconnected, relieved. At least he had one of his bases covered.

He spent the rest of the drive to Lake City thinking about what Charlee had said. After he talked to Sally and Nora, he'd go through the reports from last year one more time. He made a mental note to call the investigator on the case, too.

He pulled into Sally Jennings's driveway and saw two compact cars. The little blue one closest to the house was registered to Sally, so he figured the other was Nora's.

The small ranch house had a tidy yard and a bright-red front door. Nora Jennings opened the door a crack when he knocked, tearstained cheeks barely visible.

Hunter held up his badge. "Ma'am, I'm Lieutenant Boudreau with Fish and Wildlife. Is Mrs. Jennings here? I need to ask her a few questions."

The door flew open, and Sally Jennings stood in the doorway, hands on hips, eyes blazing. While her daughter's face was ravaged by grief, Sally's showed only fury. She looked past Hunter as though she was looking for something. Or someone. Then she stabbed a finger in Hunter's direction. "This is all Charlee Tanner's fault. She let my boy die out there, all alone, and now she let Tommy die, too."

Hunter kept his face bland. "Mrs. Jennings, may I come in?"

Sally stormed back into the house. "Fine. Whatever. You'll do what you want anyway."

Hunter walked in and followed her into the living room. Sally flopped down in an armchair, glaring, while Nora sagged onto the striped sofa and wiped the tears from her face.

"Mrs. Jennings." Then he turned to the young woman. "Nora, right? I'm so very sorry for your loss," Hunter began.

"Spare me the crap, Lieutenant," Sally spat. "Just get on with it."

"I'm trying to get a timeline of events. When was the last time either of you spoke with Tommy?"

At his question, Sally's fury deflated, and she sank into the chair, as though her anger had been the only thing supporting her. "He called me on the anniversary, drunk and sloppy, rambling about how it was all his fault."

Hunter looked up from his smartphone, where he'd been taking notes. "Did he say why he thought that?"

Sally glared at him like he was an idiot. "Our son died on that trip. Of course it was his fault."

"What time was this?"

"The first time was about eight in the morning, just as I was leaving for work."

"Where do you work?"

"For Doctor Cohen, a podiatrist. And before you ask, yes, I was there all day."

When Hunter merely sent her a questioning look, she snorted. "That is what this is about, right? To find out if I somehow caused my drunken ex-husband to off himself?"

"Mom!" Nora protested. She huddled on the couch, knees pulled up to her chest, tears streaming down her cheeks faster than she could wipe them away.

"Sorry, darling. But your father was weak." She paused, looked at Hunter. "He couldn't handle JJ's death."

"You said he called more than once. How many times did he call you that day?"

"Once more. About eight that night. Wanted me to come over."

"And did you?"

"No." She shook her head, and Hunter got a glimpse of the grief she tried to hide. She leaned forward, hands clasped in her lap, voice quiet. "He'd want to talk it all over again, every detail, and I just…couldn't."

"I understand. Did he sound like he'd been drinking then, too?"

"Yes. And to be honest, by then, I'd had a couple glasses of wine, too. It's not easy, the remembering."

"No, I can't imagine it is. Was that the last time you spoke with him?"

"Yes. I wanted to call him back, but I just couldn't bring myself to do it. Now I wish I had. Maybe then he wouldn't have...killed himself."

Hunter kept his voice bland. "Mrs. Jennings, did the deputy tell you that?"

"What? No. He said they found him facedown in the creek behind his little shack."

"While that's true, we don't think it was suicide." He paused, then added, "We believe he was murdered."

Hunter watched identical expressions of horror appear on Sally and Nora's faces.

"Oh, Daddy," Nora cried and buried her face in her knees, rocking back and forth.

Sally gripped the arms of the chair, knuckles white. "Murdered? By whom?" she demanded.

"We don't know yet. That's why we're asking questions, trying to get a sense of Tommy's movements the last couple of days." Hunter turned to Nora. "When did you last see or speak to your father?"

"Monday. On the anniversary." She glanced at her mother. "I, ah, skipped school, and Dad called my cell phone. He wanted to come get me, but he'd been drinking, and I didn't think he should drive."

"What time was that?" Hunter asked.

"About ten, I guess. I'm not really sure."

Sally walked over to the couch and sat down beside her daughter. She tried to pull Nora into her arms, but Nora scooted out of reach. "Leave me alone. You hated Dad."

Sally sighed. "Oh, honey. I didn't hate him. I hated what the alcohol made him."

"Nora, did you talk with him after that day? See him at all?"

"No. I didn't know what to say. And he kept wanting to talk about the day JJ… He wanted to go over and over every detail, and it just hurt too much. So I didn't answer when he called."

"He called several times?"

"Yeah, like three times a day."

"Why would someone murder Tommy?" Sally asked again.

"That's what we're trying to figure out. Did he have any enemies? Anyone at work he had a problem with?"

"They loved him at the shop. He could fix anything. Kept all the machines going."

"Did he ever miss work because of the drinking?"

"Yeah, some, especially lately, but the owner is a guy we've known forever. I know he cut Tommy some slack." Sally shook her head. "I can't believe he drowned. Just like his mother."

Hunter sat up straighter. "His mother drowned?"

"Back when he was little. Drowned in the bathtub."

Nora's shoulders shook with her sobs. Sally again tried to offer comfort, but Nora shrugged off her mother's touch.

"Nora, I need to ask about last year for a minute."

The teen looked up in surprise, wiped her eyes.

"After the storm started, what happened? What do you remember?"

Sally stiffened. "I don't see what this has to do with—"

Hunter held up a hand. Nora took a deep breath and said, "I don't remember much. The wind started howling, and it was raining so hard, I couldn't see the end of my kayak. I thought I felt something hit me in the shoulder, and I lost my balance and fell out of the kayak. Next thing

I knew, I was on shore, and Charlee was doing CPR. And JJ was…gone."

"You had bruises on your neck?"

Nora's hand went to her throat. "Yes. It hurt to talk for a few days. Charlee said there was a branch over me when she found me."

"Do you remember anything else, any detail?"

Nora's tears started again as she shook her head. After a moment, Sally jumped to her feet, marched over to the front door, and held it open. "It's time for you to leave, Lieutenant." Her chin came up, hands clutched the door. "Maybe you'd better check Charlee Tanner's whereabouts at the time of Tommy's murder. She already killed my son."

Hunter studied her face. "Why would you think Charlee killed either of them?" he asked.

She stiffened, as though she couldn't believe what he'd just asked. "When Charlee realized how bad the weather was getting, she should have gotten everyone to safety. Immediately. That was her job, for crying out loud. To keep everyone safe. Not to let them die." She swallowed hard, then added, "JJ's death destroyed Tommy. His drinking got out of control, and his whole personality changed. I lost them both. I'd always hoped Tommy would be able to get it together, but now…" She speared him with a look. "Tommy started talking about getting a lawyer, reopening the case. Maybe Charlee was afraid of going to jail for what she did."

Hunter thanked her and climbed into his truck, sorting and shifting the puzzle pieces around in his mind, frustration building. He still couldn't see the whole picture.

Charlee kept her focus solely on the task at hand. She made sure her guests filled out all the right forms, then let them shop while she gave the equipment a thorough once-over. She checked the first aid kit, then added a few more bandages, just in case.

Just as she started handing out the life jackets, a young couple pulled up in a Jeep, both athletic looking and fit, about midtwenties. They came bounding into the office.

The man's hair was cut military short, his demeanor casual, friendly. He propped his sunglasses up on his head and smiled. "Looks like you're getting ready to take a group out." He pointed to the loaded kayak rack. "Do you have room for two more?"

Charlee kept her professional smile in place. "Of course. Have you kayaked before?"

"We go all the time," the woman added, smiling at the man beside her.

At least they weren't unruly, inexperienced teenagers like the other day. *Focus, girl.* "Great. Let me get everyone a life jacket, then we'll get your paperwork done so we can go."

"We appreciate it, thanks." The woman smiled brightly behind her dark sunglasses, and Charlee got the feeling she was trying to tell her something, but she didn't know what.

She handed a boy of about ten a life jacket, which he immediately tossed on the ground. "I know how to swim. I'm not wearing that stupid thing."

His mother scolded him, but Charlee simply scooped

up the jacket and held it out to him. "I'm very glad to hear that you can swim. But on the river, the current can pull you along, or you could get knocked on the head if you fall out of the kayak. Either you agree to wear it—the whole time—or you can't come with us. Your choice."

The boy's mutinous expression was no match for Charlee's determination. He reached out for the life jacket, but she moved it just out of reach. "Do we have a deal? You'll wear it the whole time?"

He nodded. She waited. "Yes, I'll wear it. Geez, you're like my mother."

Charlee exchanged a glance with said mother, who smiled widely. "And no whining about it, either," Charlee added.

"Fine," he grumbled, then snatched it out of her hand. This time, she let him.

He immediately found the whistle strapped to the jacket and blew into it. Charlee yanked it out of his mouth so quick, it made him yelp. "Hey! What are you doing?"

She ignored him and said, "Gather round, everyone." She held up the whistle. "This is an emergency whistle. Which, as the name implies, is to be used in an emergency. Not any other time, ever." She eyed the boy and the other three youngsters, who were all of similar age. "Are we clear? If you're in trouble, blow the whistle. If you blow it and you're not, then you'll really be in trouble. With me."

Everyone laughed, and Charlee made sure she met the boy's eyes. "What was your name?"

"Brandon."

"Okay, Brandon, are you ready?"

He nodded, and Charlee finished the paperwork and got everyone loaded into the van, double-checking the straps on the kayak trailer as she went by.

Once they were out on the Ocklawaha River, the memories tried to force their way in, but she fought them back, tried to focus on the surroundings. She'd always loved it out here, she reminded herself. Loved the way the sunlight hit the water, the way birds watched them from shore. Still, she sat, poised to fight, eyes darting from one child to the next, like an anxious mama wood duck with newly hatched chicks. She took slow, deliberate breaths so she wouldn't hyperventilate.

She did another quick check of the group, satisfied they were all fine for now. Thankfully, both sets of parents were pretty vigilant, making sure the kids didn't do anything stupid.

Charlee looked up into the trees, then scanned the riverbank, trying, as Hunter had suggested, to find the joy she used to experience when she came out here. She missed that feeling more than she'd realized. This had always been where she'd felt most centered, most herself. Out here in her kayak, absorbing the feel of the swamp around her, listening to the birds, the wind rustling through the trees filled her with peace.

Right now, all she felt was stress.

And like she was being watched.

She turned, spun her kayak in a circle, trying to pinpoint who was watching her, grateful she'd packed her gun. She locked eyes with the young woman, who smiled. Charlee smiled back.

Then she locked eyes with the man beside her. He smiled, too, then looked around. Confident that no one was watching, he eased up the hem of his shirt and showed her his badge. Charlee couldn't tell what brand of cop he was from here, but she'd bet money Hunter had arranged this. Or maybe Pete. She nodded slightly and kept paddling.

At least now she didn't have to worry quite so much about something going wrong.

She just had to battle the ghosts of things that had already gone desperately wrong.

He lowered his binoculars and smiled. Sending an undercover cop on a kayak trip? What a lovely surprise. That meant they were worried about him, about what he would do next. As well they should. They were worried about Charlee, too. How sweet. That only made his anticipation more delicious. He cocked his head, thinking. He wondered which one had set this up? The arrogant cop who thought Charlee belonged to him? Or one of her overprotective brothers? He shrugged and kept paddling, careful to stay just out of her line of sight. It didn't really matter. In the end, he'd get Charlee right where he wanted her. They had a scene to act out, a grand finale, where he would triumph once and for all.

He could hardly wait.

He wondered where Boudreau had gone. What was so important he'd risk leaving her alone and vulnerable out here on the water? Probably a visit to that slut Sally and her mean, nasty daughter, Nora.

It should have been Nora that day. She should have died. Not JJ. Nora, who picked on her brother all the time, nagging, sniping, calling him names and making him shrink from her harsh words. Oh yes. It should have been Nora.

The good news was, it still would be. Nora and Charlee. Plus one more mean-spirited woman that this world would be better off without.

Someone had to protect boys like JJ. He'd decided a long time ago it would be him. He would save them. It was his calling and his gift.

The guilty had to pay.

He turned his kayak around and paddled back the way he'd come. *Enjoy your day, Charlee.*

It'll soon be your last.

Hunter drove back toward Ocala, determined to be at the Outpost when Charlee got back. He felt better knowing Greg and his wife were with her, but he wouldn't rest easy until he knew for sure she was fine.

He grabbed his cell phone. "Hey, Byte, it's Boudreau. Anything more on James Jennings? Okay, keep digging, would you? But I also need you to dig up whatever info you can on Tommy Jennings. Background, family, friends, any arrests, anything. Also, see what you can find out about his mother's drowning when he was a kid. See if she died in the bathtub."

"You think that's connected to what's happening now?"

"I'm not sure yet, but let's find out."

"Sure thing. I'll email you whatever I find."

"Perfect, thanks, Byte."

Hunter pulled into the Outpost and let out a relieved

breath at all the cars in the parking lot. He didn't want Charlee alone, cop or not. Not until they figured this thing out.

Several families were heading to their cars as he approached the office. Officer Wagner and his wife walked out behind them.

They stepped off to the side. "Hi, Lieutenant. This is my wife, Terry. Terry, this is Lieutenant Boudreau."

Hunter shook her hand. "Thanks for helping me out today."

"Sure, no problem."

"Everything was quiet," Greg said. "Charlee acted like she was being watched, pretty nervous, but I didn't spot anyone. Trip went off without a hitch."

Hunter clapped him on the back, then pulled out his wallet, handed him some bills. "Thanks. I owe you one. Take your lovely wife out, on me."

Greg smiled. "I'll do that." He put his hand to his wife's back and guided her toward their Jeep. Terry turned and waved as she climbed in.

"Now you're sending me undercover babysitters?" Charlee asked from behind him.

Hunter turned and saw the smirk on her face, eyebrows raised. "Would it help if I said it was—"

"For my own good?" she finished. "Um, no."

He stepped closer, rubbed his hands over her shoulders. "How about I was worried about you."

She cocked her head, considered. "Better. But still smacks of macho superiority."

"There's a killer on the loose. I'm not taking chances."

She heaved out a breath, all playfulness gone. "Yeah, there is that. Everything went fine." She nodded toward the departing Jeep. "Though I'm sure your colleague already told you that."

"He did."

Hunter's cell phone rang, and Charlee heard his murmured voice as he answered, but her attention was caught by something off in the woods behind the Outpost. From here, it looked too small to be human, but maybe it was an animal she could show the children. The two families from her tour were staying in the cabins tonight. She started in that direction, curious.

She walked into the trees, and sure enough, she found a raccoon digging in the dirt. Which was unusual for this time of day. And so close to the Outpost. When it looked up and spotted her, it took off in the opposite direction. It'd been tugging on something black, half-buried in the sand. Charlee crouched down and grabbed a stick to figure out what it was. She dug around a bit and finally pulled up a black piece of cloth. She shook the branch, leaned closer to get a better look. It took a second to register what she was seeing, and then she gasped. She was holding a crumpled T-shirt.

A shirt covered in dried blood.

"Hunter!"

At Charlee's shout, Hunter spun around. When he saw her in the woods, he muttered, "Gotta go," into his phone and took off running. "What's wrong?" He skidded to a stop and crouched down beside her.

She held a bloody shirt on the end of a branch.

Her hand shook slightly, and her face was pale. "This belongs to Travis."

"You're sure?"

"Absolutely. It's his favorite. I told him he wasn't allowed to wear it two days in a row, at least not without washing it."

"I'll be right back." He hurried over to his truck and grabbed gloves and evidence bags. He took pictures from all angles, bagged the shirt. "Call him and ask him to come back as soon as class is over. Tell him it's important."

She called him, worked to keep her voice casual. "He said he just finished his test and was already on his way back."

"Do you know what time he came to work this morning?"

"No, but I can ask Dad."

"That'd be great. Thanks."

Hunter's mind was busy sorting timelines and possibilities when Travis pulled into the parking lot in his aging little sedan. When he saw them both watching him, his eyes darted nervously from one to the other. "Hey, Charlee. What's up?"

Hunter nodded toward the building. "Let's talk inside." He didn't feel like chasing him if the kid decided to bolt. Hunter followed them in and positioned himself between Travis and the door. At his nod, Charlee reached behind the counter and pulled out the plastic bag they'd stashed there.

"Is that your T-shirt, Travis?" Hunter asked.

The kid paled but folded his arms and copped an attitude. "Maybe. So what?"

"So it's covered in blood. Whose blood is it, Travis? Tommy Jennings's?" He watched the kid's eyes to see if he'd keep trying to bluff. Since Mr. Tanner had confirmed that Travis had been at the Outpost all morning, he couldn't have killed Jennings. But those gators were another story.

Travis flung his arms wide and started pacing. "Who is Tommy Jennings? Are you crazy? Why would I have some guy's blood on my shirt?" He marched toward Hunter. "I don't even know who that is!"

Hunter merely arched a brow. "If it's not Tommy Jennings's blood, then whose is it?" He stepped closer. "The truth, Travis. Now. Or I bring you in on murder charges." He had no evidence to support it, but he needed to push the kid.

Travis paled, fear in his eyes. His voice was quiet. "I didn't hurt anyone. I swear. I'd never do that." He turned to Charlee, eyes pleading. "Tell him, Charlee. You know me."

Charlee crossed her arms. "I thought I did, but now I don't think I know you at all. Whose blood is it, Travis?"

He paced, and Hunter and Charlee exchanged a glance over his head. *Come on, kid, fess up.*

The silence lengthened, broken only by Travis's rapid breathing. His eyes darted from one to the other. "Okay, fine. It's gator blood. Not human. You happy now?"

"No, not at all. But just so we're clear, are you saying you killed those gators on the Ocklawaha, Travis?"

He stopped pacing and looked from one to the other, swallowed hard. "No. Yes. I-I—" He spun away and paced some more. "I was angry and…everything was out of control…" He grabbed his head, then spun around and jabbed a finger in Hunter's direction. "You should have stayed away from Charlee!"

"Oh, Travis," Charlee said.

Hunter called it in, then explained what would happen to a suddenly subdued Travis, who didn't say another word. Pete arrived several minutes later and arrested him for animal cruelty and drove him away in his cruiser.

Charlee looked utterly exhausted by the time they left. "I can't believe it. Or maybe I can. But either way, I hope he gets the psychological counseling he needs."

He crouched in front of the chair she had sunk into earlier, tucked a strand of hair behind her ear, leaned in, and kissed her forehead. "We'll make sure, okay?" He hated the dark smudges under her eyes that seemed to get darker and deeper by the day. Somehow, he was determined to make her smile. "You ready to head to the carnival?"

Her eyes lit up at the idea, and for a moment, he wished that's what this was. Just a normal day with a guy asking a beautiful woman to a carnival.

The spark faded from her eyes. "Right. Investigation. Question people."

He wanted to see that light in her eyes again. "Yes. But that doesn't mean we can't have a little fun while we're there, does it?"

He watched her settle into negotiation mode. "That depends. Elephant ears?"

"Of course. What's a carnival without eight pounds of grease covered in powdered sugar?"

She laughed then, and his heart felt strangely light as they stopped by her place to change clothes before they headed out to ask more questions.

Before they left Charlee's cottage, Hunter read through the report on JJ's death one more time. He'd tried to call the investigator who'd handled the case last year but found out the man had died in a car accident several months ago.

When Charlee walked into the kitchen wearing a little sundress and sandals, he almost forgot what he'd planned to ask. Almost. He couldn't get distracted. Not now.

"Sally said Tommy's mother drowned in the bathtub when he was a kid. Did you know that?"

Charlee's wide eyes softened. "Oh, those poor boys..." Then she stopped, stared at him. "Water again."

"Too soon to know if it figures into this, but we've got people checking." He nodded and held out his hand. "In the meantime, let's see if we can track down Tommy Jennings's movements at the carnival."

The sense that they were running out of time wouldn't let go, but he didn't say that out loud. He'd learned that you had to keep gathering info, keep following the bread crumbs, until finally, when you least expected it, all the pieces fell into place, and the picture suddenly became clear.

He kept her hand firmly in his, determined to keep her safe until they did.

Chapter 24

DESPITE EVERYTHING GOING ON, CHARLEE GRINNED like a kid when they arrived at the carnival. Maybe it was because she needed a break from the constant tension, but whatever the reason, there was just something about it that made her feel like she was twelve again. She looked up at the huge Ferris wheel rising up in the center, blinked at the flashing lights of the midway. Bells rang and barkers hawked their games while the smell of hot dogs and elephant ears mixed with the scent of animals and too many people. It was heavenly.

Beside her, Hunter kept a hand at the small of her back so they weren't separated in the crush. They wove their way past the merry-go-round, and Charlee couldn't help a longing gaze. She loved the merry-go-round almost as much as the Ferris wheel.

Hunter leaned close. "Later. Let's get the questioning done first."

With him in faded jeans and a crisp polo shirt that hugged his lean chest, it was easy to pretend they were just another couple out on a date. She inhaled the crisp scent of his aftershave and gave in to the urge to run her hand along the shadow of beard stubble covering his hard jaw. The envious glances women aimed her way added to the fantasy.

When he reached over and casually took her hand again, she smiled and decided not to overthink it. Not tonight. They were best friends pretending to be a couple as part of an investigation. She would just enjoy the carnival and the tender way he treated her...and keep her feelings and all thoughts of the future locked firmly away.

She spotted Sammy as soon as they entered the midway. He was tall and speaking loudly to be heard above the noise. When he spotted Charlee, his grin grew wider, and he waved. Then he spotted Hunter, and his smile faded.

"Hey, Sammy," Charlee said. She leaned over the booth to hug him.

He hugged her back, then scowled at Hunter. "What's he doing here?"

Hunter kept his smile casual, friendly. "I have to work, Sammy. You do, too, but it looks like you're having lots more fun than I am."

He frowned. "You don't have your uniform on."

"Not tonight. Have you given away lots of prizes?"

Sammy's smile came back. "One little girl won a bear like that one." He pointed above his head. "It was so big, she couldn't carry it. Her daddy helped her."

"You made her day, Sammy. That's great." Hunter eased closer, out of the path of a group of giggling teenage girls. He pulled up the photos on his phone of Paul and Wyatt Harris, Troy, Luke, Oliver Dunn, and Tommy Jennings. "Sammy, do you know these men? Have you ever seen them before?"

"Are they in trouble?" Sammy looked from Hunter to Charlee and back again.

"We just want to ask them some questions. We thought maybe they'd spent some time here. Maybe you'd seen them."

Sammy carefully studied all the photos before he shook his head. "Nope. I don't remember any of them." He looked at Charlee. "But there are lots and lots of people here. I might not have seen them."

Hunter smiled. "That is definitely possible. We'll just ask around at some of the other booths. We wanted to meet the Tool Man, too. Is he here?"

Sammy immediately became wary. "He keeps all the rides working, so he never stays in one place."

"Is he working tonight?" Hunter asked.

"Things break down all the time. People get really mad if the rides stop. One time, the one with the swings got stuck and kept going round and round, and people were throwing up, and it went all over." He giggled. "It was really funny." Then he sobered. "But people got mad at Tool Man. That wasn't funny." He turned to Charlee with a hopeful expression. "Do you want to play?"

Charlee glanced at Hunter, a question in her eyes. They were on a mission tonight.

He smiled, nodded. "Let's see what you've got, *cher*." He pulled out several bills and handed them to Sammy.

Air rifle in her hands, Charlee sent Hunter a saucy grin, then took aim and hit every single little yellow duck without stopping.

Sammy clapped, and Hunter whistled. "Not bad... for a girl."

"Now there's a challenge if I ever heard one. Your turn, Boudreau."

Hunter took the rifle and hit every duck...except the last one. Chagrined, he set the rifle down while Sammy and Charlee exchanged high fives.

"You beat him, Charlee!" Sammy crowed.

Charlee just raised an eyebrow and smirked.

Hunter looked from one to the other and grinned. "I think I've been set up."

Charlee shrugged, and her grin grew wider as Sammy held up a stuffed elephant and a bear. "Which one do you want, Charlee? Or do you want to play again and try for the big bears?" He pointed overhead.

Charlee reached for the elephant and tucked it under her arm. "I think this is just perfect." She leaned over and kissed Sammy's cheek, making him blush. "Thanks, Sammy."

Hunter stuck out his hand to Sammy. "Thank you. That was fun." Then he led Charlee to the next booth.

Charlee stopped in the middle of the crowd, gaped at him. "Wait. You don't want to play again, try to beat me?"

He shook his head, nudged her to keep moving. "We have more important things to do." He shot her one of those killer grins. "Like ride the Ferris wheel and eat grease. As soon as we finish up here."

Charlee searched his expression. "I don't understand you."

He swiped a finger down her cheek. "Stop confusing me with your brothers. That'll help." Then he kept walking.

It took another hour for them to stop at every booth along the midway and show the pictures, but they got nothing. When they reached the end, they stepped away from the crowds to a relatively quiet corner.

Charlee heaved out a frustrated breath. "That was a total waste of time."

"Not at all. It helps us narrow things down. Either

none of them came here, or they blended in well enough that none of the carneys remember them. Let's cruise by the rides, see if anyone has seen this Tool Man."

They made the rounds, but as before, all they got were blank stares and suspicious looks. Asking about strangers was one thing. Asking about one of their own? Nope. Nobody had anything to say.

"That went pretty much how I expected it to," Hunter said. "Let's go get you some—" He stopped, looked beyond the fence to where the workers' camp was set up. He took her hand. "One more stop."

They hurried along, and Hunter kept her hand clasped in his. When he smiled at her as they walked along, she felt it all the way to her heart and had the craziest urge to pull him close and kiss him, right there in the middle of the midway. To let the world know he was hers. She must have had a goofy look on her face, for he sent her a quizzical look. She shrugged. "I love carnivals. What can I say?" *And I love you, you sexy man.*

She was still trying not to think about all that as they got their hands stamped for reentry and then hiked around to where the campers were. "What are we looking for? We didn't find anything earlier."

Hunter kept walking until he came to an aging blue pickup truck. He glanced around, then pulled out his phone and took several pictures, including the license plate. Then he crouched down and took a picture of the tire treads and another of the imprint they'd left in the dirt.

"Hey, what are you doing?"

Charlee looked up to see a short, wiry man wearing

a big Stetson bearing down on them. He had a cigar clamped between his teeth, and the scent of alcohol reached them several paces before he did.

"Lieutenant Boudreau, FWC. Is this your truck?" Hunter asked. He stood in typical cop pose as he displayed his badge, looking very official.

"Yeah. So?"

"Were you driving it along SR-40 last Monday, late morning?"

He spat near Hunter's feet. "Maybe. Coulda been." He seemed to consider. "Nah, I think I was here Monday. But it coulda been anybody." He shrugged. "I leave the keys in it, so anyone who needs it takes it. The only rule is that you bring it back with the same amount of gas as when you borrowed it."

Hunter pulled out his notebook. "What did you say your name was?"

The man crossed his arms. "I didn't."

Hunter merely raised a brow and waited, pen poised.

Finally, the man huffed out a breath. "Frank Graham. They call me Shorty."

Hunter wrote that down. "And what do you do for the carnival, Mr. Graham?"

"Anything and everything. I'm the carnival boss, make sure things run smoothly while we're here."

Hunter pulled up the photos. "Do you recognize any of these men?"

Shorty scrolled through them and handed the phone back. "Never seen any of them before. But that don't mean a thing with the kinds of crowds we get here, especially on weekends."

"How long are you in town?"

"Two weeks. Every year."

"Do you know where I can find the Tool Man?"

Shorty's eyes narrowed. "He moves around a lot, fixes whatever needs fixing. Why?"

"We know Sammy is staying with him. We just wanted to talk to him."

Shorty hitched a thumb over his shoulder. "Check the rides."

"We will, thanks. Would he drive your truck?"

"Tool Man? Sure. Sammy's not supposed to. He doesn't have a license."

"But has he taken the truck?" Hunter pressed.

Shorty looked away. "I can't say for sure, but I've heard he has, a time or two. I've told him not to. He's a good kid."

Hunter stuck out his hand. "Thanks for your time."

As they walked away, Charlee glanced over her shoulder and saw Shorty whip out his cell phone and make a call.

After they showed their stamped hands at the ticket booth and headed back into the throng, Hunter smiled as he turned to her and asked, "You ready for that grease now?"

Charlee grinned back and watched as he tucked his earlier seriousness away and prepared to enjoy himself for a little while. He seemed lighter, even though the cop was still there, just below the surface, ever watchful. She knew that part never really turned off. Even though she'd resigned, it hadn't fully left her, either. It was simply part of who they were.

He pointed to a food vendor. "Hot dogs first, or straight to elephant ears? Or maybe you want to go all out and get deep-fried Oreos, or deep-fried butter?"

Charlee shook her head. "Eww. Why would I want to eat fried butter? Let's go with dogs and then the good stuff."

They got in line. "Mustard or ketchup on the dog?" Hunter asked. "But think carefully, because if you say ketchup, we can't be friends anymore."

Charlee laughed. "Deal with it, Boudreau. I put both on mine."

They managed to secure one corner of a picnic table. Hunter kept his back to the tent, eyes casually scanning the crowd as he ate. Unlike Rick, who would ignore her completely, Charlee didn't mind Hunter's vigilance. She bit into her dog with gusto and let out a little moan as the flavors exploded on her tongue.

He reached over suddenly and swiped at the side of her mouth. She leaned back, and one side of his mouth crooked up as he slowly licked his finger. "Had a blob of ketchup there."

Hunter's eyes blazed green fire as he glanced down at her lips, then back up. The smoldering look in his eyes sent electricity sizzling between them, and Charlee felt the hairs on her arms stand on end.

"I may have to rethink my stance on ketchup," he drawled. He took her chin and slowly ran his thumb over her bottom lip, eyes never leaving hers. He pulled his hand back and slowly licked his thumb, eyes hot on hers. "You taste good, *cher*."

Charlee felt his words all the way to her core, where a warmth spread out through every nerve ending. Two could play this game. She crooked her finger and leaned closer, then closer still. His eyes flashed fire as he did the same. Closer, closer. Charlee's heart rate sped up, and she was desperate to feel her lips against his.

A child's sudden cry made them both turn in that direction and broke the spell. The mother calmed the child, and everything settled back to normal.

Except none of it was normal. There was a killer on the loose.

And Charlee knew she'd lost her heart to the complicated lieutenant, who was completely oblivious to her feelings.

Hunter had to keep reminding himself that this wasn't a date, and Charlee wasn't his. He was on duty, for crying out loud. He couldn't flirt with Charlee or hold her hand except as part of their cover, or lean over the table and kiss those luscious lips as he'd almost done a few minutes ago. He shoved a hand through his hair. He had to get his head back in the game and fast.

"Let's ride the Ferris wheel," he growled, leading her in that direction.

Her quick, anticipatory smile vanished at his tone, and he felt like a jerk.

"Do you not like heights?" she asked.

"Heights are fine. We should be able to get a good look at the whole place from up there."

Charlee nodded. "Right. Got it." It was as though she was having as much trouble as he was keeping her mind on this mission.

They busied themselves watching the crowd as they

waited. When it was finally their turn, Charlee slid to the outside, but he stepped around her and sat so she was on the inside. "Just in case."

A grim understanding dawned. "You think someone might shoot at us up here?"

The attendant slammed the bar over their laps, and seconds later, the wheel started moving, sending their car up, up, up.

Hunter reached over and gave her shoulder a reassuring pat. "We should be fine. Enjoy the view."

Charlee hunched lower in the seat. "That was easier before you reminded me we're sitting ducks up here."

They inched their way higher and higher, the car swinging to a stop every time the attendants unloaded another car below them. Hunter scanned the crowds milling around, looking for anyone who was paying too much attention to them. This wheel wasn't as high as some, so he could still make out faces pretty well. Children pointed and laughed, older couples smiled fondly.

He skipped over those, focusing instead on the loners, the odd single man, anyone lurking near dark corners. He didn't see anyone who looked out of place, but he knew they were being watched.

Beside him, Charlee shivered. "Are you cold, *cher*?" He moved closer, put his arm around her shoulders.

"I think someone is watching us, but I can't figure out who."

He leaned closer. "I can't spot them either."

They stopped again, and Charlee looked around, annoyed. "This is not how I like to do the Ferris wheel. Takes all the fun out of it."

"I know. I'm sorry. We'll have to come back after all

this is over." The sudden notion that he wanted to come back, as a real date next time so he could kiss her all he wanted and proclaim to the whole world that she was his, shocked him to his core. This was Charlee. They were friends. Okay, more than friends, way more. But when had he started thinking of them as a couple?

Before he could say another stupid thing, the wheel started moving again. Something bounced off Charlee's arm, and she yelped in surprise, rubbing her arm. He tried to grab the projectile, but it slid out of the bottom of the car.

Another *thwack* and something hit his arm. On instinct, Hunter grabbed it and ended up staring at a bean bag. With a note tied to it.

Leave Charlee alone.

Oh, no. This was not how this was going to go. That stupid cop just didn't get that Charlee was off-limits. Yet that didn't seem to keep him from making eyes at her, putting his hands all over her.

No. He would pay for that. Charlee was his. They had a date with destiny.

He slipped farther into the shadows. If Boudreau wanted to be with her, then fine. He would be. He could die with her.

But first, Charlee would watch the others die.

And then the fish cop would watch her die.

Perfect.

It was time.

Chapter 25

Charlee clutched the safety bar as the car headed back down. Someone had thrown bean bags at them? Between the conflicting signals Hunter kept sending and whoever was bombarding them with freaking bean bags, her emotions were all over the map, and she hated it. Suddenly, that hot dog didn't feel so good in her stomach.

After they got off the Ferris wheel, Hunter called in what had happened and snagged a paper bag from a food vendor. He tucked the bean bag inside as evidence, and then they walked up and down the carnival grounds several more times. Charlee still felt they were being watched, but she doubted they'd find any more clues. From the look on Hunter's face, she figured he thought the same.

They stopped by to talk with Sammy, but a young teenager said Sammy was on break. He didn't know when he'd be back.

"Let's call it a night," he finally said, and Charlee breathed a sigh of relief. At least in the darkened truck, she wouldn't feel like she had a target painted on her back.

As Hunter wove through the grassy parking area toward the exit, Charlee glanced out the window and hissed out a breath. "I can't believe he's still following me," she muttered.

Hunter's gaze was sharp. "Who's following you?"

Charlee hitched a thumb over her shoulder. "I think I just saw Rick's blue pickup, not far from where we parked."

Hunter slowed, studied the truck in the rearview mirror, then did a U-turn. He pulled into an empty spot beside it, grabbed his cell phone. He slid out of the truck and took pictures of the tire treads, then climbed back in again, all without saying a word.

"You think Rick shot Brittany and me?"

"I could see him grazing you to play the hero later, but he didn't show up on scene afterward to do that. And I can't see him shooting Brittany."

She glanced at him as they drove away, sorted through what he'd said, and had to agree. Rick would have had no reason that she could see to shoot Brittany. "But bean bags? Seriously? That doesn't make sense at all."

"I don't think it's the same person. My money's on Rick or Sammy for tonight's warning."

Charlee chewed the inside of her cheek. "Rick, maybe, even though it's totally creepy, but Sammy?" Charlee asked. "Why would he do that?"

"He sees me as a threat to his crush on you. Makes sense."

Understanding dawned. "That's why you didn't search all that hard for whoever threw the bean bags. You think it was Sammy."

Hunter shrugged. "He doesn't need any trouble in his life."

Charlee cocked her head, frustrated that she couldn't see his eyes. "You feel for him."

"I guess I do."

Once back at the cottage, Charlee went into her room to get ready for bed, but the quiet of the cottage only magnified the volume of her fear and frustration. She paced her bedroom, but her frantic thoughts chased each other like hamsters on a wheel, every turn increasing her worry until her heart hammered in her chest and she was breathing like she'd run a marathon. Finally, she marched to the kitchen, too agitated to be quiet. She poured a glass of milk and had a cupcake halfway to her mouth when Hunter stepped up behind her. She jumped in surprise as he wrapped his arms around her waist and pulled her back against his bare chest, rested his chin on her head. "We're going to get whoever is behind this, *cher*."

Charlee nodded and let herself sink back into his embrace, as she slowed her breathing and rubbed the ache where her heart pounded. She was so tired. So worried. What if she couldn't find this nut job before he hurt someone else in her family? She couldn't let them down. She had to stop this cowardly piece of trash. Visions of her mother under the water and both brothers in the water flashed like strobe lights. She squeezed her eyes shut.

Her head snapped up. "I need to call Natalie."

When she would have leaped into action, Hunter tightened his hold, rubbed a hand over her arms. "It's 1:30 in the morning, *cher*."

Charlee pushed at his arms, and he instantly let go. "She might be up studying. Or partying. But either way, she'll get my text. Or she'll see it as soon as she wakes up." Charlee grabbed her phone, texted: Check in as soon as you get this. Need to know you're ok.

She gripped her hair and started pacing. "We have to figure this out. I'm afraid she'll be next."

Hunter caught her on her next pass, ran a hand down her arm. "We have someone watching her, remember?"

Charlee stopped, turned to him, eyes bright with panic. "What if it's not enough? What if he gets to her? She's not as strong as Pete or Josh. She won't—"

Hunter cupped her cheeks in his hands and silenced her with a kiss. He couldn't bear to hear the terror in her voice. He'd never seen her this way. She exuded calm in crisis situations, had been incredible every second of this whole ordeal, even after this SOB had gone after her mother. But it was thinking about Natalie in danger that pushed Charlee over the edge.

He pulled back from her lips, stroked her cheeks with his thumbs as she blinked up at him in surprise. "We'll find him, *cher*. I promise."

Her eyes flashed, and she spun out of his reach and kept pacing. "Don't you dare say something so idiotic to me, Lieutenant. You know damn good and well you can't promise me that. You can't promise anyone that. This piece of garbage has already proven he's unstoppable. He's—"

"Human," Hunter interrupted. "And he'll make a mistake. And when he does, we'll get him."

She planted her hands on her hips, chest heaving as she vibrated with fury. "How many more empty platitudes are you going to throw at me?"

He wondered if she had any idea how magnificent she looked with sparks fairly shooting from her skin. "No platitudes, *cher*. Ever. You know me better than that."

"Do I? No. I know nothing. Nothing. You keep yourself apart, hiding behind that stony mask so nobody ever knows what you're thinking or feeling."

His eyebrows climbed to his hairline. Where had *that* come from? "What are you talking about, *cher*?"

She mumbled under her breath as she spun away from him. Then she turned back, poked him in the chest, hard. "That attitude. Right there. Always calm and controlled, the man in charge." She narrowed her gaze. "Reasonable. Untouchable."

Her words jabbed at his defenses, stirred his own anger. When she tried to sidestep him again, he'd had enough. "I'll show you untouchable," he muttered. He yanked her against his chest, enjoying her little squeak of surprise. Before she could throw any more verbal missiles his way, he buried his hands in her hair and poured every ounce of his frustration with this strong, stubborn, infuriating, amazing woman into the kiss. He didn't know any other way to make her understand, especially since he didn't understand it himself.

She gasped and opened her mouth under the onslaught of his tongue. He fisted his hands in her hair and let out a little sigh of relief as her arms came up around his neck and she plastered herself against him. He hummed, low in his throat, as she moved in further, all her curves finally, finally right where he wanted them. She fit so perfectly.

His heart hammered against hers as he plundered her mouth, desperate suddenly to get closer and closer still. To touch her. Show her everything she meant to him.

Charlee gave as good as she got, and her hands slid up under his shirt, gripping his back. He spun them around and backed her up against the wall. He loved the way she felt pressed along his length, and he ran his hands up under her shirt, caressing her soft skin. He trailed kisses along the sleek column of her throat, inhaling the sweet scent of vanilla on her skin as she held him tight, as desperate as he was to get closer still.

"You feel so good, *cher*," he muttered, sliding his hands up her rib cage, caressing the underside of her breasts.

Her hands were everywhere, and they made him shiver. Soft and callused, they were part of the contradiction of Charlee. His hands stroked and caressed, propelled by the growing need to feel skin on skin. Charlee took his hand and somehow, after several more mind-numbing kisses, he found himself under those flowered sheets with her, both desperate to shed the layers that kept them apart. She looked up, and their eyes met, held, hers so dark and wide, he could drown in them. But beyond her obvious need, her eyes shredded him with a loneliness that mirrored his own. In that moment, he wanted nothing more than to take it away, forever.

When she sighed as he lowered himself over her and stretched out to his full length, all the jagged edges of his heart seemed to come back together. He kissed her mouth slowly this time, savoring the feel of her soft, soft skin against his.

He trailed more kisses over her face while he stroked her arms, then down her legs, ignoring the buzz in his head.

The sound came again, and Charlee froze. "Natalie."

He blinked, trying to get his bearings as she shoved against his chest. "I have to get the phone. It's Natalie."

She scrambled out from under him and ran to the kitchen. He raced after her, careening off the doorjamb and biting back a curse.

He blinked against the light and shook his head to clear it.

Charlee stabbed at her phone. "Come on. Come on."

The buzzing came again.

She looked up, frantic. "Not mine."

Phone. Right. He grabbed his off the counter, barked, "Boudreau."

There was nobody there. He pulled the phone away and realized it wasn't a call, but an incoming email and a text. He sagged against the counter and read both.

"Who is it?" she demanded. "What's wrong?"

The last of his brain fog cleared as the panic returned to her face.

"Byte. Frank, the carnival boss, has quite the rap sheet. One definitely worth looking into. He wanted me to know right away."

Charlee slumped against the counter.

"Nothing yet from Natalie?" When she gave a quick negative shake of her head, he held out his hand. "Come to bed, *cher*. We both need some sleep or we won't be worth spit."

Something in his heart loosened when she didn't hesitate, just put her hand in his and walked with him. He'd meant to simply hold her, but when she turned in his arms and slowly ran her hands over his face, then cupped his cheeks and kissed him, slow and deep, Hunter was lost.

"We'll figure it out," she murmured, and he felt the words like an electric shock. Shouldn't he have said those words to her? In the middle of her fears for her family, she'd reached out to comfort him, and it brought him to his knees. He tried and failed to find the right words. Finally, he simply pulled her close and stroked her soft skin as the remaining barriers between them slid to the floor, and he did his best to show her what he couldn't say. That she was beautiful and amazing and strong and fierce. That he didn't deserve her.

And that he loved her.

As their heartbeats slowed and Charlee drifted into sleep, the truth hit him, and he swallowed hard. He brushed a kiss over her shoulder and tried to sleep, but on the heels of that knowledge, fear reared its ugly head. She filled every inch of his heart and mind, and that scared him to the marrow of his bones. To keep her safe, he needed all his focus. He couldn't miss the tiniest clue. Because he realized right then that if something happened to Charlee, he didn't think he'd survive. Sappy? Yeah, definitely. But as sleep finally claimed him, he realized it didn't matter. It was the truth.

By the time Charlee stumbled into the kitchen after a quick shower, Hunter had coffee ready and was talking on his cell phone.

"Thanks. I appreciate you getting me whatever you can ASAP."

He poured Charlee a cup and then sipped his own. "Morning, *cher*. Did you get some rest?"

Charlee nodded absently as she studied him, remembering the feel of his arms around her during the night, keeping the nightmares at bay. She hadn't slept that well in a year. A stab of longing hit her at how much she liked waking up to him in her kitchen, his hair still damp from his shower. She walked over to him and pulled him close, desperate to keep reality away for just a little longer. He wrapped his arms around her and gave her a slow kiss that muddled her mind. Reluctantly, she eased away and cleared her throat. "Who was that?"

"I've had Byte run down Tommy Jennings's background."

"Did he find—" Charlee's cell phone rang, and she grabbed it off the charger. "Hey, Dad. How's Mom?"

"About the same. They keep saying she's going to fully wake up anytime, but so far, it hasn't happened." He let out a sigh. "Have you talked to your sister?"

Charlee pulled the phone from her ear and checked, a chill slithering down her spine. No calls or texts from Natalie. "I left her a text during the night to call me and check in, but I haven't heard back yet." She glanced at the clock. "She may have an early class."

"When I spoke to her yesterday, she said she'd be here in a few hours and stay with Mom overnight so I could get some sleep."

Charlee's heart rate speeded up. "She didn't show up?"

"No. That's why I'm calling. I thought she got held up at school, so I stayed here at the hospital. I didn't want to leave your mother alone."

"Of course you didn't. Let me give her a call."

"I've tried several times. She's not answering her cell phone, and I'm getting a bit concerned."

Now the hair on the back of Charlee's neck stood straight up. She tried to keep her voice calm, keep the panic from showing through. “I don’t blame you, Dad. Let me see what I can find out, and I’ll call you back, all right?”

“Sure. Thanks, hon. I just hope she didn’t have car trouble somewhere without cell service.”

Charlee fervently prayed it was as simple as that, but she couldn’t be that naive. “We’ll check it out, Dad. Don’t worry.” She hung up and met Hunter’s concerned expression. “Natalie never showed up at the hospital last night. Dad can’t reach her on her cell, and she never returned my text.” As she talked, Charlee dialed Natalie’s number, listened. “It went straight to voicemail.”

Hunter poured coffee into two travel mugs. “Why don’t you call your brothers while I check with the deputy who’s been watching her. If no one’s heard from her, we’ll have Byte ping the GPS on her phone.”

Her hand shook as she dialed Josh’s cell. “Hey, Sis. You holding up okay? I heard about Jennings. And about somebody throwing bean bags at you last night.”

Charlee didn’t have time for small talk. “Have you talked to Natalie? She didn’t show up at the hospital last night. Dad just called me.”

“What? No. Want me to call her?”

“I already did. It goes right to voicemail.”

“What about Pete? He talk to her?”

“He’s my next call.”

Charlee heard a muffled curse. “I don’t like this. Not with everything else going on.”

Hearing him mirror her thoughts made Charlee’s worry ratchet up another notch. “If Pete hasn’t talked to her, we’ll locate her phone. Maybe she had car trouble or something.”

"Then she would have called. What about Sanders? I thought he was watching her?"

"Hunter's calling him now."

"Keep me posted. I'll make a few calls on my end. She's going to be fine," he added, then hung up.

She called Pete next, but he hadn't heard from her either. Hunter walked back into the room, expression grim. "Deputy Sanders isn't answering his cell, either." When Charlee made a sound of distress, he held up a hand. "But there was a big accident near the campus yesterday, so he may have gotten called to help with that."

It was a stretch, but Charlee appreciated his effort.

His cell buzzed with an incoming text. "Byte sent GPS coordinates on her phone. Looks like it's at her apartment. You ready?"

Charlee grabbed her backpack, and they hopped into Hunter's truck, the need to hurry a living thing. She wanted to believe her sister was merely sleeping in, maybe overdid it at a party last night. But her mind kept going to a far greater concern. What if the killer had Natalie?

Hunter climbed into the driver's seat, handed her a travel mug and two pieces of toast slathered in peanut butter wrapped in a napkin. "You need to keep your strength up."

Charlee tried to keep the panic at bay as Hunter made the hour-long trip to Gainesville in record time. She usually enjoyed driving through the University of Florida campus, with its redbrick buildings and stately live oaks. Since it drew thousands of students from all over the world, most of the businesses in town obviously catered to the university one way or another. But today, she wished everyone would just get off the road already.

Hunter drove about a mile past the main campus to an apartment complex wedged up against other apartment complexes. "Easy, *cher*. We're almost there."

"Turn right here, then go past the mailboxes to the third building on the left."

Hunter drove past bicycle racks and a swimming pool to a three-story building at the back. Since only a small number of summer classes were in session, he found an open guest spot without a problem. He leaned over the steering wheel and scanned the woods that backed up to the buildings.

Charlee followed his gaze, then looked away. Until they had proof, she was going under the assumption that her sister had gotten tied up with homework, forgot to charge her phone, fell asleep, had car trouble. Any plausible explanation that didn't include the person who had targeted her family.

They climbed out of the truck, and both scanned the parking lot. "Her car's not here," Charlee said. When Hunter opened his mouth to respond, she added, "I know it may not mean anything."

Charlee led the way to the apartment her sister shared with a girl from Ohio, Calisa. She knocked. "Natalie. It's Charlee. You home?"

They waited, and Charlee's nerves stretched thin. How would they get in if Natalie or Calisa weren't home? Finally, they heard rustling inside, and then the dead bolt opened. Calisa's sleepy face appeared, red hair matted on one side.

She managed a wan smile. "Hey, Charlee." She looked past her to Hunter. "Who's the hunk?"

"This is Hunter; he's a friend of mine. Is Natalie here?"

Calisa shrugged. "Not sure. I got in pretty late. Or I guess it was early."

She opened the door wider and led the way down the short hall into the main living area. Charlee went to Natalie's room, tapped on the closed door. "Nat? You here?" When she didn't get an answer, she opened the door to chaos. Clothes, shoes, books littered the floor and the unmade bed. The closet doors hung open, clothes spilling out there, too.

Hunter stepped into the room behind her. "Is this typical for Natalie? Or did someone toss the place?"

Charlee almost smiled. "No, this is typical Nat. If it had been neat, I'd have wondered if I were in the wrong room." Hunter crouched down and started sifting through the stuff on the floor while Charlee went to the closet, pushed some clothes aside. "Her favorite overnight bag from the designer outlet is missing. She must have packed it to head home." Charlee grabbed her phone, dialed Natalie's number, and scanned the room as she waited to hear it ring. Her worry ramped up another notch when she heard nothing.

She met Hunter's eyes, then turned and saw Calisa hovering in the doorway. "What's going on? Why are you wondering about her overnight bag?"

"Did you see Nat yesterday at all?"

"Um, yeah, for a few minutes, maybe eleven or so? We were both heading for an afternoon class."

"Did you come back to the apartment during the afternoon?" Hunter asked.

Calisa looked from one to the other. "No. After class, I went to work and then hung out with some friends till pretty late. Why? What's wrong?"

"Our mom is in the hospital. Natalie said she was heading there, but we haven't seen her."

Calisa covered her mouth with her hand. "Oh my gosh. Is she okay?"

"That's what we're trying to figure out." Hunter pulled out his little notebook. "Do you know what class she had yesterday?"

"Um, not really. Summer school is weird, you know. The schedules are different. Except for the one yesterday, I don't know. I don't think she had another one. You could maybe ask at the registrar's office."

"Was she supposed to work last night?"

Calisa shrugged. "We're roommates, but we don't, you know, hang out. We both just do our own thing."

Hunter tucked his notebook in his pocket. "Thanks, Calisa. Here's my card. Will you call me if you hear from Natalie?"

She nodded solemnly. "Of course. I hope she's okay."

"We do, too, thanks." Charlee gave the girl a quick hug, then they left.

"Try her phone again," Hunter said when they reached the parking lot. They both spun in a slow circle, straining to listen, but heard nothing. Hunter kept walking, expanding the circle. "Call again," he said.

Charlee kept pace, letting the phone ring several times before hanging up and dialing again.

Finally, as they rounded the corner of the building, they both heard it. Faint, but there. "Natalie!" Charlee yelled, but there was no answer. Her eyes landed on the dumpster, and she shouted "No!" and leaped toward it.

Hunter grabbed her around the waist before she got there. As Charlee tried to free herself, he said, "Let me look first."

Charlee met his eyes, knew what he was trying to do, and shoved out of his arms. "Natalie!" She reached the dumpster and pushed the lid up, steeling herself against what they might find.

It was empty. Except for Natalie's phone.

Charlee let out a breath she hadn't realized she was holding. Hunter put an arm around her to steady her. "Take a breath, *cher*."

Charlee's relief turned to panic. "She'd never ditch her phone, especially since Mom's stroke." She swallowed hard. "He has her."

Hunter didn't agree or disagree. Instead, he said, "Let me bag her phone, see if we get lucky and he left prints on it." He started for his truck.

"We need to find her, now!"

"Agreed. Which means we take it step-by-step, so we don't overlook something obvious and end up wasting time." He scanned the area around the building, walked several feet, scanned the other direction. "No security cameras."

Charlee huffed out a frustrated breath, fighting to stay calm, think logically. They hurried over to the registrar's office and found out Natalie had checked in to her class yesterday. But it was a three-hour class, so she could have left partway through, and no one would have noticed.

Before they left town, they stopped at the funky

boutique in a converted Victorian where Natalie worked. As soon as Charlee and Hunter walked into the incense-heavy front room, an older woman in flowing, colorful robes glided in their direction. "Charlotte." She air-kissed both of Charlee's cheeks and then smiled at Hunter. "And who might you be, handsome?"

"Lieutenant Boudreau, Fish and Wildlife, ma'am. And you are?"

"Delores Fairbanks, but you can call me anytime." At Hunter's smile, she laughed. "Or just call me Delores. What brings you here, Charlotte? How's your mother? Natalie said she had to get home, so she couldn't come in to work yesterday afternoon."

"That's why we're here. What time did she call you, Delores?"

"Well now, it was the middle of the day. I know we were quite busy. Lots of gals pop in during their lunch hour to pick up a wedding or shower gift this time of year. Must have been between noon and one or so, I'd say." Her penciled eyebrows rose. "Why? What's wrong?"

"Nat didn't show up at the hospital. Nobody has seen her since yesterday."

Delores put a hand to her ample bosom. "Oh, dear heaven. What could have happened?"

"That's why we're here." Hunter produced another card and handed it to Delores. "Please call me immediately if you hear from her."

"Sugar, I may call you even if I don't." She grinned, then sobered as she saw their expressions. She cleared her throat. "Please let me know when you find her so I won't worry."

"We will." Charlee leaned in for more air-kisses and then they climbed back into Hunter's truck.

Hunter turned them toward Ocala and called Josh, asked him to meet them at the hospital with his fingerprint kit. Charlee leaned back against the headrest and turned to look at him. "We have to find her."

"And we will. We'll take I-75 back, in case we're wrong and she went that way. Keep an eye out for her car."

Charlee nodded, desperate for something besides her fear to focus on. They scanned the roadside as they headed south, Charlee hoping against hope they would find her sister's car, maybe a note inside that she'd hitched a ride...something.

But they reached the hospital in Ocala without finding a single trace. Charlee called Pete as they pulled into the parking garage. "Anything?"

"That's what I was going to ask you," Pete said.

"Her roommate hasn't seen her since yesterday. The deputy keeping an eye on her isn't answering his cell. And Delores hasn't heard from her since she called in around lunchtime to say she had to get home because of Mom. We checked Route 441 and I-75 between here and her apartment and didn't find any sign of her."

"I called all the area hospitals. She hasn't been brought in under her name or a Jane Doe, either. FHP hasn't reported any accidents."

"So where is she?" Charlee couldn't keep the worry out of her voice.

"We'll keep looking, squirt. Be tough. Is Josh there yet?"

Charlee looked in the rearview as her brother pulled up behind them. "He just got here."

She hung up, then squeezed her eyes shut for a second, rubbed at the ache in her chest before she looked at Hunter. "He has her."

He met her gaze without flinching. "It looks that way. But we can't be sure. Let's see if Josh can get any prints from the phone while we check in with your dad."

She hugged Josh before she and Hunter headed through the hospital. Outside her mother's room, Charlee summoned her best smile. No way did she want to add to the burden her folks already carried.

When they walked into the room, her father's eyes lit with hope. "Did you find her?" His smile faded as he saw Charlee's face. He looked from one to the other. "Did you find out anything? Where could she be?"

Charlee hugged him, then guided him away from the bed, in case their mother could hear them. "We're still working on it. Pete and Josh are, too."

Her father glanced over at the bed, then back, his face bleak. "You have to find her. I couldn't bear it if something happened to her, too."

With that, her big, strong bear of a father wrapped her in his arms and burst into silent sobs that tore Charlee's heart to tiny little bits. She'd never seen him cry. Never seen him anything other than the solid rock that held their family together. Whatever it took, she'd stand by him and help hold him up.

She ran a hand down his back and hung on tight. "We'll find her, Dad. I promise. We won't stop until we do."

"See that you do." After a few minutes, he eased away and sat back down by her mother's bedside.

Charlee went to the other side and placed a gentle

kiss on her mother's cheek. "Come back to us, Mama. We need you. We love you."

Her father clasped Hunter's hand. "You keep my girl safe. If something happens to her..." He let the thought trail off.

"Yes, sir. I'll do whatever it takes." The two men exchanged a nod, and Charlee and Hunter left the room.

"Let's go check in with your brothers," Hunter said.

Chapter 26

HUNTER JOGGED TO KEEP UP WITH CHARLEE ON THE way back to the parking garage. He understood her frantic need to *do* something, to find Natalie right this minute. But he also knew—as did she—that if they didn't take the time to think it through, to figure out who had her—or at least make a really good guess—they'd waste time running in circles. And that they couldn't afford.

"Anything?" she asked as soon as she reached Josh, who had the tailgate down and was using it as a worktable.

Josh shook his head. "The phone has been wiped completely clean. Not even Nat's prints are on it." His cell phone rang. "Tanner."

"Meet us at Charlee's cottage," Hunter said as he climbed into the truck. Josh looked up from his call and nodded that he understood. Hunter headed back toward Charlee's place.

She growled when he pulled up to a fast food drive-through. "I really can't eat," Charlee said when he handed her a burrito.

Hunter unwrapped his with one hand while he drove. "I know. But we need to think, *cher*, and for that we need fuel."

She nodded, took a small bite and choked it down, then took another and another until she had finished the whole thing. He gave her major points for that. She did what needed doing for the sake of her loved ones, every time. He would do no less for her. And that meant finding Natalie, ASAP.

As soon as they reached her cottage, he walked around the outside, grabbed the palm frond, and climbed up to access the camera's SD card, hoping they'd get lucky this time. Once back inside, he opened his laptop on the kitchen table. "Talk me through what happened a year ago, would you?"

Charlee sank into the chair opposite and took a sip of her sweet tea, rubbed her eyes. "Haven't we been over it enough?"

"No. Because like you, I think we're still overlooking an important piece somewhere."

"What do you want to know?"

He picked up the newspaper clipping she'd been sent. "You said Tommy looked a lot different then. How so?"

"Well, he wasn't broken then, if you know what I mean. His hair was groomed, he took care of himself."

He inserted the SD card while he spoke, loaded the photos. "What about JJ and Nora? We saw their yearbook pictures. Did they look pretty much like that?"

"Yeah, why?" She jumped up. "Wait. I have a picture."

She hurried into her room and came back carrying a photo. She held it out, and Hunter took it from her. "We took a group shot before we left that day. It, ah, it was my first solo trip as guide, so..." She shrugged.

Hunter studied the photo. "Okay, so there's JJ and Nora with you in the front. There's Tommy and Sally." Hunter pointed. "Who's that?"

"That's James, Tommy's brother."

Hunter switched from the photos to the report

from last year, started scrolling. "He wasn't with you, though, right?"

"He was supposed to be, but he didn't go with us, no." Charlee slid back onto the chair, frowned as she thought back. "There was some bad blood between Sally and James. He started ragging on Nora about how she was talking to JJ, so Sally jumped in and told him to stay out of it. It wasn't his job." Charlee waved her hands. "The whole thing escalated in a hurry, and before I knew it, Sally stormed off one way and James the other. She came back, but James didn't. After a while, Tommy said we should just go on without him."

Hunter was working out the logistics in his mind when his email chimed. He read the short message, then looked up at Charlee. "Tommy and James Jennings's mother drowned in her bathtub when James was seventeen, Tommy was ten. At the time of her death, the boys' biological father was in prison."

Hunter could see Charlee's mind racing down the same track as his. She drummed her fingers on the table. "You think James is behind all this? Because of the water connection?"

Hunter fired off another email, then stood and paced, his mind working through the possibilities. He leaned both arms on the table. "What if James didn't leave? Or what if he came back and killed JJ? Or maybe JJ's death was an accident, but he tried to kill Nora?"

Charlee's eyes went wide as she followed the thought. "And I interrupted him." She wrapped her arms around her middle and started rocking back and forth. "I-I never even thought about it. I should have. Dear God, what if it's been him all along? He's got Natalie."

Hunter came around the table and placed a hand on her shoulder. "Easy. Take a breath. Let's make sure before we go off half-cocked. It's still just a theory, albeit the best one we've got."

He went back to the photos from the trail camera and scrolled through them. "Come on, come on," he muttered, flipping back and forth between photos. He squinted, leaned closer.

"What did you find?" Charlee leaned over his shoulder. "Can you make it any clearer? Or is there a better shot of his face?"

Hunter kept flipping back and forth, frustration roiling in his gut. "No, not really, but maybe Byte can work his magic." He snapped a photo of Charlee's group shot, then sent that and several different shots from the trail camera to Byte to run through facial recognition, see if they matched. Then he used the dates Byte had sent and ran a search on James Jennings. While he waited, he drummed his fingers on the table as Charlee flipped through the pages of the old case file, both of them searching, desperate.

"Yes." He read the report that popped up and shot Charlee a look of triumph. "James was questioned in his mother's drowning death in the bathtub. His fingerprints are on file. He was a juvenile then, but we should be able to access his prints, given the nature of the situation."

He fired off an email request for that, then picked up his cell. "Hey, Sanchez, listen, do me a favor. I know it's a real long shot, but run down to the Outpost and dust the canoe and kayak registration forms filled out the day Brittany died for prints, would you? Thanks."

Charlee felt like she was going to burst out of her skin. She escaped Hunter's concerned gaze by taking refuge in her room, desperate to settle her mind, force the panic away. Her hands tingled, and her heart raced like a runaway train. She sat down on the side of her bed and put her head between her knees so she wouldn't hyperventilate. Slow, deep breaths. In, out...in, out.

She had to be strong. After a few minutes, she stood and paced, still taking slow, deep breaths. She wouldn't be able to help anyone if she didn't calm down.

As she paced, she turned toward her dresser and stopped. Sunlight filtered through the sheer curtains and glinted off something on the dresser top. She stepped closer to investigate, surprised to find a gold, heart-shaped charm lying there. It looked like it should be on a charm bracelet or necklace—and she'd never seen it before in her life.

Maybe it belonged to Natalie? No. Her sister never wore gold, only silver, and only chunky, funky modern pieces. This necklace was more old-fashioned. She turned it over. Fourteen carat gold. Not costume jewelry, so definitely out of her sister's price range. Their mother used to wear gold all the time. Had she given this to Natalie, and Nat had left it here?

That didn't make sense either. Natalie hadn't been to the cottage recently.

Her heart started racing again, so she sat on the edge of the bed, repeating her slow-breathing routine. If Hunter saw her now, he'd know she'd turned into a complete weakling.

"Yes! We got him! Charlee?"

She ran to the kitchen, heart pounding all over again. "What did you find?" She leaned over his shoulder and took a deep, calming breath, inhaling his clean male scent. She did it again. He exuded utter calm, and everything inside her settled as she absorbed his strength.

He pointed to two images on his laptop, side by side. "Byte got a hit through facial recognition. Byte used what we sent, plus a photo Troy had taken on the river the day Brittany died. Despite the bleached hair and beard, Oliver Dunn and James Jennings are the same person."

Charlee leaned closer, stunned. Her eyes bounced back and forth between the two images, merging them in her mind. "Unbelievable. I never even guessed. He didn't act the same or move the same or anything." She shook her head. "I should have seen it."

Hunter looked up. "Stop. You shouldn't have. You weren't supposed to. That's the whole point of a disguise. Besides, how much time did you spend with Oliver, I mean James, that day last year?"

Charlee thought back. "None, really. Just enough to get introduced, collect paperwork, and go over the safety check. After his fight with Sally, I never saw him again." She banged her fist on the table. "We have to find him!"

The charm popped out of her hand and hit the table.

"What's this?" Hunter asked.

"I just found it on my dresser, but it's not mine. I don't think it's Natalie's either. Not her style."

Hunter thought a moment, then picked up his cell phone. "Mrs. Jennings, may I speak to Nora? No, ma'am, I just have a quick question for her."

Charlee froze as she realized what he was thinking. *No, oh, please no.*

"When was the last time you saw her? Okay, take a deep breath, ma'am. You said the window to her room is open. Is there any sign of a struggle? Good, that's good. My guess is she just snuck out of her room. Does she do that often? Then it's a safe bet she's done it again." He paused. "Ma'am, does your daughter wear a gold, heart-shaped charm on either a necklace or bracelet?"

Charlee leaned closer so she could hear the conversation.

"Her father gave it to her for her last birthday," Sally said. "Actually, two gold charms on a bracelet. One for Nora. And one for…JJ. It's here on her dresser. But… one of the charms is missing. How do you know this?" Her voice rose. "What's going on? What's happening with Nora?"

"Nothing that we know of yet. But I'd like you to call your daughter, Mrs. Jennings, and check in. Let me know when you hear from her. I just want to be sure there's nothing more going on here than normal teenage behavior."

Charlee could hear Sally Jennings yelling more questions and accusations as Hunter disconnected the call.

She met Hunter's troubled gaze. "You think he has Nora, too?"

"Not necessarily. He might have taken the charm to make us think that."

"But you think he has Natalie. And he's the one behind everything."

"It all fits."

James wouldn't hesitate to kill, not after Brittany.

That's the part Hunter wouldn't say. She knew exactly what she had to do, how to end this thing. She also knew he'd never go for it. Her heart pounded, and she sat on her hands to stop the trembling. The whole idea sounded crazy, even to her, but it would work.

"We'll find her, *cher*. You have my word on that."

"I don't doubt it." She straightened, met his gaze head-on. "But I'm not sure you'll find her in time."

Hunter studied her, folded his arms over his chest. "What are you scheming in that beautiful head of yours?"

"We use me as bait to draw him out."

Hunter froze, didn't move a muscle, but fury exploded in his eyes. When he spoke, his voice was utterly calm and controlled. He stood, leaned over her. "Over. My. Dead. Body."

Charlee stood and forced him back a step. He wouldn't intimidate her, not now. This mattered too much. Her sister's life hung in the balance. "Just hear me out."

"This is not open for discussion."

"It absolutely is. I am not done talking about this."

"Well, I'm damn sure done listening." He grabbed her upper arms and hauled her close. "I won't lose you to this lunatic, *cher*, do you understand? I won't risk you, too."

He pulled back when he realized what he'd said. Charlee seized the opportunity. "I'm not your brother, Hunter." When would he finally realize that?

"No, you're not. But you're just as important to me."

The words dropped like a ticking bomb into the sudden silence.

Charlee's breath caught. Oh, this so wasn't the time

for this conversation, even though his words made her heart sing. "Then you have to trust me to do what I need to do."

He made a slashing motion with his hands. "This doesn't have a thing to do with trust. It has to do with skill sets and strategy. This guy is a cold-blooded killer. I know you're trained law enforcement, but one person is no match for this guy, Charlee. Let your brothers and me do our jobs and get this scumbag."

"While I stay here and bake cupcakes for the team?" she asked sweetly.

Hunter started to respond, then saw her face. "I'm not trying to be condescending, *cher*."

"Trying or not, you're doing a fabulous job."

"I'm trying to keep you alive!" His roar echoed in the small room.

She leaned in until they were nose to nose. "And I'm trying to keep my sister alive."

The silence lengthened. Finally, he sighed, scrubbed a hand over the back of his neck. "How about we work together?"

Charlee crossed her arms. "And that would be how, exactly?"

"Once Pete, Josh, Fish, and Sanchez get here, we'll come up with a plan."

She narrowed her eyes at his easy acceptance. "You're not shutting me out of this, Lieutenant."

He nodded. "I won't. But if you try to run off on your own, I'll truss you up like a hog on a spit until this is over."

"Don't threaten me."

"Oh, this isn't a threat, *cher*. I can guar-an-tee I will

do exactly that if you try to put yourself in this killer's sights."

Within a few minutes, Pete, Josh, Fish, and Sanchez were crowded into Charlee's kitchen. Hunter kept an eye on her as she prepped a batch of cupcakes. He hadn't meant to insult her. He knew baking helped her clear her mind. Running generally did the same for him.

How to keep her involved in finding and saving Natalie without her getting killed? That question circled round and round in his brain until he had a raging headache. No way would he let a civilian—never mind her law-enforcement experience—get in the middle of the hunt for a ruthless killer. Especially since she was the victim's sister. What was she thinking?

As he watched her pour the batter into the muffin tin, he sighed. He knew exactly what she was thinking. The same thing he would be if their positions were reversed. She would do whatever it took to save her sister. Just like he would do whatever it took to protect her. He'd meant every word of his earlier threat.

Everyone pulled up chairs at the kitchen table while Charlee slid the pans into the oven, then she sat down beside him.

"What have we got?" Pete said.

"Facial recognition says Oliver Dunn is really James Jennings, Nora and JJ's uncle who walked away from the kayak launch the day JJ died and hasn't been seen since."

Sanchez shook his head. "You mean there was someone else on the river with Charlee last year??"

All eyes turned to Charlee, and her face flamed.

"Maybe. He and Sally Jennings fought before we left, and he stormed off. It was in my report, but both the investigator and Rick pretty much blew it off, since JJ's death was ruled an accident."

There were muttered curses from the others, then Josh asked, "He wasn't there when you came back?"

"No, I never saw him again." Charlee cocked her head, thinking. "The whole time we were questioned by the police, Tommy just rocked back and forth, mumbling, 'Oh, Jimmy, oh, Jimmy.'" She looked up, expression anguished. "I thought he meant JJ. His legal name was James Junior, he'd said. Did that mean Tommy suspected his brother killed his son?" She shuddered. "Is that why he was killed? To keep him from talking?"

"We'll look into all that, *cher*. Later," Hunter said. "But first, we need to find him."

"None of this should ever have happened." Charlee wrapped her arms around her middle.

The way she curled in on herself made him mad. He took her hand, ignoring Pete and Josh's exchanged glance. "I'll keep saying it until you believe it, *cher*. None of this is your fault. You didn't cause any of this."

Josh nudged Hunter's hand aside and took Charlee's in his own. "He's right, you know. You didn't kill anyone, Sis. The opposite. You saved Nora. Brittany, too."

"But JJ died. So did Brittany."

"Charlee." Pete's harsh tone had everyone looking his way. "If we're right about all this—and I'd stake my life that we are—then James Jennings killed Brittany and Tommy. On purpose. There is no way you could have saved them. He had a definite agenda."

Everyone at the table agreed.

Charlee swallowed hard, then met Hunter's gaze. "So how do we save Natalie?" She looked around the faces at the table, and Hunter watched her expression harden. "I am going to be part of the plan, so keep that in mind."

Both her brothers immediately launched a protest, but she held up her hands, sent them each a steely glare. "Don't try to stop me. Include me, or I'll do it on my own." She waited, glaring at both of them, not giving an inch.

Hunter finally spoke up. "Every murder—or attempted murder—involves water, usually drowning. Except Brittany's. Which may have been to keep her from talking, so it messed with his original plan. I think he's holding Natalie near water."

"But which water?" Charlee asked. "Everything that's happened has been somewhere different."

"He could be anywhere," Josh agreed. "I think we need a way to draw him out, get him to let us know where he is."

"Use me as bait. Set up a trade." Charlee's stubborn chin jutted out at a challenging angle. "I'm the piece that connects all this."

"Absolutely not," Pete and Josh said instantly, seconded immediately by Sanchez and Fish.

Hunter watched Charlee. Her scowling siblings presented a rather intimidating front, but she didn't look cowed in the least. "So far, you've all said exactly what Hunter said. I'm still waiting for someone to offer up a better idea."

"Can we get a location through his phone's GPS?" Fish asked.

Hunter shook his head. "He had a burner phone and

turned it off the same day Brittany died. I've had Byte set up an alarm if he turns it back on for any reason, but he won't. Jennings is too smart for that."

"He use a debit or credit card anywhere?" Sanchez asked, but his expression said he already knew the answer.

"He told Charlee he didn't trust 'big brother' and paid cash for everything."

"Do we have a BOLO out on his truck?" Fish asked.

Hunter nodded. "I already called it in."

Fish studied Charlee from head to toe as she took the cupcakes out of the oven. "How about this? Why don't we modify Charlee's idea a bit? We let the killer think he's getting Charlee in trade for Natalie, but it'll be me instead."

"How are we going to let him know any of this? We have no idea where he is. He hasn't contacted anyone." Charlee's voice rose with every sentence.

"He will," Hunter said. "And we'll be ready." His phone rang. "Boudreau. What have you got?" He listened for several minutes, then hung up. "Dispatch got a call from a cop up in Lake City who saw the BOLO. Says he chatted with a guy matching Jennings's description at a small gas station just outside of town."

Hunter looked around the room, his excitement starting to build. "I'm guessing he's headed back to Tommy's place. He doesn't know we're onto him yet, so we'll have the element of surprise."

Everyone jumped up from the table, cell phones to their ears, calling for reinforcements, getting a plan together.

Charlee grabbed Hunter's arm. "I'm coming with you."

"*Cher*, I—"

"Don't. If you try to leave me behind, I'll find a way to follow you."

He studied her face and knew she meant every word. Memories of his brother's death flashed through his mind, and he knew a bone-deep terror he'd never felt before. He couldn't lose her to this lunatic. This beautiful, tough woman had burrowed into his heart in ways he'd never expected and had only just begun to explore. If something happened to her, he'd never be able to forgive himself.

He glanced around the room, realized the others were already outside. Options, alternatives, plans ran through his mind as he pulled her close. But then he shoved all that aside, just for a minute, and kissed her with every bit of the emotion crowding his heart. He gave her all of it, every single feeling surging through him. Want. Affection. Fear. Apology. Love, most of all.

As she melted against him, into the kiss, he absorbed the taste and feel of her, tucked it away to savor in the days ahead. He knew he'd never get another taste of her.

His brother's lifeless face flashed through his memory, and his resolve hardened. She could hate him forever if it meant she'd be alive to do it. He cupped her face for one last kiss, imprinting the memory on his heart. Then he reached around her neck and used a pressure point to render her unconscious.

He caught her as she sagged in his arms and carried her to her room, gently tucked her under the covers. He kissed her forehead, brushed the hair back from her face. "I love you, *cher*."

He pocketed her car keys as he hurried outside. Then

he raised the hood on her Jeep, yanked out enough spark plug wires that it wouldn't run, and hopped in his truck.

With this one decision, he knew he'd lost any chance to be part of her life. She'd never forgive him, ever. He understood. Agreed with her, even. But he didn't regret it. Her life mattered too much.

Chapter 27

Charlee woke to an annoying buzz. It grated on her nerves, pulling her out of a really sweet dream in which Hunter stood in the ocean, water sluicing off his finely sculpted muscles, that killer grin on his face. He crooked a finger, inviting her to join him in the water. She shed her cover-up and raced to the water's edge, toes in the warm blue water, ready to dive in to meet him. *I'm coming*.

The persistent noise came again, and the dream vanished.

No. Come back.

She opened her eyes, blinked as she tried to orient herself. Bedroom. Cottage.

The sound came again. Phone.

She automatically groped around the nightstand, then realized the sound came from the kitchen. She hopped up and raced into the room. She scooped up the phone just before it stopped ringing. "Hello?"

"So where did all the law-enforcement types rush off to, Charlotte? It seems they left you behind?"

Charlee froze as she realized several things at once. Hunter had indeed left her behind. He'd knocked her out, the dirty, rotten, lousy scoundrel. And she recognized the voice. Goose bumps popped out on her skin, and she wrapped one arm around her middle. Somehow James knew they'd left. She eased away from the windows, chilled to the bone. Was he out there right now, watching?

And how had James gotten her cell number? She had to get him talking, see if she could hear any background noise, get some information she could pass along that would help them catch him. "Who is this?" she asked.

He laughed. "Oh, come now, Charlotte. Don't be coy. I figure by now your lieutenant and his cronies would have discovered my identity."

"Fine. Should I call you James? Or Oliver?" She refused to show any hint of fear, even though her knees were banging together like a couple of old bones.

"Oh, good. You have figured it out. That will make things easier. I thought for a moment the other day—the day dear Brittany left this earth—that you'd recognized me, but no. Guess you're just not that smart, eh?"

Charlee clenched her jaw to keep from saying the wrong thing. She'd let him lead the conversation. "I guess not. Just out of curiosity, how did you get my number?"

He laughed, an ugly sound. "It's amazing how helpful eavesdropping can be. Dear old Dad gave it to Travis the other day."

Charlee wouldn't think about this guy being anywhere near her father. "What do you want, James?"

"Aren't you going to ask about your sister? She's a lovely girl. All that pretty skin and sheen to her hair."

Charlee's hand shook so hard, she almost dropped the phone. "Let me talk to her."

He laughed again, a chilling, evil sound. "*Tsk, tsk.* You're not calling the shots here. Best remember that."

"What do you want with Natalie?"

"Nothing, really. She's just here to serve as a way

for us to get reunited. You upset me that day, Charlotte, showing up when you did. Now it's time to make things right."

Charlee wasn't playing his game. "I'll do whatever you want. Just let me talk to Natalie." She gritted her teeth. "Please."

He sighed, and then she heard struggling in the background.

"Charlee? Is that you? Help me, please. He's crazy."

"I'm coming to get you, Nat. Just hang on."

Charlee heard a muffled scream. Seconds later, James came back on the line. "See? She's fine." He paused while Charlee thought through what that scream might mean. She pushed the terrifying images away, or she wouldn't be able to think, to plan.

"Here's what's going to happen, Charlotte. First, you're going to tell me where your law-enforcement friends are headed right now."

She wouldn't let Hunter and her brothers walk into a trap. "They got a call and rushed out of here. I don't know where they went."

"I don't believe you, but it won't really make a difference. I'll figure it out, and afterward, you'll pay for lying to me. That's never a good idea, Charlotte."

"Just tell me what you want. I'll do anything, as long as you let Natalie go."

"Are you proposing a trade? Your life for hers?"

Charlee didn't hesitate. "If that's what it takes."

He laughed long and hard. "You Tanners. And Boudreau. What a loyal bunch. It would be quite amusing, really, if it weren't so stupid."

She heard a loud noise, another muffled scream, and

she jumped up, pacing. "Let her go, James. Please. It's me you want."

"It is. And I will get you." He paused, and Charlee gripped the back of a chair, straining to pick up any background noise. There was nothing, so she figured he had Natalie inside somewhere. Which didn't help much. She tried another tack.

"Is Nora there, too?" she demanded.

The silence lengthened, and she feared she'd said the wrong thing.

"Nora should have been nicer to her brother. She should have been the one who died. Not JJ."

Her instincts had been right. He *had* tried to kill Nora last year. But had he snatched her now? Charlee's hands started tingling, and she forced herself to take slow, deep, even breaths. She needed all her wits about her.

"Is she there?" Her voice was hard, demanding. "Answer the question."

He laughed. "Silly Charlotte, still trying to take charge. You. Are. Not." He hissed the last, then lowered his voice. "Get in your car and start driving. Take SR-40 to CR-326 to US-301. Head north for exactly forty miles and pull over into the Shell gas station. I'll call you with more instructions. If you're not there in an hour, your sister dies. And if I find out you called Hunter or any of your family members, well, same thing. Natalie dies a very painful death."

"Don't hurt her. Just...don't hurt her." Charlee raced around the room, searching for her keys while he talked. She checked her purse, the hook in the kitchen where she usually kept them. Nothing.

"Do you understand?"

"I can't find them. Oh God."

"What?"

"I can't find my keys. They're not here." She ran outside to her car and checked the ignition. No keys. She stopped. Looked at the car. The hood wasn't quite shut. She pulled it up and glanced at the engine, saw the wires sticking up. Hunter had not only taken her keys, he'd disabled her car. She slammed the hood. "I'll need more time. My car won't run."

"Then you'd better think fast, Charlotte. The clock is ticking."

He hung up.

Dammit, Hunter. Charlee's heart pounded, and pictures of Brittany's and JJ's still faces flashed before her eyes. This couldn't be happening. Panic threatened to buckle her knees.

NO! She straightened, swallowed back the fear, and let her training kick in. *Think, Charlee*. First, she needed a car. Her parents' place was closest. She'd take her mom's. She rushed inside for her tennis shoes and then sprinted toward their house.

Natalie's life depended on her. And maybe Nora's, too. *Oh God*.

As Hunter, plus Pete and Josh, along with Sanchez and Fish, raced toward Lake City, guilt rode shotgun beside him. Hunter knew Charlee would be beyond furious when she woke up. She'd never forgive him, and he couldn't blame her. But he wasn't sorry. He'd do it again if it meant keeping her safe.

He'd think later about how much he'd miss her. After they had Jennings in custody.

As they neared Tommy Jennings's cabin, they pulled off into a restaurant parking lot. Hunter spread a hand-drawn map on the hood of his truck. "We'll drive part-way down the dirt track, then go the rest of the way on foot. Otherwise, Jennings will see the cloud of dust a mile away. Pete, Josh, and I will approach from the front. Sanchez and Fish, you come from behind."

They needed the element of surprise.

Josh came up beside him as Hunter climbed into his truck. "If this piece of garbage hurts a hair on Nat's head..." He let the thought trail off.

"I hear you. We'll find her."

Josh narrowed his eyes. "How'd you get Charlee to agree to stay behind? She'd been pretty adamant up until that point."

Hunter put his sunglasses back on. "Let's just say I convinced her to take a little nap instead."

For a moment, Josh said nothing. Then his eyes widened. "You didn't."

Hunter nodded, braced for a blow. "I did. I couldn't risk anything happening to her."

Josh shook his head. "She will tear you limb from limb."

"I know."

Josh studied him as though he'd just figured something out, then one corner of his mouth kicked up in a small smile. "I think my sister may have met her match in you."

Hunter shrugged. "She means the world to me." It surprised him how easily the words slipped out, along with the knowledge that he meant every one.

Josh slapped him on the shoulder. "Good luck with that, man. At best, I foresee a severe beating followed by major groveling in your future."

"I don't think it'll be that easy, but let's get Natalie home safe first."

"Absolutely." Josh hurried back to his vehicle, and they headed out.

Hunter knew the cabin was empty before he reached the front door. Every instinct screamed that this wasn't the place.

Still, they circled the house and burst in, guns drawn, just to make sure. No Jennings. No Natalie, either. They searched the perimeter of the property, but thankfully found no blood or other evidence of more recent violence.

Hunter walked away from the others, pulled out his phone to call Charlee. Again. But again, he stopped before he finished dialing. If she was still out cold—please, God—he didn't want to wake her. Because the foolishness of what he'd done had just fully occurred to him. The minute Charlee's eyes popped open, she'd find a way to go after Natalie herself. And that was even scarier than having her with them.

"Where to now, Lieutenant?" Sanchez asked as they all gathered outside the cabin.

Hunter yanked his focus back to Natalie and the map. "The next logical choice is Big Shoals, where JJ died."

"What if you're wrong?" Pete sounded like he was working hard to keep the panic at bay. "Maybe he took her back to the Ocklawaha, where he tried to kill Brittany."

Hunter nodded, understanding Pete's panic. He wouldn't add his worry about Charlee. "It makes as much sense as anything. We know everything he does revolves around water." He nodded to Josh. "Your boat blowing up, forcing Charlee and me off the bridge, your mom in the bathtub."

"What if he went back to the Outpost? Hiding in plain sight?" Fish asked.

"Also possible," Josh said.

"I agree," Hunter said. "So let's cover all our bases. You and Pete head back to the Ocklawaha. Fish, you and Sanchez head for the Outpost, check that whole area, river and land."

"Where are you going?" Pete asked.

"Back to Big Shoals. But first I need to check on Charlee." He grimaced. He hadn't meant to say that last out loud.

Josh just shook his head and snorted.

"What's going on?" Pete wanted to know.

"He knocked her out so she couldn't come with us."

Pete's eyes widened, and he whistled. "She'll be eight miles past spitting mad when she gets hold of you."

Hunter met his gaze. "I know. But I couldn't risk it." And now he was more worried she'd rush off on her own, without anyone to watch her back.

Josh glanced over at Pete. "He loves her."

Hunter nodded, then climbed back in his truck, ignoring Pete's shocked expression. He picked up his phone, set it down again. He muttered a prayer that Charlee would stay asleep for a while longer and then hit the gas, determined to stop this scumbag before he hurt Natalie.

Chapter 28

Charlee's side ached, and sweat poured down her skin by the time she reached her parents' house, found the hidden key under the frog, ran inside, and grabbed the keys to her mother's car. It took another few minutes to get the car out of the garage and pointed toward the highway.

After the first half hour, she hadn't gone twenty miles, and anxiety clawed at her skin with every single red light and slow-moving vehicle. That was the trouble with two-lane roads. You were at the mercy of every pokey Joe and farm vehicle. She pounded the steering wheel in frustration when she hit the speed trap section of Waldo. She kept one eye on the speedometer as she inched past the flea market, then she opened it up when the speed limit went back to sixty.

Her fury and frustration with Hunter and his high-handed ways grew with every mile. Ranting and raving didn't allay her fears but gave her something else to think about as the minutes ticked by. He'd had no right to knock her out in some misguided attempt to keep her safe, the macho, testosterone-driven idiot. She wasn't a child. She was trained law enforcement.

She'd hate him if she didn't love him so much.

And part of her understood his bone-deep need to protect her. She might have resorted to the same thing in his place. Still.

She glanced at the dashboard clock. Less than thirty minutes to go.

She swallowed hard and inched the accelerator up. *Don't let me be too late.*

When she stopped at the next light, she picked up her phone to call him, let him know what was happening. Then set it down again. How was Jennings tracking her? Since she'd taken her mom's car, chances were good he hadn't put a tracker on it. Or installed any kind of camera or recording device to see if she made any calls.

So that left tracking her phone. She glanced in the rearview mirror. No sign of anyone following her since she'd left the Outpost, either. Since she didn't know how tech-savvy Jennings was, whether he had some way to know if she'd talked to Hunter against his orders, she'd just send a text.

Traffic started moving again before she could figure out how to word the message, how to let Hunter know what was happening, without Jennings knowing. Hands gripping the steering wheel, Charlee drove as fast as she dared, while her mind spun with possible clues to give Hunter. She didn't have time for a speeding ticket.

She couldn't be late, either.

She kept driving north.

~

Hunter hadn't gone more than ten miles when his radio crackled. "719-Ocala, I've got a woman on the line, says you need to come to her house right away. Name is Sally Jennings, says it's about her daughter. I'm inputting her address into CAD."

"10-4. I'm on my way."

Hunter wanted to ignore Sally's flair for the dramatic, but he couldn't ignore her—and Nora's—connection to Jennings. He made a quick U-turn and headed the ten miles back to Lake City and Sally's ranch house. As he pulled into the driveway, the front door flew open, and Sally ran toward his truck.

"She's gone. You have to find her. Please."

Hunter stepped out of the vehicle and scanned the area as he guided her back toward the house. "Take a deep breath and tell me what's going on, Ms. Jennings."

"You asked me about Nora, so I tried to call and text her, but I got no response. I thought she was just mad, typical teen. But then a friend of hers showed up, saying she was here to pick up Nora. They were supposed to go shopping today."

"Would Nora have blown her off? Are they good friends?"

"They've been best friends for years, and they've been planning this for weeks. Ashley tried to contact her, too, and checked all her social media in case she missed a message, but there's nothing. She's just gone."

Sally stopped pacing and gripped Hunter's arm, face pale. "Does this have something to do with Tommy's death?"

Hunter kept his voice and expression calm. "We're not sure yet. How well do you know Tommy's brother, James?"

She snorted. "He's a controlling bully, and I tried to keep Tommy as far away from him as possible. But Tommy said James was the only family he still had. They got together every year, but I didn't go with them. They usually took the kids, though."

"Took the kids where?"

She looked at him in surprise. "To the carnival. James is a carney, mechanic or something. I have no idea. I didn't want to know. He and Tommy met up every year when the carnival came to town."

Hunter's mind raced, shuffling and sorting facts in his head. "We found a ride wristband at Tommy's cabin."

Sally ran her hands through her hair, eyes darting around the room. "Yes, Tommy called and asked Nora to go with him, but she said no."

"Mrs. Jennings, if Nora decided to get away from everything for a day, where would she go? Who would she call?"

"She would call Ashley. And they would go to the old quarry outside of town. The kids think we don't know about it, but they sneak in under the fence and go swimming."

Again, water. "Can you tell me exactly where at the quarry they hang out?" It had once been a huge operation. He didn't have time to check all the possible locations.

"I can draw you a map." She grabbed a piece of paper and sketched out directions and landmarks, then handed it to Hunter. "You'll find my baby?" Her chin quivered. "She's all I have left."

Hunter nodded and headed for the door. "Call me the minute you hear from her. I'll do the same."

He radioed dispatch and told them where he was headed, though his instincts said he wouldn't find Nora—or Natalie—there. Still, he had to check. He couldn't skip the obvious.

Charlee arrived at the gas station Jennings had directed her to with less than three minutes to spare. She pulled right up to a pump, since she needed gas anyway, and sat for a moment, head on the steering wheel, trying to catch her breath.

Someone knocked on the window, and she yelped. She looked up to see an elderly gentleman peering in at her. She lowered her window a fraction.

"Are you all right, Miss? I didn't mean to startle you."

Charlee took a deep breath. "I'm fine, thank you for asking." She dredged up a smile and stepped out of the car when it appeared the man wasn't leaving until she'd convinced him.

She stuck her credit card into the slot and started pumping gas, just as her cell phone rang.

She forced her emotions back. *Think. Be smart.* "Hello?"

"Oh, good. You made it on time. Cutting it pretty close, aren't you?"

The hair on the back of Charlee's neck lifted, and she looked around the small gas station in the middle of nowhere. Was he watching? Or was he tracking her phone's location?

"What now?" she demanded. On the way here, she had decided that confident beat sniveling, no matter what. She'd keep him just a little unsure of her compliance. She had the sense he enjoyed the back-and-forth, so she'd give him that, if it bought her time.

"Has loverboy been calling to check on you?"

She snorted. "Why would he? He's all worked up about some case, and I guess since I'm not FWC anymore, he doesn't feel the need to tell me anything."

There was a pause, and Charlee wondered if she'd laid it on too thick.

"Poor Charlotte, never quite good enough to keep up with the big boys. By the way, did you find the charm?"

She ignored the jab and focused on keeping him talking. She knew the minute Hunter figured out she was gone, he'd have her cell phone traced. "What charm?"

"Come now, Charlotte. You're a terrible liar. You know, the pretty gold one I left on your dresser. Did you ask the lieutenant about that?"

Charlee swallowed the bile in her throat. He'd not only been watching, but he'd been in her cottage, again. "Why would I ask him about it?"

"It's such a lovely piece. Nora wears one just like it."

Oh, dear God. They were right.

He waited.

"Where did Nora get it?" Would he tell her?

He giggled then, and the sound scared her more than anything he'd said so far. "Her father gave it to her. One charm for her. And one to remember JJ." He paused, and his voice turned low, angry. "You remember JJ. The boy you let die out there, alone. It should have been Nora. But I'll set that right soon enough."

Fear hit Charlee square in the gut. She gripped the pump handle until her knuckles turned white and waited.

"Are you still there, Charlotte?"

She straightened her shoulders, kept her voice firm. "Of course. Let me talk to Natalie."

"Hmm. I think not. You haven't earned it yet. I want you to keep driving north. Another forty miles. This time, though, you'll only have forty-five minutes. There will be another gas station. Left side of the road this time. Don't be late."

Charlee took a deep breath. She had to let Hunter know what was happening.

She sent him a quick text, closed the gas cap, and made a quick stop inside the gas station. Then she climbed back into the car and sped out onto the highway. She shoved the fear away. She couldn't let it in, or she wouldn't be able to focus. She had to stay calm and clearheaded.

Jennings had killed his own brother. And had meant to kill Nora.

Jennings had Natalie. And probably had Nora, too.

Charlee gripped the wheel tighter. This story would not end like the others, not as long as she drew breath. She had to save Natalie and Nora and herself, too.

She might be angry enough with Hunter to clock him upside the head, but she'd make sure he never had to watch someone else he cared about die.

Somehow, she'd fallen in love with the macho warrior with the sense of honor and hot body and piercing green eyes. She wouldn't let him find her dead body.

She refused to let her sister and Nora die, either.

All she had to do was figure out how to save them all.

Hunter hopped out of his truck in the makeshift parking area by the abandoned quarry. The other two cars were empty. He stepped over the chain and ran toward the sound of laughter.

He broke through the trees to see seven or eight teenagers playing on a rope swing. Several cheered from shore as a young man leaped, swung out over the water, and let go of the rope.

One of them spotted his uniform and hissed, "Cop."

"Everybody stay put." He waited while the last guy swam to shore. "I need to ask a couple questions."

One young man stepped forward, clearly the leader. "We weren't doing anything wrong, man. Just cooling off."

"Nothing except trespassing." When they started to protest, Hunter held up a hand. "I don't care about that right now." He pulled out his phone, showed them Nora's picture. "Do any of you know her?"

One girl said, "Sure. That's Nora Jennings."

Several others nodded.

"Has she been here today? Have you seen her?"

They looked at one another. The same girl said, "Not today, no."

"But she's come out here other times?"

Shrugs and averted glances all around.

"How long have you been here today?"

The leader checked a waterproof watch. "About three hours."

"Is she in trouble?" one of the other girls asked.

"We can't find her, so we just want to be sure she's okay." He pulled out his card. "Will you call me if you see or hear from her? It's important."

"It bites that her dad just died. You think she tried to…?"

Hunter zeroed in on the girl. "Was she suicidal?"

They all shook their heads. "She was pretty torn up about her dad, you know? But I don't think she'd try to hurt herself or anything."

"Thanks for your help. Let me know if you see or talk to her."

He jogged the path that wound around this side of the quarry to check for any sign of her. The path was obviously well used, but he saw no sign of a struggle, no discarded items except cigarette butts and beer bottles, a condom.

When he got back to the teens, they eyed him with dread. "There's no sign of her. Keep me posted." As he hurried away, he turned. "And stay off private property."

As he headed back to the main road, his cell phone rang. "Boudreau."

"Hunter? This is Liz. Charlee's friend?"

"What's up, Liz?"

"I'm here at Charlee's cottage. Her car is here, but she's not. I had told Charlee I was dragging her antique shopping today. Are you guys out investigating? She's not answering her cell phone."

The dread in Hunter's gut dug deeper, but he kept his voice calm. "She's not with me right now, but I'll call you if I hear from her."

"That sounds good. Thanks. Oh, hey, Sammy," she said before the line went dead.

Sammy made him think of the carnival and James Jennings. Was James the Tool Man? The pieces of the puzzle were dropping into place.

His cell phone buzzed with an incoming text from Charlee: Not sitting around while you do your stupid FWC stuff. Going kayaking. Might even see a friend I haven't seen in a year.

Hunter froze as he reread the text. If he understood, she was trying to tell him she was headed for Big Shoals, where JJ Jennings died last year. And the "friend" had to be Nora Jennings. He called Brad.

"Hey, Byte. Run a check on the GPS in Charlee Tanner's phone, would you?"

"On it."

He hadn't gone more than two miles down the road when Byte called him back.

"She's heading north, right?" Either on her own or with Jennings.

"Got it in one, boss. How'd you know?"

"I think Jennings is headed back to the rapids at Big Shoals, where JJ Jennings died."

"Are you sure?"

"As sure as I can be. Get me exact coordinates on last year's scene and send them to my laptop. Where is Charlee now, exactly?"

"She just left what looks like a gas station. Want me to send backup?"

"Not just yet."

"But this is—"

"Call Pete and Josh and give them Charlee's location," he interrupted. "Tell them to head this way and call me en route. We'll get a plan together."

"Don't bust in alone, boss." Byte sounded worried.

"Just call them." Hunter hung up and threw the phone onto the seat beside him.

Then he flipped on his light bar and hit the gas. He passed several state troopers, and when questioned via radio, said he was on the trail of a suspect, thanked them for the offer of help, and kept going. After what seemed like forever, he pulled into the gas station. Playing a hunch, he went inside and flashed his badge at the young Indian man behind the counter.

Hunter held up his phone and showed him

Jennings's photo. "I'm looking for this guy. Have you seen him?"

The clerk shook his head.

He flipped through his phone and offered Charlee's picture. "How about her?" He flipped through more photos. "Or her?" he asked, showing Natalie's picture. "Or how about this girl?" He showed him Nora's photo.

The clerk squinted at Nora's photo and shook his head. "Go back to the other one. No. The first one. Yes, she was here a little while ago."

Just then, another clerk, an older man, came in. He looked Hunter's uniform up and down. "Are you perhaps Lieutenant Boudreau with Fish and Wildlife?"

"I am. How do you know my name?"

Hunter's hand went to his weapon as the man reached under the counter. He relaxed slightly when the man handed him a folded piece of paper with his name on it. "A young lady was here before and asked me to give this to you if you stopped by."

"Was she alone?" When the man said yes, Hunter held up his phone and the picture of Charlee. "Is this her?"

The man nodded, and Hunter unfolded the note.

He says he'll kill Natalie if I don't come alone. He's tracking me, but I'm not sure how. He might have Nora, too. Be careful.

Hunter thanked them both and hurried back to his truck. The knot in his gut tightened. A killer had her in his sights, and she was worried about him. First, he texted Pete and Josh: Heard from Charlee. She's headed north. Jennings monitoring her phone, maybe car. I'm in pursuit.

He wanted to call her but didn't want to risk alerting Jennings. Byte had sent the coordinates of last year's incident to Hunter's dash-mounted laptop, and he glanced at the map as he sped in that direction, various scenarios and possibilities to take down Jennings running through his mind. He switched to satellite view to get a better feel for the location and put those details together with the photos of the scene he'd seen earlier. He'd figure it out. No way would he let Charlee die. Or Natalie and Nora, either.

Charlee headed farther north, one eye on the rearview mirror, one eye on the speedometer. If she got pulled over for speeding, it would make her late, and that couldn't happen.

She came around a bend in the road and slammed on her brakes, along with every other car ahead and behind her. Flashing lights from several emergency vehicles let her know this wasn't just a routine traffic stop. Within moments, traffic on the 60-miles-per-hour stretch of four-lane highway came to a complete standstill. Charlee eyed the dashboard clock and forced the fear back.

She had no doubt Hunter had figured out where she was heading and wasn't far behind. Which both reassured and terrified her. As a cop, and Marine Corps before that, Hunter had mad skills. Her brothers were no slouches, either. But Jennings was one determined lunatic.

Her cell phone rang. She picked it up and saw the blocked number. "What?" she barked. He seemed to like weakness, so she wouldn't show him any.

"*Tsk, tsk*. Why so grouchy, Charlotte?"

"Because there's been an accident, and traffic isn't moving. I can't make your crazy deadline if I'm sitting here stuck in traffic."

Charlee listened to the silence and worried she'd gone too far.

"Where are you, exactly?"

"I'll check." Charlee opened the GPS window on her phone and read out the nearest cross streets.

"I see you. Glad you know better than to lie to me, Charlotte."

"Why would I do that? You have what I want."

"Ah, yes. The lovely Natalie. Do you know what I want?"

Charlee swallowed the panic. "Me," she bit out. "But I won't go quietly."

Jennings laughed. "We are going to have such a good time together, Charlotte. Before. I. Kill. You."

Charlee gripped the steering wheel harder to keep her hands from shaking. "Why are you calling me?"

"Do you know where you're going yet?"

Charlee was betting her life on it, but she wouldn't give him the satisfaction. "I'm waiting for you to tell me."

"I'm sure you've already guessed." He purred the words, and Charlee felt her skin crawl. "We're meeting back where it all began. The same spot on the river where sweet JJ was swept away and died. And where nasty Nora was supposed to die." His tone changed, became hard. "You have until nine p.m. to show up there in your kayak. Alone."

Charlee pulled off into a little strip mall parking lot, where she took several deep breaths. She had to think, plan. She used the map function on her phone to pinpoint exactly where she'd been last year. It would take at least another hour to reach the outfitter where she used to work. She knew how to get onto the property, knew their security was nonexistent, and figured they wouldn't mind if she borrowed a kayak. She changed the map view, trying to remember if there was a better place to put a kayak in to get to the shoals faster. She didn't relish the idea of navigating the rapids in the dark, but she didn't have a choice.

Her best chance was to get ahead of him and get to the spot before he and Natalie got there. Otherwise, she didn't know how she'd get the drop on him.

Her phone rang. Hunter. She wasn't sure if Jennings could hear what she said, but she wouldn't chance it. She feigned anger as she picked up the phone. "What? You done playing with your FWC friends and now you're checking up on me?" *Come on, Hunter, play along.*

"Look, *cher*, I had things to do, you know?"

She snorted. "Right. Well, so do I. I'm not waiting around for you to have time for me."

"Touché. You still going kayaking?" he asked.

"Yep. You know how much I love it, especially in the dark."

There was a pause. "You want to go get some ice cream at the yogurt place later?"

Hunter hated yogurt, and they used to joke about the yogurt place near the outfitter where she worked, saying they were getting "ice cream." So he knew where she was heading. "Yeah. I still have a couple errands to run before I put my kayak in."

"Ok, I'll call you later. Be safe, *cher*."

She disconnected and murmured, "You, too," even though she knew he couldn't hear her.

Charlee kept driving until she saw a sign for a big-box outdoor store. She hurried inside and bought a backpack, high-powered flashlight, a wearable headlamp so she could see where she was paddling, two knives, extra bullets for her Glock, and some sturdy freezer bags to keep everything dry, just in case.

She wasn't a former marine like Hunter, but this wasn't her first day in the woods.

Chapter 29

Hunter checked in with Byte, who said Charlee was still heading in the same direction. Just as he hung up, Pete called for an update. "I just talked to Charlee. She's okay. Rattled but hiding it well. Says she still has a couple errands to run tonight before she puts her kayak in."

Pete bit back a curse. "He wants her on the rapids in the dark."

"That's my guess. It also means he's betting her skills are sharp, because if she's the ultimate target, he won't want anything happening to her that he didn't cause."

"She'll handle it. Charlee's amazing on those rapids. She laughs and shouts like a little kid. It's always been her favorite thing." Pete sobered. "It used to be, anyway. Before."

"I know. And it will be again. We're going to get her out of this, make sure she can enjoy them any time she wants. Stay focused, Pete. You have to think like a cop, not a brother."

"This is my sister—both my sisters—we're talking about."

"I know. Believe me, I know. But we have to leave emotion out of it if we're going to get them out alive."

Pete muttered several choice words. "Hate that you're right." He heaved out a breath. "What now?"

"The outfitter she worked for was Suwannee Paddlers, right?"

"Right."

"Meet me there as soon as you can. Tell Josh. I'll call Sanchez and Fish. Do not try to get out there without me, or I'll shoot you myself. We clear?"

"Clear, Lieutenant."

"We're going to get this guy."

Sammy sat in the passenger seat of the dusty old pickup truck, trying to figure out what was happening. The windows were rolled down, and the wind blew in his face, just like always, but something was wrong. Tool Man was acting really different today. He wasn't smiling or saying nice things; he was just grumpy.

"Can we stop for cupcakes? I bet Charlee brought in some more today." Maybe cupcakes would make Tool Man smile. They always made Sammy smile. They were so good.

Tool Man shot him a look. "No cupcakes. Not today."

Sammy's face fell, and he nodded. "Okay."

He got socked in the arm. "Don't worry, Sammy, we'll get some tomorrow. Today, we have some things to do, important things."

"What things? Do I get to help?"

Tool Man smiled then, but it wasn't the right smile. This smile was scary and made Sammy want to hide. "Yes, Sammy. You are definitely going to help me."

Sammy nodded. "I'm hungry." He peeked sideways to be sure Tool Man wasn't going to hit him. Sometimes he didn't like it when Sammy reminded him that he needed food.

The truck pulled off the road and into the parking lot

of a fast food joint. "You stand next to the truck. Don't let anyone near the stuff in the back, okay?"

Sammy climbed out and stood by the tailgate. Inside the bed was some big lumpy stuff, but it was covered by a tarp, so he couldn't tell what it was. He reached in to lift a corner of the tarp, and Tool Man smacked his hand away. Hard. "Ouch."

"Hands off. And no peeking, or you'll be sorry. Got it?"

Sammy nodded miserably as Tool Man went inside. He didn't know what was happening, but he wanted to go home.

Charlee arrived at Suwannee Paddlers long after the chain had been hung across the entrance and the padlock secured for the night. She climbed out of the car and let out a relieved breath when she turned the tumblers and the lock popped open.

She pulled through and then locked the gate behind her. If Jennings came this way, she wasn't making things easy for him. She parked in the gravel parking area by the office, loaded her backpack, and quickly sprayed deet all over herself before she headed for the canoe/kayak launch. She didn't want the bugs that swarmed at dusk ruining her concentration on the rapids.

The kayaks were kept on racks, also locked, but Charlee was betting the combination hadn't been changed on these either. She was right.

She hauled one of the kayaks off the lowest rack, grabbed paddles and a life jacket from the nearby storage cabinet, and dragged the kayak to the water's edge.

She strapped on the life jacket, secured the headlamp

to her forehead, and tucked the backpack on her lap, making sure the pocket holding her loaded gun was open for easy access.

Hang on, Natalie. I'm coming.

She pushed off and headed into the water, her phone in a plastic bag, GPS showing her location.

~

Hunter and the team rendezvoused in the parking lot of a dentist's office just south of White Springs.

"This scumbag is smart, so we have to be smarter. We don't know why he killed his brother, Tommy, or why he attempted to kill you and Pete." He nodded to Josh.

"You think JJ's death goes back to his mother's dying somehow?" Sanchez asked.

"There's a lot we don't know. JJ's death could have been an accident. What we do know is that he has both Charlee and Natalie. I think it's safe to say he has Nora, too. My gut says he wants Charlee at the place where JJ died."

"Agreed," Pete said, and everyone nodded.

"So here's what I'm thinking." Hunter pulled up a map of the area and outlined his plan. Within minutes, they were back on the road. Hunter just prayed they got there in time.

~

Sammy's worry increased as they kept driving and it started to get dark. "Don't we have to get ready for work?"

"We have other work to do tonight, Sammy."

"But who will give the kids their prizes?"

Tool Man laughed. "Don't worry. They'll all get what they deserve. Promise."

Sammy wanted to believe him, but that didn't sound...right.

A little while later, when Sammy thought his bladder would burst, they finally pulled off the paved road and onto a dirt road. The road kept getting narrower and narrower, and branches swept into the cab of the truck and scratched his arms. He rolled up the window a little and tried not to pee his pants, but the bumpy road was making it really hard.

They finally stopped in a little clearing, and Tool Man turned off the ignition. "Time to go, Sammy. You're going to learn a lot tonight. I'm going to need your help. Are you ready?"

"Yes, sir," Sammy said, but just then, he wasn't sure. Something in his tummy was telling him things were really wrong. But he trusted Tool Man, so he got out. "I have to pee," he whispered.

"Go on. Make it quick."

Sammy went a few feet into the woods, then came back to where Tool Man stood by the bed of the truck. He dropped the tailgate and flipped up the tarp. At first, Sammy didn't know what he was looking at, but then Tool Man turned on a great big flashlight, and the ache in Sammy's tummy got real bad.

There were ladies in there, two of them, and their hands and feet were tied with duct tape, and there was duct tape over their mouths. But it was their eyes that got to Sammy; they were wide and scared, and they made Sammy scared, too.

"Who are they? Why are they tied up?"

"You'll find out soon enough." Tool Man nodded to the smaller of the girls. "You grab that one, and I'll get the other."

Sammy did as he was told and swung the girl over his shoulder just like Tool Man did with the other one. But his hands were shaking, and he wanted to run away and hide.

Something bad was going to happen.

Chapter 30

It was dark by the time Charlee approached the rapids. Not exactly ideal conditions. Before she went any farther, she secured her phone and gun in the backpack and put it into the dry cubby behind her seat. It meant she'd have to find the location from memory, but she hoped the headlamp would provide enough light that she could find her way.

Flashbacks from a year ago kept wanting to steal her breath, but she pushed them back. She had to focus on paddling. On getting to the right location and then figuring out a way to free Natalie before this loony tune killed her. That Charlee would give her life for her sister's wasn't even in question. She was prepared to die for her, planned on it, even. Natalie was going to be a teacher, and the world needed more good teachers, caring ones like their mom had been. She wouldn't, couldn't let her die. Wouldn't be able to live with herself if she did.

She took a deep breath and plunged into the churning water ahead of her, relying on muscle memory and years of kayaking to keep her upright as she navigated the rocks and currents in the dark. The headlamp illuminated just past the end of her kayak, but not far enough for her to clearly see anything or anyone who might be standing along the shoreline.

It took all her concentration to navigate, but she made

herself scan the shore regularly to make sure she didn't pass the spot. If she did, there was no way she could get back there easily. If at all.

She thought she was close to where she needed to be. Now all she had to do was figure out how to get to shore. Finding a way around the trees and rocks and the eddies surrounding them would be tricky. Especially in the dark.

Suddenly, something hit her in the arm, hard. She pulled back in shock, tipping the kayak to one side. She tried to rebalance her weight, but the current grabbed her wrong, and before she could stop it, she'd flipped out of the kayak and was shooting down the river face-down. She immediately spun to her back and spit out what seemed like gallons of water. With her feet out front, she tried to steer herself toward the edge where she could grab a rock or branch. Anything.

She felt the whoosh of air as something passed by, and then she was yanked to a stop, hard. She clawed at whatever was around her neck, choking her.

A rope.

The pressure increased as someone tugged on the other end of the line. Charlee wedged her hands under it to keep it from tightening around her neck, but it wasn't working. She used her feet to kick, trying to duck, to escape, something.

"Hold still, and I'll pull you in."

Jennings! No! Charlee tugged harder, trying to get the rope off so she could escape. But he'd rigged a slip knot, so the more she tugged, the tighter it got.

"Don't fight me, Charlotte, or you'll die before all the fun starts. Then where will we be?"

Charlee stopped fighting. Let him bring her to Natalie. She gasped for breath as he dragged her toward shore, banging her on rocks as he pulled. She stepped in a hole and fell into the water, only to be yanked upright by the rope.

"Keep moving."

He would pay for this, the slimy monster. Charlee grimly reached out for rocks and branches and used them to lever herself up and over. She finally collapsed on the shore on all fours, coughing and gasping for air. She threw off the rope, took off her life jacket, and climbed to her feet, fury in her eyes.

"I'm here, you lunatic. Now let my sister go. I'm what you want."

He laughed, and Charlee realized she'd forever hate that cackle, deep and evil and sounding like it came from the pit of hell itself.

He clicked on a flashlight, and Charlee bit back the shout when she saw Natalie kneeling by the water's edge, tape over her mouth, hands and feet bound. She looked at Charlee, utter panic in her eyes, and Charlee smiled, trying to offer what reassurance she could.

Then he turned the light to the right. Nora. Also tied up and kneeling by the water.

"What do you want with Nora? She's no part of this."

He spat in the dirt. "Show's what you know, Miss Smarty Pants." For the first time, Charlee noticed the gun he held, and another chill raced over her skin. He tucked the gun under Nora's chin and raised her head. The same panic swirled in her eyes as in Natalie's. Charlee smiled at her, too. *Be brave. We're going to get through this.*

"Nora is my niece, in case you haven't figured that

out yet. But she was supposed to die that day, not JJ. Never JJ. So you see, this is as much her fault as yours."

"Why Nora and not JJ?" Charlee was desperate to keep him talking, to figure out how to take him down.

His face distorted, and he smacked Nora with the gun. Her head snapped back, and she screamed behind her gag as she landed in the sand.

"Oh no, you don't." Jennings dragged her back to a kneeling position. He fixed Charlee with a curious gaze. "Didn't you hear the way she talked to him? Always belittling him and making fun of him. She showed him no respect whatsoever."

"But don't all brothers and sisters talk to each other like that? I don't understand."

"No; they're supposed to protect each other! To be good to each other and take care of each other!" His voice rose with every sentence, spit flying. "Get over here. Now." He held the gun to Nora's temple and motioned Charlee over with his other hand. "You're going to do what should have happened last year. You'll drown Nora. It seems only fitting."

Behind her gag, Nora struggled to get away, yelling behind the tape. Charlee's heart rate sped up. This was her one chance.

She walked over to Nora slowly, sliding the knife out of the sheath at her waist, hoping the shadows would hide what she was doing.

As she slid down next to Nora, she whispered, "Stay put until I tell you to run." She used her body to hide the quick slice she made through the bindings on Nora's feet, grateful the girl understood. She didn't move a muscle.

"Yank off the gag," Jennings instructed. "But if she screams, I'll shoot her right there."

Charlee met Nora's eyes, and the girl nodded. Charlee yanked off the tape, ignoring the tears that ran down the girl's cheeks.

"Hold her head under the water until I say stop."

Charlee hesitated, trying to come up with another plan, until Jennings screamed, "Do it now!"

Charlee put her left hand behind Nora's neck and quietly counted to three. She made sure the girl sucked in air before she stuck her head under the water, then held her own breath, waiting for Jennings to take a step closer. Praying he would.

Time seemed to slow down as she counted silently. One. Two. Three... Thirty-five...forty-six. Her lungs were starting to burn, and she knew Nora's were, too.

Come on, Jennings. One more step.

Just when she thought her lungs would burst, he took that last step closer to watch Nora die. Which was exactly what Charlee was banking on.

The second he did, she spun around and jabbed her knife into his midsection with all her strength while she tried to knock the gun away with the other arm. "Run, Nora!" she shouted.

She let go of the knife and used both hands to try to wrestle the gun away from him, but he was a lot stronger than she'd given him credit for. Charlee used every bit of her strength, but in one blinding move, he twisted her arm behind her back while his other hand came around her neck. Next thing she knew, he had the gun jabbed against her temple.

He was breathing hard as he muttered, "You will pay

for that, Charlotte. After you're dead, who will protect Nora from all I have planned?"

"What are you doing, Tool Man? Is that Charlee?"

Charlee's blood ran cold as Sammy stepped out of the woods, stumbling a little, looking even more confused than usual. He raised a hand to the back of his head and then gave a little shriek when it came away bloody. "You hit me, Tool Man. Why did you hit me?"

Beside her, Tool Man's voice gentled, and Charlee wanted to scream at Sammy to run and hide. "I'm sorry, Sammy. I never meant to hurt you. But you kept asking questions, and I needed to think."

"Why are you holding Charlee like that? I don't think she likes it." Sammy's eyes widened. "Is that a gun? Why are you holding a gun on Charlee?"

"Do I have to hit you again, Sammy?"

"N-no." He shook his head, then winced. "I'll be quiet."

"Good boy. Now come here."

Charlee's mind scrambled for what to do next. Her eyes met Natalie's panicked ones, and she fervently hoped if Hunter was nearby, he'd get over here already. She needed backup.

But as soon as the thought formed, she rejected it. She'd do whatever she had to do, with or without backup.

Sammy inched closer, clearly confused by what Jennings was saying.

"Come closer, Sammy. That's it. Now, bend down by Natalie. She's been a bad girl, and you're going to punish her."

"What did she do? Why is she a bad girl? I don't know Natalie."

"She's my sister, and she hasn't done anything wrong, Sammy," Charlee said. "Don't listen to him."

Jennings tightened his grip and aimed his gaze at Sammy. "You'll do as I say, or I'm going to hurt Charlee. You don't want that to happen, do you?"

Sammy shook his head, clearly miserable. Charlee tried to think, to come up with something, anything.

"Bu-but I don't want to hurt anyone. It's not nice to hurt anyone. And Charlee's always nice to me."

Jennings's control snapped, and he lunged for Sammy. Charlee bent down and whipped her second knife from its ankle holster. She leaped up on Jennings from behind and wrapped her legs around his waist. He had the gun trained on Sammy, but this time, it was Charlee who had her arm around his neck, and her knife was pointed just below his ear.

"Drop the gun or I slice you open," she hissed.

"I'll shoot him—or your sister—before you can get it done."

"I wouldn't bet on that," Hunter said, stepping out of the shadows. Charlee breathed a quick sigh of relief, especially when she saw his body armor. "Drop the gun, Jennings. It's over."

"It's not over until I say it's over. Drown her, Sammy. Do it NOW!"

"He's lying to you, Sammy. Don't do it," Charlee said.

Sammy stood, frozen in indecision.

Hunter kept walking closer, never taking his eyes off Jennings. "I understand why Brittany had to die, and why you think Nora should, too. They were mean to their brothers, weren't they?"

"Yes. Sisters should protect their brothers. And mothers should never be mean to their sons. Never. They should love them and protect them."

"Just like you protected Tommy from your mother."

"Yes. She called him names, told him he was worthless. She was a terrible mother. She ruined Tommy."

"So why did you kill him, then? You've protected him all his life."

Jennings struggled to break Charlee's hold. "It's all her fault! Tommy saw me try to kill Nora last year, and he threatened to tell. My own brother who I protected his whole life. How could he do that to me?" His eyes filled with tears, and he started crying. "All I ever tried to do was protect him. That's all. And he threatened to betray me, to turn me in. I couldn't let him do that."

Charlee met Hunter's eyes, saw him nod toward Sammy. She hoped she understood what he meant, what he wanted her to do. She uncrossed her legs and slid down so she was standing behind Jennings. She met Hunter's eyes and counted to three. On three, she gulped in a breath and spun away from Jennings, grabbing Sammy and rolling into the water with him. "Get down," she shouted to Natalie.

As Charlee pulled Sammy behind a big rock in the water, she heard a shot, then another, followed by a third. The silence seemed to go on forever. Then she heard splashing and Hunter's voice. "Charlee? You okay?"

She stood up, dragging a confused Sammy up with her. He swiped at the water running down his face. "What happened? Why were people shooting?"

Hunter positioned himself so Sammy couldn't

see Jennings lying on the bank. Josh appeared beside Hunter, also wearing body armor. "You okay, Sis?"

Charlee smiled. "I am now. Thanks." Then she turned to Sammy, tried to find the right words. "Sweetie, I know that Tool Man gave you a place to stay and took care of you, but he was a bad man."

Sammy swallowed hard. "He wanted me to hurt Natalie. And he was going to hurt you."

Charlee hugged him. "Yes, but you tried to save us. Thank you, Sammy."

He tried to look past them. "Is Tool Man coming home?"

Charlee met his eyes. "No, Sammy, he's never coming home."

Pete showed up to give Charlee a hug. "You okay, squirt?"

Sammy eyed him. "I'm glad you didn't die."

Pete stopped, stared at Sammy for a long moment. "Somebody rolled me over, that day along the Ocklawaha. That was you, wasn't it, Sammy?"

Sammy ducked his head. "You looked like you needed help. And I knew you were Charlee's brother."

Pete held out his hand. "Thank you, Sammy. You saved my life."

Sammy looked from one to the other, then back at Charlee. "I never wanted to hurt anybody. Tool Man told me to shoot his gun and scare you a little the day you were on the river with those people, but I didn't want to. When somebody started shooting back at me, I ran away before something bad happened."

Charlee exchanged glances with Hunter, who put a strong arm around Sammy's shoulders. Was it possible

Sammy didn't realize he'd actually hit her and Brittany that day?

Sammy's eyes were wide, and his chin quivered. "What will happen to me now? Where will I go?"

"Why don't you let Josh find you a blanket and look after you for a while, and then later, you can come home with me until we figure something out. Okay?"

Sammy looked Hunter up and down. "You saved Charlee."

"We all did."

Sammy thought about that. "Then you're not a bad man." And with that, he hugged Hunter until he couldn't breathe.

Once Josh led Sammy away, Charlee rushed over to hug Natalie, who sat on a log beside Sanchez and sobbed. She leaped up and wrapped Charlee in a bone-crushing hug. "Oh, thank God, Charlee. You were amazing, and I've never been so scared in my whole life."

"I'm just glad you're okay." She looked over Nat's shoulder at Pete. "Is Nora okay?"

He hitched a thumb over his shoulder to where Nora sat on a rock with Fish, who had an arm wrapped around her shoulders.

Satisfied they were all okay, Charlee turned and marched over to Hunter, who was talking with Sanchez.

He reached out to hug her, but she wasn't having any of that. Not yet. She pulled back her fist and punched him in the jaw with enough force to land him on his butt in the sand. He looked up at her, a little dazed. He shook his head to clear it, worked his jaw.

"Don't you ever, ever knock me out again to get me

out of the way." She stood, hands on hips, and glared at him while her brothers burst into applause.

Hunter just stared up at her for another dazed moment, then climbed to his feet. "Look, Charlee, I'm sorry, I—"

"Why?"

He looked confused. "Why what?"

"Why did you knock me out?"

"Because I didn't want you to die. Why do you think?"

She narrowed her eyes at him. "Not because you didn't think I could take care of myself?"

He spread his hands around the area. "Obviously, you can take care of yourself. And then some."

"Why else?"

He fisted his hands on his hips. "Why else what?"

She waited.

His eyes met hers for a long moment, then darkened to green fire as he took a step in her direction. Then another. Until he stood right in front of her. "Because I love you, Charlotte Tanner. And I couldn't bear the thought of losing you."

She cocked her head, considered, as his words sank deep into her heart. Then she shot him a cheeky grin. "Then kiss me, you overbearing idiot, before I deck you again."

"Yes, ma'am," he said before he swept her into his arms and into a kiss that had her feeling like a movie star, never mind that she was soaking wet and standing in the middle of a crime scene.

Chapter 31

In the end, Charlee finally took Natalie and Sammy home with her, while Hunter and her brothers finished processing the crime scene. Sally Jennings came for Nora, and instead of cursing this time, she hugged Charlee and thanked her over and over for saving her daughter.

It was near dawn when Hunter slipped into her room and slid under the covers. He pulled her back against his chest and wrapped her tightly in his arms, like he'd never let go. "Don't ever scare me like that again, *cher*," he muttered before he dropped into a dead sleep.

Charlee cradled her head on his shoulder and drifted back to sleep herself, smiling.

Later that morning, her dad picked up Natalie to take her to the hospital before driving her back to Gainesville. Their mom had woken up, finally, and the doctors were confident she would recover. Liz had called, twice, to make sure Charlee was okay.

Sammy prowled Charlee's small kitchen, unsure of himself. He smiled shyly when Hunter walked in.

"Hey, Sammy." Then he walked right over to Charlee and kissed her soundly. "Good morning, beautiful."

Charlee leaned back. "Wow. That was nice. Good morning to you, too."

"You guys want to go to the Corner Café for some coffee?"

"And cupcakes?" Sammy asked hopefully.

"Maybe. Charlee hasn't had time to bake any lately. But I'm sure Liz will have other goodies."

Smiling, Sammy led the way outside. The café was crowded when they arrived, and they again spent longer than Charlee would have liked answering questions and getting hugged. Charlee was exhausted and just wanted a bit of quiet time to process it all. But apparently, that would have to wait.

The bell jangled, and Sammy's face split into a wide grin as Frank Graham, the carnival boss, and the heavy-set lady they'd met the other day stepped through the door. "Frank! Ida! It's good to see you. I'm having a cupcake. Liz had a special stash, just for me."

"We're glad to see you, too, Sammy." They exchanged glances with Hunter and pulled up chairs at their table.

Sammy grinned, a bit of frosting on his cheek. Ida handed him a napkin and signaled, so he wiped it away. "Did you hear about Tool Man? Hunter said he was a bad man. And he's not coming back, ever."

Ida patted Sammy's hand. "We heard that, sugar, and we're sorry. We know you two was close."

Sammy shrugged and focused on peeling another cupcake wrapper. "I don't know what to do now."

The adults exchanged glances, then Ida said, "Well now, that's why we're here. We talked with Lieutenant Boudreau, and he said it'd be a right fine idea if you came and stayed with me." Ida paused. "What do you think about that, Sammy?" Even though Sammy had confessed to shooting at Brittany and Charlee that day on the river, everyone, including the ADA, believed he'd only meant to scare them, not hurt anyone. They were all hopeful that Sammy would get a suspended sentence or community service rather than jail time.

He scrunched up his eyes, thinking. “I could keep my job?”

“Of course you could. And you could stay with me as long as you like.”

“That would be good.” He finished his cupcake and stood, held out his hand to Hunter. “Thank you, Mr. Copper.” Then he turned and hugged Charlee. “Thank you, Charlee.” He looked from one to the next. “I have to go now. But you were my friends, and you saved me.”

“We’ll always be your friends, Sammy,” Charlee said. “You come see us next time you’re in town, okay?”

“You’ll have cupcakes?”

“Of course.”

Sammy smiled and followed Ida and Frank out the door.

Charlee cocked her head as she looked at Hunter. “I think you’re nothing but a softy under that tough exterior, Lieutenant.”

He shifted uncomfortably in his chair, then looked around the café before aiming his gaze back at her. “You ready to tell your parents you’re trading your kayak paddle for a mixer?”

Charlee smiled. “Actually, I told Dad this morning that I’m ready to take over the Outpost full-time, whenever they’re ready. Liz is okay with me supplying cupcakes when I can.”

“What changed your mind?”

“Big Shoals. You.”

“How so?”

“When I was out on the rapids, I remembered how

much I loved it. How much I love being outside and on the water. The guilt, the fear, it blocked out the love for a long time. I'm finally ready to put the past behind me, to move forward."

"Is there room for a—what was it you called me, an overbearing idiot?—in that moving-forward plan?"

"Maybe. What did you have in mind?"

He looked down and unclasped the thick silver bracelet he always wore. "I gave this to my brother for his high school graduation. It's not a ring, but maybe it will do until I can buy you one." He looked at her, love and trust and admiration shining in those green, green eyes, just for her. "I love you, Charlee Tanner. Marry me?"

With those simple yet heartfelt words, the last of the fear slipped away, and her heart soared. This man would always have her back. He probably would never take her to the symphony—not that she wanted to go—but he'd let her know she was loved and protected every day of her life. What more could a girl want?

"I think I can put up with you for a lifetime, Lieutenant."

"Then kiss me before I change my mind," he quipped and cupped her face in his hands before he kissed her thoroughly.

Everyone cheered as they left the café. They drove back to the Outpost, where they took two kayaks out on the Ocklawaha River and had their very own celebration. Together.

If you love action-packed romantic suspense like Connie Mann's Beyond Risk, *you'll love the thrilling new series from beloved author Katie Ruggle, featuring a family of bounty hunter sisters—and the men who get away with their hearts. Read on for a sneak peek.*

IN HER SIGHTS

"I'm headed to the park," Molly called as she let the screen door slam behind her. It slapped against the edge of the frame, too warped to close properly. She absently made a mental note to fix it later...along with the hundred other things that needed doing around the house.

"You want backup?" Charlie yelled back, and Molly resisted the urge to roll her eyes. Her sister would do anything to get out of paperwork, but Molly wasn't about to enable her, even if it would be nice to have someone along to help relieve the boredom.

"Nope, this should be easy-peasy."

"You're taking Warrant though, right?" Cara, Charlie's twin and the worrywart of the family, peered at Molly through the screen door.

Their enormous, hairy Great Pyrenees mix cocked his head when he heard his name. "Yes." Leash in hand, Molly allowed Warrant to tow her down the porch steps as she gave Cara a wave over her shoulder, wanting to get out of earshot before her sisters thought of any more questions. If Molly was delayed long enough, Charlie would somehow finagle her way into coming along, and that meant Molly would be stuck sorting her sister's expense reports. That prospect wouldn't be so bad, except that Charlie was terrible about taking care of her receipts. They were always sticky or stained or wrapped around chewed gum. *Nope*. Charlie could do her own expense report. It was a beautiful afternoon for a walk to the park, and Molly was going to enjoy it.

Warrant trotted at her side as they passed their neighbor's scarily perfect yard. Mr. Petra silently watched from his wide, immaculate porch, his narrow-eyed glare boring into her.

Baring her teeth in a wide smile, Molly waved. "Hey, Mr. P! Beautiful day, isn't it?"

As he continued to glower, Molly felt her forced smile shift to a real grin. Being passive-aggressively friendly to her sourpuss of a neighbor was oddly satisfying. She felt his disapproving glare follow her until she reached the end of their street and turned the corner. Warrant happily bumbled along next to her, although his broad, pink tongue was already hanging out of his mouth.

"We've gone a *block*," she said. "You can't be getting tired already."

Warrant just blinked his oblivious dark eyes at her, and she sighed.

"You're the laziest dog in the world. It's a good thing you're cute, or we wouldn't put up with your shenanigans." That last part was a lie. Molly and her sisters would put up with Warrant even if all of his fur fell out and he sprouted leathery, bat-like wings. They'd probably even get specially made sweaters with appropriately placed holes for his new appendages. She smiled at the mental image as she ran a hand over his silky-soft head.

The sun beamed down warmly on them as they walked, light filtering through the trees that lined the residential street. Langston was close enough to Denver—just an hour's drive from downtown to downtown if traffic was light—that commuters were snapping up new cookie-cutter homes on the northern edge of the small city as fast as they could be built. Set tucked against the foothills of the Rocky Mountains, the new suburbs had wide stretches of fresh sod and spindly saplings that cast barely any shade, but Molly's house was in the older, richer, southern part of town. That meant neighbors eyed her family's worn and comfortably raggedy property from their own perfectly restored Victorians with lush, Mr. P-approved lawns, but it also meant that the trees were old enough to spread their sheltering branches over the yards and quiet streets, protecting Molly and Warrant from the strong Colorado sun.

Although it was mid-September, it still looked—and felt—like summer. The only hint that fall had begun was the absence of kids running around at two thirty on a Tuesday afternoon. Despite Warrant's slowing pace, the mile-long walk went quickly, the peace of the quiet, warm day soothing Molly's too-busy brain.

After much coaxing and a minimal amount of dragging her increasingly lazy dog, Molly made it to the park. Only a handful of people were there, mostly parents watching their preschool-age kids play. Warrant perked up once the dog run came into view, but Molly towed him in the opposite direction toward an empty bench next to the swings, doing her best to pretend she couldn't see his sad look. She failed miserably.

"I know, Warrant." She sat and tried to ignore the guilt swamping her. "We need to make some money, though. You eat a lot, and it's not the cheap stuff, either. Your food is the equivalent of dog caviar, so I don't think it's too much to ask for you to help out occasionally."

With a soul-deep sigh, he lay down next to the bench and rested his chin on his front paws. Molly turned her attention away from the dog and eyed the shops across the street. Her spot on the bench was the perfect vantage point.

She pulled her phone from her pocket and pretended that she wasn't watching the door next to the cute ice cream parlor. The apartment above the shop was leased by Maryann Cooper, who seemed to be a law-abiding, responsible citizen. The same couldn't be said about her younger brother, Donnie. He had a habit of taking things that didn't belong to him—like wallets and cell phones and the occasional car—and he hadn't shown up for his most recent court date.

Molly had a strong suspicion that Maryann knew where Donnie was hiding, and she would leave for her shift at the turkey-processing plant in an hour or so. Since Maryann had been dodging all of her calls and refusing to answer the door, Molly would have to take a more direct approach. She started playing a game on her phone to pass the time while keeping one eye on the apartment across the street, just in case Maryann decided to leave early. Warrant stretched out on his side and dozed, snoring softly.

After a peaceful half hour drifted by, Molly stood and stretched, knowing it was time to move closer to the ice cream shop. Warrant provided an excuse to hang out at the park without looking like a lurker—and he'd also proven to be an excellent conversation starter with people who wouldn't have given her the time of day if she'd tried approaching them alone—but having the dog along did require some additional planning. Warrant's top speed was a slow amble, so she had to allow enough time to get him through the park and across the street.

Before she could make her move, an all-too-familiar voice made her groan and plop back down in her seat.

"Molly Pax. Just the person I wanted to see." John Carmondy started rounding the bench but paused to rub Warrant behind the ears. The dog—traitor that he was—thumped his heavy tail against the ground and rolled over in a plea for belly scratches. To Warrant's obvious delight, John complied.

"John Carmondy. Just the person I *didn't* want to see." If she'd known that he was going to be at the park, she would've stopped and talked at Mr. P, or even helped Charlie with those sticky receipts. Molly sent a quick text and then slid her phone into her pocket. "Why are you here?"

Still crouched to pet Warrant, John grinned up at her. Her dog's back foot pedaled in the air as John found just the right spot. Molly wasn't surprised. She was well aware that the man knew exactly how to hit everyone's buttons. Too bad he seemed to take as much pleasure in pestering her as he did in playing with her dog. "Why am I at the park?" he asked. "Why does anyone go to the park on such a beautiful day?"

Across the street, Maryann slipped out of the door next to the ice cream shop and hurried toward her ancient Honda parked on the street. She was leaving early today. Molly watched her go, holding back a growl when she saw Maryann get in her car and pull away from the curb. There went her chance to talk to the bail-jumper's sister.

"You're such a happy dog, aren't you?" John cooed. "Not all crabby like your owner."

Molly rolled her eyes hard enough that she was surprised they didn't spin right out of her skull. "I'm not crabby." She hesitated, honesty pushing her to add, "Well, not to most people."

With a snort, John gave Warrant a final belly scratch before straightening to his full—and significant—height. Crossing over, he took the spot next to her on the bench, and Molly fought the urge to shift to give him more room. He was just so darn *huge*, with biceps as big as her head and thighs like muscled tree trunks. His ridiculously enormous body took up almost the entire bench. "I'm special, then?"

"Special's one word for it," she muttered. *Aggravating* was another. So were *flirty*, *distracting*, and *confusing*, although she wasn't about to admit to any of the last three. Forcing her brain back to the job at hand, she snuck another quick glance across the street. Even though Maryann had left, Molly kept a furtive eye on the shops as she pretended to watch the kids playing on the jungle gym. She hoped that her unwelcome companion would wander away if she ignored him.

"So...how've you been?"

Of course he didn't wander away. She should've known better. John Carmondy was as hard to get rid of as head lice—and twice as irksome. The fact that her pulse did a weird skittery hop of excitement every time she saw him just annoyed her more. Shooting an irritated glance his way, she saw he was gazing across the street at the ice cream shop, the corner of his mouth tucked in as if he was trying to hold back a grin. He wasn't fooling anyone, though. The deep crease of his dimple gave him away.

Her sigh sounded more like a groan. "Did you want something, or do you have some kind of daily annoyance quota you need to fill?"

When he laughed, she couldn't help but dart another quick look in his direction. The harsh lines of his face—the square jaw and dark, intense eyes and bumpy nose that had obviously been the target of a fist or two in the past—were softened by his full lips, the lush sweep of his long eyelashes, and that stupidly appealing dimple. Someone that attractive shouldn't be so incredibly irritating, but that was John Carmondy in a nutshell: ridiculously pretty and just as ridiculously obnoxious.

"Oh, Pax...such a jokester." He continued before she could protest that she was completely serious. "What's happening in your life? It's been a while since we last got together, and I want to know everything. That's what good friends do. They share thoughts and ideas and feelings with each other. So share, my good friend. Whatcha up to?" He turned toward her, slinging his arm over the back of the bench so that his enormous hand rested behind her. Although she tried to ignore it, she couldn't help but shiver. She tried to tell herself it was her imagination, but it felt like the heat from his arm was burning the skin of her back like a brand.

"First of all," she started, even as the adult in her brain told her not to encourage him, to just ignore him until he gave up and left, "I saw you only three days ago, when I grabbed that bail jumper from the hardware store."

"The one *I* tracked down? The one you stole while I was in the bathroom? *That* bail jumper?"

Ignoring his—accurate—comment, she continued. "Second, we're not friends, so there will be no sharing of any kind. Third, please go away."

She did her best to keep her gaze forward, but it was like her eyes had a mind of their own. In her peripheral vision, she saw him clutch at his chest dramatically. "How can you say we're not friends? We share all the time. Skips, jokes...we're even sharing a park bench right now. We're sharers, Pax. That's what we do."

"No, that's *not* what we do." *Quit encouraging him*, the smart part of her brain warned.

"We should share an office," he continued, proving she shouldn't have said anything. "I don't know why you're fighting this so hard. We would be incredible together. A dream team, you might say."

Losing the battle over her self-control, she turned her head to look. Instantly, she regretted it when her brain went blank at the sight of him. As annoying as he could be, even she had to admit that he was a beautiful, beautiful man. Tearing her gaze from his amused face, she scowled hard at the ice cream shop across the street, trying to regain her composure—and her ability to speak. "One of us would be dead within a week. The other would be in jail for murder."

"But think how much fun that first week would be. Totally worth it." His chuckle was low, with a growly undertone that made her shiver. *Don't be stupid*, that practical portion of her brain warned. This talk about killing each other and stealing skips and their mutual antagonism wasn't some weird, twisted version of flirting. He might enjoy riling her up, and he was most likely sincere about wanting her to work for him—she and her sisters were very good at what they did, after all—but he wasn't interested in her like that. He was just a very, very attractive guy who was used to getting what he wanted. When she refused his job offers and stole his skips and responded to his teasing with snark rather than utter adoration, he wanted her even more.

Heat rushed to her belly, even as she hurried to correct the thought. *Wants me to* work *for him, not wants me in any other way*.

Wrestling her mind away from that line of thinking before she could get even more flustered, she focused on the playground. A toddler who'd been playing on the base of the slide was swept up by her mom, and the two walked toward the ice cream shop. Even though it was the middle of the day, the place seemed to be doing a brisk business. An older couple entered the shop while a young woman in running clothes peered through the front window, as if tempted by the thought of a cone.

John chuckled and shifted on the bench, drawing her attention once again. "Has it only been three days since we saw each other last? It *feels* longer, probably because I missed this." From the corner of her eye, she saw him gesture back and forth between the two of them, and she had to swallow an amused snort. He was persistent; she'd give him that. When she didn't respond, he turned to follow her gaze, although his arm remained stretched behind her. "So…? Who are you hunting these days?"

And there it was…his true motivation. While she'd been dithering about whether he was actually flirting with her, he'd been focused on stealing her latest job. She gave herself a mental shake. When would she learn that John Carmondy was only interested in what benefited John Carmondy? "Who says I'm working? Why couldn't I just be walking my dog on a beautiful day?" Even as she spoke, she scolded herself for encouraging him. John was the human manifestation of *give an inch, take a mile*.

He laughed again in that low, husky way that she refused to think of as sexy. "Because you have that look you get when you're on the trail of a skip. You're a bloodhound, Miss Molly Pax, and you don't lift your nose from the ground until you find your target."

Sighing in a deeply exaggerated way, she stood, and he immediately followed suit. Of course it was too much to ask that she could lose him that easily. She was going to have to get creative. "As much as I would love to stay and listen to you compare me to a dog, Warrant and I have things to do."

Although Warrant got to his feet reluctantly, he perked up as she headed toward the dog park and walked willingly at her side.

"When are you going to come work for me, Pax?" John asked, catching up easily.

"Never ever." She paused and then added for good measure, "Ever."

"I offer a really good health insurance plan," he said in the tone of someone dangling candy in front of a toddler. The sad thing was that Molly would've been tempted by that…if this were anyone but John. She enjoyed being a bail recovery agent more than she'd ever expected, but the paperwork of owning a business was much less fun. There was no way she'd ever accept a job from John, though. Forget a week—she'd murder him before she completed her first *day*.

"Good for you." As they drew closer to the dog run's gate, Warrant trotted in front of her, eager to get inside. Molly's phone buzzed in her pocket, and she pulled it out to glance at the text. Showtime. Get over here. She held back a smile at the perfect timing. Sometimes things really did work out beautifully, even when John was sticking his nose where it didn't belong. "Here. Hold him a second."

She tossed the end of the leash to John, and he caught it automatically. Turning, she jogged toward the road. In front of the ice cream shop, the runner who'd been peering wistfully through the window now looked to be flirting with a scruffy-looking white guy in his midthirties.

As Molly paused by the side of the road to let a car pass, she typed Donald Cooper, ice cream shop on Walnut St. NOW and sent the text before glancing behind her. She couldn't hold back a smirk. John was trying to follow her, but Warrant had put on the brakes. He'd plopped his fluffy hundred-pound butt down in front of the dog park entrance and braced his front legs, refusing to move. *That's right, baby*, she thought gleefully. *Earn your expensive dog food*.

"Don't you want to go with your mama?" The distance between them made his voice faint, but Molly could still hear John's cajoling words. "I bet there's some bacon over there. Wouldn't you like some bacon? Mmm...salty and meaty?"

A laugh escaped Molly as she glanced at the text that had popped up on her phone.

On our way from Clayton and Fifth. ETA four minutes.

Four minutes is doable, she thought, jogging across the road while adopting her game face. "Felicity!" she said, the last syllable rising in a well-practiced squeal as she trotted over to the runner to give her an exuberant hug. "I thought that was you." Keeping an arm around Felicity's back, she turned toward the man who was not even trying to hide the way he was checking her out. She gave him a small smile that he returned with a leer.

"Are you two twins?" he asked.

"Just sisters," they chorused, before bursting into practiced giggles.

Molly kept her expression as dumb and happy as possible. "Who's this?"

"This," Felicity said, "is Donnie. I dropped my apartment key without realizing it, and he picked it up for me. The stupid tiny pocket in these shorts is useless." She flipped the waistband of her shorts over, revealing the small inside pocket and a smooth, bronze patch of hip. Donnie's gaze locked onto the exposed skin, and his eyes bugged out a little.

"That's so sweet of you, Donnie," Molly cooed.

"It's *so* sweet." Felicity tossed her glossy, dark hair over her shoulder, and Donnie's eyes followed the movement as he swallowed visibly.

"You should buy him some ice cream as a thank-you." Molly gave him an approving smile, carefully not looking over his shoulder. Surely four minutes had passed by now.

Pouting a little, Felicity said, "I'd love to, but I left all my money at home."

"I have money." Molly patted her pocket. "You can pay me back later, Fifi."

Felicity gave her a quick, covert glare at the hated nickname, but the expression disappeared as quickly as it arrived, replaced by a beaming smile. "Thanks, Moo!"

Hiding her grimace, Molly accepted that as well-deserved payback.

"I should..." Donnie trailed off as he glanced over his shoulder, his whole body going stiff as he saw the approaching sheriff's deputies. "Shit! Gotta go!"

He bolted.

"Wait!" Molly tried to grab his arm, but he slipped past her outstretched hand.

"Sorry, ladies!" he shouted over his shoulder. "You can buy me that ice cream some other time!"

Sharing an exasperated glance with her sister, Molly took off after him, Felicity close behind. "Way to be stealthy, Deputies!" she called back over her shoulder before focusing on the chase.

"Why do they always run?" Felicity grumbled as they sprinted past a Mexican restaurant followed by a bank, weaving between people who were trying to enjoy the early fall day. Donnie shoved through a group of young teens, ignoring their protests, and disappeared as the boys clustered back together. Molly muttered a breathless curse as she jumped into the road to skirt the group, not rude enough to knock the teens out of the way as Donnie had done.

"Hey!" one of the boys called, puffing out his narrow chest as he trotted after them. "What's the hurry? Stop and talk to us."

The others in the group laughed and made *oooh* noises. Mentally thanking the universe the she only had to deal with sisters, Molly didn't break stride as she barked out, "Get back to school!"

As Felicity choked back a laugh behind her, the boy deflated and returned to his hooting group. Molly barely noticed his retreat or her sister's amusement, completely focused on finding which direction Donnie had run. A yelp from a middle-aged man as he stumbled sideways caught her attention, and she dashed in his direction. Spotting the back of Donnie's blond head, she called out, "This way!" and took off after him again.

Up ahead, two moms faced each other, chatting as they leaned on their baby strollers, blocking the sidewalk completely. Molly sucked in a worried breath, concerned that Donnie would plow right through, sending the babies flying, but he went into the street to go around them. Molly started to do the same, but a garbage truck barreled toward her, and she returned to the safety of the sidewalk. She was going too fast to stop, so she jumped over the front wheels of the strollers.

Behind her, she heard Felicity calling apologies to the furiously shouting moms, but Molly focused on Donnie's back. He was fast, the slippery doofus.

"Why do they always run?" Felicity asked again as she lengthened her stride to pull level with Molly.

"Because they know they're going to jail?" Unlike

her sister, Molly was already sucking air, and she cursed her love of pastries and hatred of exercise for the hundredth time. "At least...*you're* wearing...appropriate clothes."

"Could be worse," Felicity said as they chased Donnie across an empty lot. "You could be in a dress and heels, like when we crashed that wedding to bring in the maid of honor."

"True."

Donnie darted sideways, grabbing the edge of a recycling bin and pulling it down behind him.

"Someone's been watching too many movies!" Molly shouted at his back as she dodged around the tipped bin. "Are you going to run...through an open-air market next?"

Except for a frantic glance over his shoulder, Donnie didn't reply. He took a sharp left turn between two large Victorian houses, and Molly skidded in the dry dirt as she tried to follow. Her feet slid out from under her, sending her down to one knee and her hands. Tiny pebbles bit into her palms as she grunted, pushing herself back up to her feet without missing a beat.

The fall had only cost her a second or two, and she took off after Felicity. Determined to bring Donnie in, Molly increased her speed, her legs churning even faster until she started catching up to her sister. They wove through yards, skirting evergreens and even a cupid-bedecked fountain that looked much too tempting. Molly's lungs heaved with effort, her skin slick with sweat and gritty from salt and dust. She knew she was reaching the end of her endurance, so she pushed herself to go just a little bit faster, knowing that they had to bring down Donnie within the next few seconds, or he would get away.

Her molars clicked together at the thought. There was no way she was going to let Donnie escape. Not after all of this. Her latest burst of speed shot her past Felicity, who glanced at her with a bared-teeth grin. The crazy woman loved foot chases. If Molly had any energy to spare, she would've rolled her eyes.

Instead, she focused on the sweat-soaked back of Donnie's shirt. Digging deep, she slowly closed the gap between them until they were only ten feet apart. Giving her another hunted glance, he turned abruptly and headed for a six-foot wooden fence enclosing someone's backyard. Molly and Felicity groaned in unison.

"Not it," Molly said quickly, just before Felicity said it.

"But I'm in shorts and a sports bra!"

She sighed, her heaving lungs making it come out in an uneven rush. "Fine. I'll do it." Although Molly would much rather be the one who gave her sister a leg up rather than dropping into a stranger's backyard, Felicity had a point. Molly's T-shirt and capris were slightly more suited to hurdling a fence.

Donnie didn't slow down as he approached the wooden barricade, using his momentum to haul himself up the side. Driven by the intense desire to avoid doing the same, Molly scraped up the very last of her energy and surged forward, leaping up to latch her arms around his waist. Her weight unbalanced him, and his grip on the top of the boards slipped, sending them both tumbling to the ground.

Molly hit the sunbaked earth first, grunting as the air

was driven out of her lungs from the force of the fall. Although she managed to twist slightly so that his entire weight didn't land on her, he'd still pinned her right arm and shoulder to the weedy ground. Then Felicity was flipping him over, and Molly was free of his weight.

Rolling over and pushing to her knees, Molly blinked a couple of times to orient herself. "You good?" she asked, and Felicity gave her a fierce grin. Her knee was pressing firmly into Donnie's spine, and she had a strong grip on his hand, using it to twist his arm behind his back. Donnie was swearing and muttering, his words muffled by the thick thatch of weeds his face was shoved into.

"Never better."

"I'm not," Donnie whined. "Who the hell *are* you?"

With a breathless chuckle, Molly stood up and did a quick inventory, checking for any injuries of her own. Although her shoulder was throbbing where Donnie had landed on it, she knew there was no major damage done. She'd just be bruised and sore for a few days.

The two deputies ran toward them, barely winded, and she raised her eyebrows. "You were slow on purpose, weren't you?"

"I'm admitting nothing." Maria winked at her as she and her partner, Darren, took over, allowing Felicity to climb off Donnie. "Just think of it as a measure of trust in you. We knew you'd run him down. You always get your guy."

"Besides," Darren said as he cuffed Donnie's hands behind his back, "this way you really feel like you earned the payout."

"I'm fine with not earning it," Felicity said, and

Molly nodded in agreement. "If we'd ended up having to go over that fence, I would've been *annoyed*."

"I'll leave the acrobatics to you youngsters," Maria said, helping Donnie to his feet.

"Youngsters?" Molly exchanged a skeptical look with her sister. "What are you? Thirty?"

"Thirty-*two*."

Rolling her eyes, Molly fell in behind the trio as they headed back in the direction of the park. "Okay, Grandma."

"No one read me my rights." Donnie's voice was a winded mix of complaint and triumph. "That's illegal. I'm going to sue you all."

"We're only required to let you know your Miranda rights if you're being questioned while in police custody," Maria explained with more patience than Molly could muster after that chase.

"*We* never have to read you your rights, dummy." From Felicity's gleeful tone, she had just about as much sympathy for Donnie as Molly did. "We're not cops."

"I can't believe you played me like that," Donnie whined from his spot between the two deputies. "That's why I don't trust chicks."

Darren gave him a look. "How were you not suspicious when they started paying attention to you? Those two are *way* out of your league."

Molly tuned out Donnie's indignant sputters and turned to her sister. "Thanks for getting here so fast after I texted. How'd you sneak away without Charlie tagging along?"

Felicity grinned. "I asked her to help me clean the garage. That's the one thing she hates more than paperwork. There's no way she'll go out to check if I'm in there. She'll be too worried that I'll make her help."

"Genius."

"Yep."

As they reached the ice cream shop, a shout from across the street caught Molly's attention. When she turned her head and saw John and Warrant, both looking equally stubborn and annoyed, she pressed her lips together to hold back a laugh.

"Talk about genius." Felicity sounded just as amused as Molly felt. "You finally figured out a way to ditch Carmondy. Nice one, Molls."

"Thanks. I just wish he'd give up on following me around and chase his own skips."

Her sister's eyebrows bobbed up and down comically. "I've told you about a thousand times why he's really always trailing after you."

"Not that again." Molly groaned. This was a regular joke that Felicity—all of her sisters, actually—teased her with, but it was as far from reality as it could possibly be. "He wants me to work for him. Since I keep refusing, he wants to steal my skips out from under me. That's all there is to it."

"He's in *loooove*," Felicity cooed, and Molly jabbed her sister in the side with her elbow. "How have you not realized this? He basically has cartoon hearts where his pupils should be whenever he looks at you."

"Hush." Even though Molly knew it wasn't true and that her sister was just trying to get a rise out of her, the running joke still made her squirm...mainly because the teeniest, tiniest, stupidest part of her felt a ridiculous surge of hope.

Although Felicity smirked at her, she did fall silent, to Molly's relief.

"Would you mind finishing up with Maria and Darren?" Molly asked. "I need to retrieve our dog."

"Sure." Felicity jogged to catch up with the deputies, who were ushering Donnie around the corner to where they must've parked their squad car.

"You're my favorite sister!" Molly called after Felicity before crossing the street. Her pace slowed as she neared John and Warrant, their twin accusing stares making her feel a bit guilty, even as she had to bite back a grin.

"Thank you for holding him," she said, taking the leash. "I just had to take care of something."

Instead of yelling about getting ditched, however, John's attention ran over her grass-and-dirt-stained clothes and settled on the scrape on her forearm. His eyes narrowed. "What happened?"

She flapped her hand to dismiss his concern. "I just didn't feel like climbing over a fence today."

"That makes no sense." He eyed her carefully, as if searching for other injuries. "You okay?"

"Of course. All in a day's work." She couldn't help smiling at him. No matter how aggravating John Carmondy was, it was kind of nice having someone worry about her.

She quickly nipped that thought in the bud. If she allowed herself to get mushy where John was concerned, he'd start stealing jobs from her left and right. Even worse, if she didn't stay on her guard around him, she'd end up agreeing to work for or with him, and one of them would surely end up dead in short order. It was important for their continued safety that she resist any urge to soften toward her biggest rival.

"You *are* hurt, aren't you?" His voice was full of concern as he took a half step closer, as though ready to administer first aid. Molly didn't find the idea of John's big hands on her as repugnant as she should have. In fact, the thought of him taking care of her, of letting her lean against his broad chest as he checked her scrapes and bruises was almost...nice.

That thought brought her back to reality, and she turned sharply away, tossing him a muttered "bye." That was why it was important to not let Felicity's insinuations take root in her brain. Molly had to be careful, since she had a bad habit of playing the sucker for a pair of puppy-dog eyes and a sob story. Although she'd been forced to develop a hard shell when she and her sisters started their bail recovery business, there was nothing she could do about her soft, marshmallowy center. She was pretty much stuck with that.

Acknowledgments

Books may be written in isolation, but it takes a whole team to bring them to life. My heartfelt thanks to Amanda Leuck, agent extraordinaire, and to Deb Werksman, Susie Benton, Rachel Gilmer, and the whole team at Sourcebooks who so warmly welcomed me into the family. What a joy to work with all of you.

Huge thanks to Greg Workman, Chad Weber, and Mindy Workman of the Florida Fish and Wildlife Conservation Commission, who were kind enough to answer my endless questions. Anything I got right is due to their expertise. Any mistakes are entirely my own.

I can't imagine writing a book or doing life without Leslie Santamaria, Harry Neumann, and my amazing family and friends who keep me encouraged, fed, and watered. As always, my thanks to the Great Creator, who gives the gift of stories, and to you, dear readers, for inviting my stories into your lives. Happy reading!

About the Author

Connie Mann is a licensed boat captain and the author of the Florida-set Safe Harbor romantic suspense series, as well as *Angel Falls*, *Trapped!*, and various works of shorter fiction. She has lived in seven different states, but this weather wimp has happily called warm, sunny Florida home for more than twenty years.

When she's not dreaming up plot lines, you'll find "Captain Connie" on Central Florida's waterways, introducing boats full of schoolchildren to their first alligator. She is also passionate about helping women and children in developing countries break the poverty cycle and build a better future for themselves and their families. In addition to boating, she and her husband enjoy spending time with their grown children and extended family and planning their next travel adventures.

You can visit Connie online at conniemann.com.